Knights Club

THE MESSAGE OF DESTINY

SHUKY · WALTCH · NOVY

QUIRK BOOKS
PHILADELPHIA

Originally published in France as *Chevaliers: Le Message*
in 2013 by Makaka Éditions.
Copyright © 2012 MAKAKA. All rights reserved.

First published in the United States in 2019
by Quirk Productions, Inc.

Translation copyright © 2019 by Quirk Productions, Inc.

Library of Congress Cataloging in Publication Number:
2018943032

ISBN: 978-1-68369-065-8

Printed in China
Translated by Carol Klio Burrell
Cover design by Andie Reid
Typeset in Sketchnote
Production management by John J. McGurk

Quirk Books
215 Church Street
Philadelphia, PA 19106
quirkbooks.com

10 9 8 7 6 5 4 3 2 1

Halt!

THIS IS NOT A REGULAR COMIC BOOK!

In this comic book, you don't read straight through from first page to the last. Instead, you'll begin at the beginning and soon be off on a quest where you choose which panel to read next. You'll go on an adventure, answer riddles, solve puzzles, and face down mighty foes—because YOU are the main character!

It's easy to get the hang of it once you see it in action. Turn the page to see an example of how this comic book plays like a game!

HOW TO PLAY COMIC QUESTS

1 Pick where you want to go—doors, paths, signs, and objects can all have numbers, so keep your eyes peeled!

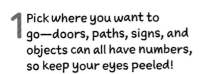

2 Flip to the panel with the matching number.

3 Continue reading from there, making more choices as you go to complete the quest!

HOW TO PLAY COMIC QUESTS

As you go, use the handy Quest Tracker sheets on the next few pages to log your progress. Use a pencil so you can erase. (You can also use a notebook and pencil, or download extra sheets at comicquests.com.)

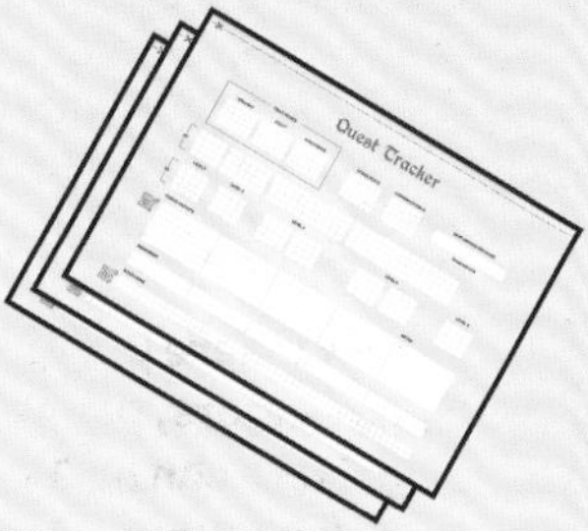
Quest Tracker

THE RULES OF KNIGHTHOOD

While playing the game, be sure to follow these rules to preserve your honor as a knight.

REMAIN VIGILANT: Always examine your surroundings for hidden passages, objects, and people—they may be hard to spot.

KEEP TRACK OF YOUR PROGRESS: Your Quest Tracker has squares to represent your Experience points (XP) and your Strike points (SP). When you have enough XP to level up, you'll gain the corresponding amount of SP for that level, and a special ability point you can use for strength, agility, or intelligence. Only a potion or leveling up will get you back your lost SP!

KNOW YOUR ATTACK: Your weapon or your spell will have a certain number of attack points that you can keep track of on your Quest Tracker. If you get new weapons or spells, their points will wipe out and replace the ones you have, so choose wisely.

STAY TRUE TO YOUR STRENGTHS: You may only carry as many objects as you have strength points. However, you can unload an object whenever you need to make room for a new one. Your main weapon, jewelry, armor, and clothes don't count against your strength points. Your purse can hold up to 98 gold pieces—but no more!

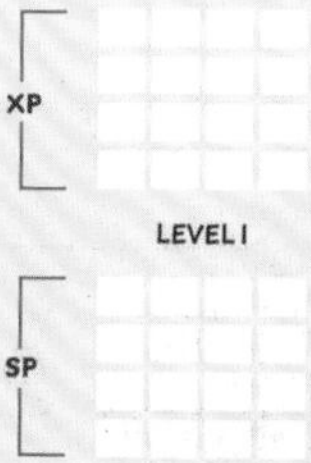
XP
LEVEL I
SP

FIGHT WITH HONOR: Use the combat wheel at the end of the book to fight enemies when they appear. The effectiveness of your attacks and spells will be determined by how you turn the wheel. Fight through the first battle in the beginning of the book to learn how combat works!

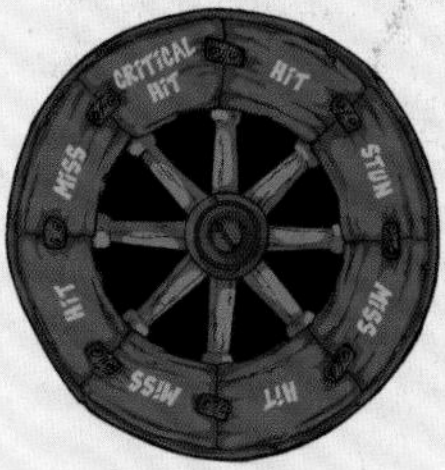
CRITICAL HIT
HIT
STUN
MISS
HIT
MISS
HIT
MISS

COLLECT MAGIC CARDS: Throughout the kingdom are 20 types of magical cards that will give you a boost in battle. Check them off on your Quest Tracker as you acquire them.

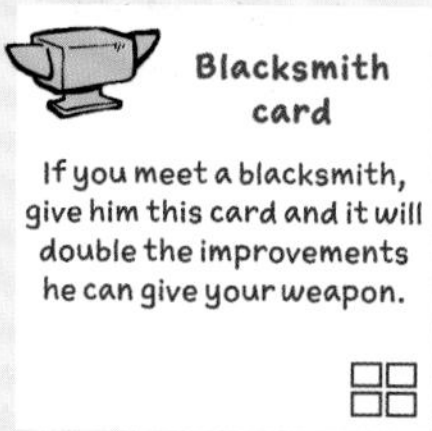
Blacksmith card
If you meet a blacksmith, give him this card and it will double the improvements he can give your weapon.

GOOD LUCK! LET THE ADVENTURE BEGIN . . .

Quest Tracker

CHARACTER NAME

(MAKE UP YOUR OWN NAME)

TRAIT POINTS

STRENGTH	AGILITY	INTELLIGENCE		ATTACK	RESISTANCE

XP

LEVEL 1	LEVEL 2	LEVEL 3	LEVEL 4	LEVEL 5

SP

NOTES

ITEMS IN YOUR PACK

ITEMS YOU ARE CARRYING/WEARING

GOLD PIECES

Quest Tracker

CHARACTER NAME

(MAKE UP YOUR OWN NAME)

TRAIT POINTS

STRENGTH	AGILITY	INTELLIGENCE	ATTACK	RESISTANCE

XP

SP

LEVEL 1   LEVEL 2   LEVEL 3   LEVEL 4   LEVEL 5

ITEMS IN YOUR PACK

NOTES

ITEMS YOU ARE CARRYING/WEARING

GOLD PIECES

Quest Tracker

TRAIT POINTS

STRENGTH | AGILITY | INTELLIGENCE

ATTACK

RESISTANCE

CHARACTER NAME

(MAKE UP YOUR OWN NAME)

XP

LEVEL 1 | LEVEL 2 | LEVEL 3 | LEVEL 4 | LEVEL 5

SP

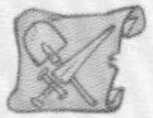

ITEMS IN YOUR PACK

NOTES

ITEMS YOU ARE CARRYING/WEARING

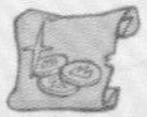

GOLD PIECES

Quest Tracker

CHARACTER NAME

(MAKE UP YOUR OWN NAME)

TRAIT POINTS

STRENGTH

AGILITY

INTELLIGENCE

ATTACK

RESISTANCE

XP

LEVEL I

LEVEL 2

LEVEL 3

LEVEL 4

LEVEL 5

SP

NOTES

ITEMS IN YOUR PACK

ITEMS YOU ARE CARRYING/WEARING

GOLD PIECES

Card of Resistance to Fire Spells

This card can be used before a battle against a fire mage to lower their Attack points by 3.

5 gold pieces for squires

Card of Protection +2

If you meet a blacksmith who asks for this card, it multiplies by two the bonuses he can give your shield.

10 gold pieces for squires

Card of Power

This card doubles your Attack points for one battle.

Blue card

(must be used immediately) 3 extra Ability points until the next level.

Card of Evasion

This card can be used before a battle against an archer to evade their first two attacks.

5 gold pieces for squires

Card of Confusion
Use this card for one puzzle, but only if you're given that option.

Card of Quantity

This card allows you to make twice as much of a potion from the same ingredients.

Orange card
Gives one protection an extra 10 points during your current level

+3 permanent attack points for squires

(must be used immediately) Doubles your experience points during your current level

+3 permanent attack points for squires

Card of Concealment

If you encounter a foe, whatever your level, this card lets you hide and continue on your way without having to fight.

Card of Lock Picking
This card allows you to pick certain locks.

10 gold pieces for squires

Card of Experience x2

You must decide to use this card before a battle begins. If you use it, your experience points are doubled.

+2 permanent Attack points for squires

Green card
Gives one protection an extra 10 points during your current level.

+3 permanent attack points for squires

Card of Healing
This card restores all your Strike points.

10 gold pieces for squires

Card of Double Attacks
Before a battle, you can choose to use this card to double your strikes until the end of the fight.

10 gold pieces for squires

Card of Taming
Where you have the option, you can tame one creature.

Red card
(must be used immediately) Doubles your Attack points during your current level.

Card of the Forge x2
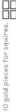
If you meet a blacksmith who asks for this card, it multiplies by two the bonuses that the can give your weapon.

Card up Your Sleeve

Use this Ace of Hearts if you have the opportunity.

Card of Dissipation
Remove all of an enemy's special resistance

10 gold pieces for squires.

Yellow card

(must be used immediately) Doubles the capacity of your pack for your whole trip (note, it does not double your Strength points).

Begin Your Quest!

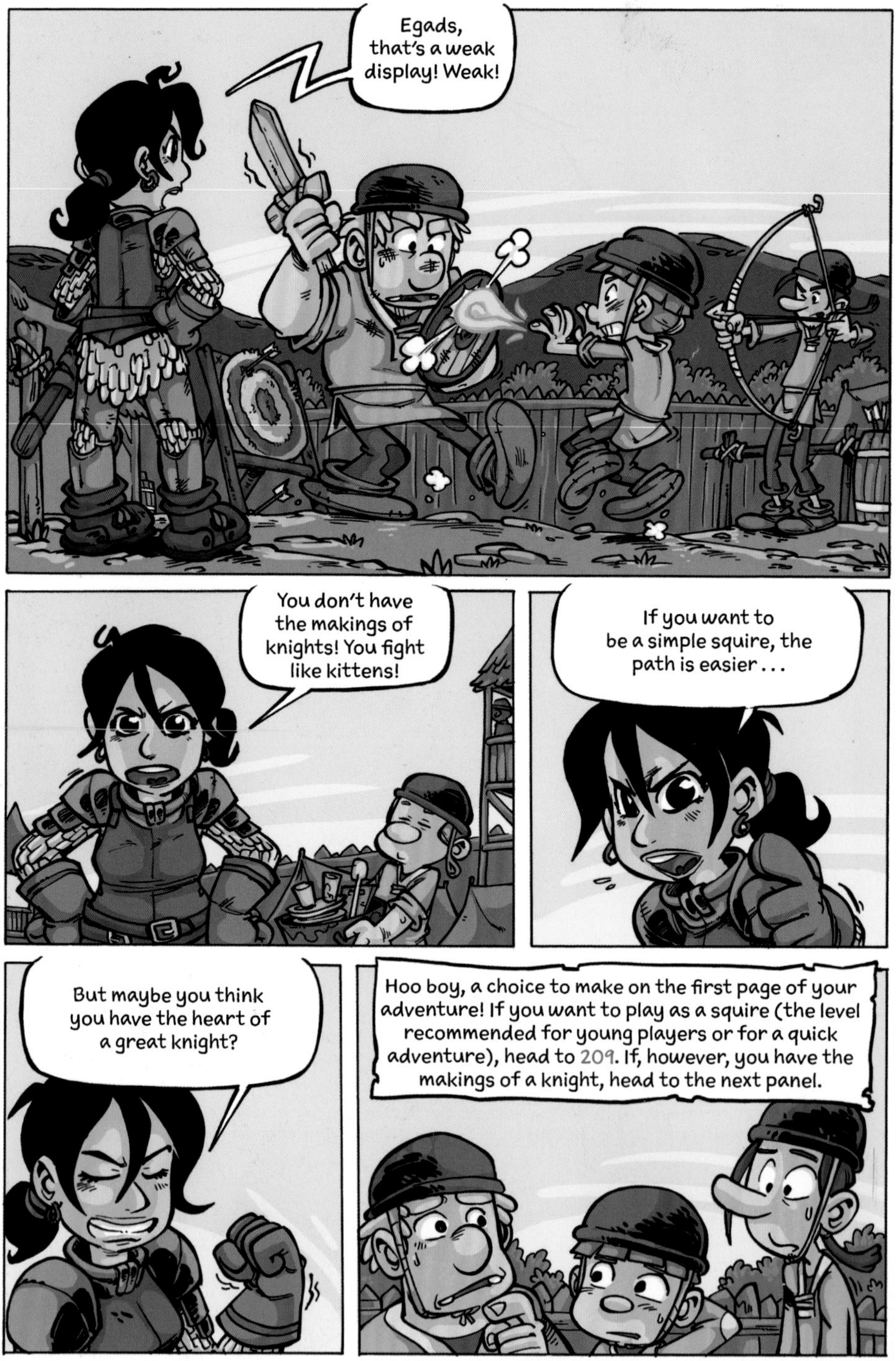

Egads, that's a weak display! Weak!
You don't have the makings of knights! You fight like kittens!
If you want to be a simple squire, the path is easier . . .
But maybe you think you have the heart of a great knight?
Hoo boy, a choice to make on the first page of your adventure! If you want to play as a squire (the level recommended for young players or for a quick adventure), head to 209. If, however, you have the makings of a knight, head to the next panel.

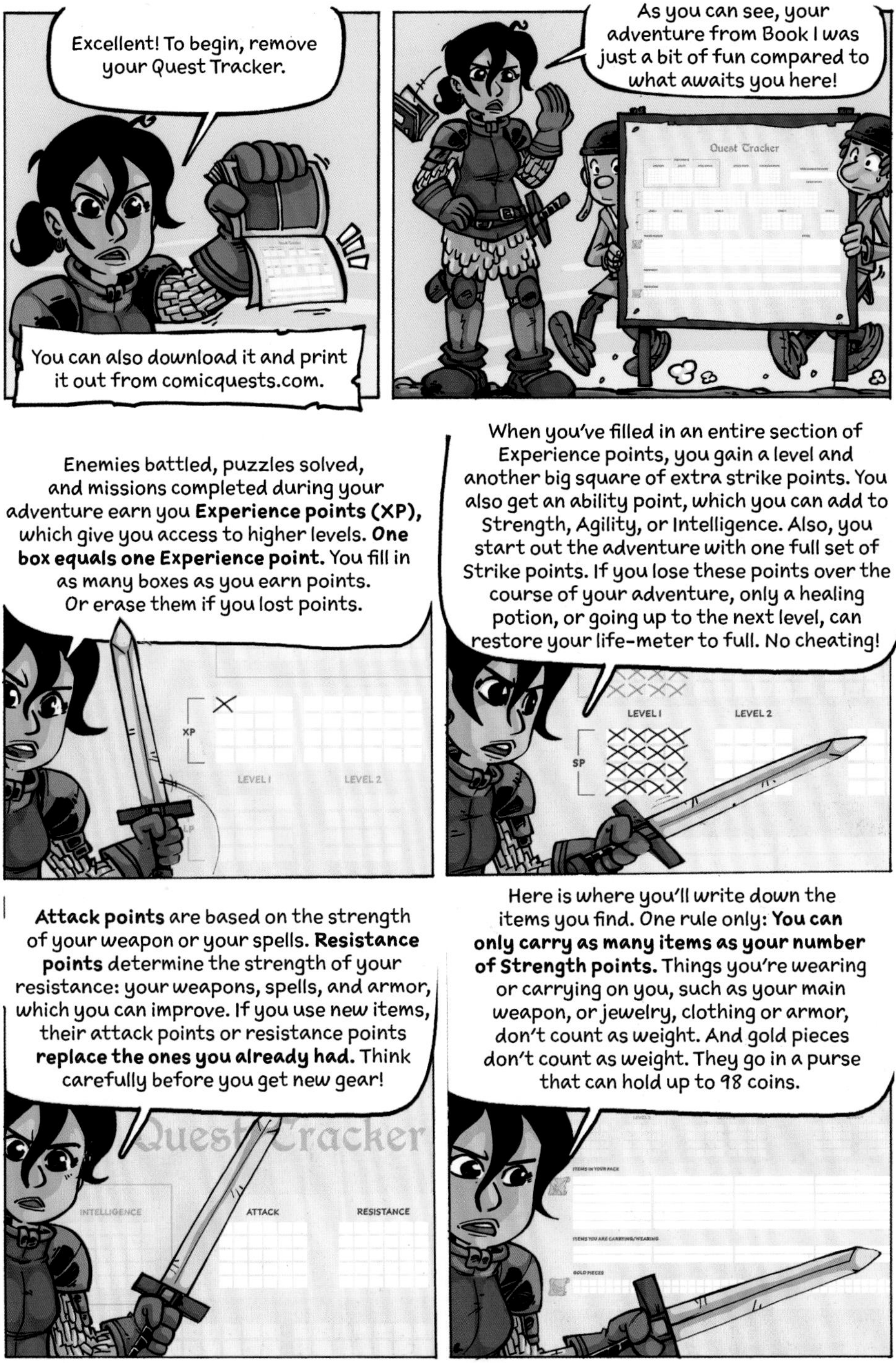
Excellent! To begin, remove your Quest Tracker.
You can also download it and print it out from comicquests.com.
As you can see, your adventure from Book I was just a bit of fun compared to what awaits you here!
Quest Tracker
Enemies battled, puzzles solved, and missions completed during your adventure earn you Experience points (XP), which give you access to higher levels. One box equals one Experience point. You fill in as many boxes as you earn points. Or erase them if you lost points.
XP
LEVEL 1
LEVEL 2
When you've filled in an entire section of Experience points, you gain a level and another big square of extra strike points. You also get an ability point, which you can add to Strength, Agility, or Intelligence. Also, you start out the adventure with one full set of Strike points. If you lose these points over the course of your adventure, only a healing potion, or going up to the next level, can restore your life-meter to full. No cheating!
LEVEL 1
LEVEL 2
SP
Attack points are based on the strength of your weapon or your spells. Resistance points determine the strength of your resistance: your weapons, spells, and armor, which you can improve. If you use new items, their attack points or resistance points replace the ones you already had. Think carefully before you get new gear!
Quest Tracker
INTELLIGENCE
ATTACK
RESISTANCE
Here is where you'll write down the items you find. One rule only: You can only carry as many items as your number of Strength points. Things you're wearing or carrying on you, such as your main weapon, or jewelry, clothing or armor, don't count as weight. And gold pieces don't count as weight. They go in a purse that can hold up to 98 coins.

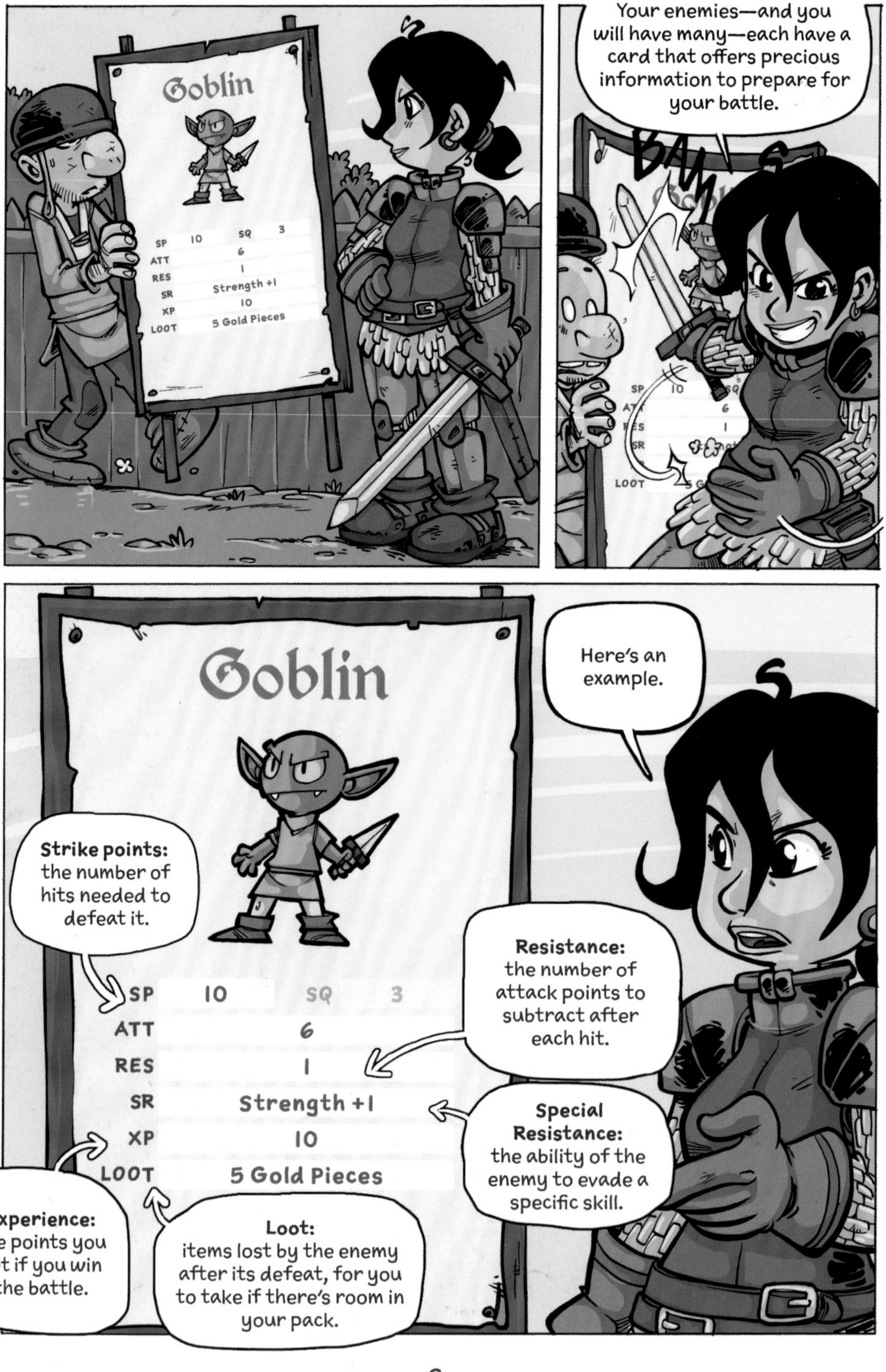
Goblin
SP 10 SQ 3
ATT 6
RES 1
SR Strength +1
XP 10
LOOT 5 Gold Pieces
Your enemies—and you will have many—each have a card that offers precious information to prepare for your battle.
Goblin
Here's an example.
Strike points: the number of hits needed to defeat it.
SP 10 SQ 3
ATT 6
RES 1
SR Strength +1
XP 10
LOOT 5 Gold Pieces
Resistance: the number of attack points to subtract after each hit.
Special Resistance: the ability of the enemy to evade a specific skill.
Experience: the points you get if you win the battle.
Loot: items lost by the enemy after its defeat, for you to take if there's room in your pack.

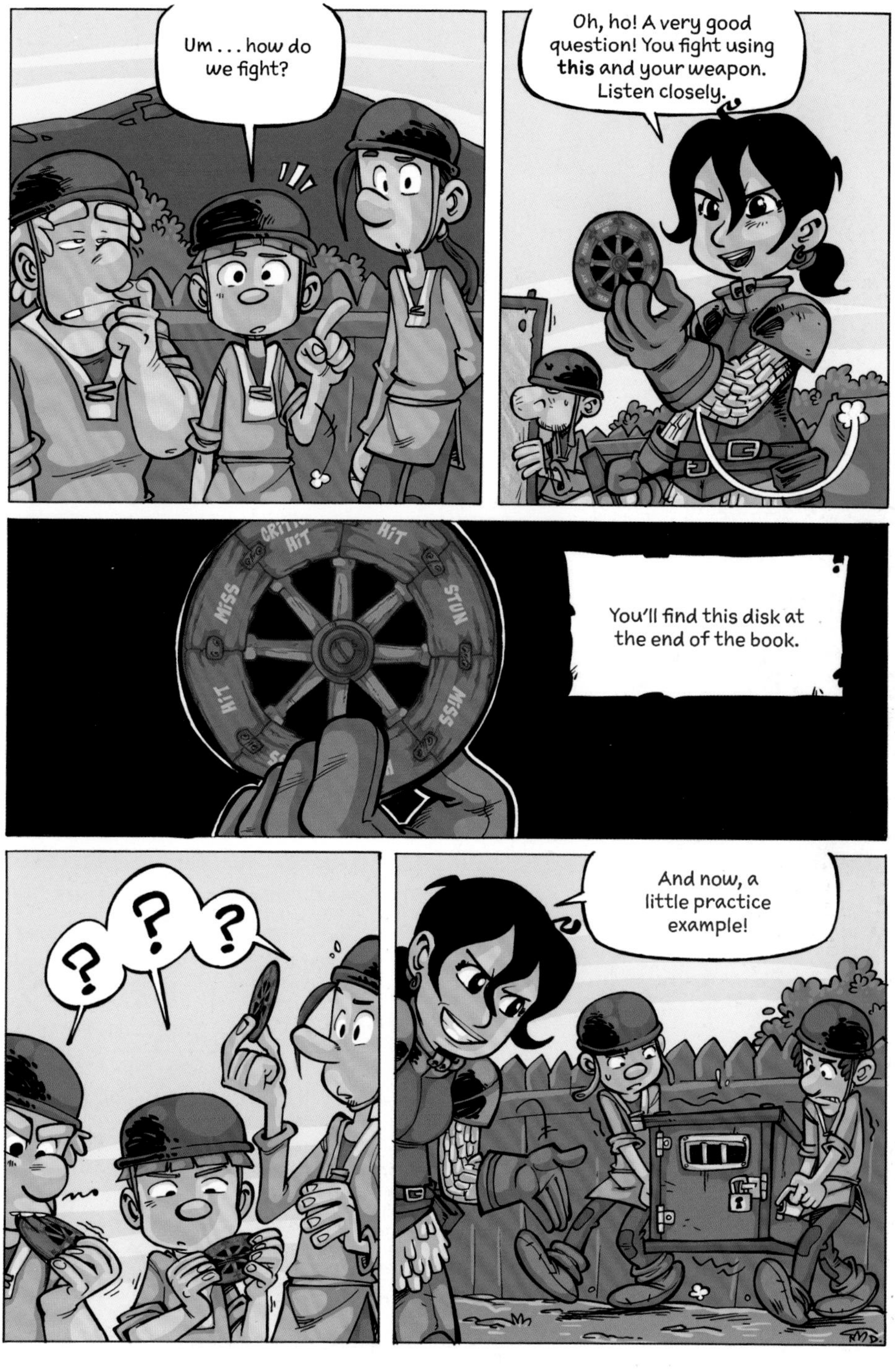
Um . . . how do we fight?
Oh, ho! A very good question! You fight using **this** and your weapon. Listen closely.
CRITICAL HIT
HIT
STUN
MISS
HIT
MISS
You'll find this disk at the end of the book.
? ? ?
And now, a little practice example!

Unless it says differently, I always strike first. Let's start by saying that I have a weapon with 5 Attack points... I spin my disk with my eyes closed...

SP	10	SQ	3
ATT		6	
RES		1	
SR		Strength +1	
XP		10	
LOOT		5 Gold Pieces	

When I decide to stop the disk, my index finger is on **Hit**. That means I struck the first blow, so I take 5 Strike points from the goblin...

But the goblin has 1 point of Resistance—so he only loses 4 points. Now, say that my main ability is Strength—then I would only cause 3 points of damage with each blow because he has a Special Resistance of "Strength +1."

-4

The only way I can strike a 5-point hit on him is to land on **Critical Hit**, which defeats all Resistance.

Stun means your adversary has to miss a turn. After you spin for yourself, you have to spin for your opponent, following the same rules. **Miss** means your turn passes with no damage to your foe.

E

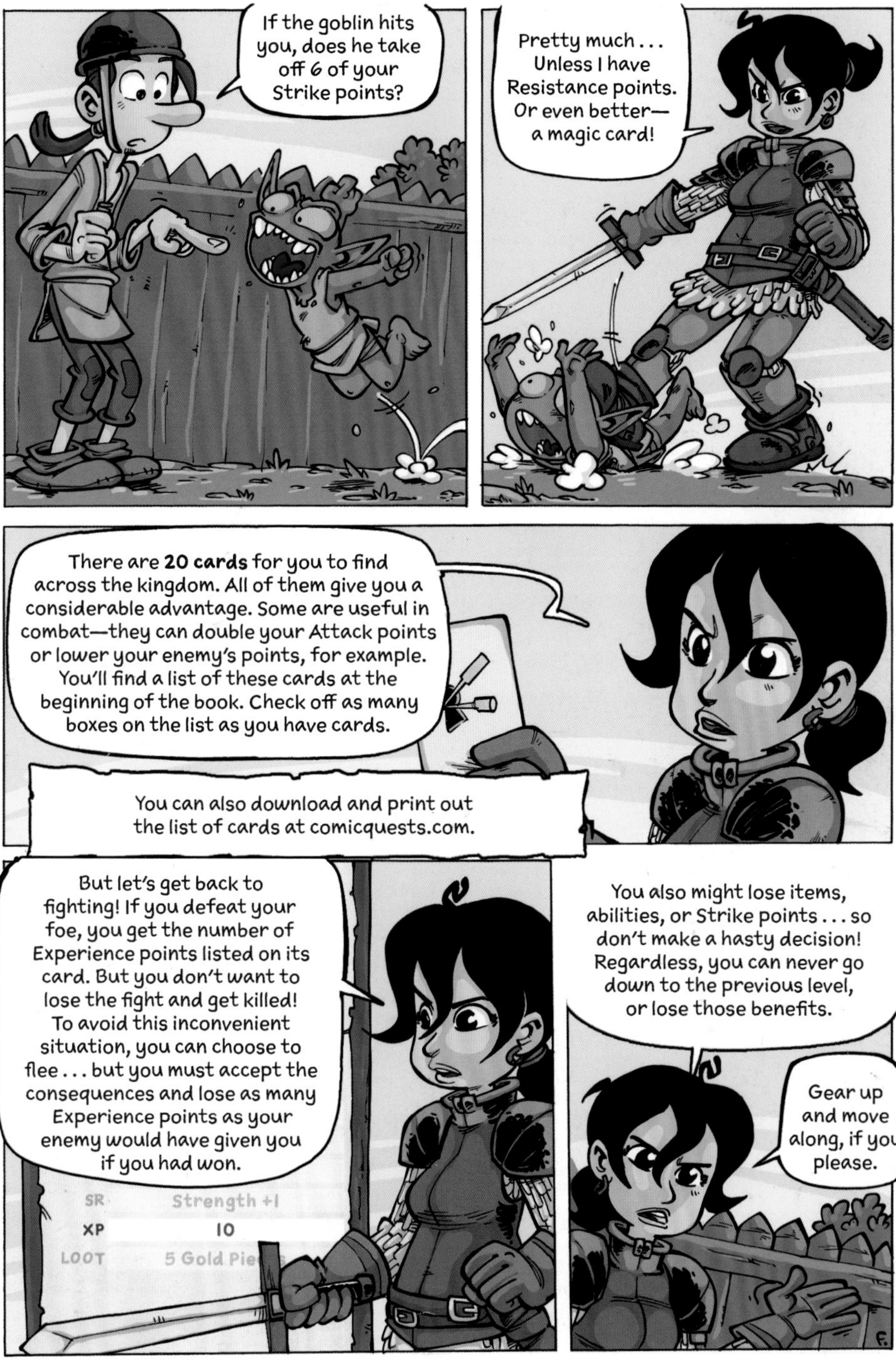

If the goblin hits you, does he take off 6 of your Strike points?
Pretty much . . . Unless I have Resistance points. Or even better— a magic card!
There are **20 cards** for you to find across the kingdom. All of them give you a considerable advantage. Some are useful in combat—they can double your Attack points or lower your enemy's points, for example. You'll find a list of these cards at the beginning of the book. Check off as many boxes on the list as you have cards.
You can also download and print out the list of cards at comicquests.com.
But let's get back to fighting! If you defeat your foe, you get the number of Experience points listed on its card. But you don't want to lose the fight and get killed! To avoid this inconvenient situation, you can choose to flee . . . but you must accept the consequences and lose as many Experience points as your enemy would have given you if you had won.
SR Strength +1
XP 10
LOOT 5 Gold Pie
You also might lose items, abilities, or Strike points . . . so don't make a hasty decision! Regardless, you can never go down to the previous level, or lose those benefits.
Gear up and move along, if you please.
F.

And now it's time to choose. Who will you play as?

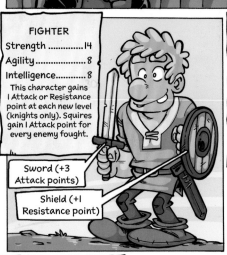

FIGHTER

Strength 14

Agility 8

Intelligence............ 8

This character gains 1 Attack or Resistance point at each new level (knights only). Squires gain 1 Attack point for every enemy fought.

Sword (+3 Attack points)

Shield (+1 Resistance point)

ARCHER

Strength 8

Agility 12

Intelligence........... 10

This character can strike twice at the beginning of a battle, spinning the disk twice (knights only). The Archer can also pick certain locks (all players).

Bow (+2 Attack points)

MAGE
(cannot carry a weapon)

Strength 5

Agility 8

Intelligence.................. 17

This character has the ability to recognize certain plants for making potions. If you choose, go to 179 to learn how to recognize these plants (knights only). The Mage can also tame some creatures (all players).

Fire Spell (+2 Resistance points)

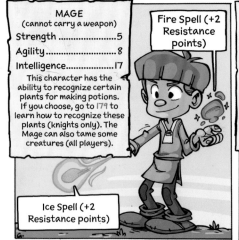

Ice Spell (+2 Resistance points)

KARINKA

Strength 10

Agility 10

Intelligence.............. 10

The captain? Really? Sure, why not . . . This character has the ability to regain 10 Strike points after each new battle (knights only). The captain also adds 1 point to the Ability of your choice when you set out (all players).

Full Armor (+2 Resistance points)

Sword (+2 Attack points)

Choose your character, write down your abilities and other characteristics on your Quest Tracker (weapons, shield, Attack, etc.), and go to PAGE H. If you completed "Knights Club: The Bands of Bravery," you can—if you want—copy over all your abilities from there and keep all your items.

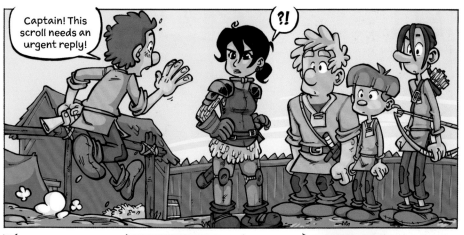

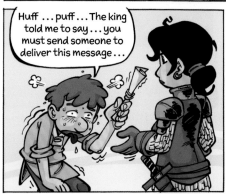

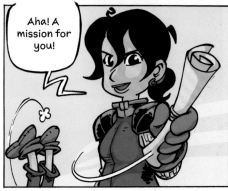

Captain! This scroll needs an urgent reply!
?!
Huff . . . puff . . . The king told me to say . . . you must send someone to deliver this message . . .
Aha! A mission for you!
Leave the camp discreetly and head across the country to the north. Get to the city of Rebourg as quickly as possible, and deliver this message to the count. Do not delay!
Remember: If you come across the same panel twice during the same adventure, you don't have to fight enemies you've already battled or count items you've already collected. Write everything down in your Quest Tracker. Be very alert and observant so you don't miss anything. Be patient, don't cheat!

Before you begin your mission, the captain gives you three healing potions that you can use at any time to regain 32 Strike points. If you won a weapon or a mage's robe in Book 1, add one extra Attack point before you start the adventure. **Go to 258 to set off on your quest.**

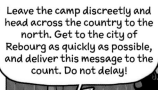

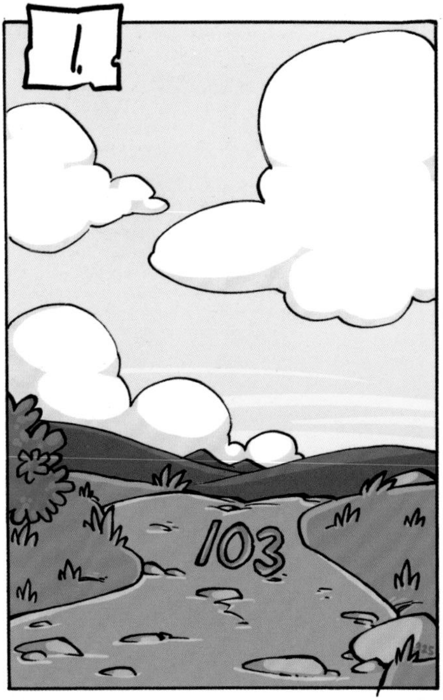
1.
103

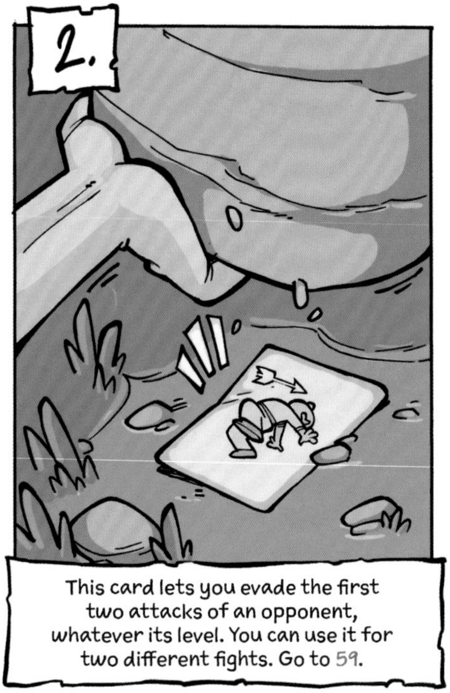
2.
This card lets you evade the first two attacks of an opponent, whatever its level. You can use it for two different fights. Go to 59.

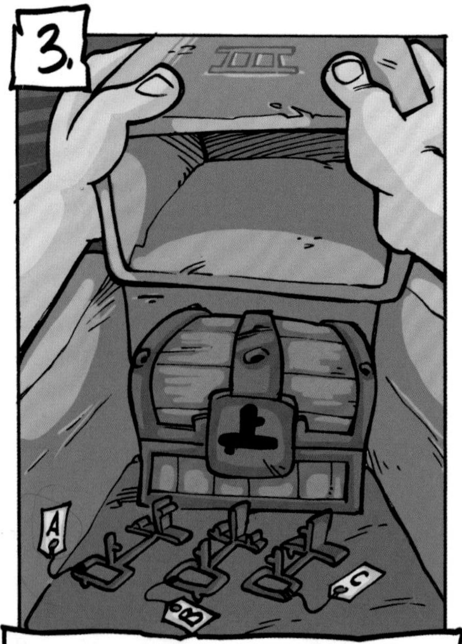
3.
A
B
C
If you know how to pick locks or if you've figured out which key to use, head to 137.

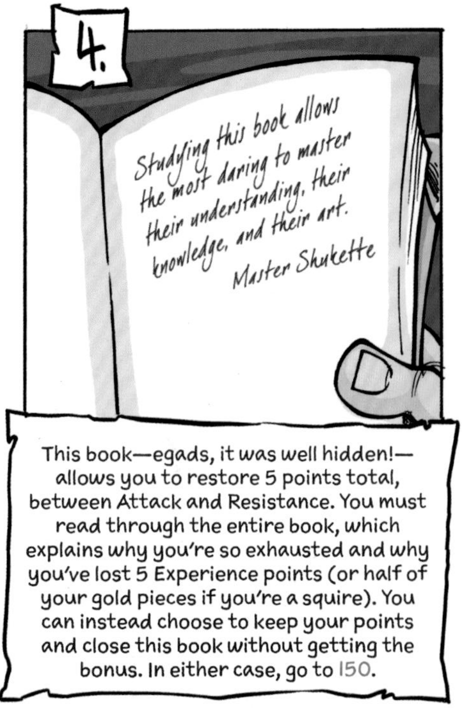
4.
Studying this book allows the most daring to master their understanding, their knowledge, and their art.
Master Shukette
This book—egads, it was well hidden!—allows you to restore 5 points total, between Attack and Resistance. You must read through the entire book, which explains why you're so exhausted and why you've lost 5 Experience points (or half of your gold pieces if you're a squire). You can instead choose to keep your points and close this book without getting the bonus. In either case, go to 150.

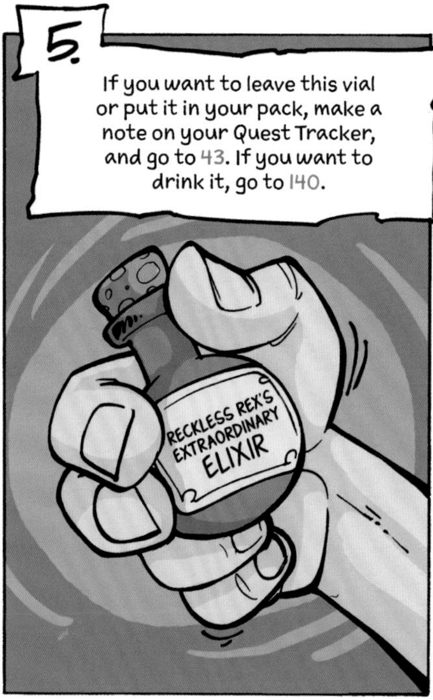
5.
If you want to leave this vial or put it in your pack, make a note on your Quest Tracker, and go to 43. If you want to drink it, go to 140.
RECKLESS REX'S EXTRAORDINARY ELIXIR

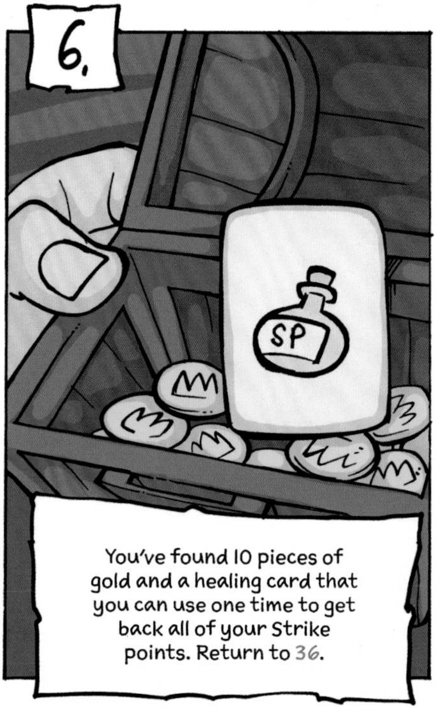
6.
SP
You've found 10 pieces of gold and a healing card that you can use one time to get back all of your Strike points. Return to 36.

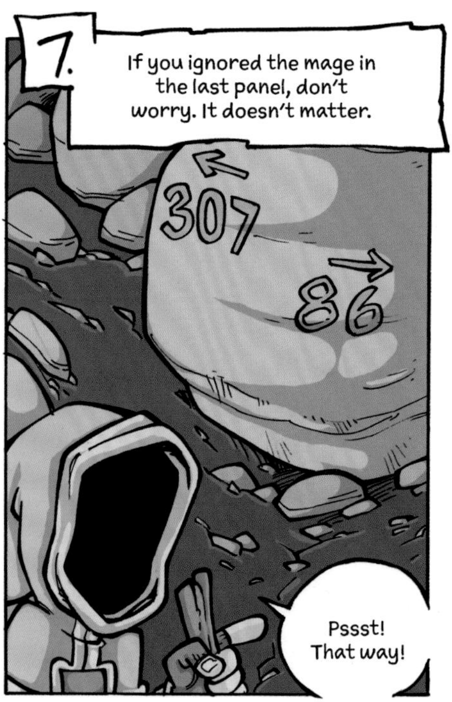
7.
If you ignored the mage in the last panel, don't worry. It doesn't matter.
307
86
Pssst! That way!

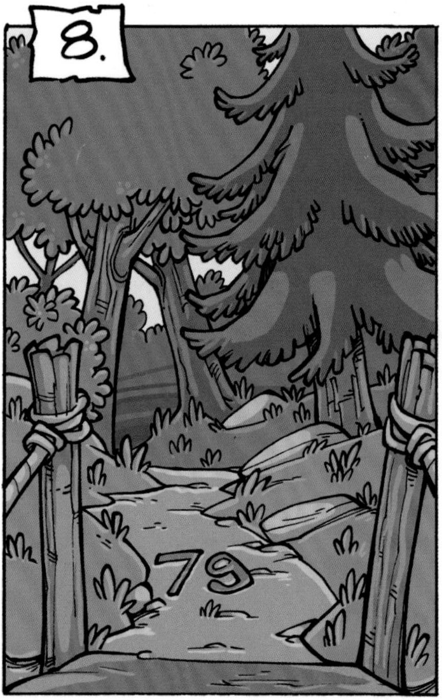
8.
79

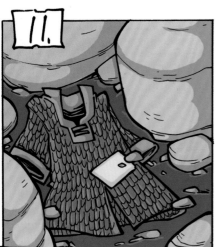

An amazing discovery! You've gotten your hands on a mail shirt that gives you 5 extra Resistance points. As for the yellow card, it doubles how much your pack can hold (note! it doesn't double your strength points). Now go on to 307.

SP	7	SQ	3
ATT		6	
RES		0	
SR		0	
XP		8	
LOOT		0	

Fight or flee, as you wish. Unless you've mastered the art of animal taming? In that case, you hold out one hand toward the beast to calm it. It will follow you, and you can add its Attack points to yours in the next battle.

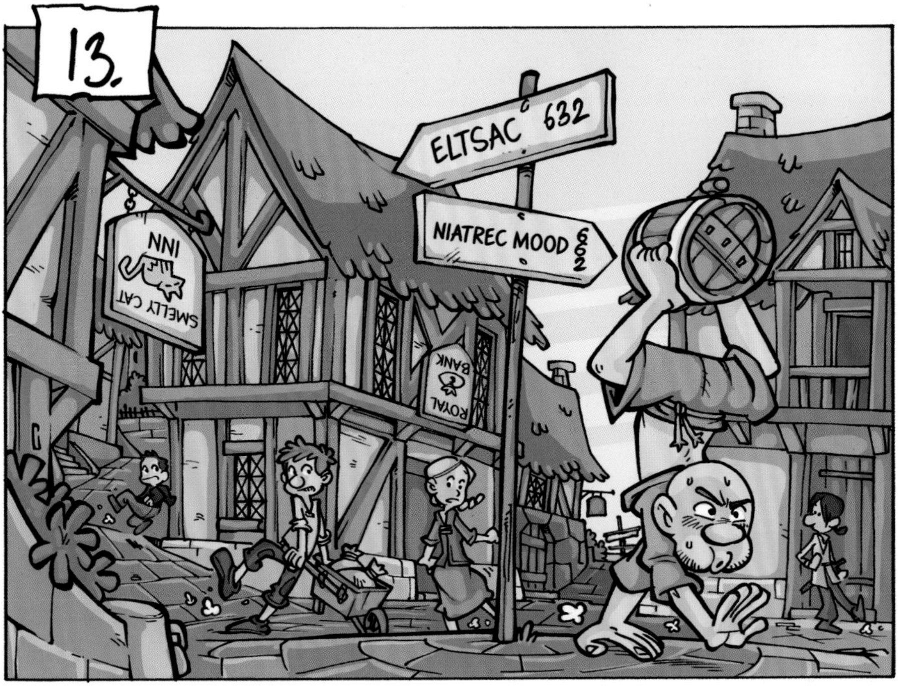

13.
ELTSAC 632
NIATREC MOOD 602
SMELLY CAT INN
ROYAL BANK

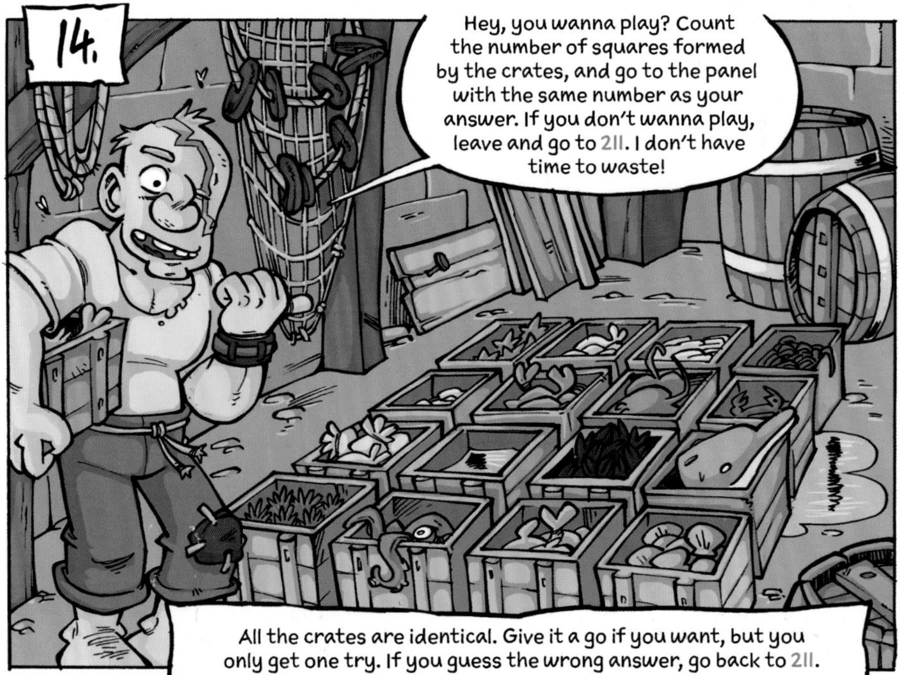

14.
Hey, you wanna play? Count the number of squares formed by the crates, and go to the panel with the same number as your answer. If you don't wanna play, leave and go to 211. I don't have time to waste!
All the crates are identical. Give it a go if you want, but you only get one try. If you guess the wrong answer, go back to 211.

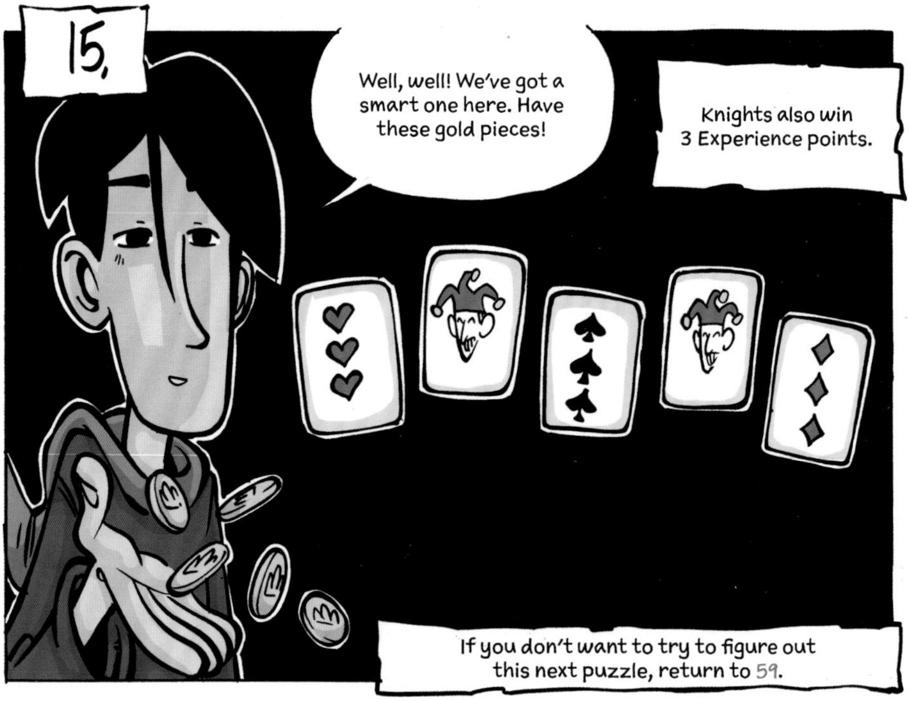
15.
Well, well! We've got a smart one here. Have these gold pieces!
Knights also win 3 Experience points.
If you don't want to try to figure out this next puzzle, return to 59.

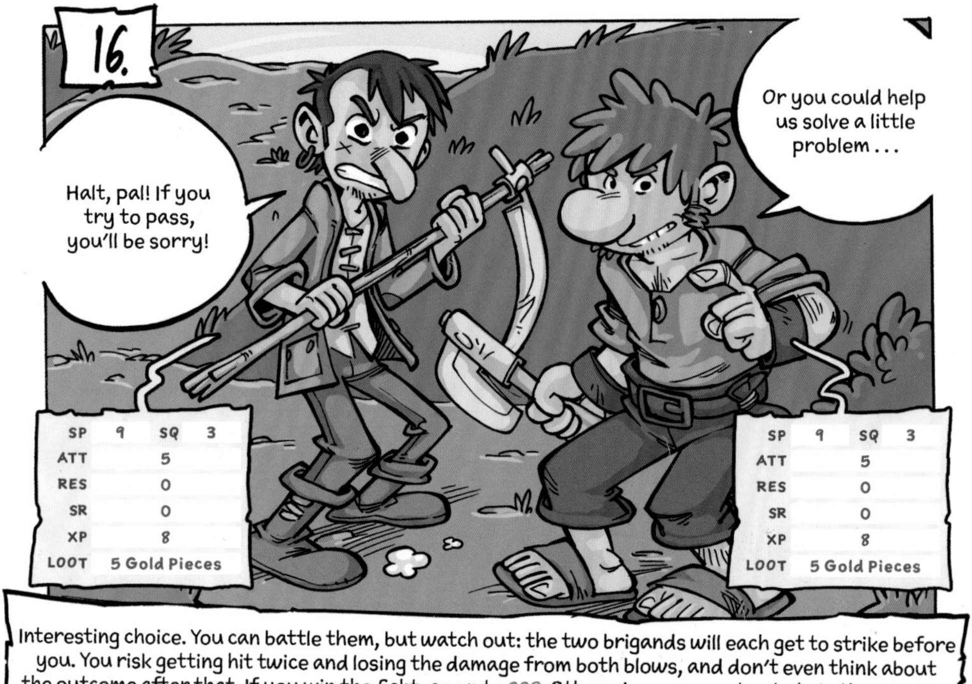
16.
Halt, pal! If you try to pass, you'll be sorry!
Or you could help us solve a little problem . . .
Interesting choice. You can battle them, but watch out: the two brigands will each get to strike before you. You risk getting hit twice and losing the damage from both blows, and don't even think about the outcome after that. If you win the fight, go on to 298. Otherwise, you can try to help them in 342.

SP	9	SQ	3
ATT	5		
RES	0		
SR	0		
XP	8		
LOOT	5 Gold Pieces		

SP	9	SQ	3
ATT	5		
RES	0		
SR	0		
XP	8		
LOOT	5 Gold Pieces		

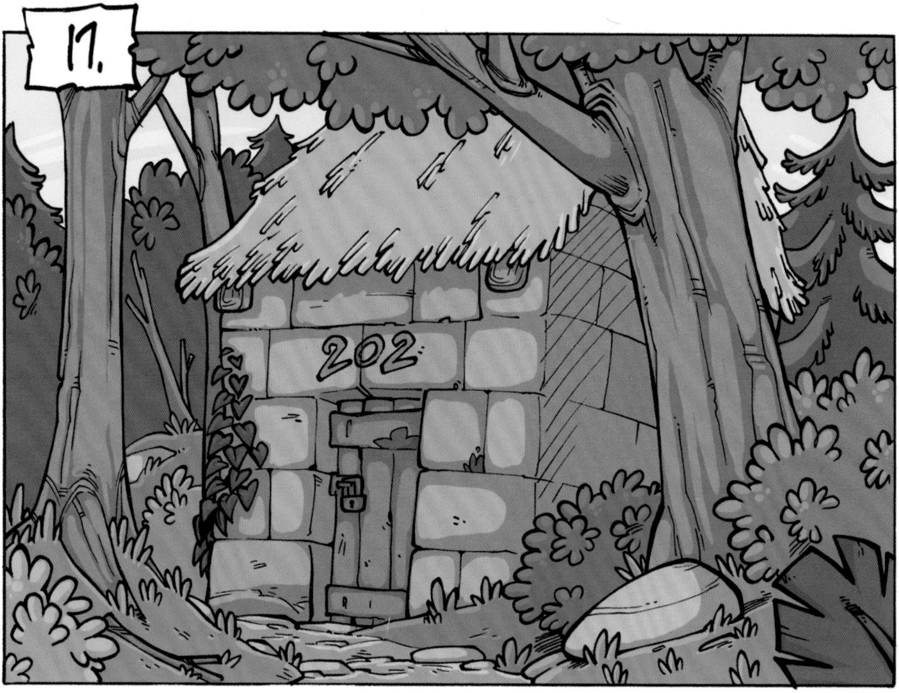
17.
202

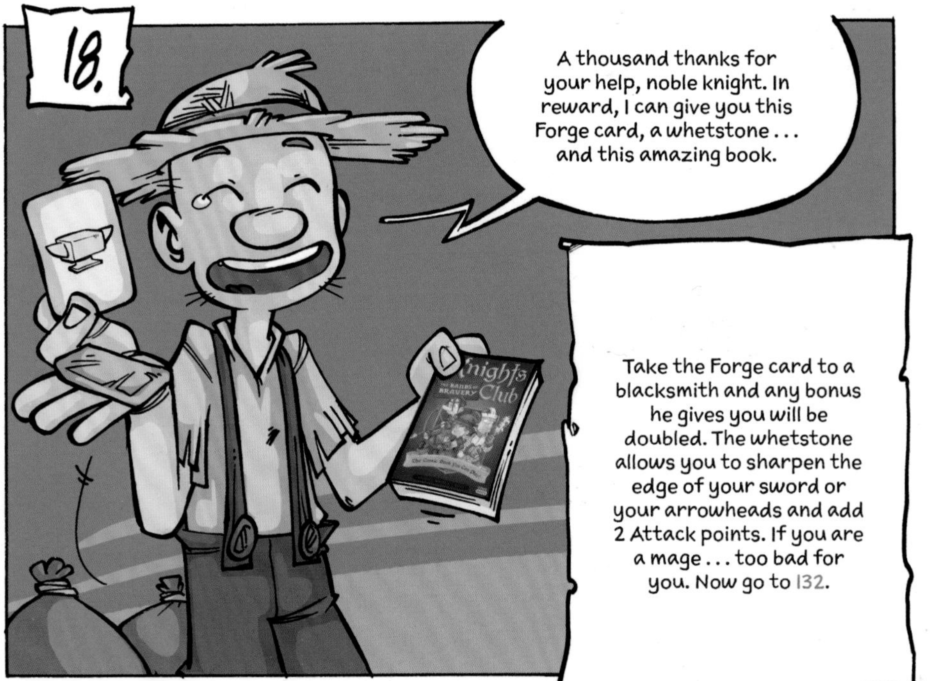
18.
A thousand thanks for your help, noble knight. In reward, I can give you this Forge card, a whetstone . . . and this amazing book.
Take the Forge card to a blacksmith and any bonus he gives you will be doubled. The whetstone allows you to sharpen the edge of your sword or your arrowheads and add 2 Attack points. If you are a mage . . . too bad for you. Now go to 132.

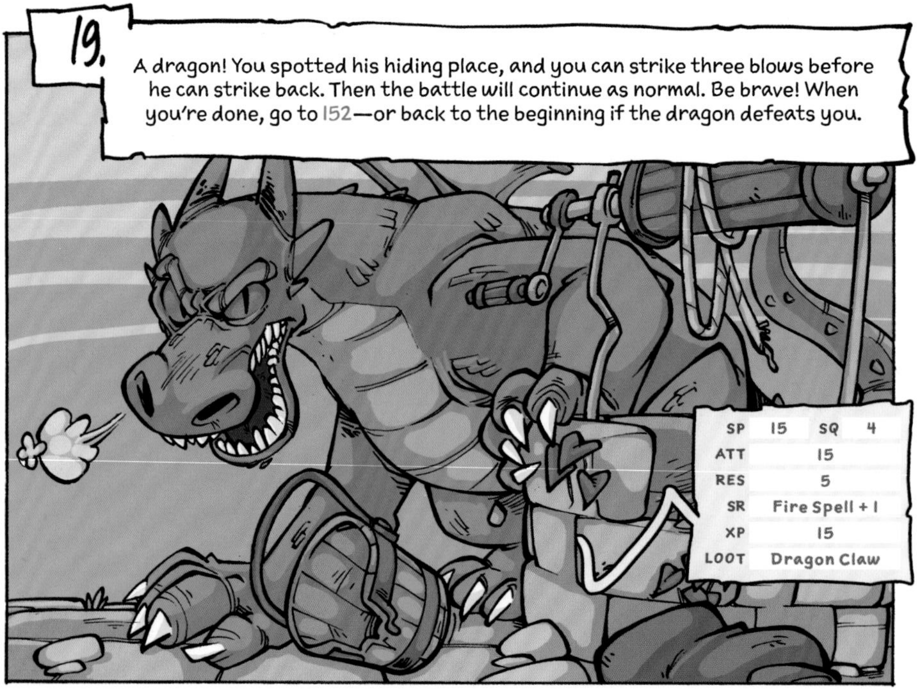
19.
A dragon! You spotted his hiding place, and you can strike three blows before he can strike back. Then the battle will continue as normal. Be brave! When you're done, go to 152—or back to the beginning if the dragon defeats you.

SP	15	SQ	4
ATT	15		
RES	5		
SR	Fire Spell + 1		
XP	15		
LOOT	Dragon Claw		

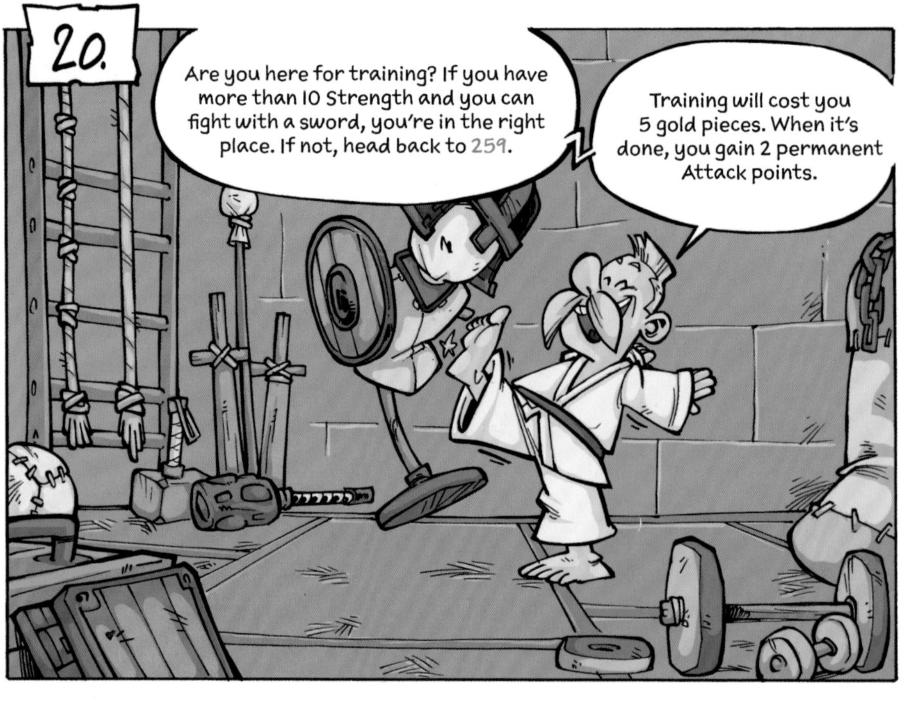
20.
Are you here for training? If you have more than 10 Strength and you can fight with a sword, you're in the right place. If not, head back to 259.
Training will cost you 5 gold pieces. When it's done, you gain 2 permanent Attack points.

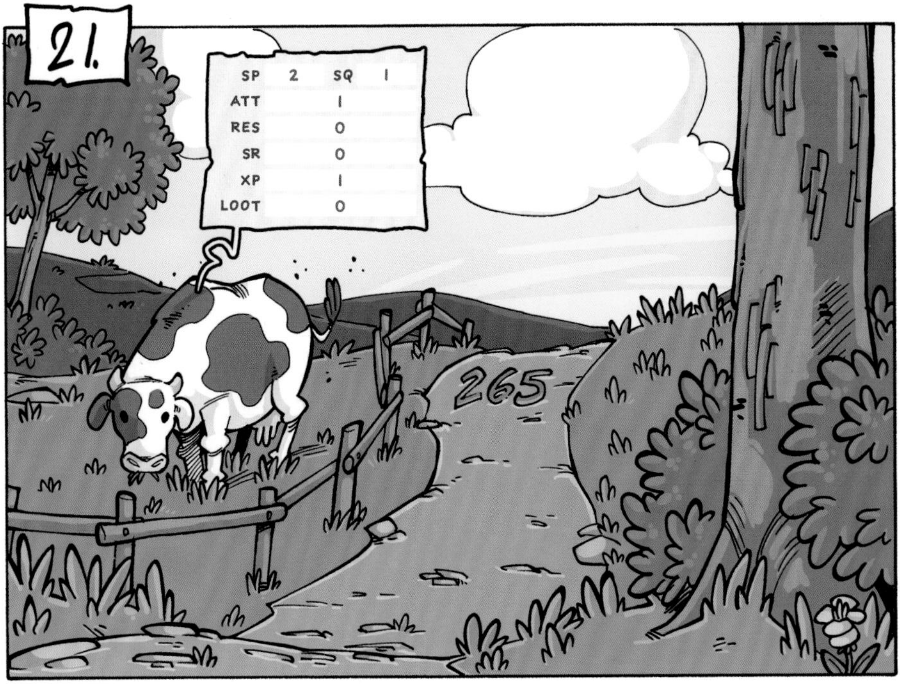
21.
SP 2 SQ 1
ATT 1
RES 0
SR 0
XP 1
LOOT 0
265

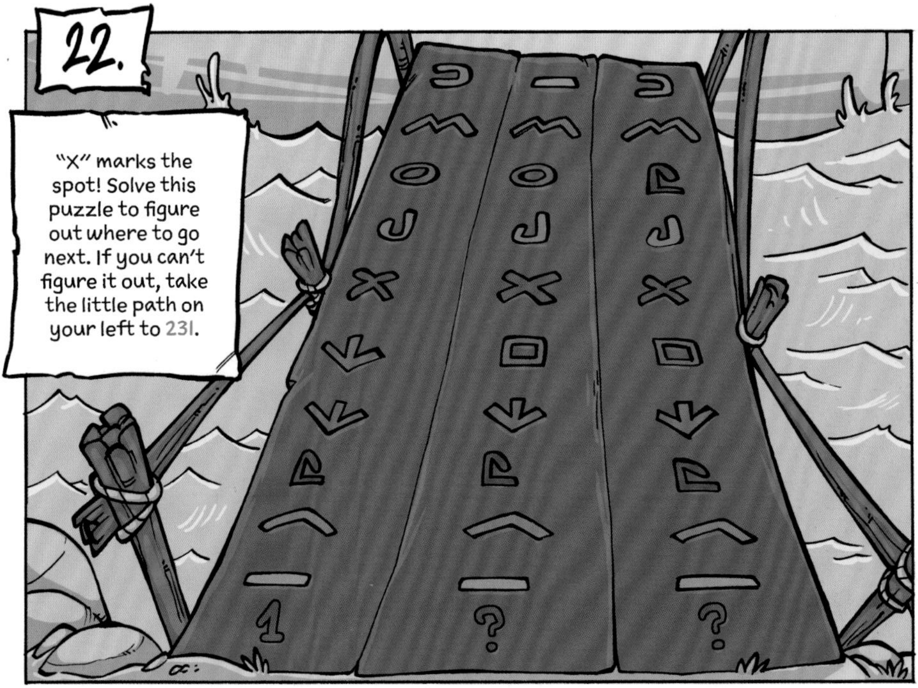
22.
"X" marks the spot! Solve this puzzle to figure out where to go next. If you can't figure it out, take the little path on your left to 231.
1
?
?

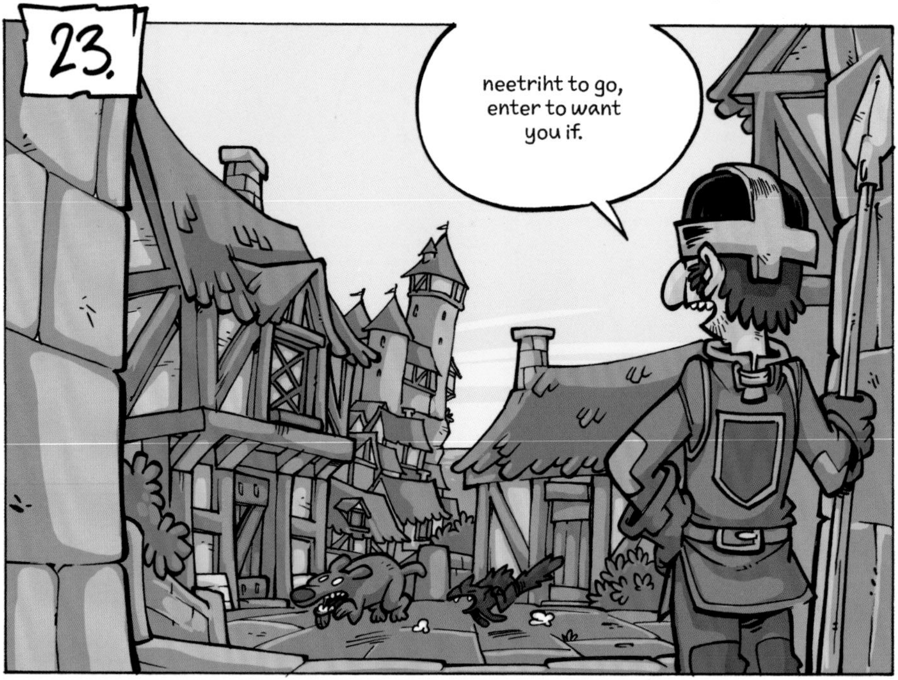
23.
neetriht to go,
enter to want
you if.

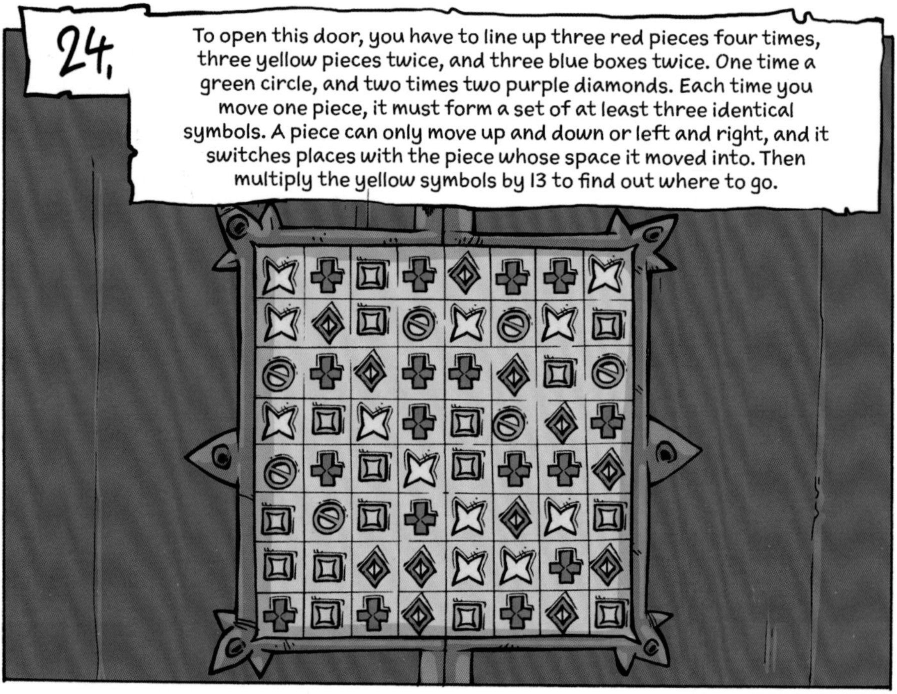
24.
To open this door, you have to line up three red pieces four times, three yellow pieces twice, and three blue boxes twice. One time a green circle, and two times two purple diamonds. Each time you move one piece, it must form a set of at least three identical symbols. A piece can only move up and down or left and right, and it switches places with the piece whose space it moved into. Then multiply the yellow symbols by 13 to find out where to go.

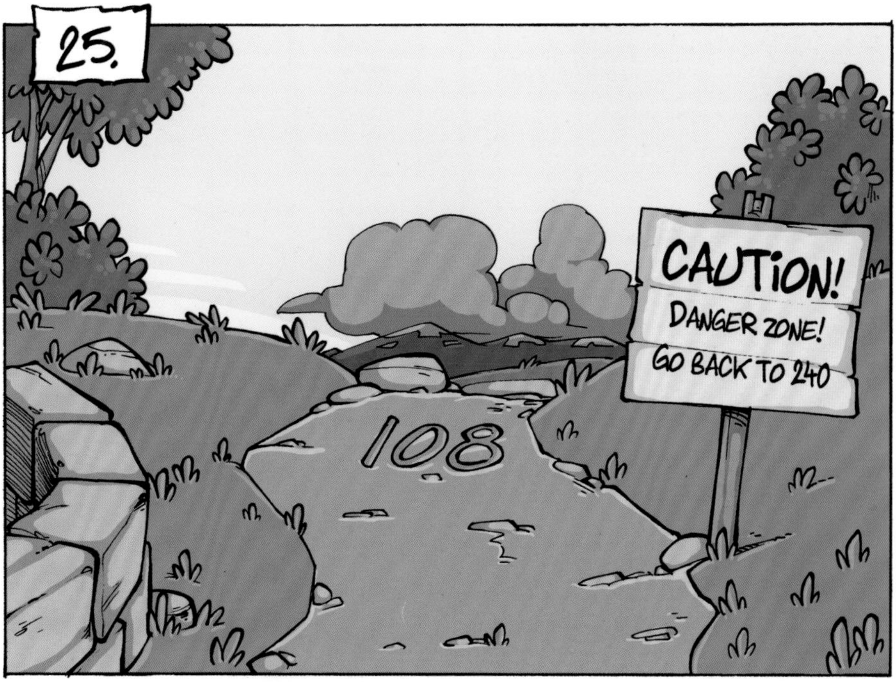
25.
CAUTION!
DANGER ZONE!
GO BACK TO 240
108

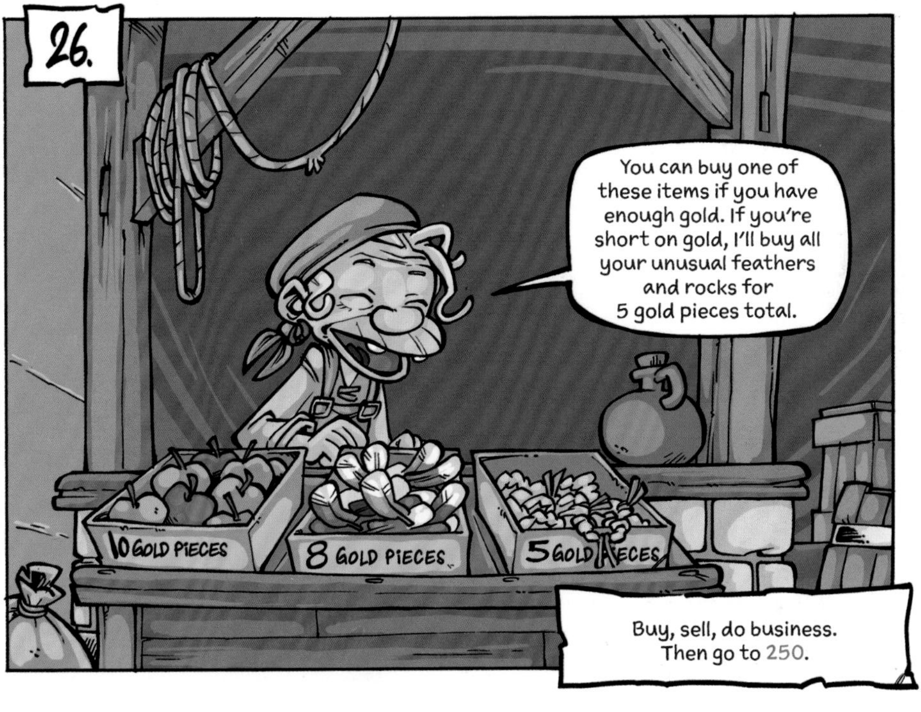
26.
You can buy one of these items if you have enough gold. If you're short on gold, I'll buy all your unusual feathers and rocks for 5 gold pieces total.
10 GOLD PIECES
8 GOLD PIECES
5 GOLD PIECES
Buy, sell, do business. Then go to 250.

21. Can't run away from this one! You have to battle the badger. If you win, go to 168. If you lose all your Strike Points, you die and have to restart your adventure. If you know how to charm animals, you can forego fighting this creature and tame it instead. Its attack points will be added to yours, for the next battle only. Good luck!

SP	8	SQ	2
ATT		4	
RES		1	
SR		0	
XP		5	
LOOT		0	

28.

29.

30. Oh yeah, you're awesome! Well, if you leave the village and head north, you'll find a small hidden path on the right that leads to Yannick's caravan. He loves games—but tell him Olaf sent you, or he won't play a game with you. Now go back to 211. I have things to do.

31.

	SP	7	SQ	2
	ATT		4	
	RES		0	
	SR		0	
	XP		4	
	LOOT		Black Feather	

CAW

Go on your way to 97,
but first (if you wish)
pick a fight with this crow.

32.

33.

Whoo! Whoo-
hoooo! Yes! That's it!
Yow-hoo! Yowza
wowza!

Both of you get
out and go to 104
right now!

34.

Where do you think
you're going? Can't you
read? I suggest you turn
back around, unless you're
here to give us back our
pendant?

A pendant? What pendant? If
you're curious, go on to 339. If you
have no fear, fight and go to 271.
Or you can head back to 318.

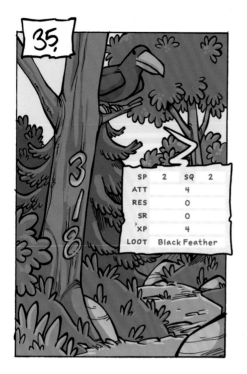

SP	2	SQ	2
ATT		4	
RES		0	
SR		0	
XP		4	
LOOT		Black Feather	

Fleeing was costly. You lose 1 Attack point during the next battle, whatever your rank. If you fought that horrible rat and killed it, bravo to you!

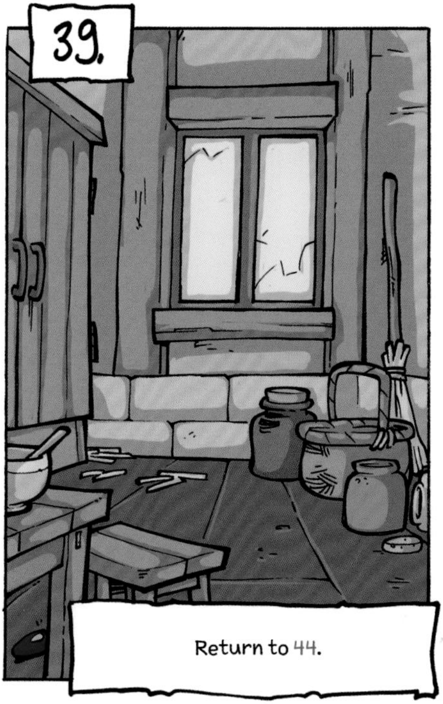
39.
Return to 44.

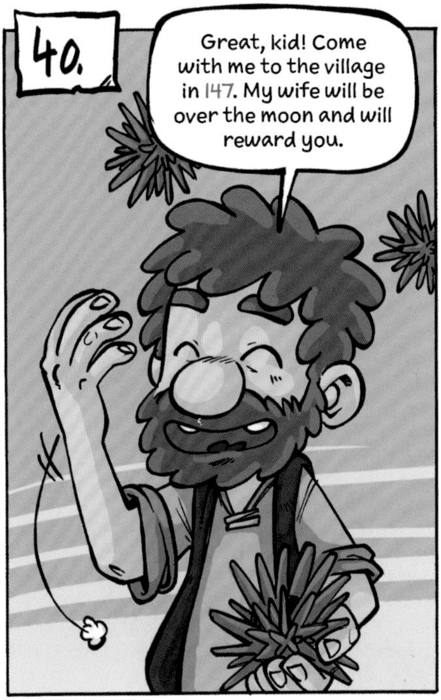
40.
Great, kid! Come with me to the village in 147. My wife will be over the moon and will reward you.

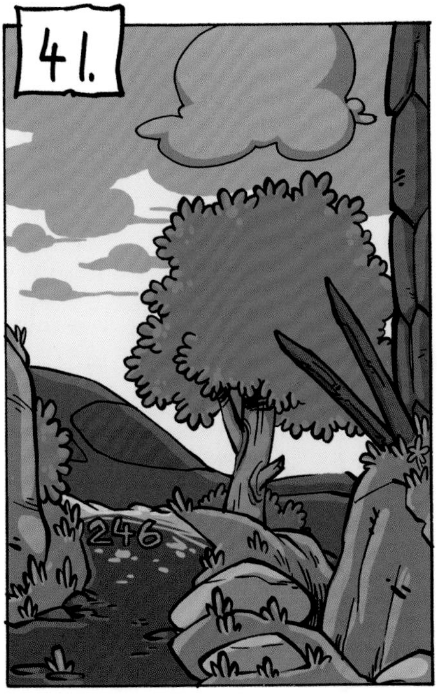
41.
246

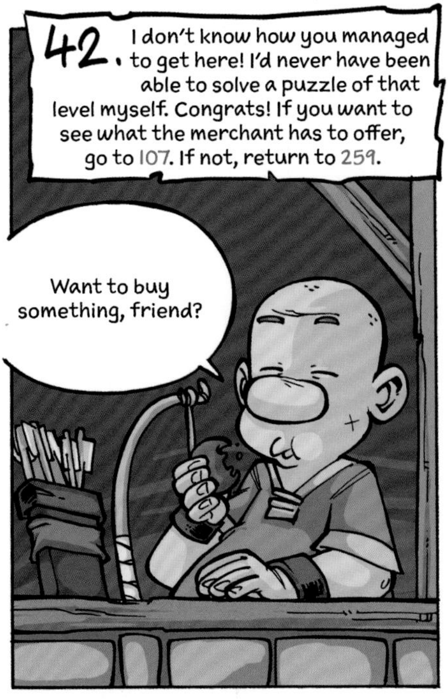
42.
I don't know how you managed to get here! I'd never have been able to solve a puzzle of that level myself. Congrats! If you want to see what the merchant has to offer, go to 107. If not, return to 259.
Want to buy something, friend?

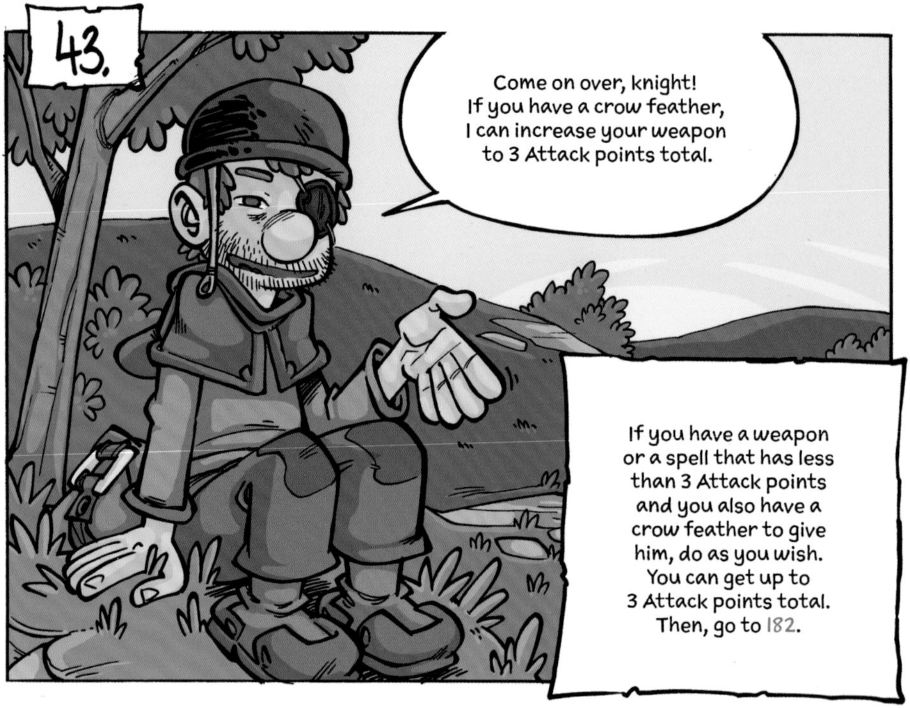
43.
Come on over, knight! If you have a crow feather, I can increase your weapon to 3 Attack points total.
If you have a weapon or a spell that has less than 3 Attack points and you also have a crow feather to give him, do as you wish. You can get up to 3 Attack points total. Then, go to 182.

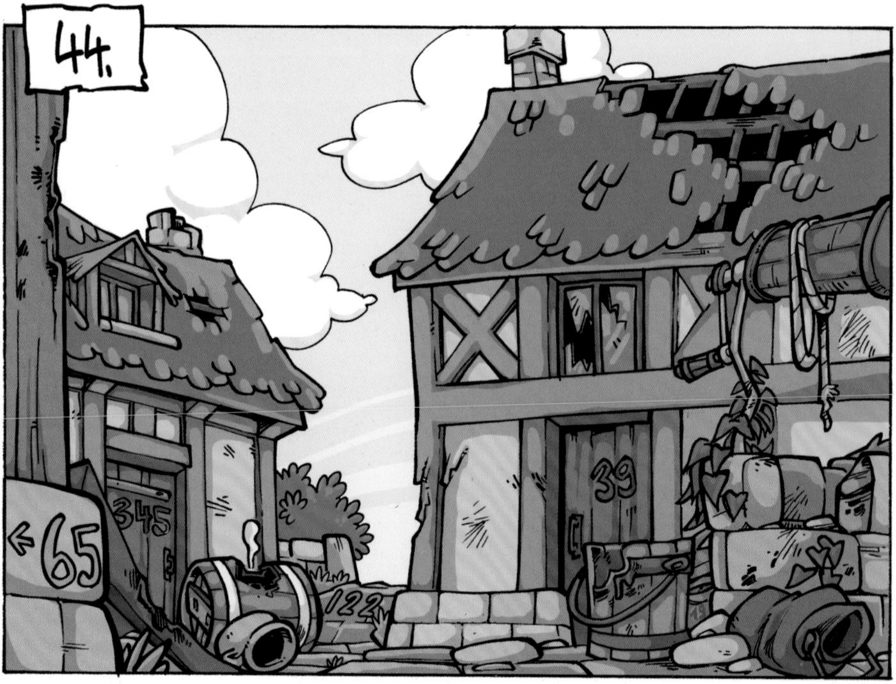
44.
39
345
65
122

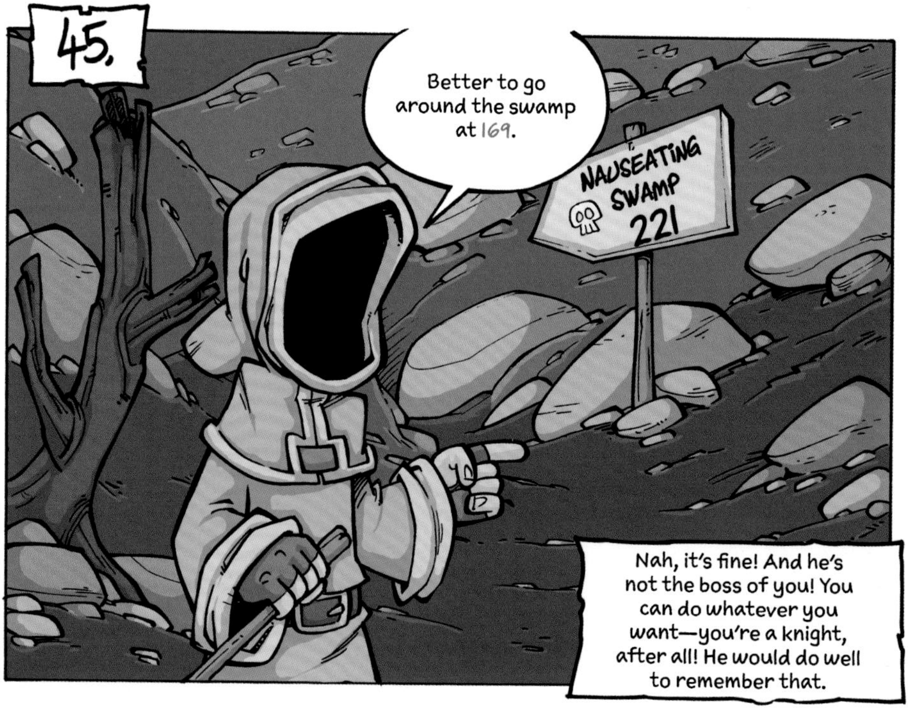
45.
Better to go around the swamp at 169.
NAUSEATING SWAMP 221
Nah, it's fine! And he's not the boss of you! You can do whatever you want—you're a knight, after all! He would do well to remember that.

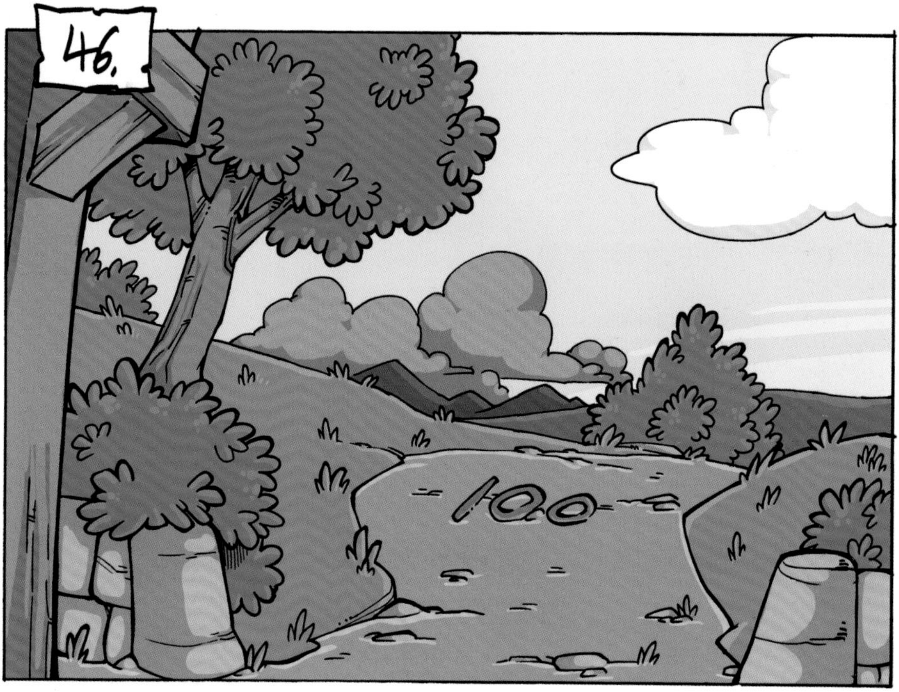
46.
100

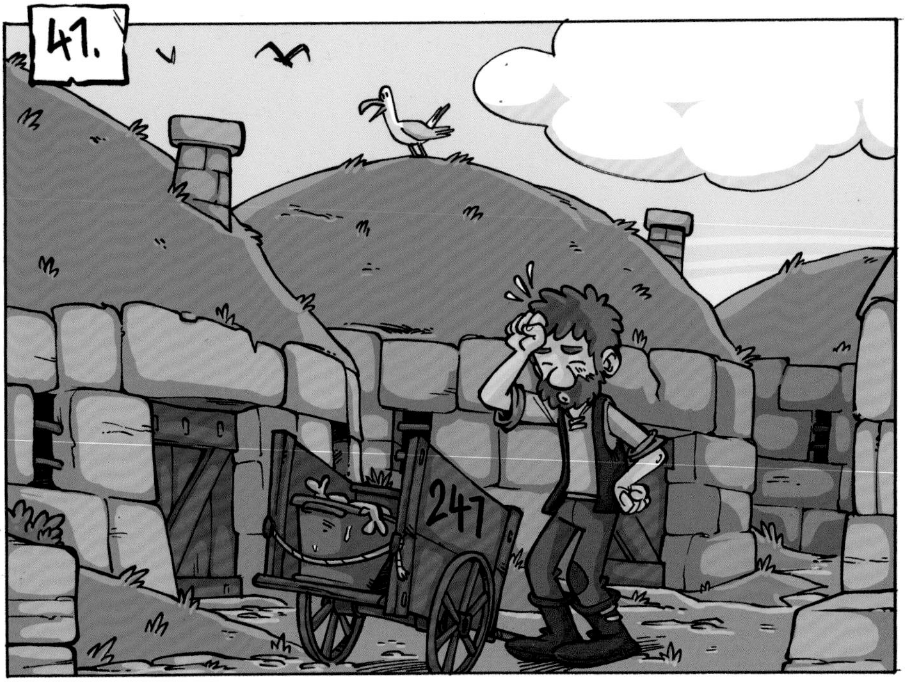
47.
247

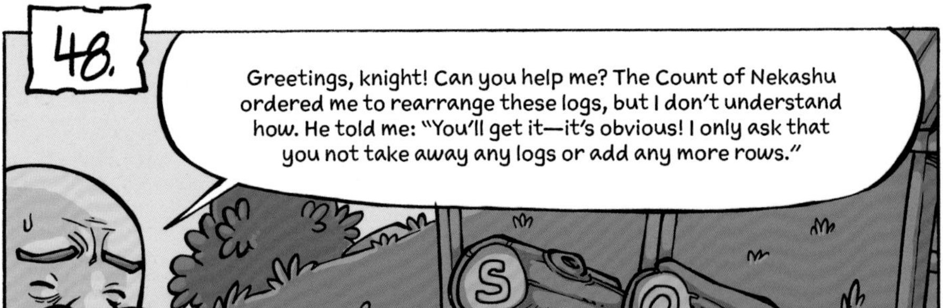
48.
Greetings, knight! Can you help me? The Count of Nekashu ordered me to rearrange these logs, but I don't understand how. He told me: "You'll get it—it's obvious! I only ask that you not take away any logs or add any more rows."
S O
M W G R
F A R E D
P
S G L S O E L E

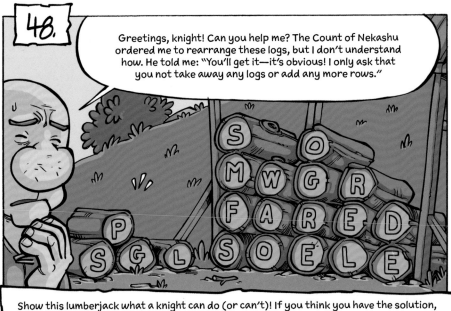

Show this lumberjack what a knight can do (or can't)! If you think you have the solution, go to 165. If you have more than 11 in Intelligence, go to 326. If you're dying of boredom from having to solve all these puzzles and would rather thump a monster, go to 190.

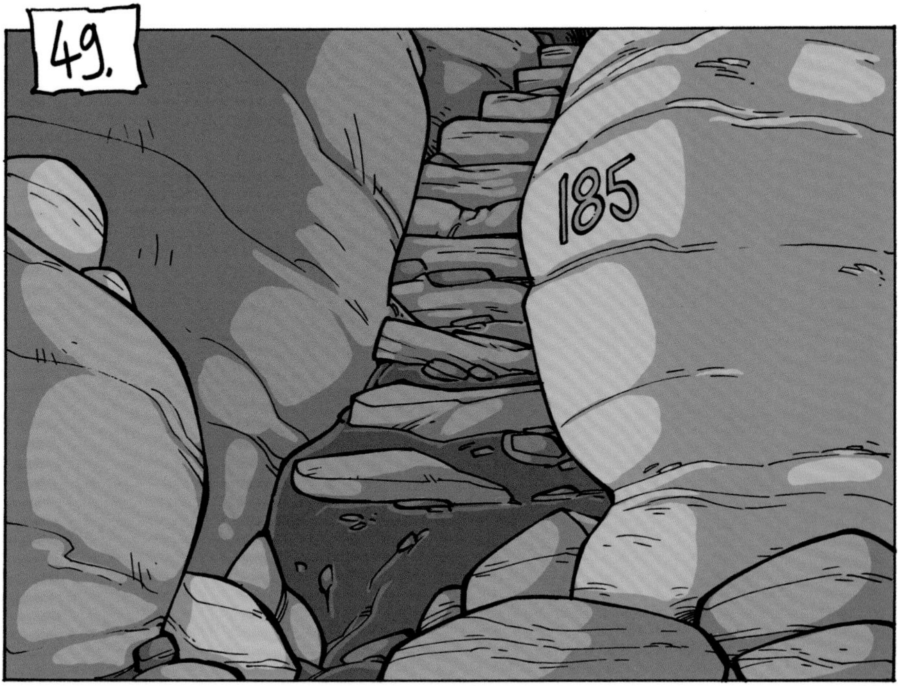
49.
185

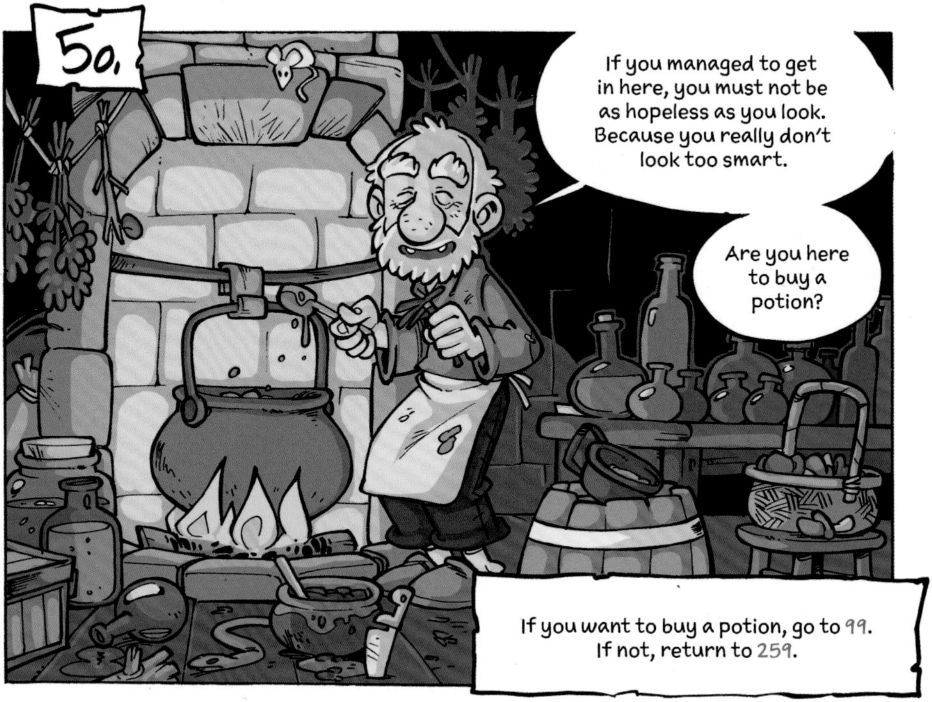
50.
If you managed to get in here, you must not be as hopeless as you look. Because you really don't look too smart.
Are you here to buy a potion?
If you want to buy a potion, go to 99.
If not, return to 259.

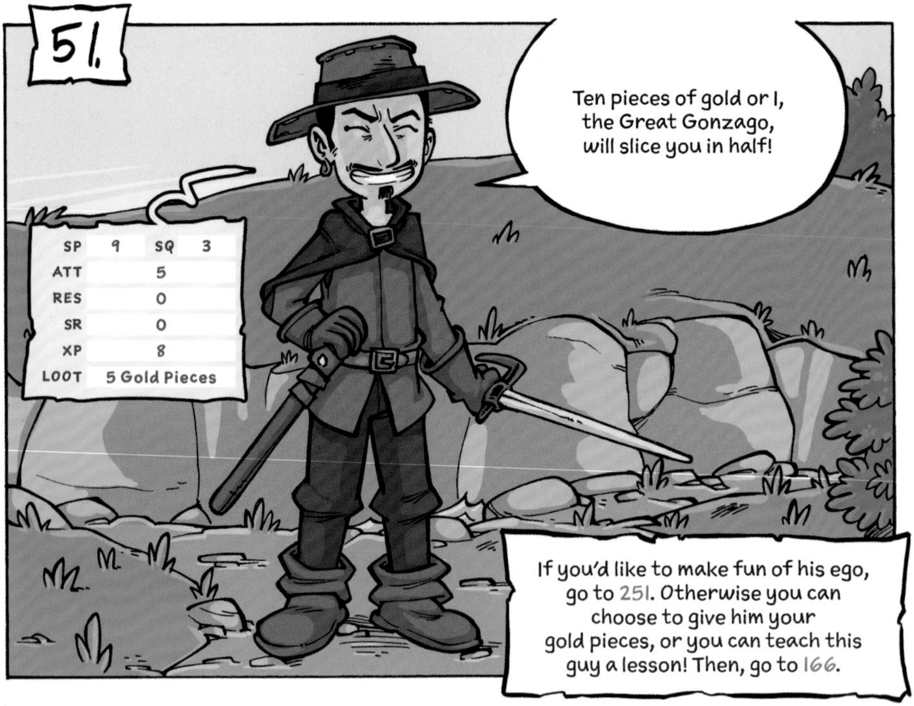
51.
SP 9 SQ 3
ATT 5
RES 0
SR 0
XP 8
LOOT 5 Gold Pieces
Ten pieces of gold or I, the Great Gonzago, will slice you in half!
If you'd like to make fun of his ego, go to 251. Otherwise you can choose to give him your gold pieces, or you can teach this guy a lesson! Then, go to 166.

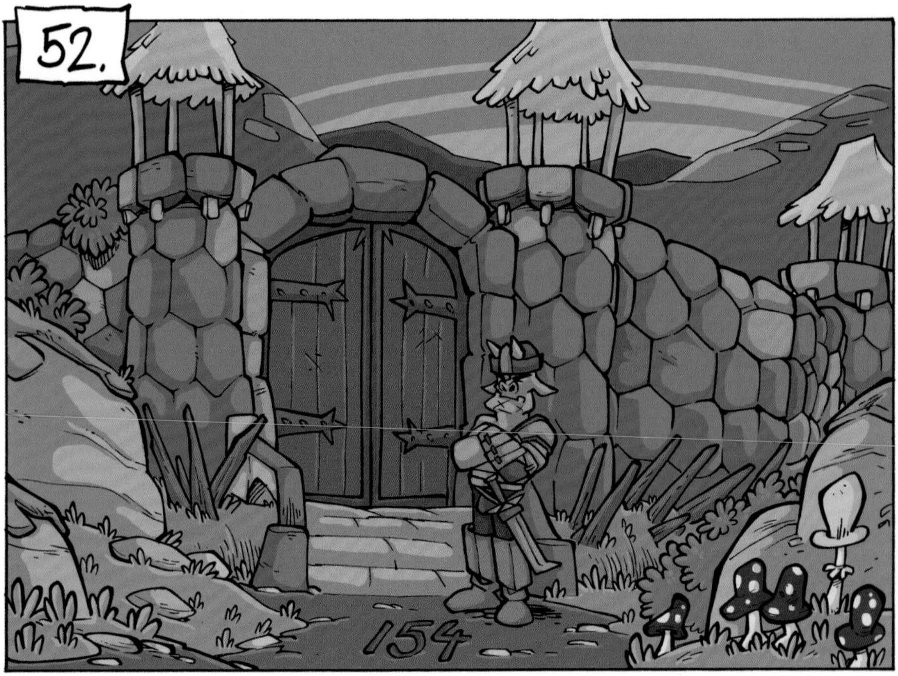
52.
154

53.

Hmm. Not bad for a human! I say that, but in fact none of my people have been able to answer my little question, so I've been left in peace to read some masterpieces of medieval literature. So, what can I do for you? I can only find one book for you before closing time!

If you want to ask for a book that will help you improve your spells, go to 274. If you want a book about precious stones, go to 129. If you want something from Quirk Books, go to 218. You can also just go to 239 and leave.

54.

You can't escape from this zombie, but if you defeat it, you get all the stuff in 281. If you have greater than 15 Strength, you get a first Stun blow that considerably slows down your enemy. As a result, you can now spin your wheel three times in a row!

SP	30	SQ	7
ATT	20		
RES	0		
SR	0		
XP	5		
LOOT	0		

55.

56.

Hello. Do you have a library card? I can't let you in if you don't. Sorry.

If you have successfully won a library card during your adventures in Knights Book I, you can go to 150 and enter. If not, turn back to 241. (And listen, don't even think of trying to force your way in.)

57.

Rare are the humans we can rely on. You won't be able to keep the pendant, but it matters not. Here instead is an amulet we enchanted ourselves. It will not only give 5 extra Attack points, but also the same in Resistance.

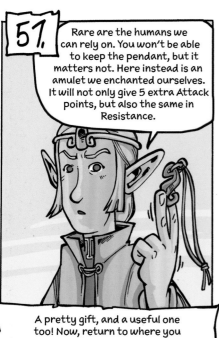

A pretty gift, and a useful one too! Now, return to where you were before you went to 94.

58.

SP	7	SQ	2
ATT	4		
RES	0		
SR	0		
XP	4		
LOOT	Black Feather		

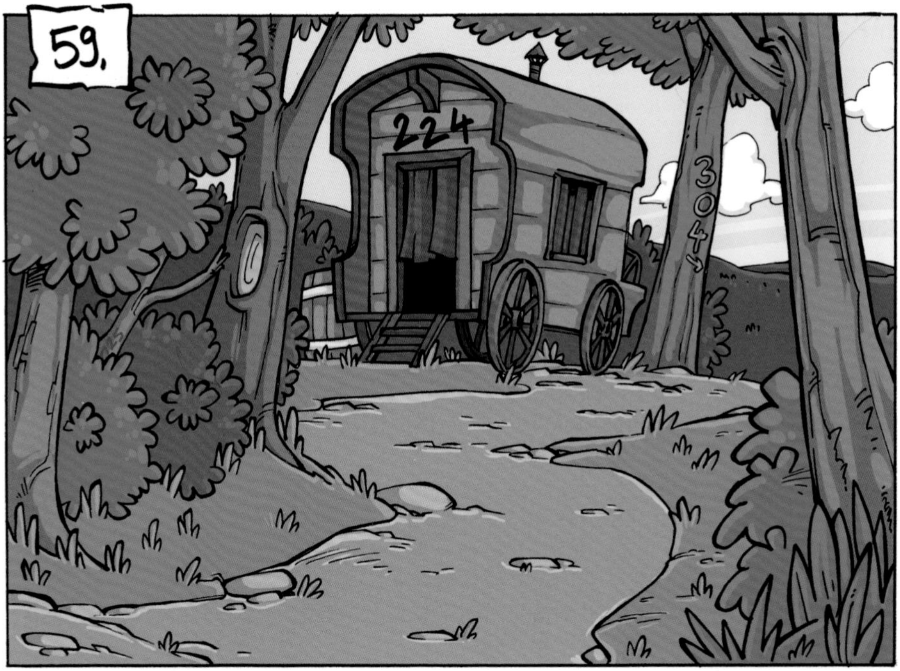
59.
224
3041

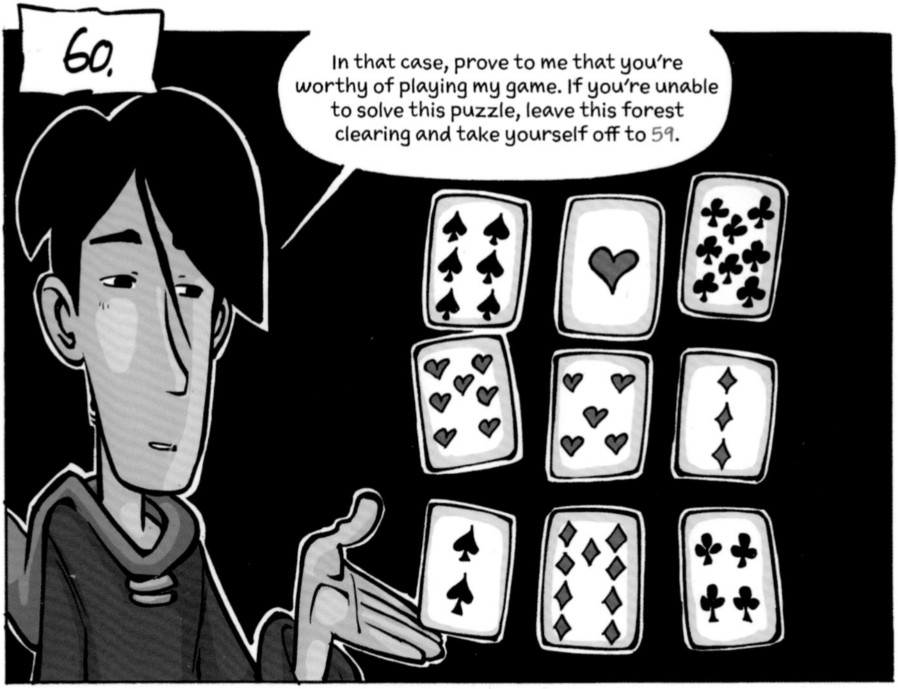
60.
In that case, prove to me that you're worthy of playing my game. If you're unable to solve this puzzle, leave this forest clearing and take yourself off to 59.

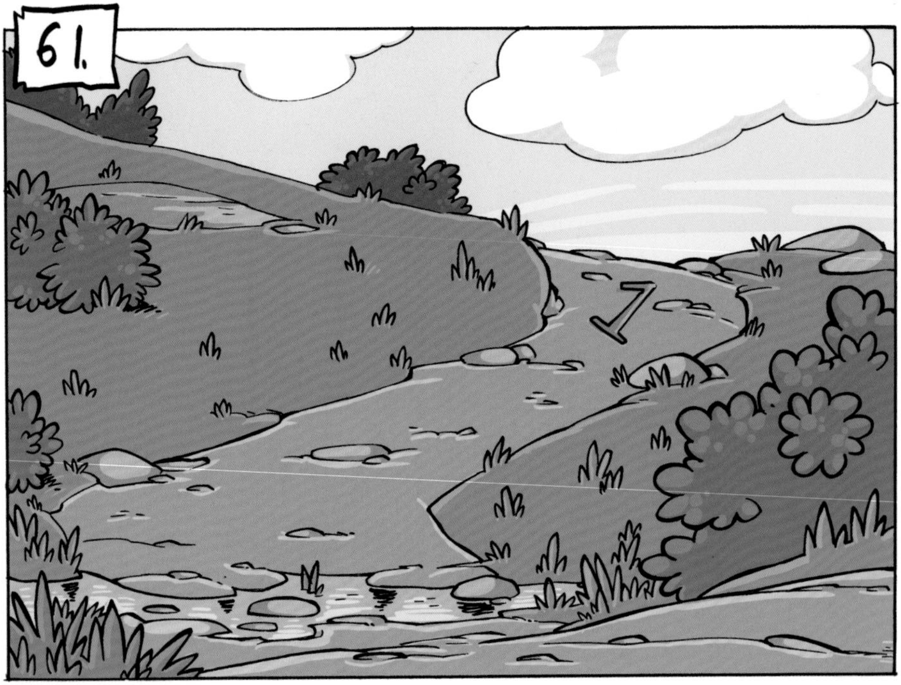
61.
7

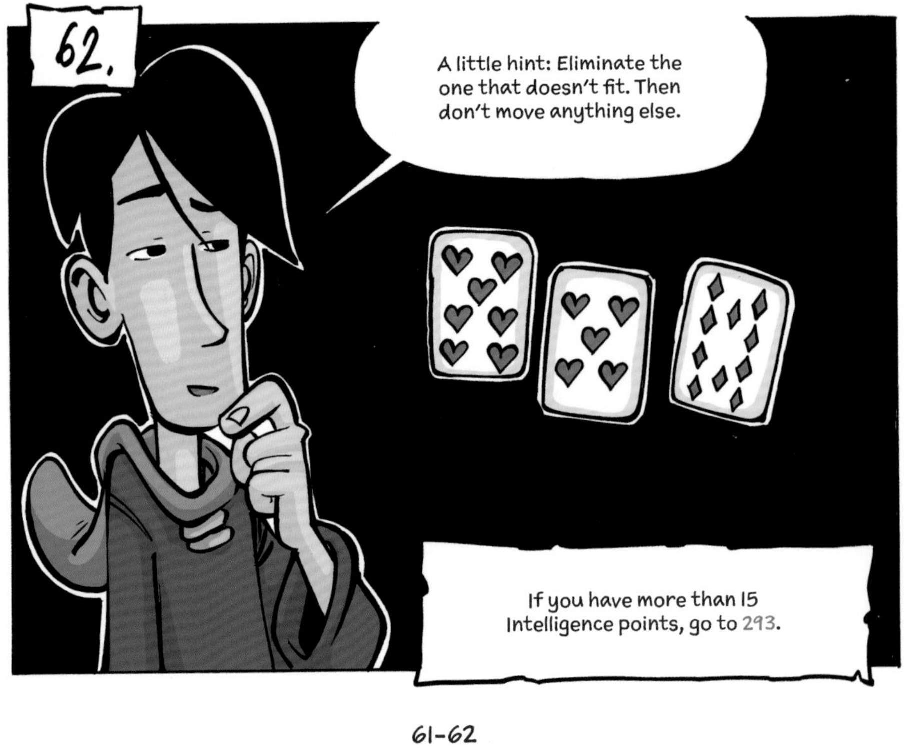
62.
A little hint: Eliminate the one that doesn't fit. Then don't move anything else.
If you have more than 15 Intelligence points, go to 293.

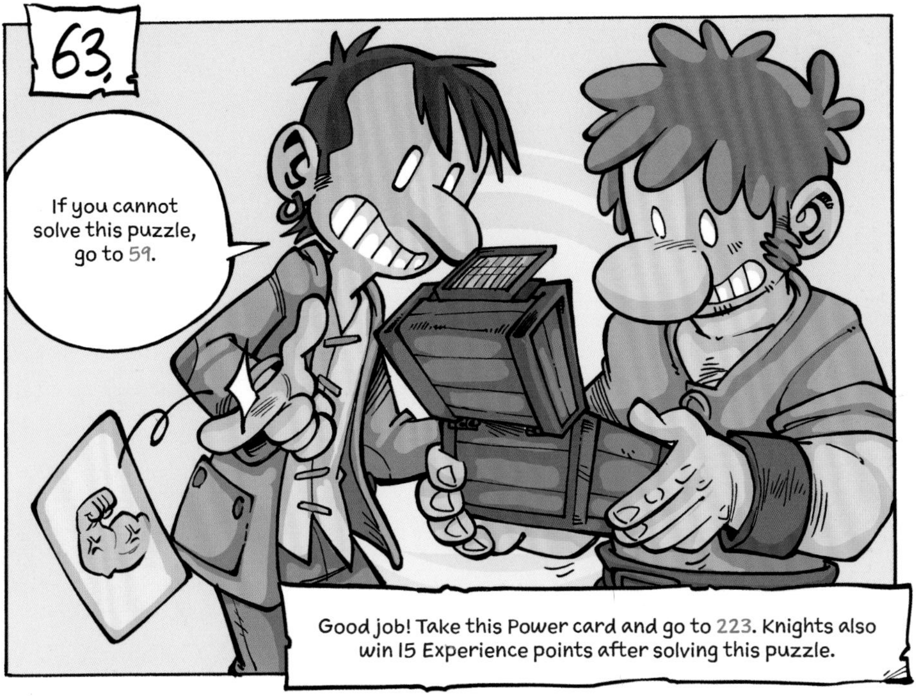
63.
If you cannot solve this puzzle, go to 59.
Good job! Take this Power card and go to 223. Knights also win 15 Experience points after solving this puzzle.

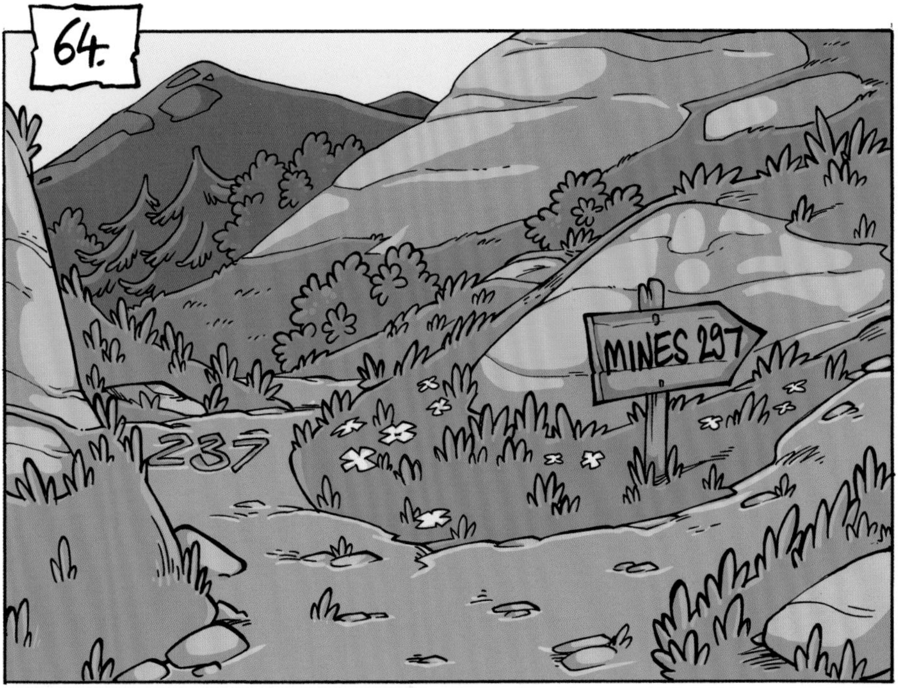
64.
MINES 297
237

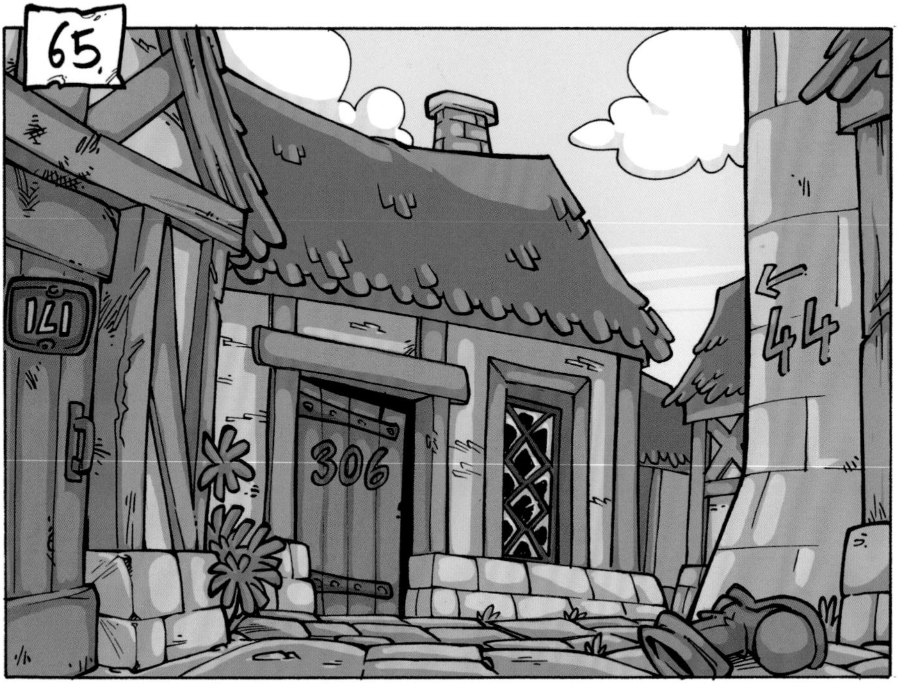
65.
171
306
44

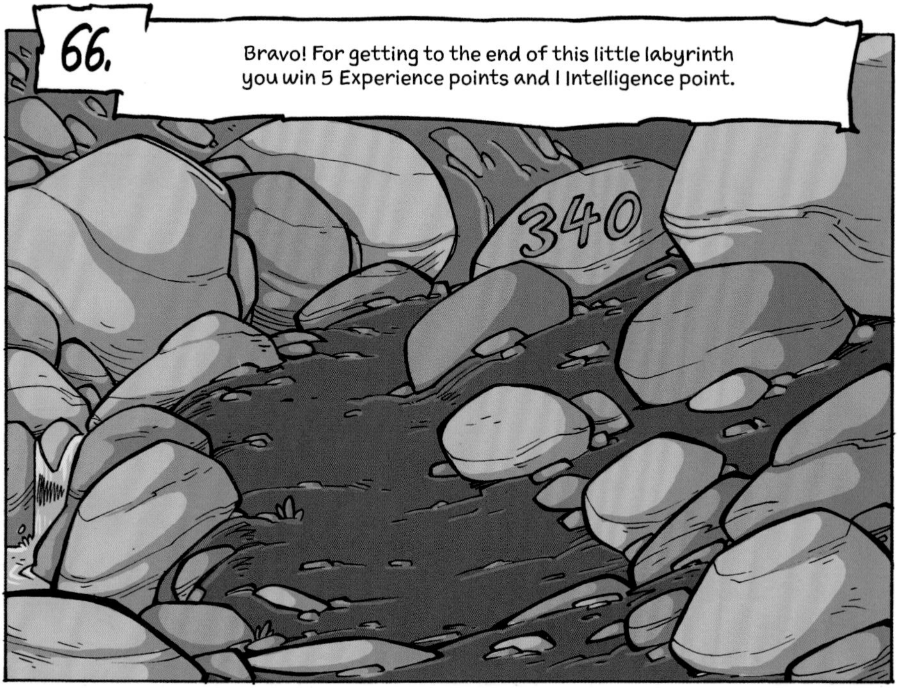
66.
Bravo! For getting to the end of this little labyrinth you win 5 Experience points and 1 Intelligence point.
340

67.

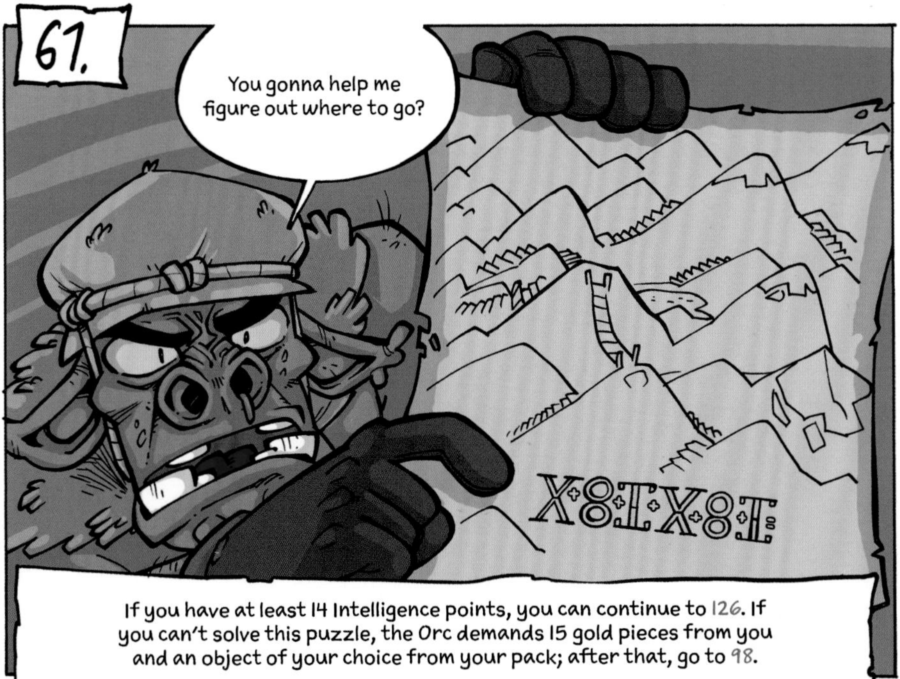
You gonna help me figure out where to go?

If you have at least 14 Intelligence points, you can continue to 126. If you can't solve this puzzle, the Orc demands 15 gold pieces from you and an object of your choice from your pack; after that, go to 98.

68.

Did you pass a crow before you came here?
If so, it pecked your nose and you lose 10 Strike points.
If you're a squire, the crow plucked 5 gold pieces from you!

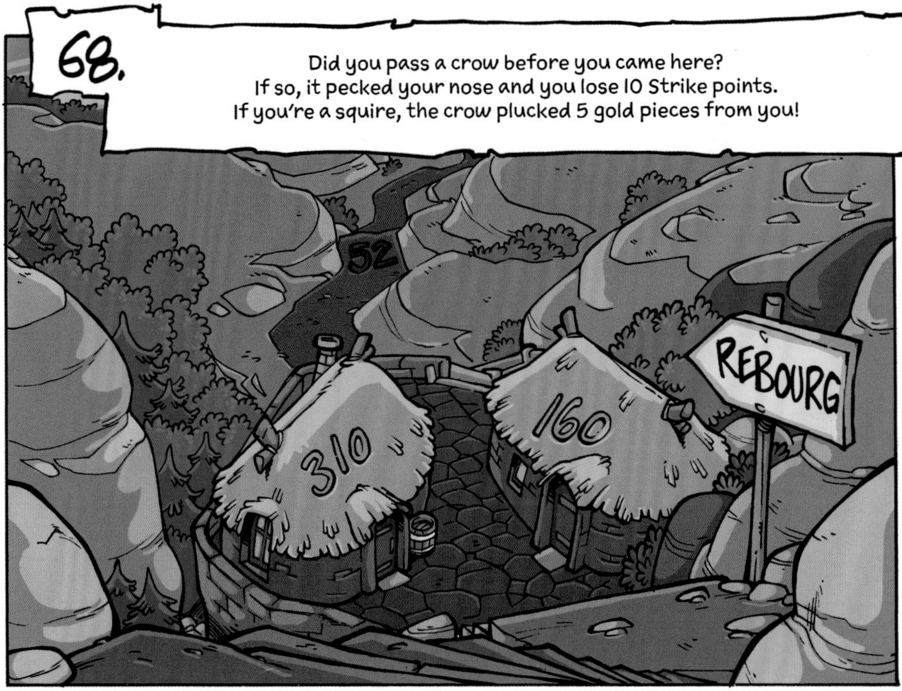
52
REBOURG
310
160

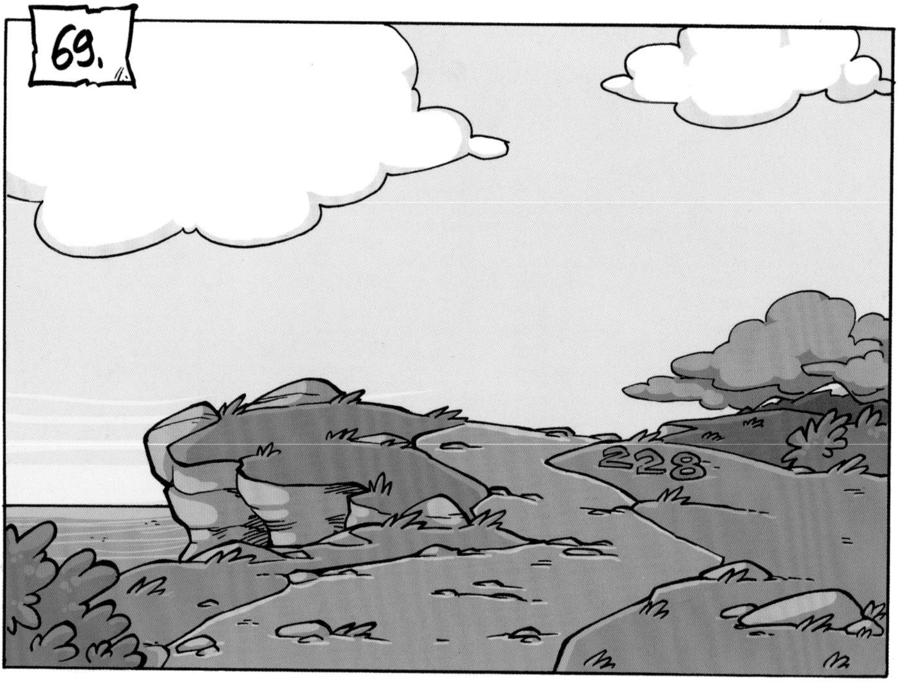
69.
228

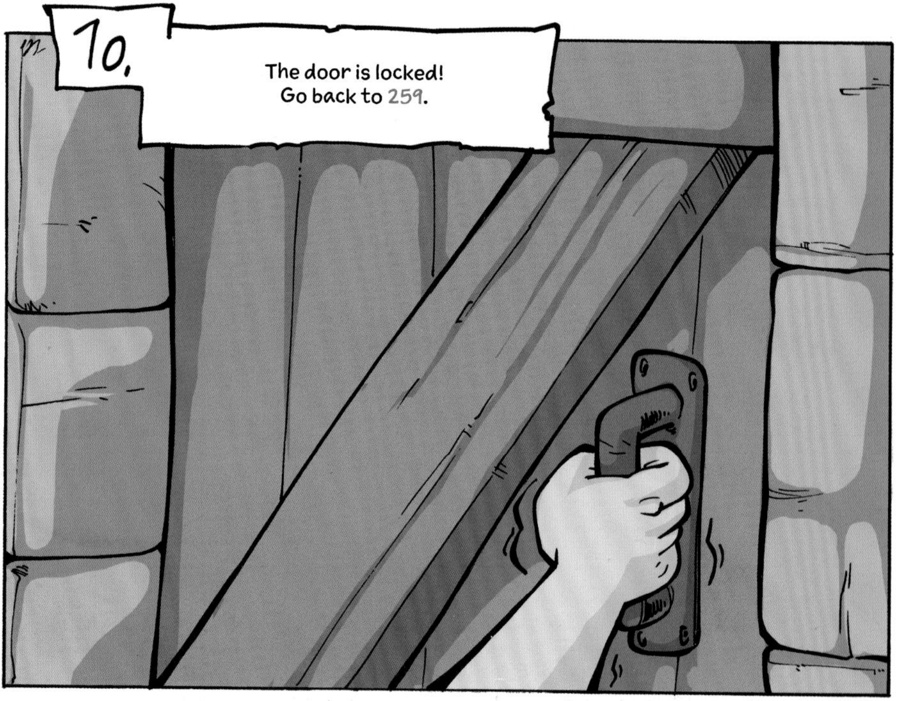
70.
The door is locked!
Go back to 259.

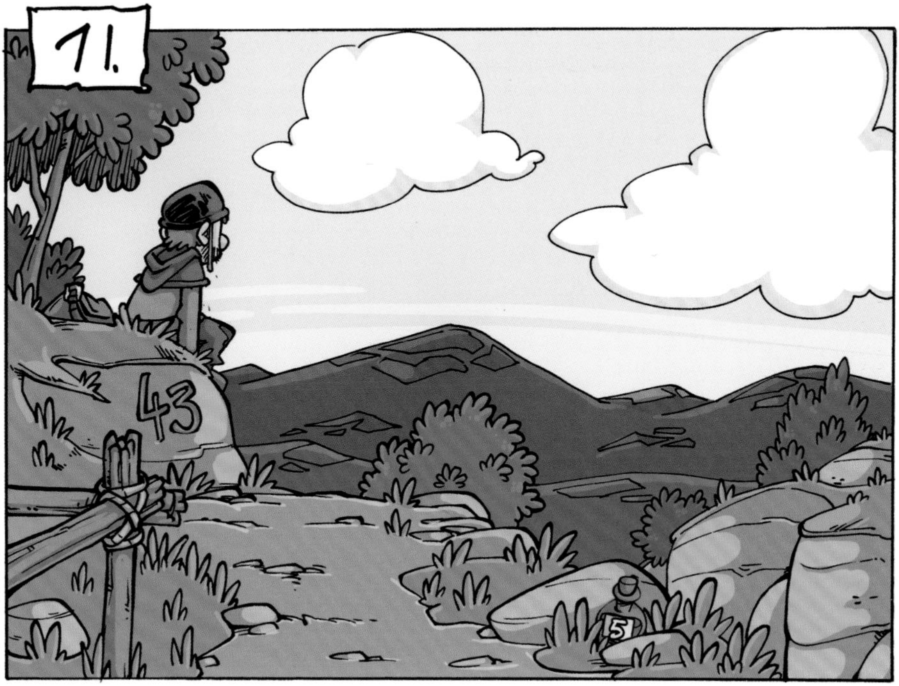
71.
43
5

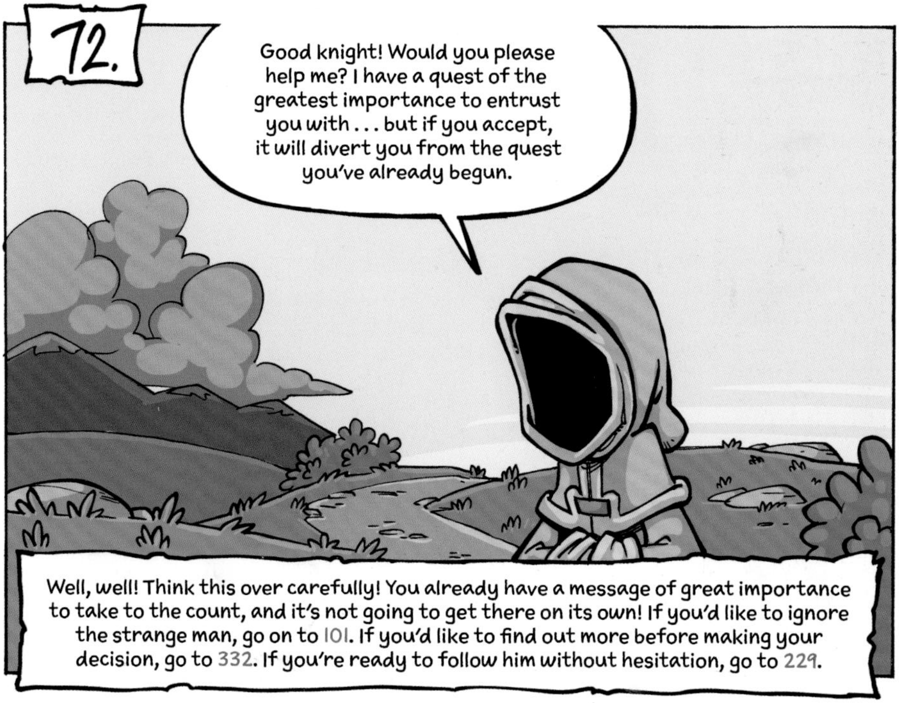
72.
Good knight! Would you please help me? I have a quest of the greatest importance to entrust you with . . . but if you accept, it will divert you from the quest you've already begun.
Well, well! Think this over carefully! You already have a message of great importance to take to the count, and it's not going to get there on its own! If you'd like to ignore the strange man, go on to 101. If you'd like to find out more before making your decision, go to 332. If you're ready to follow him without hesitation, go to 229.

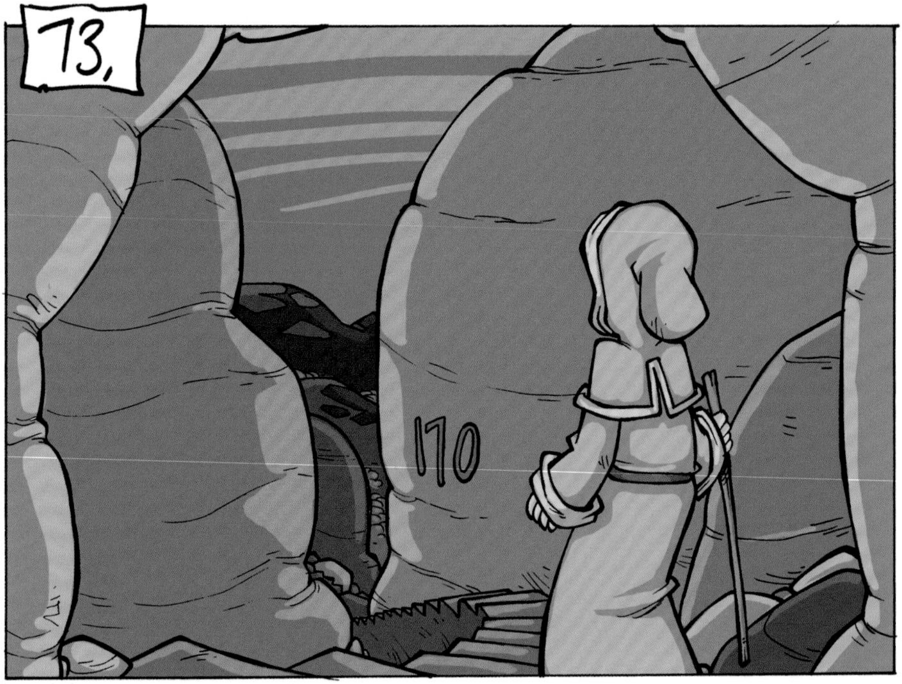
73.
170

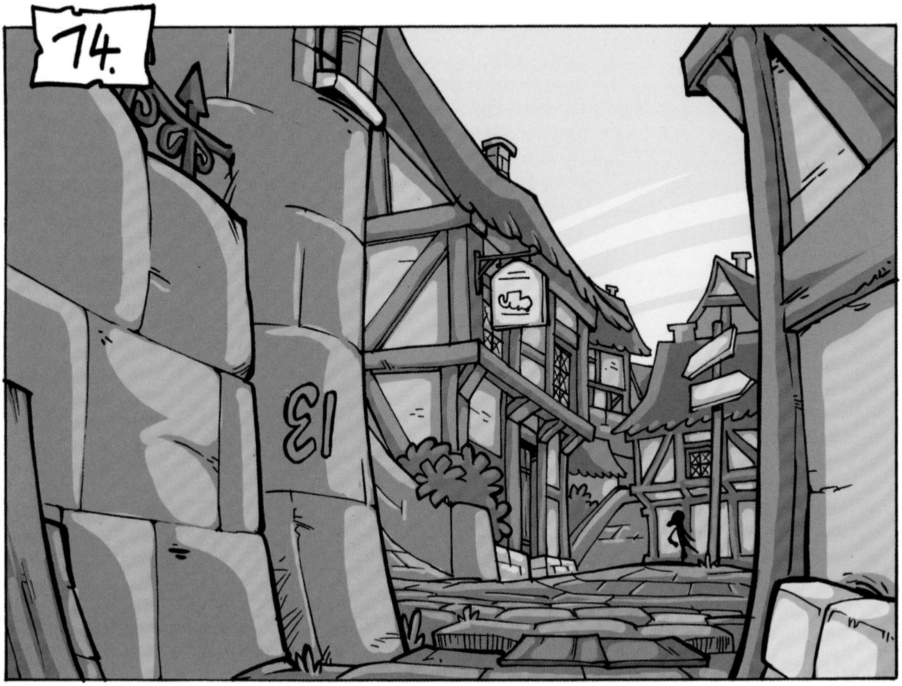
74.
13

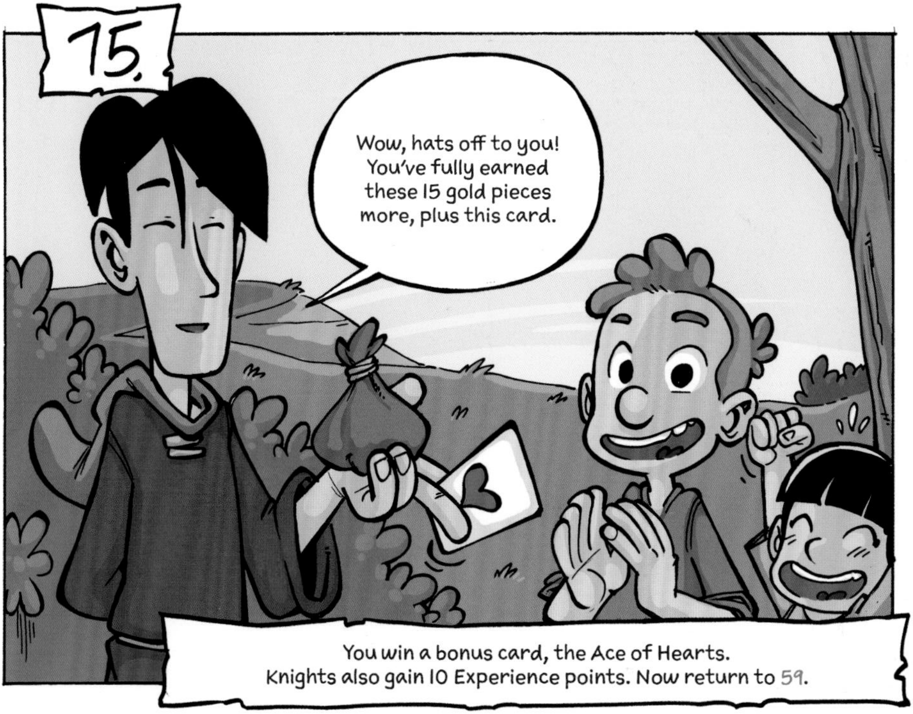
75.
Wow, hats off to you! You've fully earned these 15 gold pieces more, plus this card.
You win a bonus card, the Ace of Hearts.
Knights also gain 10 Experience points. Now return to 59.

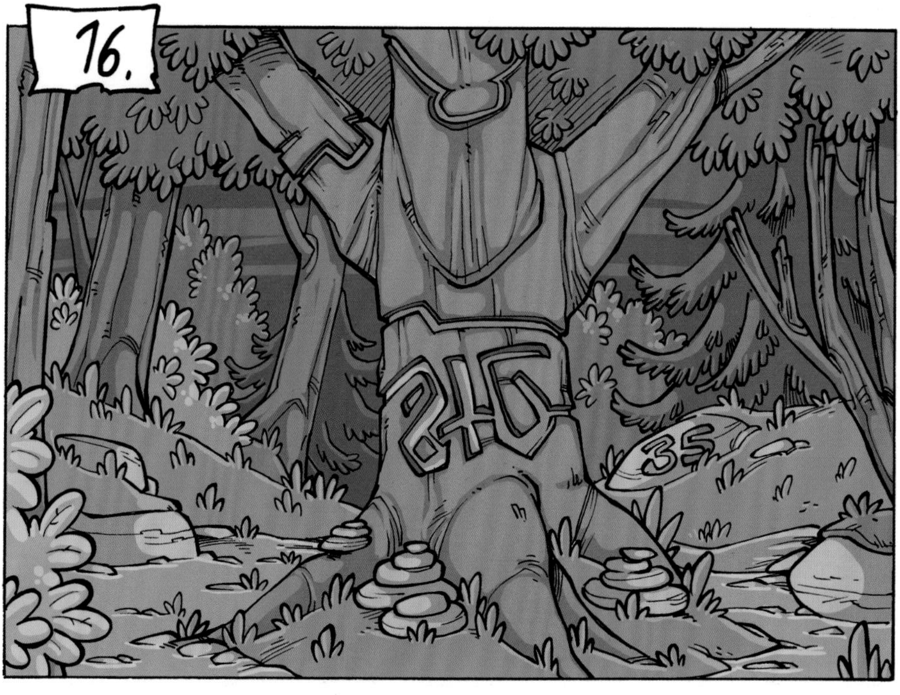
76.
35

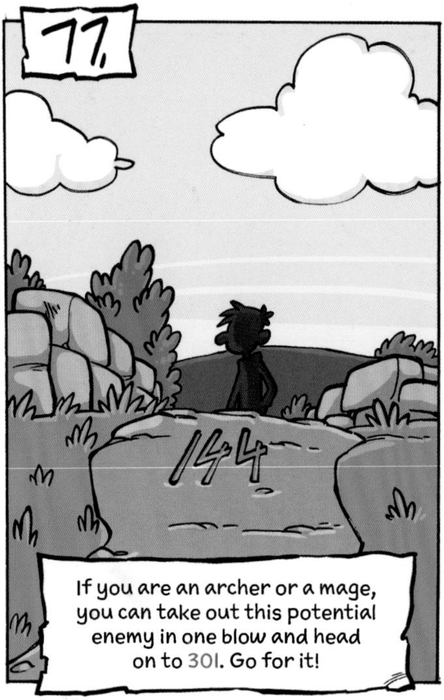
77.
144
If you are an archer or a mage, you can take out this potential enemy in one blow and head on to 301. Go for it!

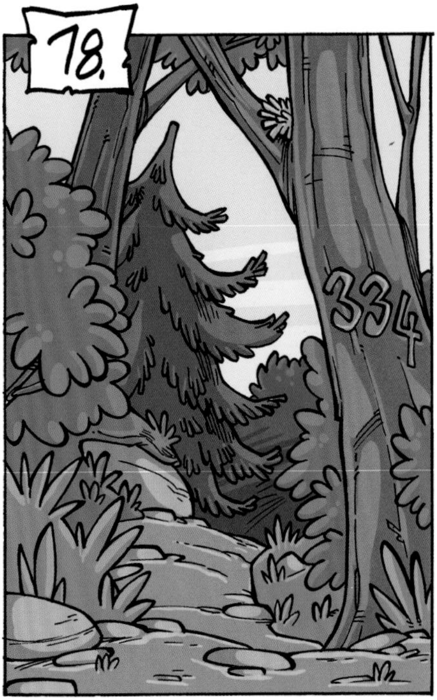
78.
334

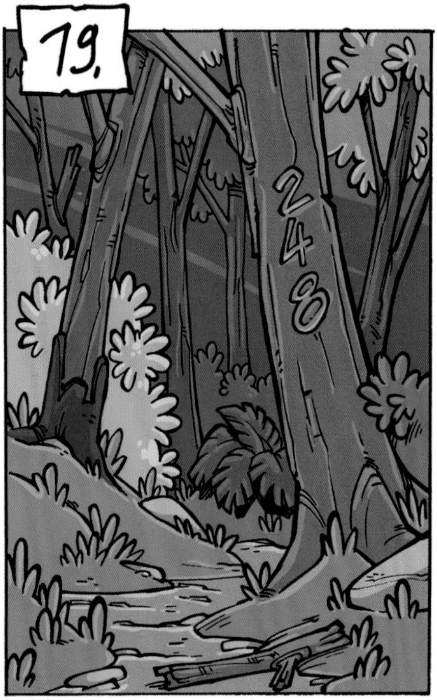
79.
248

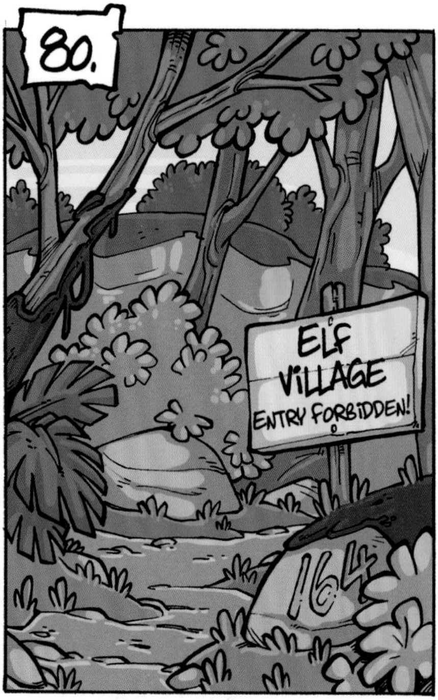
80.
ELF VILLAGE
ENTRY FORBIDDEN!
164

81.

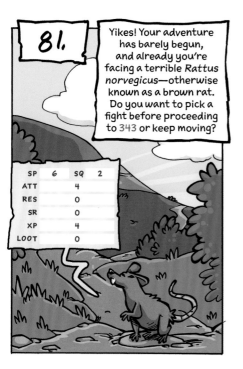

Yikes! Your adventure has barely begun, and already you're facing a terrible *Rattus norvegicus*—otherwise known as a brown rat. Do you want to pick a fight before proceeding to 343 or keep moving?

SP	6	SQ	2
ATT		4	
RES		0	
SR		0	
XP		4	
LOOT		0	

82.

Still no idea? Go back to 36.

83.

84.

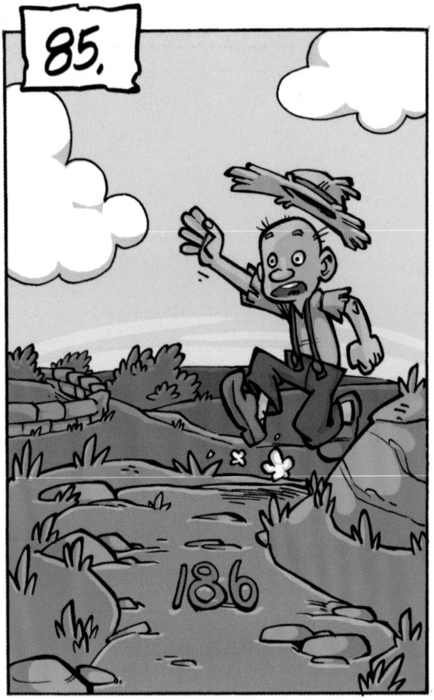
85.
186

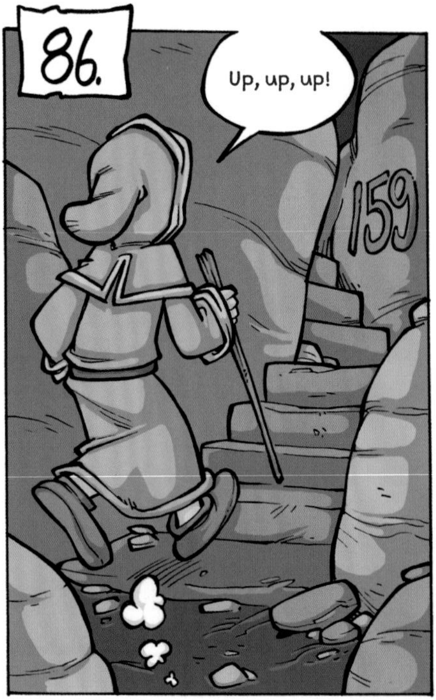
86.
Up, up, up!
159

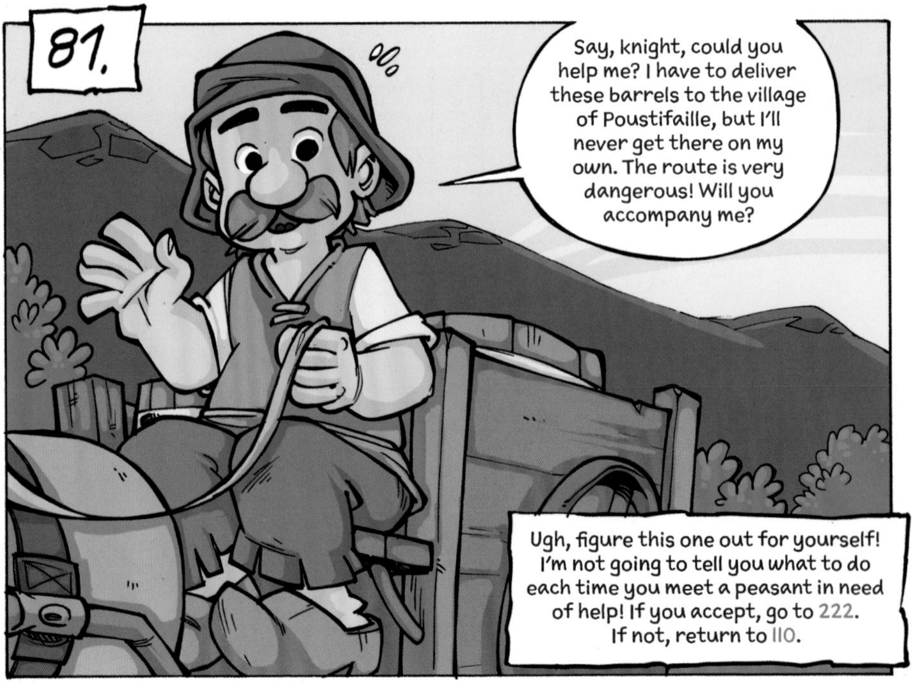
87.
Say, knight, could you help me? I have to deliver these barrels to the village of Poustifaille, but I'll never get there on my own. The route is very dangerous! Will you accompany me?
Ugh, figure this one out for yourself! I'm not going to tell you what to do each time you meet a peasant in need of help! If you accept, go to 222. If not, return to 110.

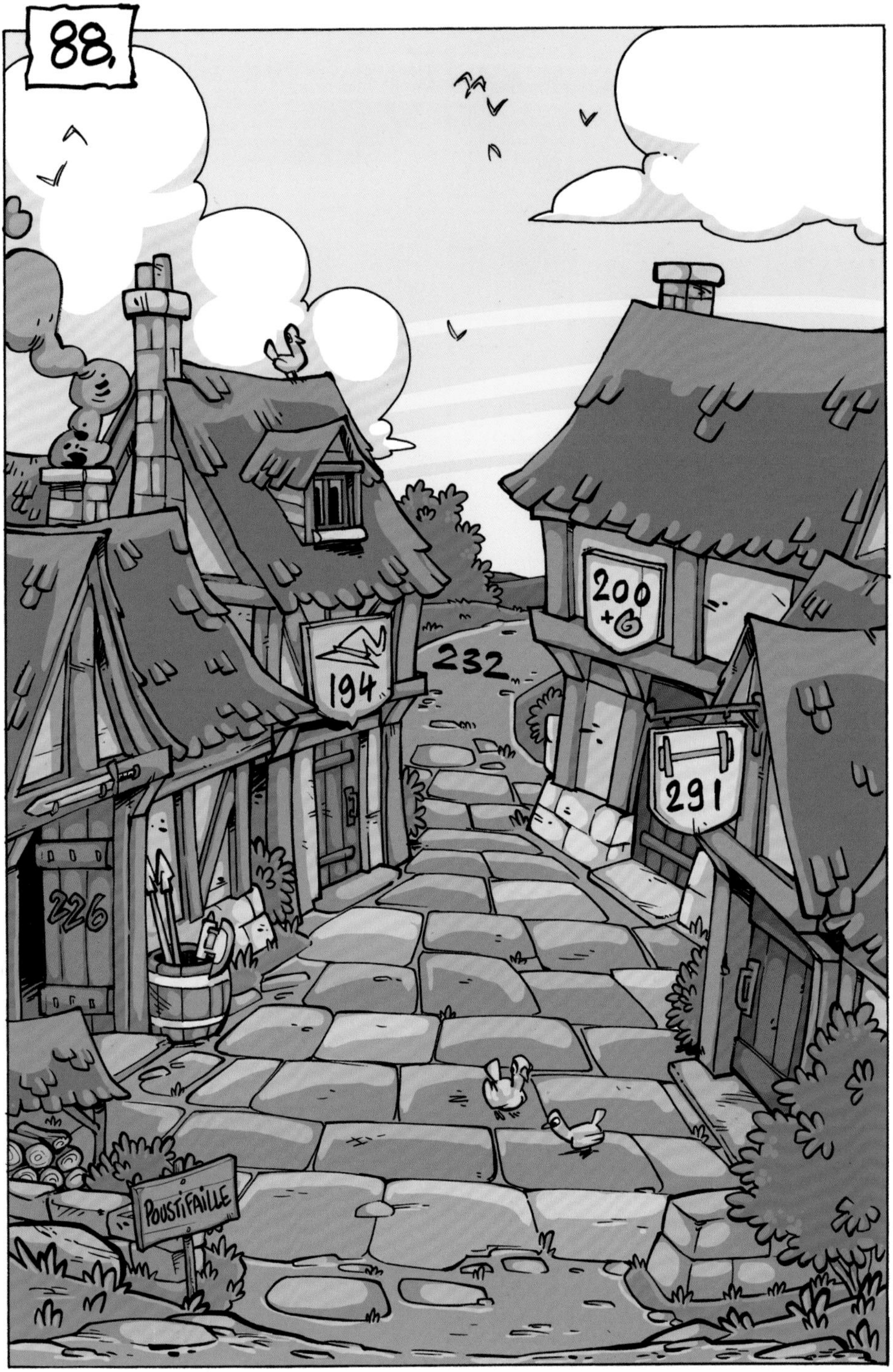
88.
194
232
200 +
291
226
POUSTIFAILLE

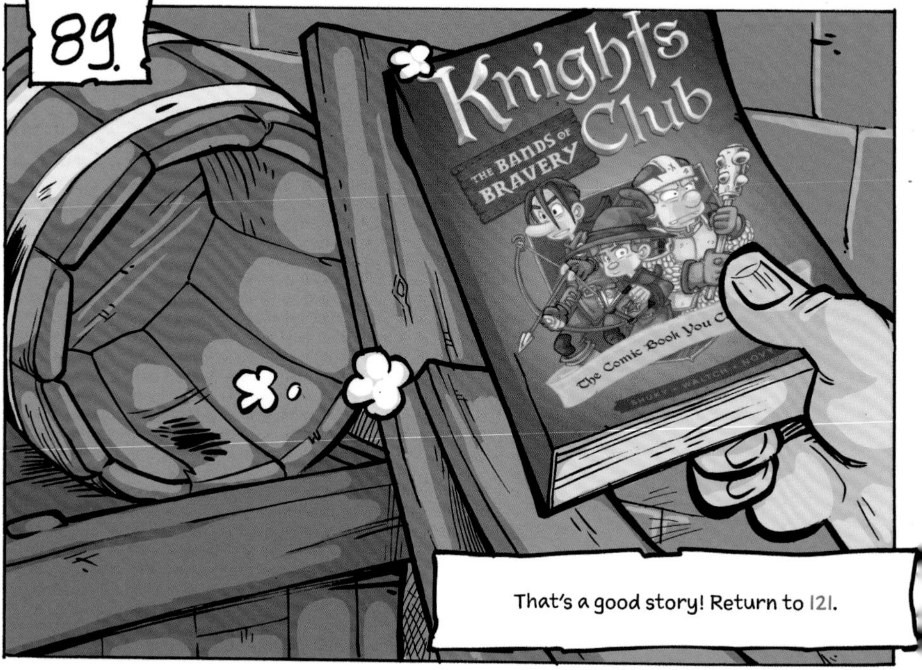
89.
Knights Club
THE BANDS OF BRAVERY
The Comic Book You C
That's a good story! Return to 121.

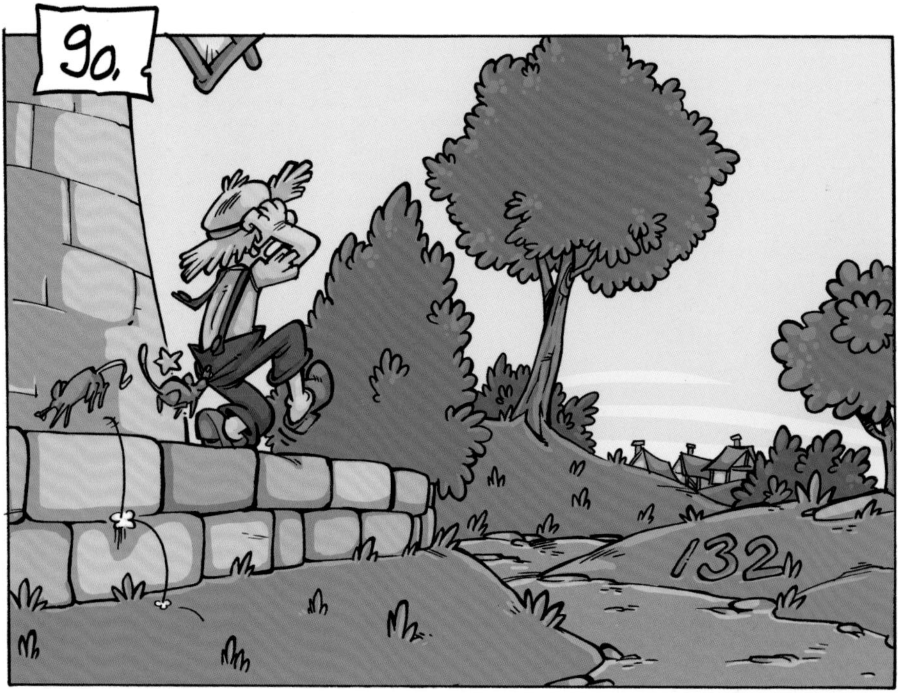
90.
132

91.

"Greetings, knight! It's lucky you're here. There's a problem with the fireplace. Can you help?"

Hey, you're a knight, not a chimney sweep! If you choose to help, go to 253. Otherwise return to 211.

92.

It's not always easy to flee... You lose 5 Strike points and 8 Experience points. If you're a **squire**, you lose 3 gold pieces.

93. Darned pest! Battle it or flee, but act quickly! I'll be waiting for you in 166. If you have more than 13 Agility, you can shoot 3 arrows before the rat has a chance to move.

SP	8	SQ	3
ATT		6	
RES		0	
SR		0	
XP		8	
LOOT		0	

94.

"You're back? You really found the pendant? Follow me to 242. The king will be delighted."

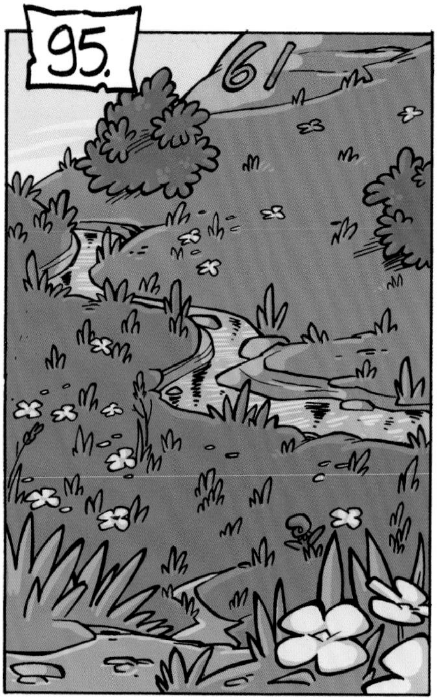
95.
61

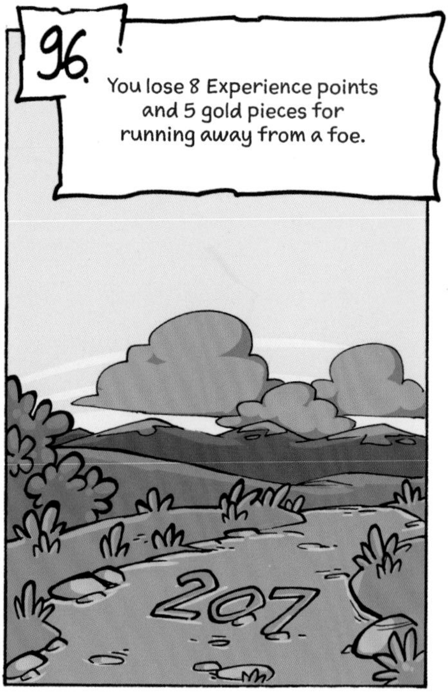
96.
You lose 8 Experience points and 5 gold pieces for running away from a foe.
207

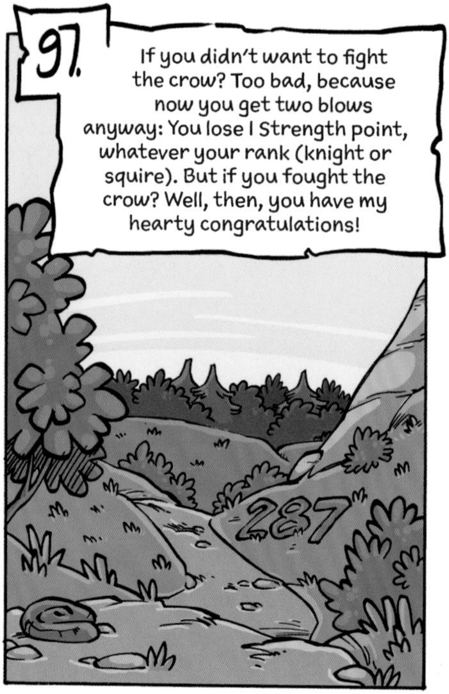
97.
If you didn't want to fight the crow? Too bad, because now you get two blows anyway: You lose 1 Strength point, whatever your rank (knight or squire). But if you fought the crow? Well, then, you have my hearty congratulations!
287

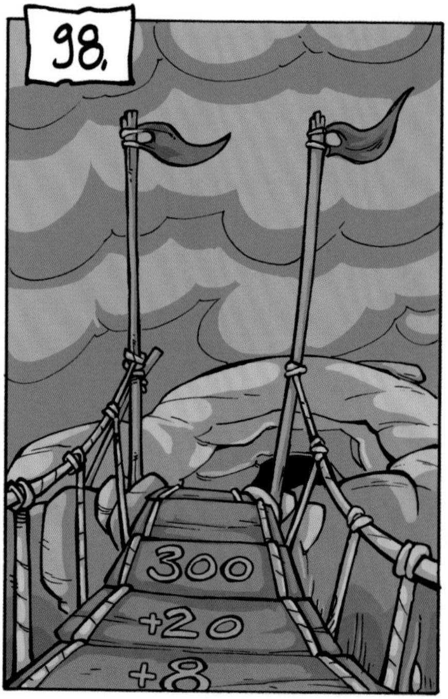
98.
300
+20
+8

99. These potions won't add any weight to your pack. If you have a little gold burning a hole in your pocket, spend away. Then return to 259.

100.

101.

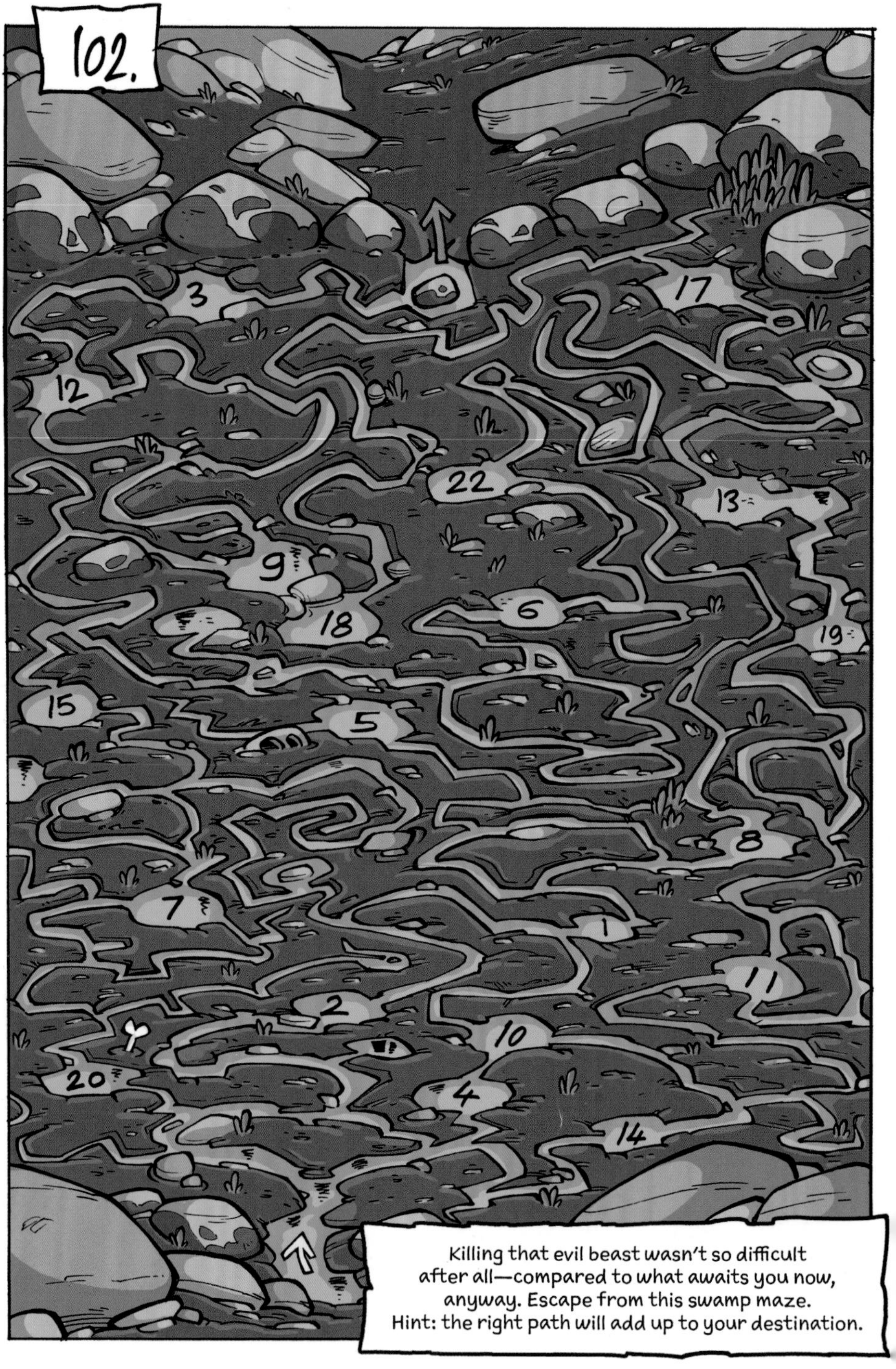

102.
3
17
12
22
13
9
6
18
19
15
5
8
7
1
11
2
10
20
4
14
Killing that evil beast wasn't so difficult after all—compared to what awaits you now, anyway. Escape from this swamp maze. Hint: the right path will add up to your destination.

103.

SP	7	SQ	2
ATT	4		
RES	0		
SR	0		
XP	4		
LOOT	Black Feather		

104.

Here, you've earned it. This card doubles your Attack points during the rest of the time you're at your current level. And thank you again!

You can now return to 241. It will be impossible to go into the library again—you will be refused entry. You have to admit, you made a pretty big disturbance!

105.

The beast chased you off without the least bit of trouble. Bravo!

106.

I can improve your gear for 10 gold pieces. Whaddaya say? And if you have a Forge card, terrific! I'll do it all for free, if you hand over the card as a tip.

If you accept, the blacksmith upgrades your attack and defense equipment by 1 point. You also benefit if you're a mage, since this man offers you a special handmade ring that gives you the same bonus. Next, go to 304.

107.

Remember: These weapons add no weight if you carry them in your hand. Any weapons you already have in your pack each weight 1 point. You can sell them back to the merchant; they will get you 5 gold pieces in total. Make a note of the panel number for this armory on your Quest Tracker, and you can return at any time, to sell or buy weapons. Now return to 259.

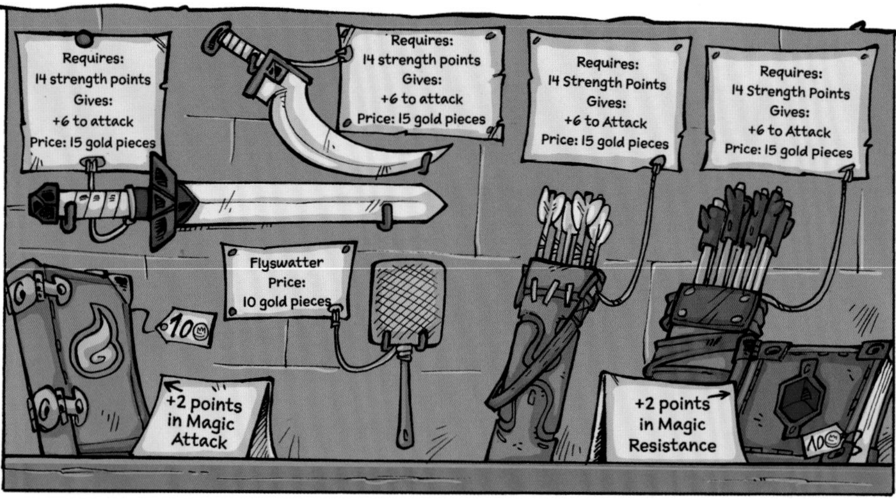

Requires:
14 strength points
Gives:
+6 to attack
Price: 15 gold pieces
Requires:
14 strength points
Gives:
+6 to attack
Price: 15 gold pieces
Requires:
14 Strength Points
Gives:
+6 to Attack
Price: 15 gold pieces
Requires:
14 Strength Points
Gives:
+6 to Attack
Price: 15 gold pieces
Flyswatter
Price:
10 gold pieces
10
+2 points in Magic Attack
+2 points in Magic Resistance
10

108.

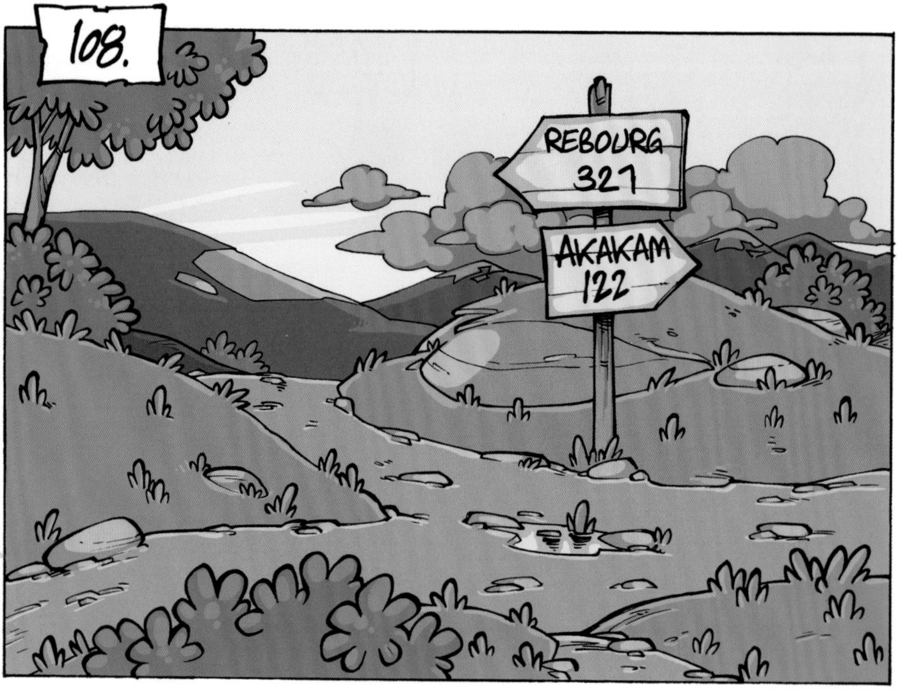

REBOURG
327
AKAKAM
122

109.

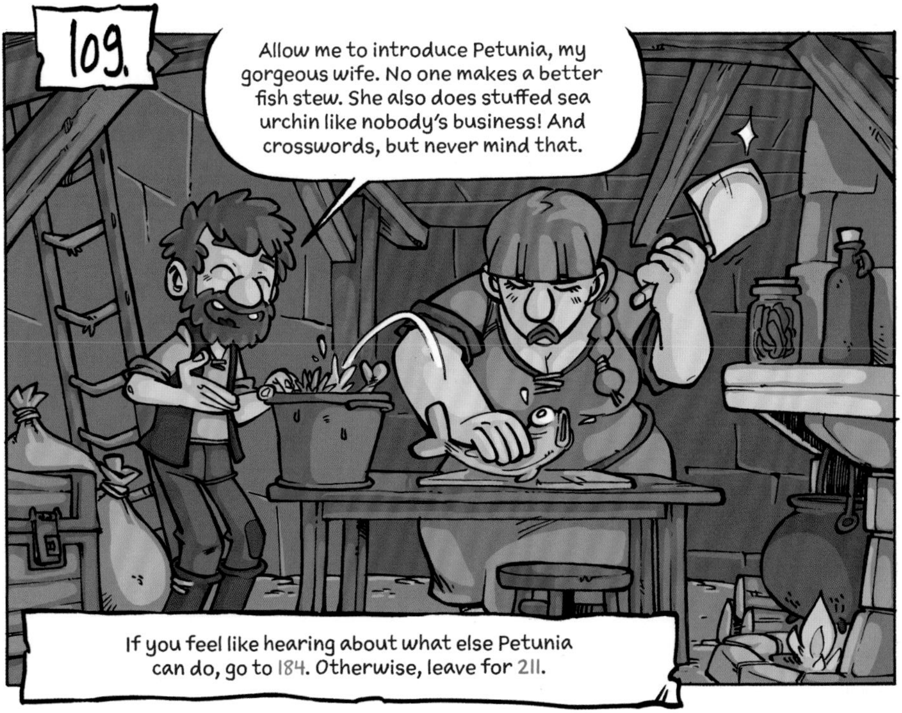
Allow me to introduce Petunia, my gorgeous wife. No one makes a better fish stew. She also does stuffed sea urchin like nobody's business! And crosswords, but never mind that.
If you feel like hearing about what else Petunia can do, go to 184. Otherwise, leave for 211.

110.

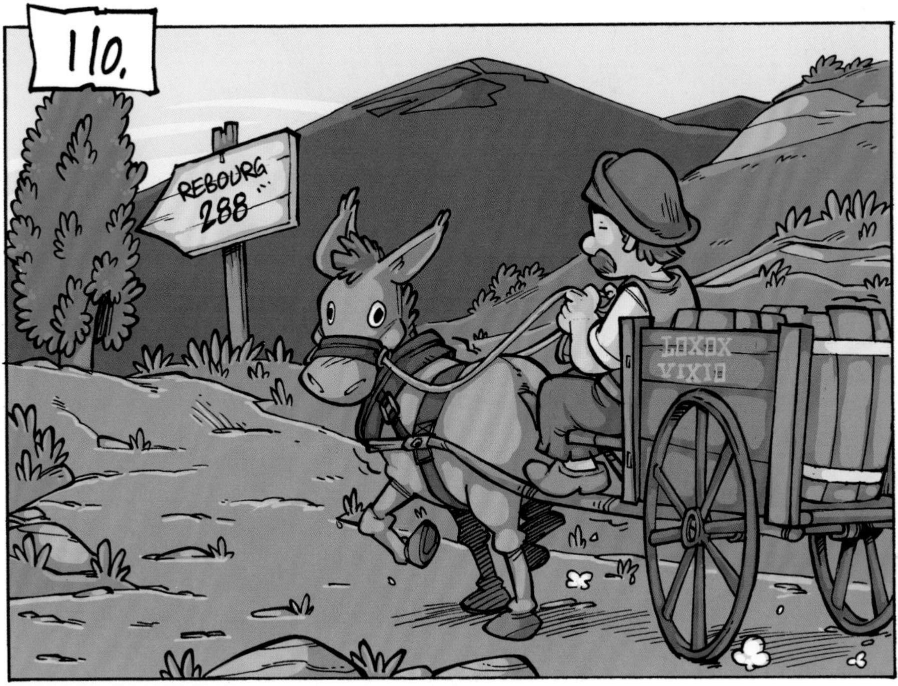
REBOURG
288

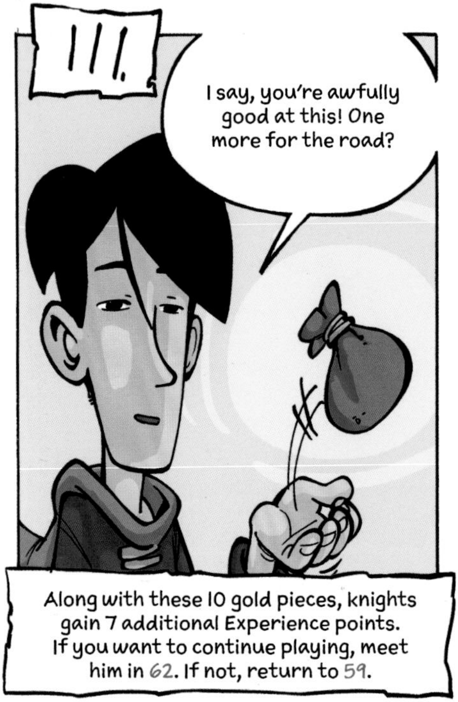
111.
I say, you're awfully good at this! One more for the road?
Along with these 10 gold pieces, knights gain 7 additional Experience points. If you want to continue playing, meet him in 62. If not, return to 59.

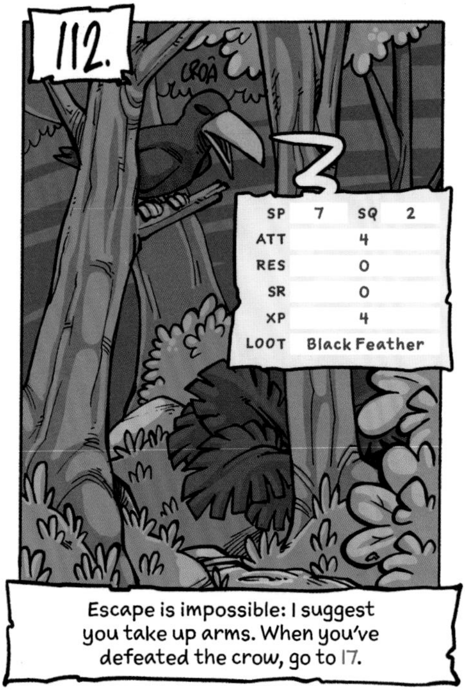
112.
3
Escape is impossible: I suggest you take up arms. When you've defeated the crow, go to 17.

SP	7	SQ	2
ATT	4		
RES	0		
SR	0		
XP	4		
LOOT	Black Feather		

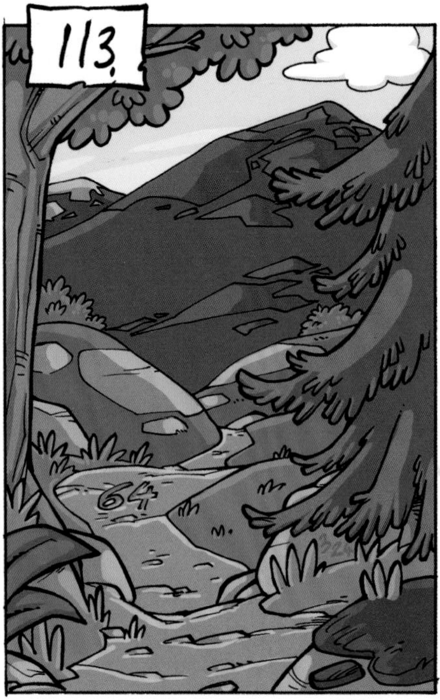
113.
64

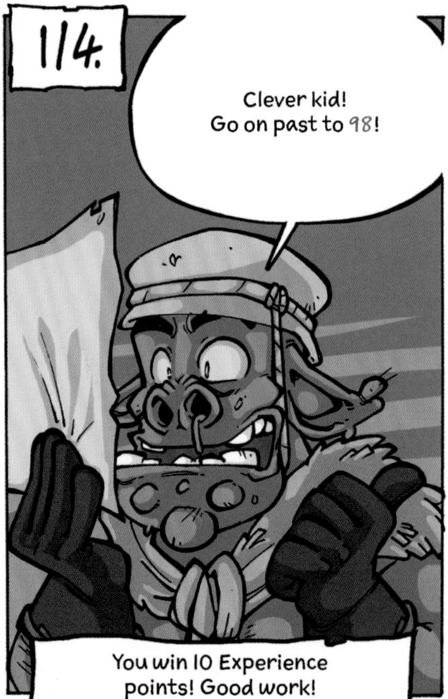
114.
Clever kid! Go on past to 98!
You win 10 Experience points! Good work!

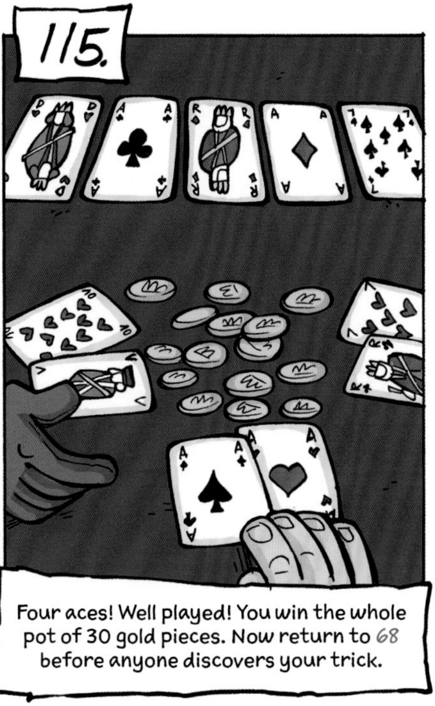
115.
Four aces! Well played! You win the whole pot of 30 gold pieces. Now return to 68 before anyone discovers your trick.

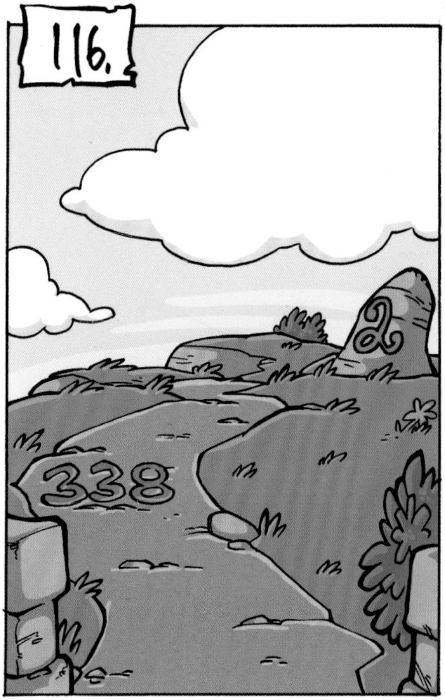
116.
338

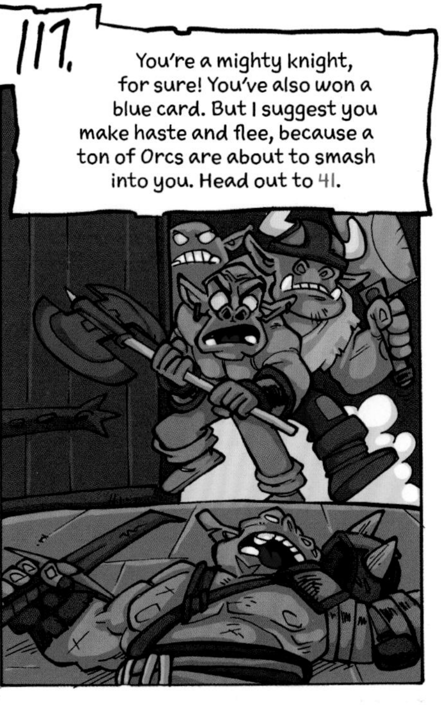
117.
You're a mighty knight, for sure! You've also won a blue card. But I suggest you make haste and flee, because a ton of Orcs are about to smash into you. Head out to 41.

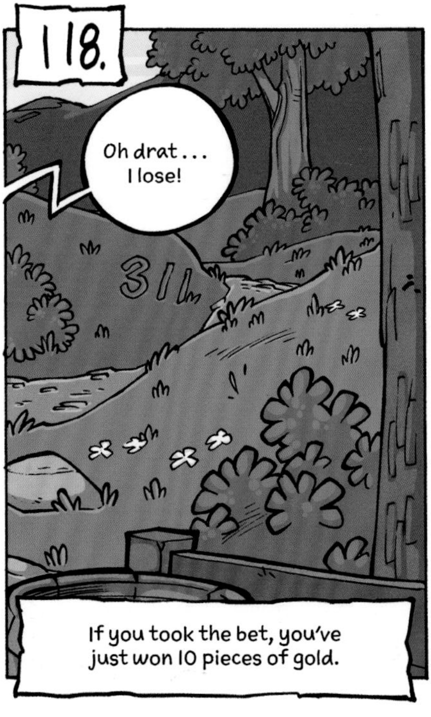
118.
Oh drat . . . I lose!
311
If you took the bet, you've just won 10 pieces of gold.

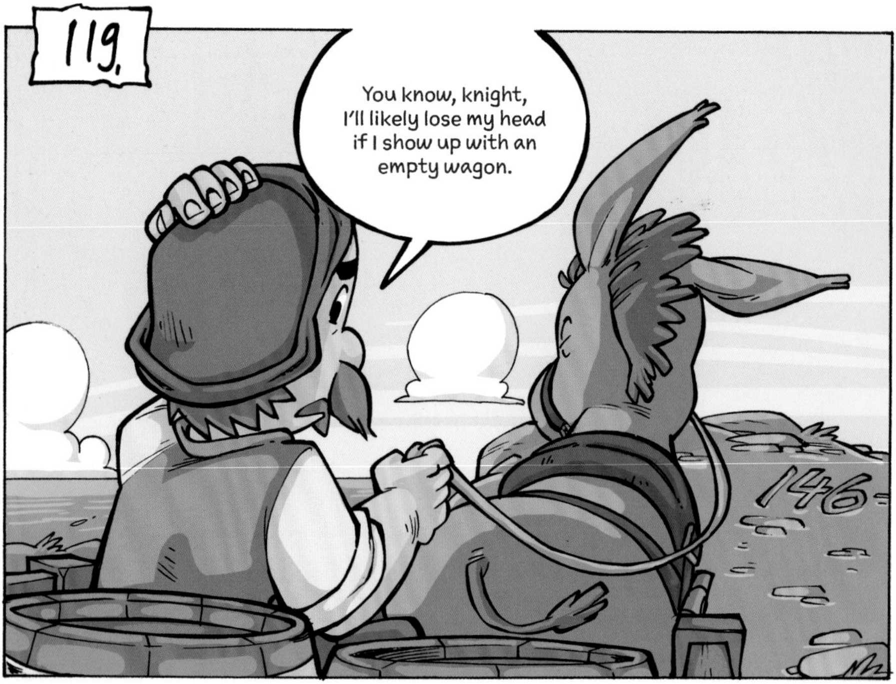
119.
You know, knight, I'll likely lose my head if I show up with an empty wagon.
146

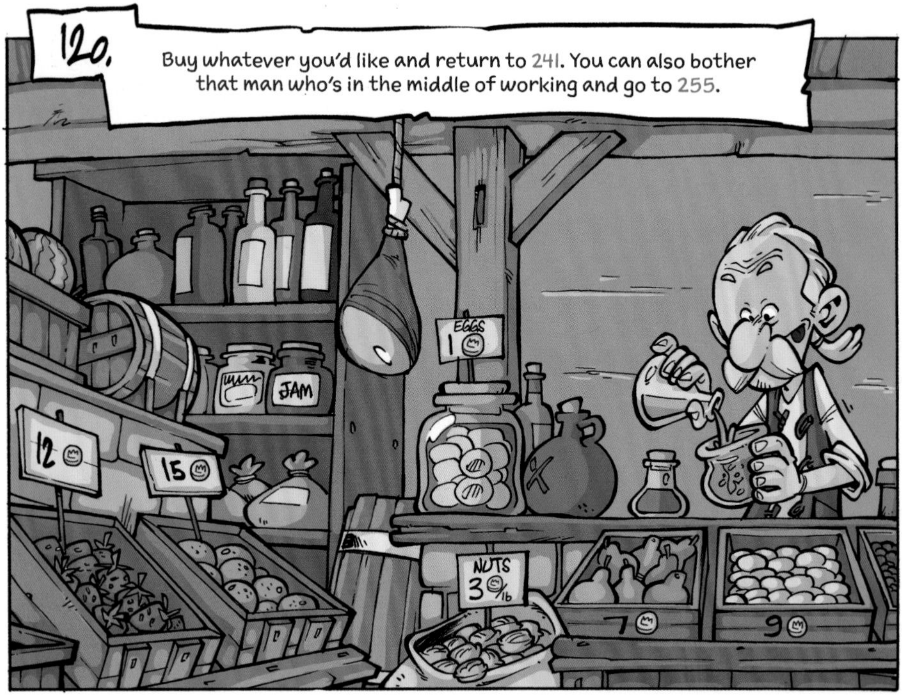
120.
Buy whatever you'd like and return to 241. You can also bother that man who's in the middle of working and go to 255.
EGGS 1
JAM
12
15
NUTS 3 /lb
7
9

121.

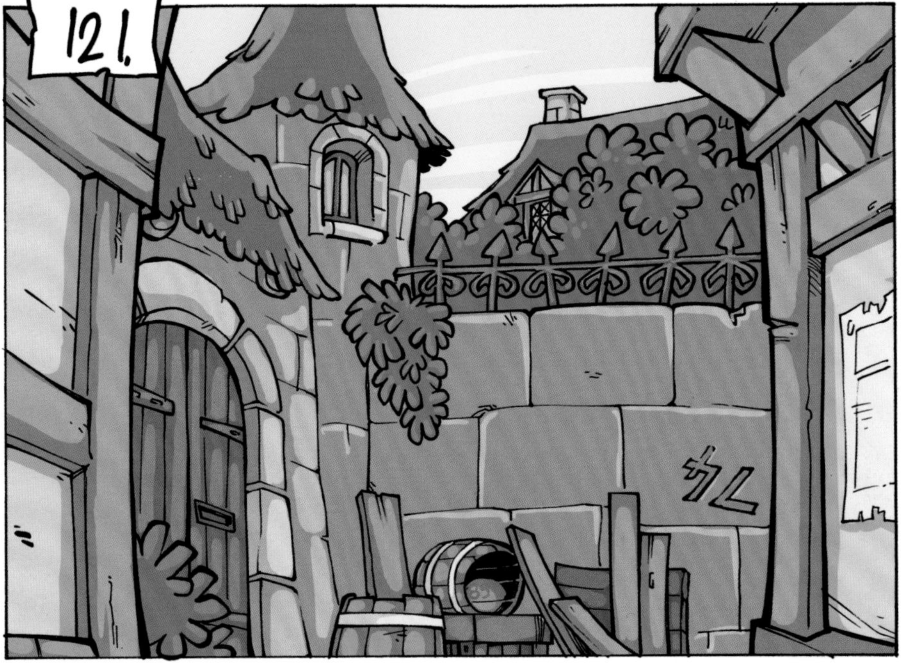

122.

Where did this guy come from? Dragons are tough beasts. I recommend you run away really fast to 268. If you flee, you lose 5 Strike points, or 10 gold pieces if you're a squire. If you have more than 18 Strength points, you can strike a first Stun blow, which doesn't subtract any of his Strike points, but does daze him. You can then spin your wheel three times before it's his turn!!

SP	15	SQ	4
ATT	15		
RES	5		
SR	Fire spell +1		
XP	15		
LOOT	Dragons claw		

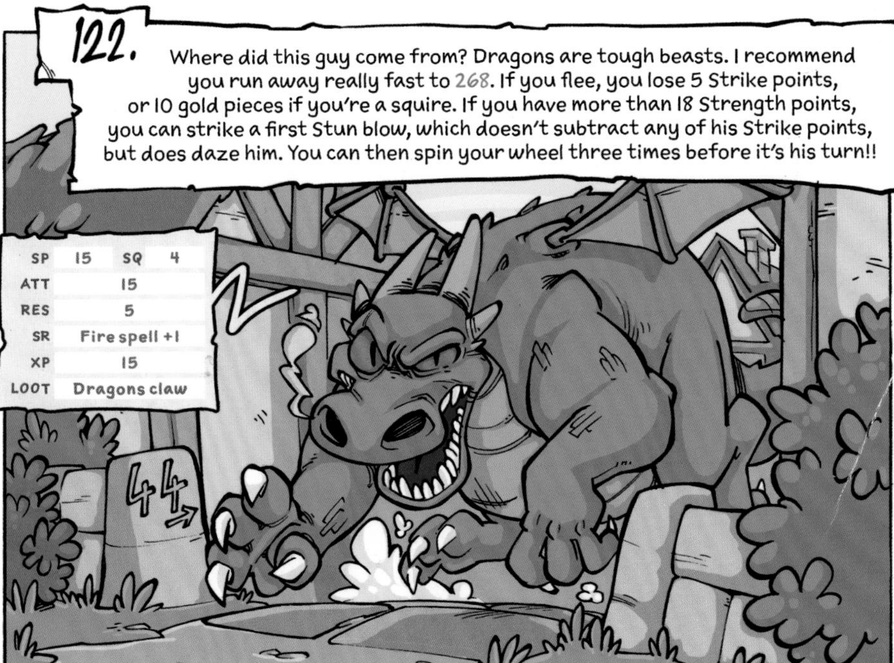
44

This rat is just passing by, but feel free to battle him. If you'd rather avoid it, carry on along your way. If you know how to tame animals, the rat can accompany you until your next battle. His 4 attack points will be added to yours. But remember: he can only help you for one fight!

SP	6	SQ	2
ATT		4	
RES		0	
SR		0	
XP		4	
LOOT		0	

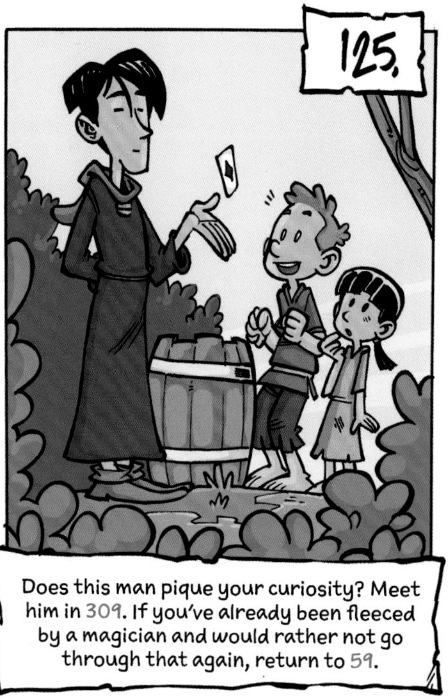
125.
Does this man pique your curiosity? Meet him in 309. If you've already been fleeced by a magician and would rather not go through that again, return to 59.

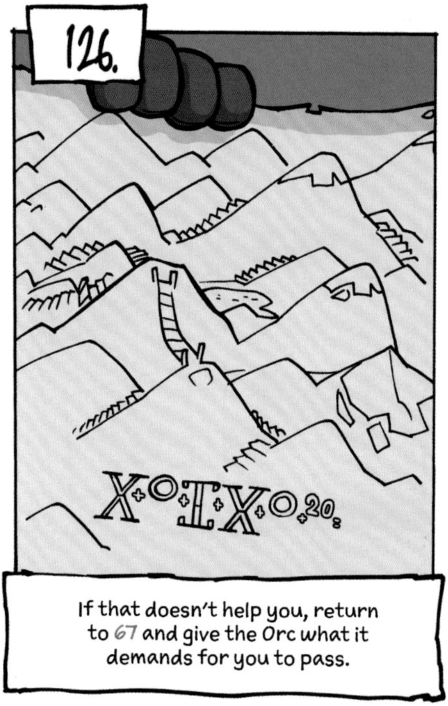
126.
If that doesn't help you, return to 67 and give the Orc what it demands for you to pass.

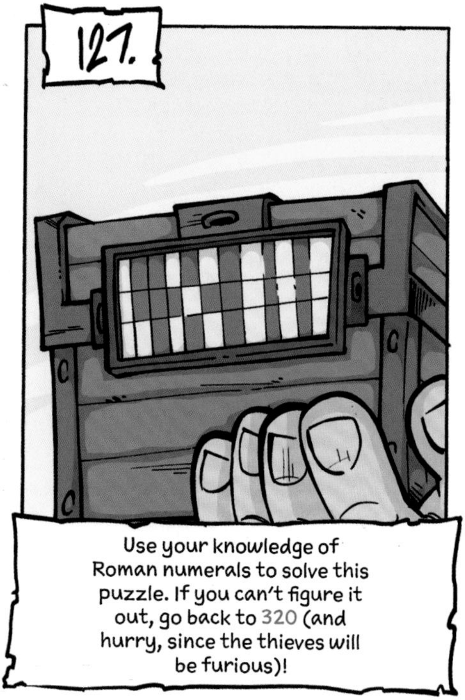
127.
Use your knowledge of Roman numerals to solve this puzzle. If you can't figure it out, go back to 320 (and hurry, since the thieves will be furious)!

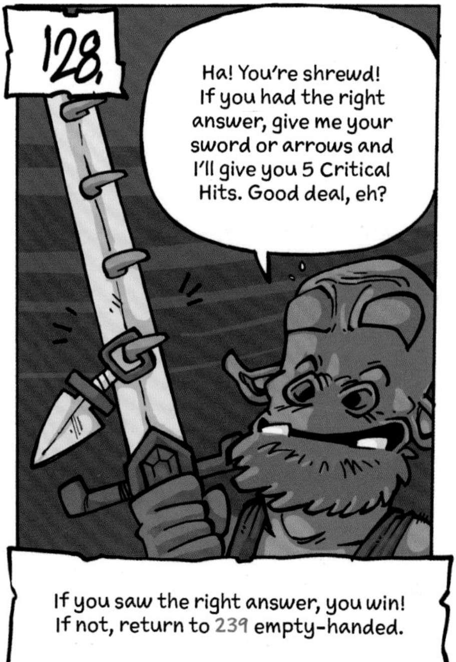
128.
Ha! You're shrewd! If you had the right answer, give me your sword or arrows and I'll give you 5 Critical Hits. Good deal, eh?
If you saw the right answer, you win! If not, return to 239 empty-handed.

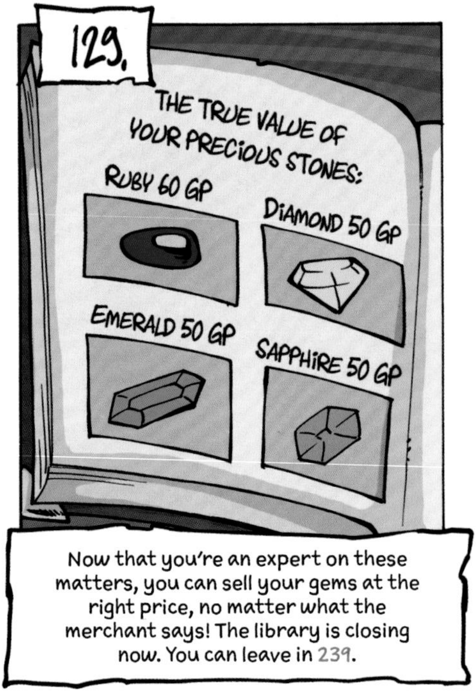
129.
THE TRUE VALUE OF YOUR PRECIOUS STONES:
RUBY 60 GP
DIAMOND 50 GP
EMERALD 50 GP
SAPPHIRE 50 GP
Now that you're an expert on these matters, you can sell your gems at the right price, no matter what the merchant says! The library is closing now. You can leave in 239.

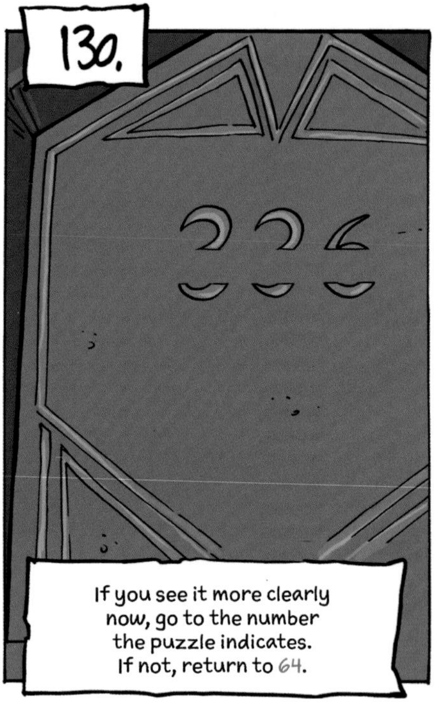
130.
If you see it more clearly now, go to the number the puzzle indicates. If not, return to 64.

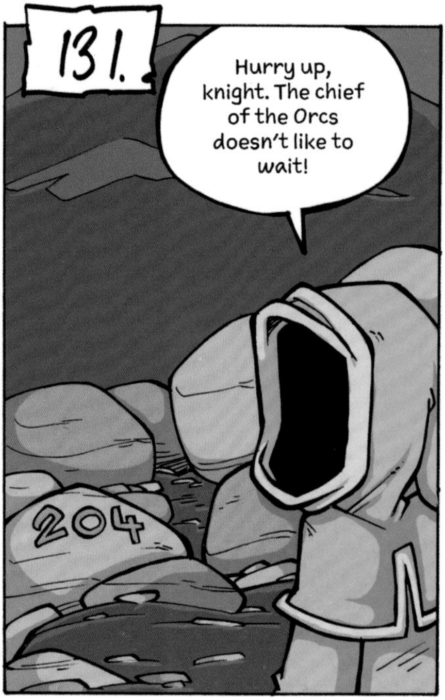
131.
Hurry up, knight. The chief of the Orcs doesn't like to wait!
204

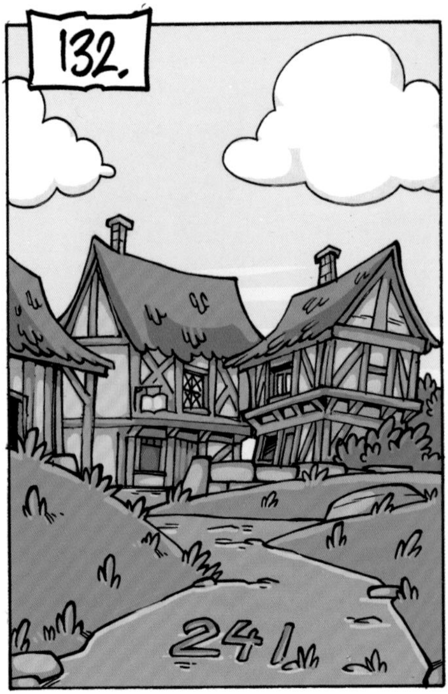
132.
241

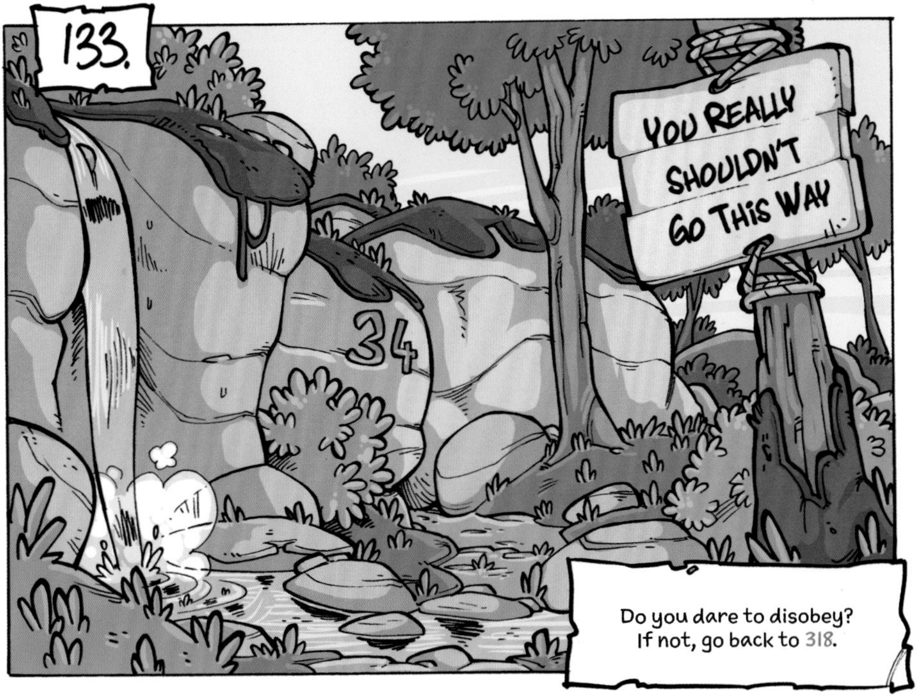
133.
YOU REALLY SHOULDN'T GO THIS WAY
34
Do you dare to disobey?
If not, go back to 318.

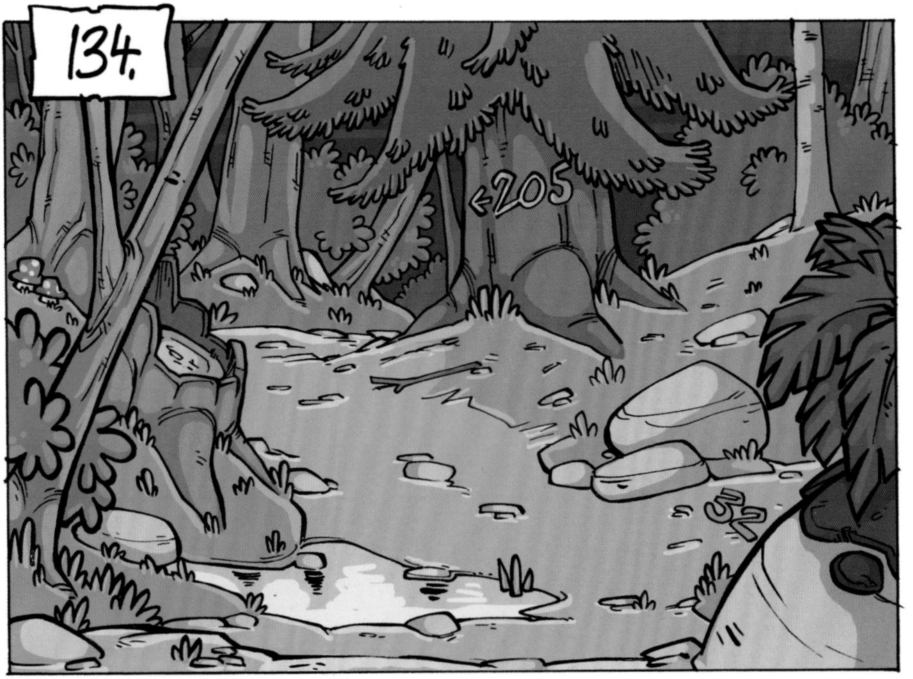
134.
←205
52

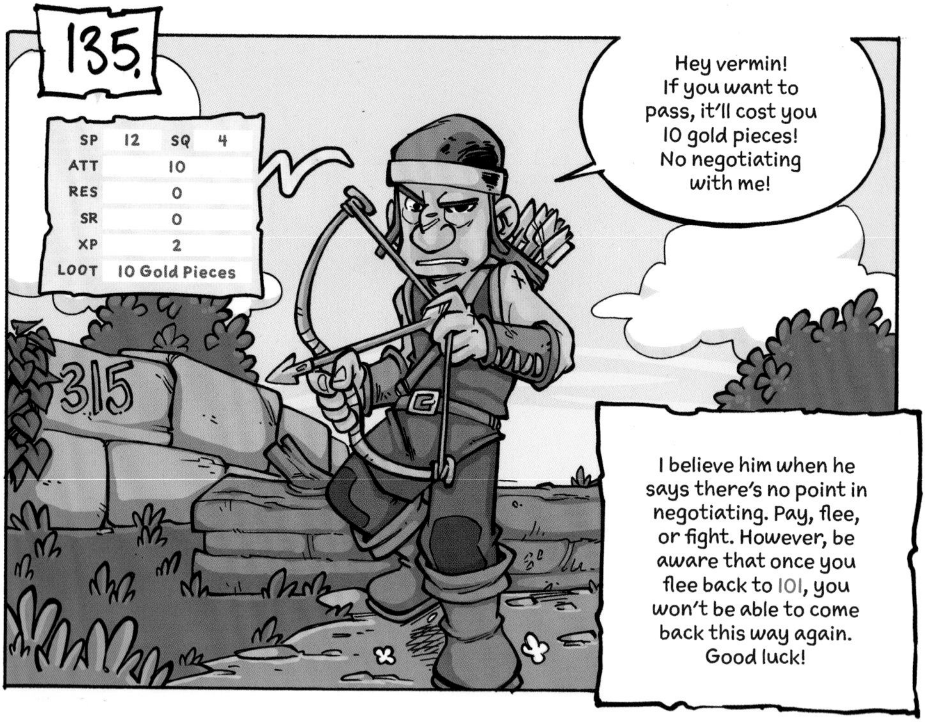
135.
SP 12 SQ 4
ATT 10
RES 0
SR 0
XP 2
LOOT 10 Gold Pieces
315
Hey vermin! If you want to pass, it'll cost you 10 gold pieces! No negotiating with me!
I believe him when he says there's no point in negotiating. Pay, flee, or fight. However, be aware that once you flee back to 101, you won't be able to come back this way again. Good luck!

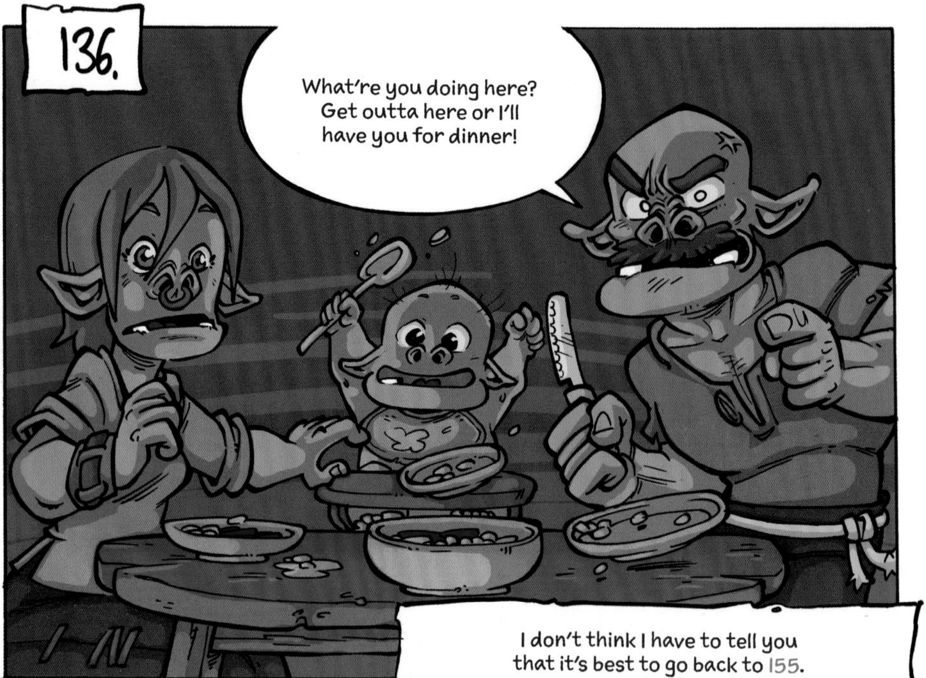
136.
What're you doing here? Get outta here or I'll have you for dinner!
I don't think I have to tell you that it's best to go back to 155.

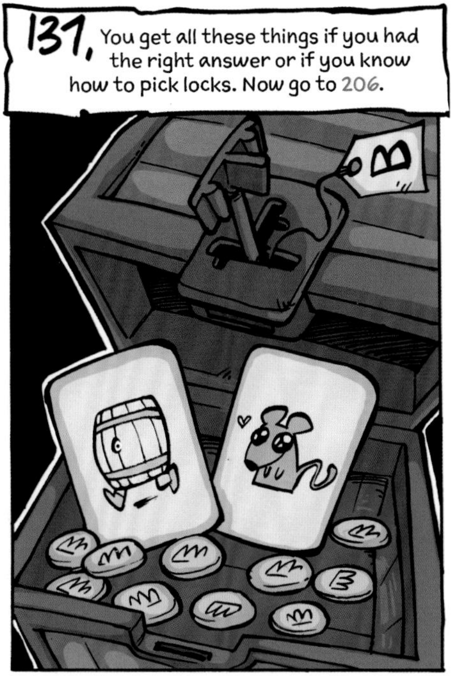
137.
You get all these things if you had the right answer or if you know how to pick locks. Now go to 206.

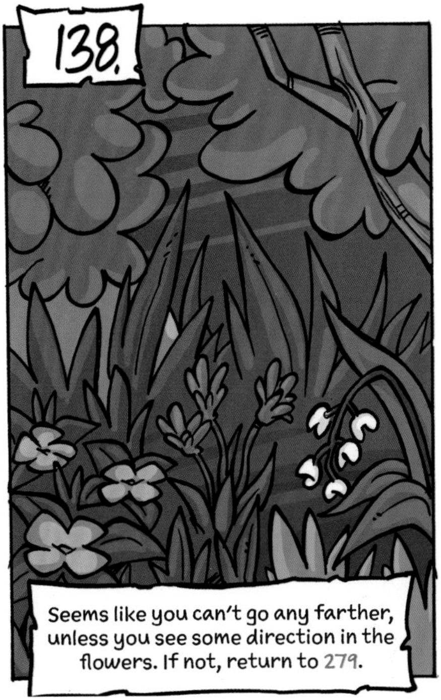
138.
Seems like you can't go any farther, unless you see some direction in the flowers. If not, return to 279.

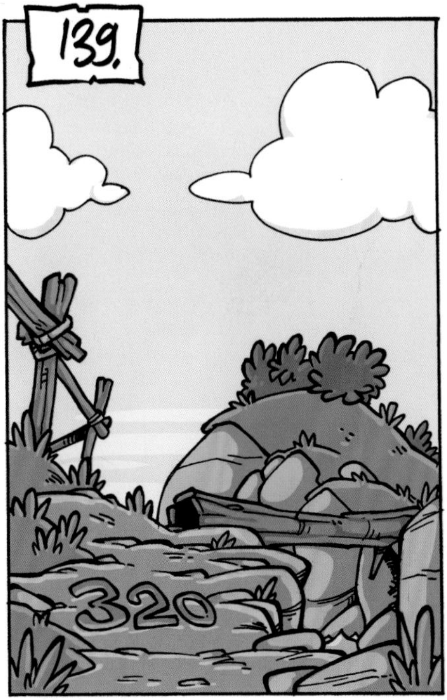
139.
320

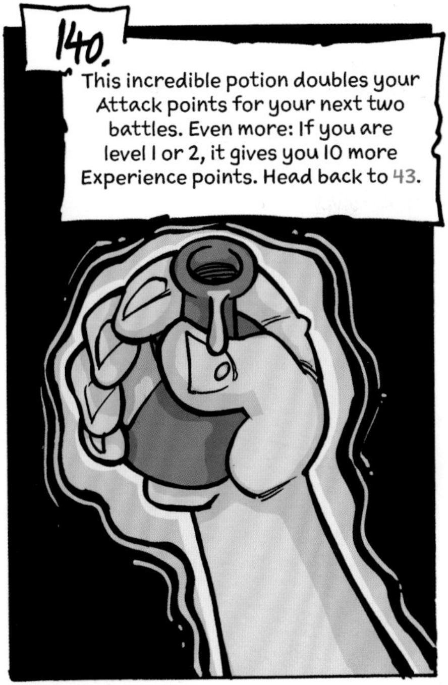
140.
This incredible potion doubles your Attack points for your next two battles. Even more: If you are level 1 or 2, it gives you 10 more Experience points. Head back to 43.

141.

You can engage in battle with this terrible creature or run to 77.
If you win the battle, go to 28.

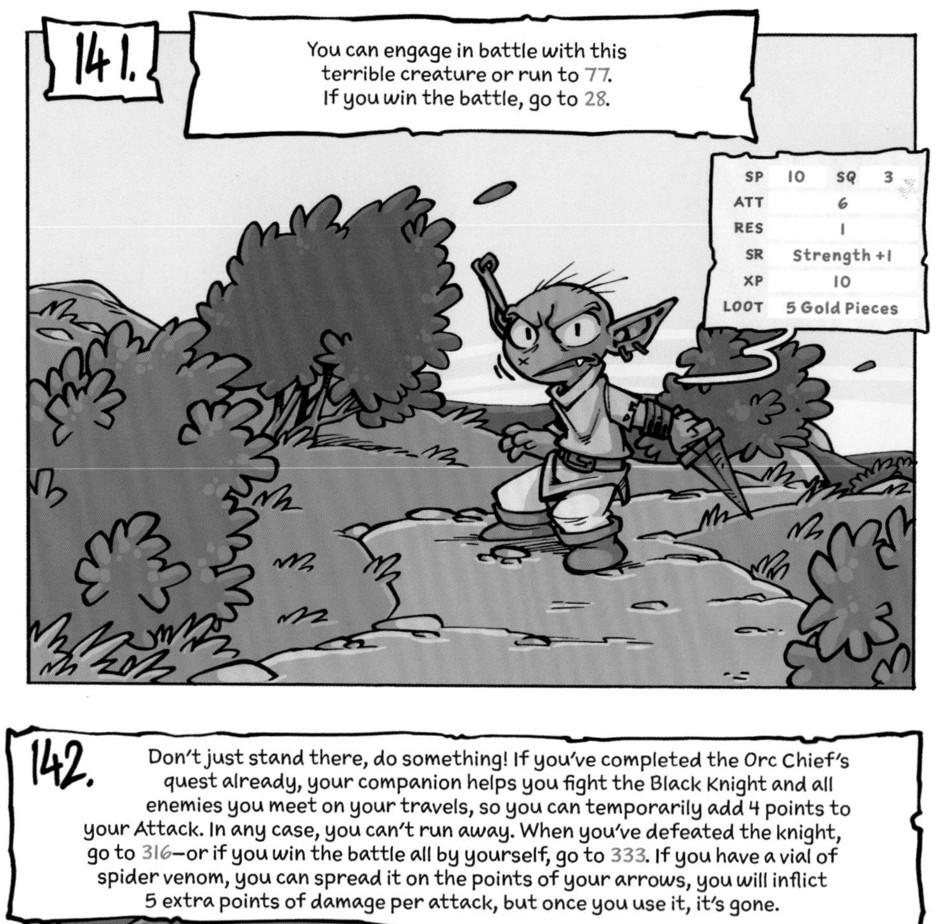

SP	10	SQ	3
ATT	6		
RES	1		
SR	Strength +1		
XP	10		
LOOT	5 Gold Pieces		

142.

Don't just stand there, do something! If you've completed the Orc Chief's quest already, your companion helps you fight the Black Knight and all enemies you meet on your travels, so you can temporarily add 4 points to your Attack. In any case, you can't run away. When you've defeated the knight, go to 316—or if you win the battle all by yourself, go to 333. If you have a vial of spider venom, you can spread it on the points of your arrows, you will inflict 5 extra points of damage per attack, but once you use it, it's gone.

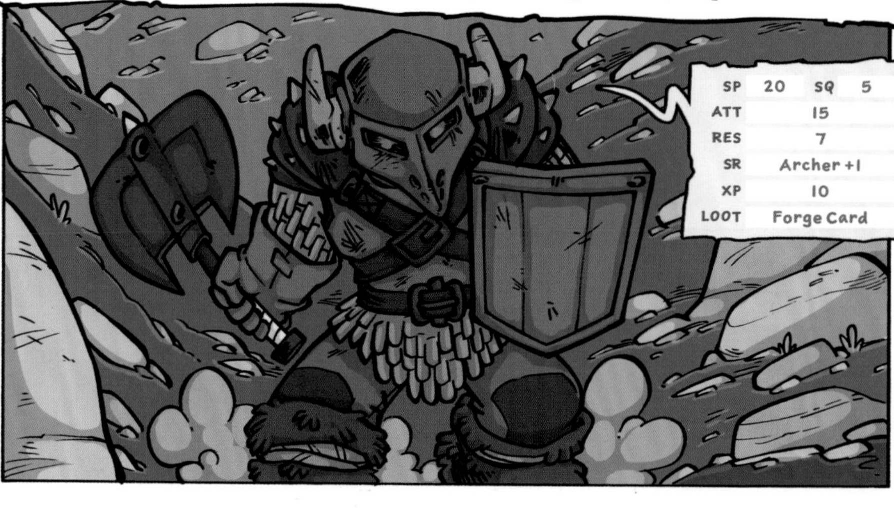

SP	20	SQ	5
ATT	15		
RES	7		
SR	Archer +1		
XP	10		
LOOT	Forge Card		

143. Truly amazing! You get 15 experience points.

144.

SP	11	SQ	3
ATT		8	
RES		1	
SR		0	
XP		8	
LOOT		1 Pouch of Powder	

Fight, then go to 10 if you win. Or ignore him and go to 189 . . . it's up to you!

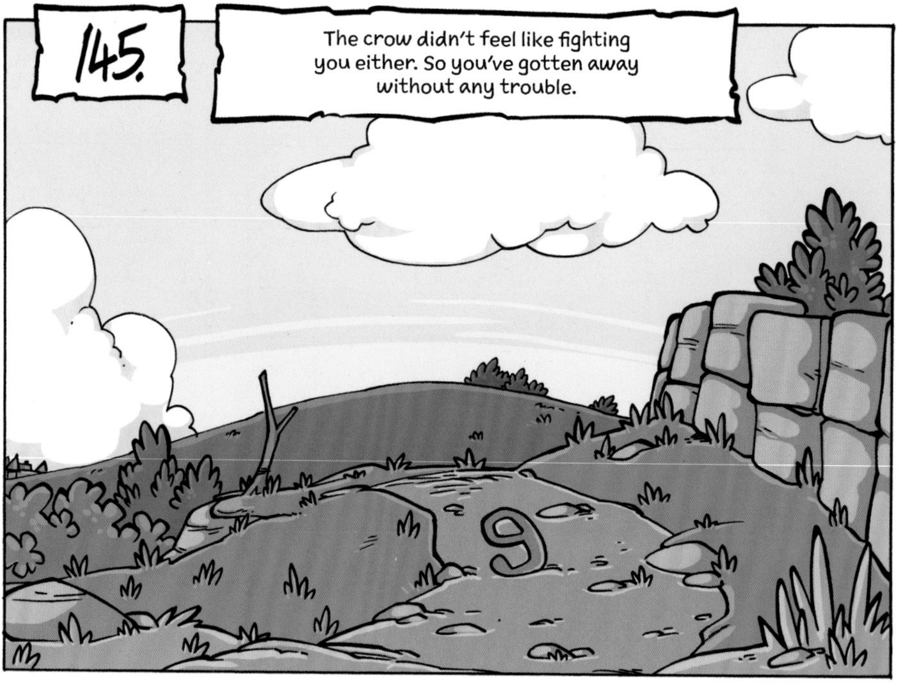
145.
The crow didn't feel like fighting you either. So you've gotten away without any trouble.
9

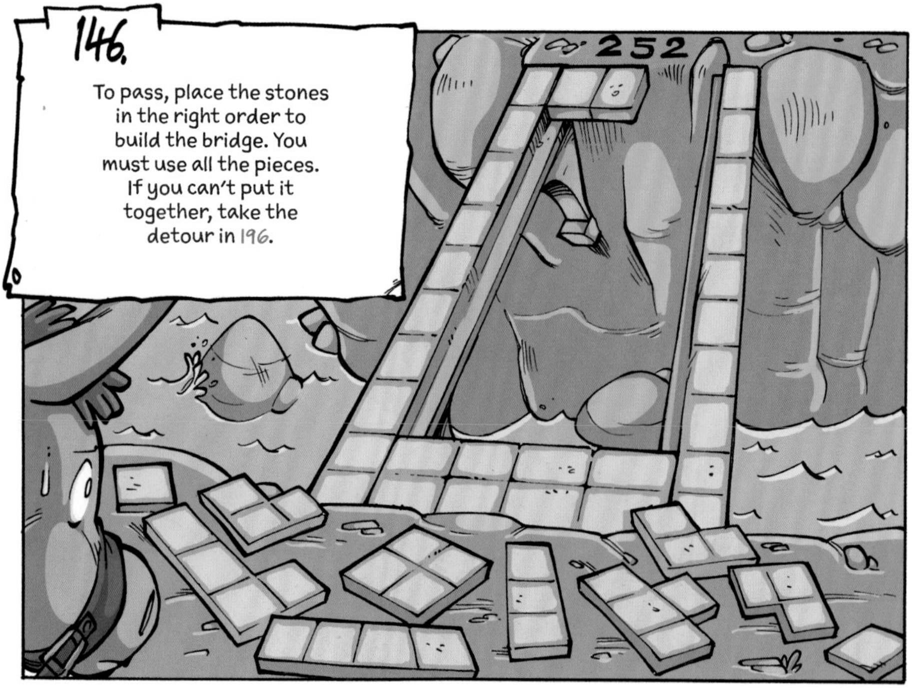
146.
To pass, place the stones in the right order to build the bridge. You must use all the pieces. If you can't put it together, take the detour in 196.
252

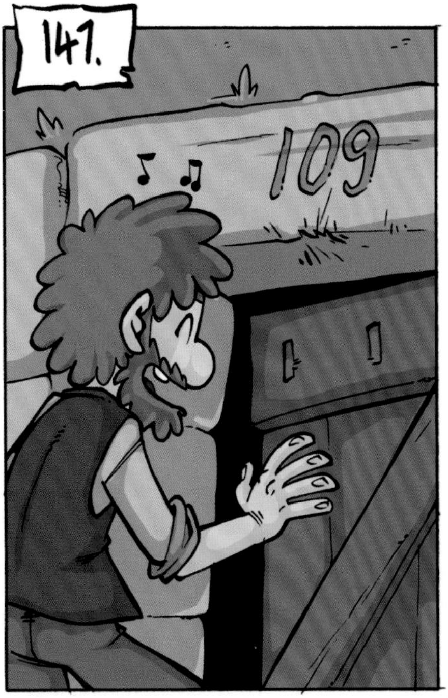
147.
109

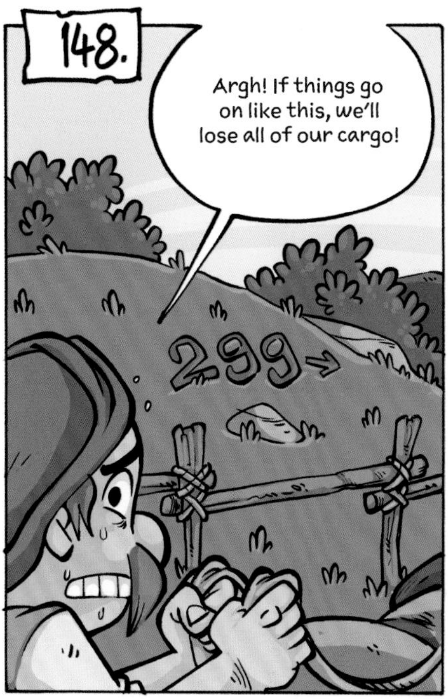
148.
Argh! If things go on like this, we'll lose all of our cargo!
299

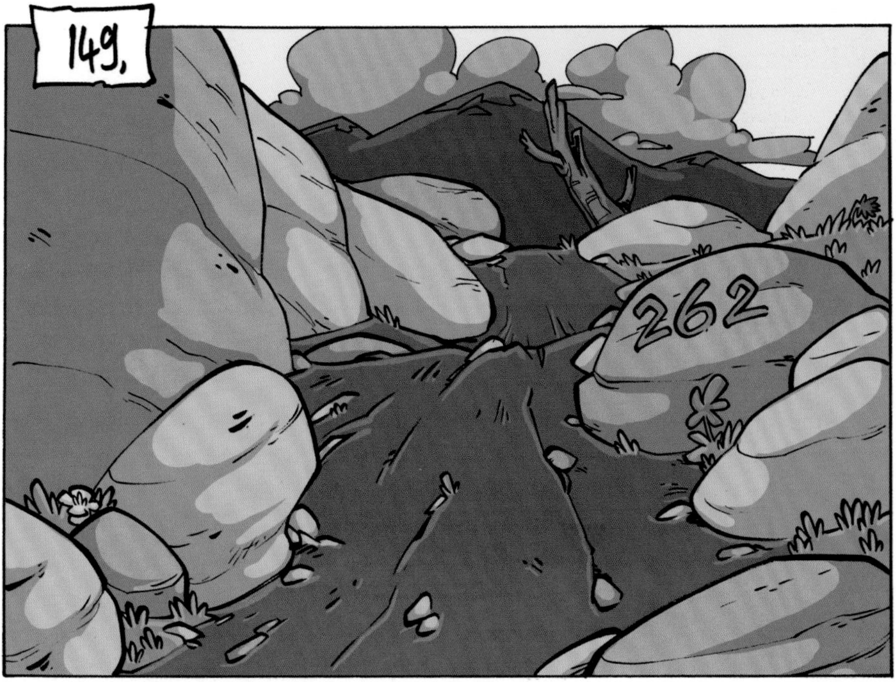
149.
262

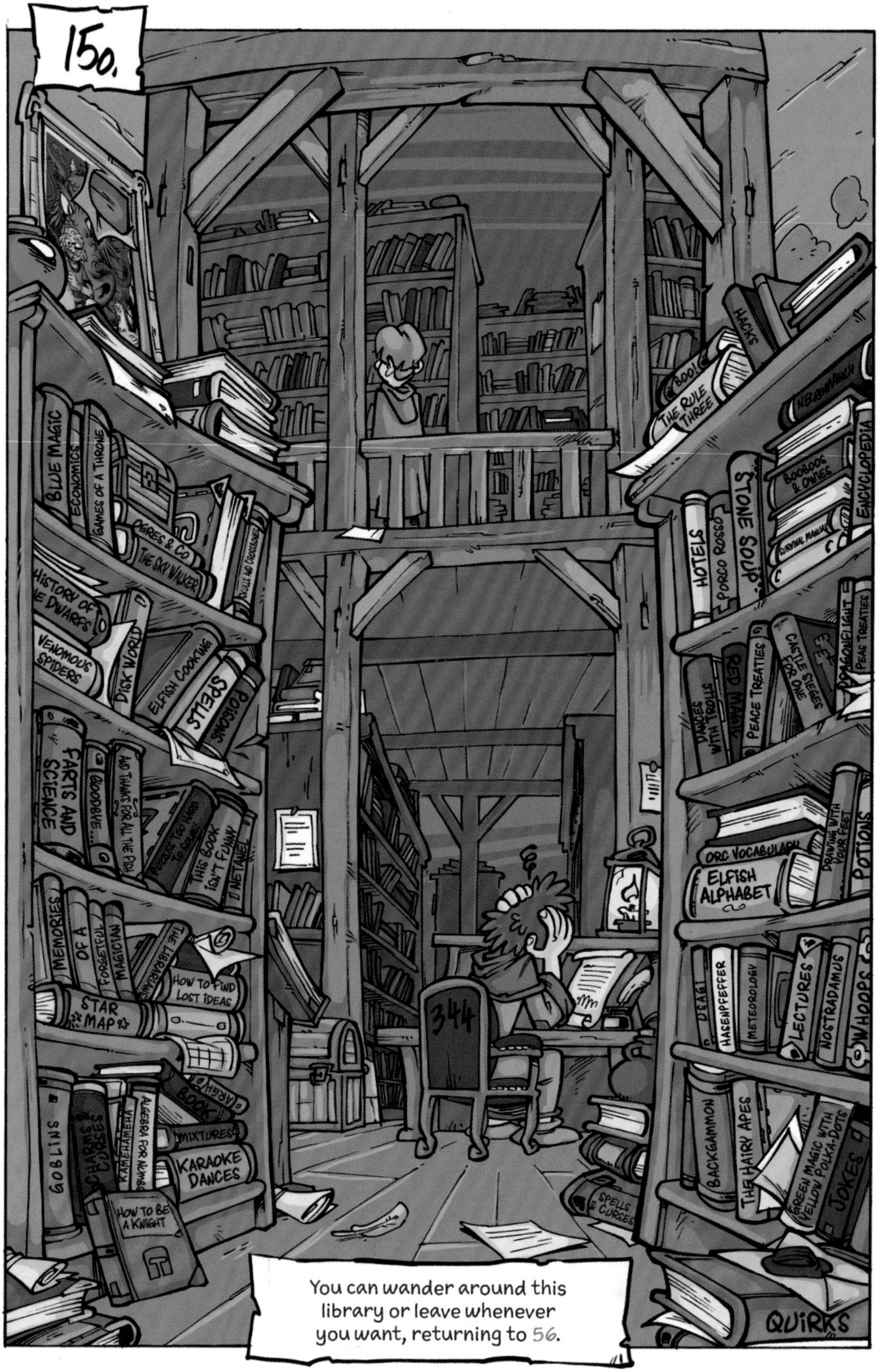
150.
BLUE MAGIC
ECONOMICS
GAMES OF A THRONE
OGRES & CO
THE SKY WALKER
HISTORY OF THE DWARFS
VENOMOUS SPIDERS
DISK WORLD
ELFISH COOKING
SPELLS
POISONS
FARTS AND SCIENCE
GOODBYE...
AND THANKS FOR ALL THE FISH
PUZZLES TOO HARD TO SOLVE
THIS BOOK ISN'T FUNNY
MEMORIES OF A FORGETFUL MAGICIAN
THE LIBRARIAN
HOW TO FIND LOST IDEAS
STAR MAP
GOBLINS
CHARMS & CURSES
KAMEHAMEHA
ALGEBRA FOR NUMBS
BOOK
MIXTURES
KARAOKE DANCES
HOW TO BE A KNIGHT
HACKS
BOO!
THE RULE OF THREE
NECROMANCY
BOOBOOS & OWIES
ENCYCLOPEDIA
SURVIVAL MANUAL
STONE SOUP
HOTELS
PORCO ROSSO
RED MAGIC
PEACE TREATIES
CASTLE SIEGES FOR ONE
DRAGONLIGHT
PEACE TREATIES
DANCES WITH TROLLS
ORC VOCABULARY
ELFISH ALPHABET
DRAWING WITH YOUR FEET
POTIONS
USAGI
HASENPFEFFER
METEOROLOGY
LECTURES
NOSTRADAMUS
WHOOPS
BACKGAMMON
THE HAIRY APES
GREEN MAGIC WITH YELLOW POLKA-DOTS
JOKES
SPELLS & CURSES
QUIRKS
344
You can wander around this library or leave whenever you want, returning to 56.

151.

Did you run away? The rats bit at your feet; you lose 8 Strike points. If you're out of Strike points and you don't have a potion, you've died and you must begin the adventure again. If you are a squire, your weapon loses 1 Attack point during your next battle. If, however, you fought the rats and won, well done—you just gained a level. In this case, don't forget to add 1 point to the characteristic of your choice, plus the bonuses that go with your character. Also, you've won 5 gold pieces, and that's pretty good news!

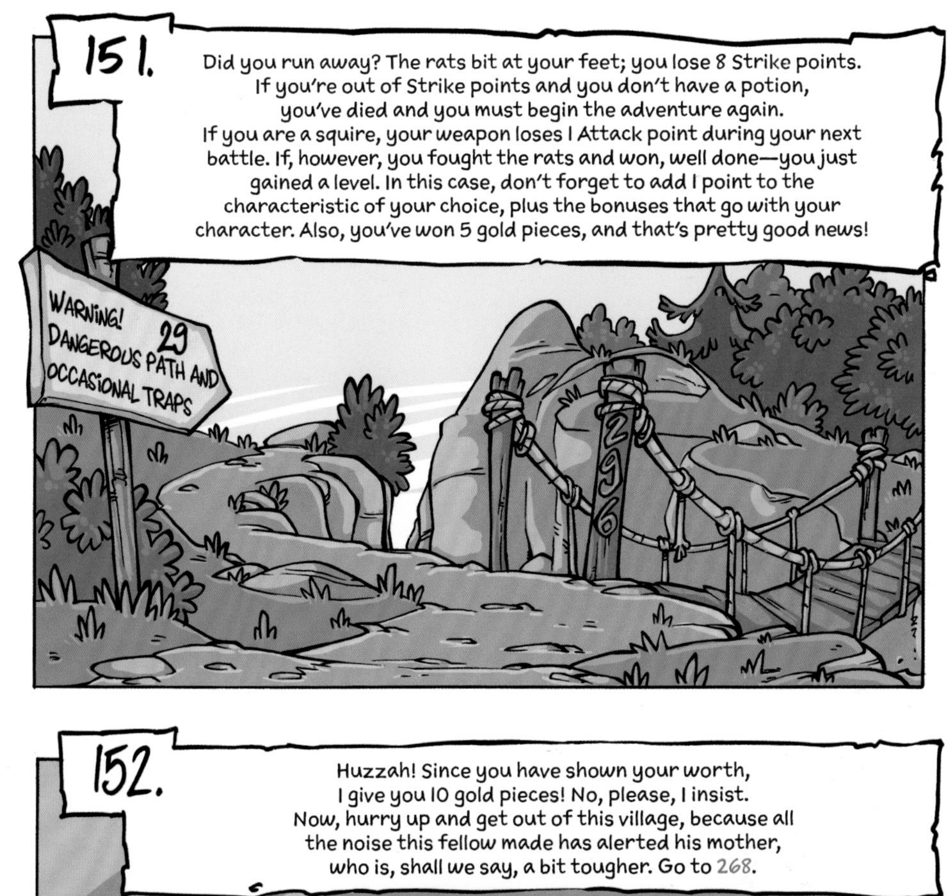
WARNING! 29
DANGEROUS PATH AND OCCASIONAL TRAPS
296

152.

Huzzah! Since you have shown your worth, I give you 10 gold pieces! No, please, I insist. Now, hurry up and get out of this village, because all the noise this fellow made has alerted his mother, who is, shall we say, a bit tougher. Go to 268.

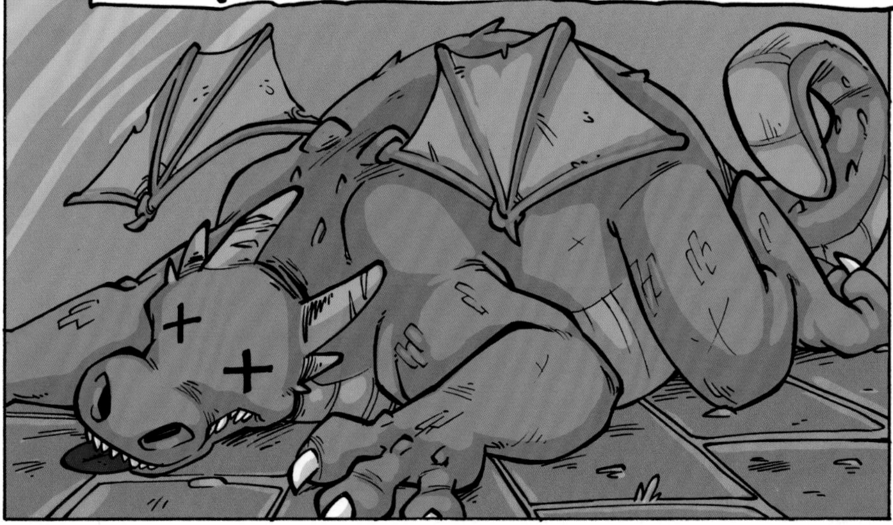

153.

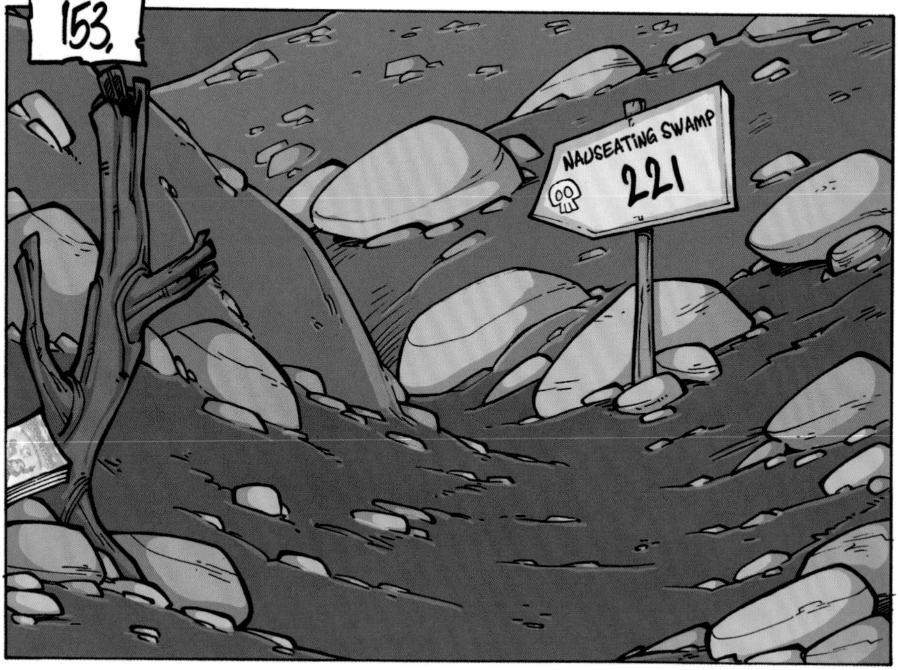
NAUSEATING SWAMP
221

154.

Fight this mighty Orc if you wish and then go to 117—if you win. If you'd rather not go up against this warrior and instead want to take the path that bypasses the Orc camp, go to 41.
If you've completed the orc chief's quest, pass along undisturbed to 303.

SP	100	SQ	10
ATT	35		
RES	5		
SR	0		
XP	30		
LOOT	Blue Card		

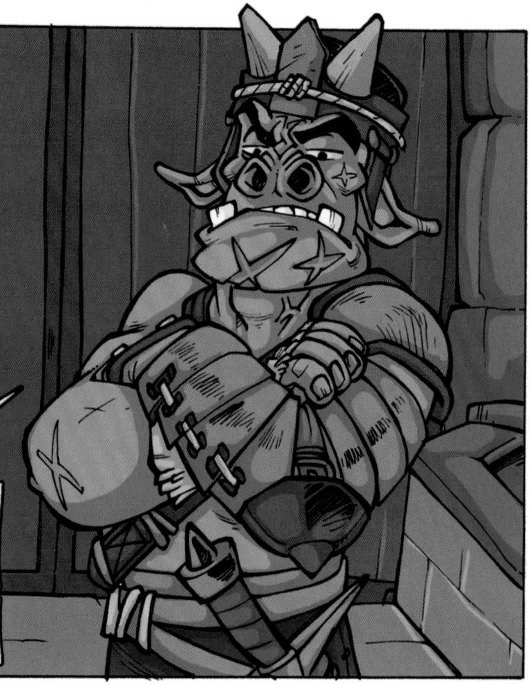

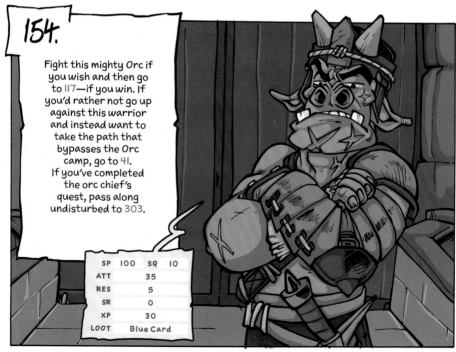

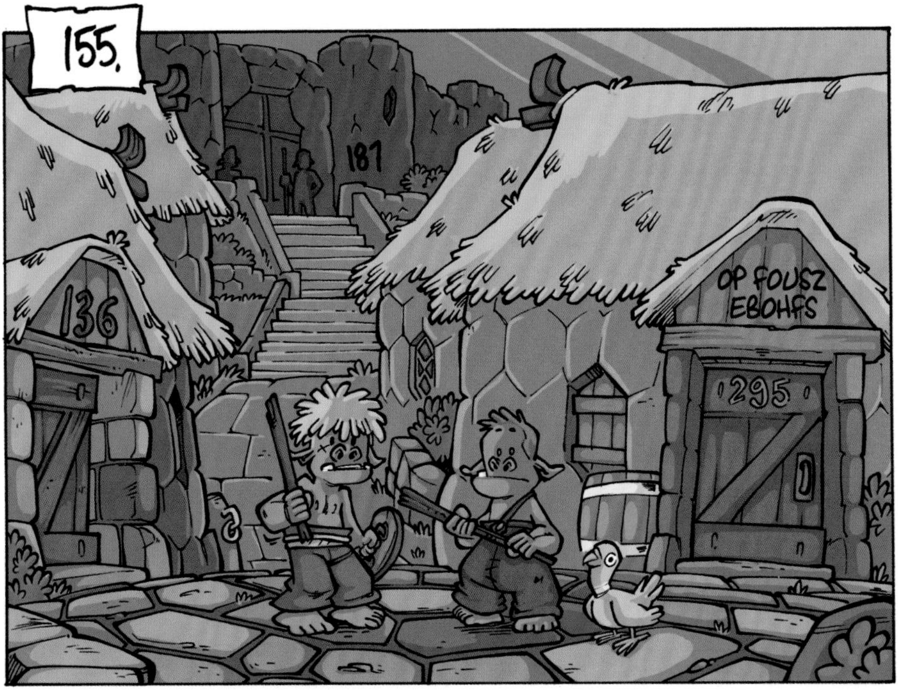
155.
187
136
OP FOUSZ
EBOHFS
295

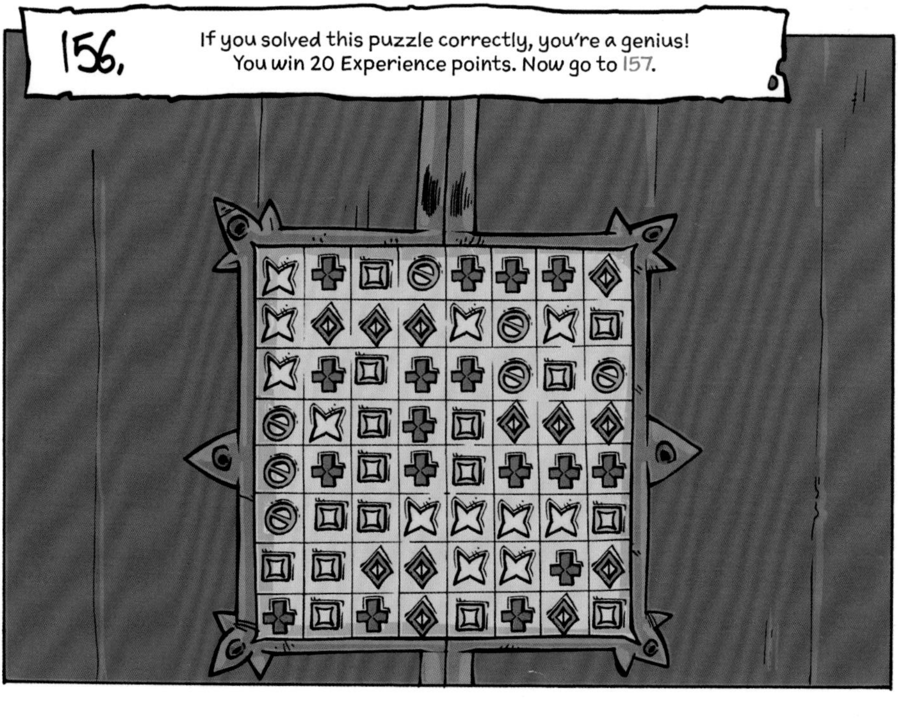
156.
If you solved this puzzle correctly, you're a genius!
You win 20 Experience points. Now go to 157.

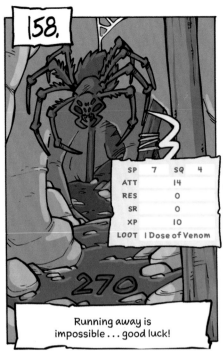

SP	7	SQ	4
ATT		14	
RES		0	
SR		0	
XP		10	
LOOT		1 Dose of Venom	

Running away is
impossible . . . good luck!

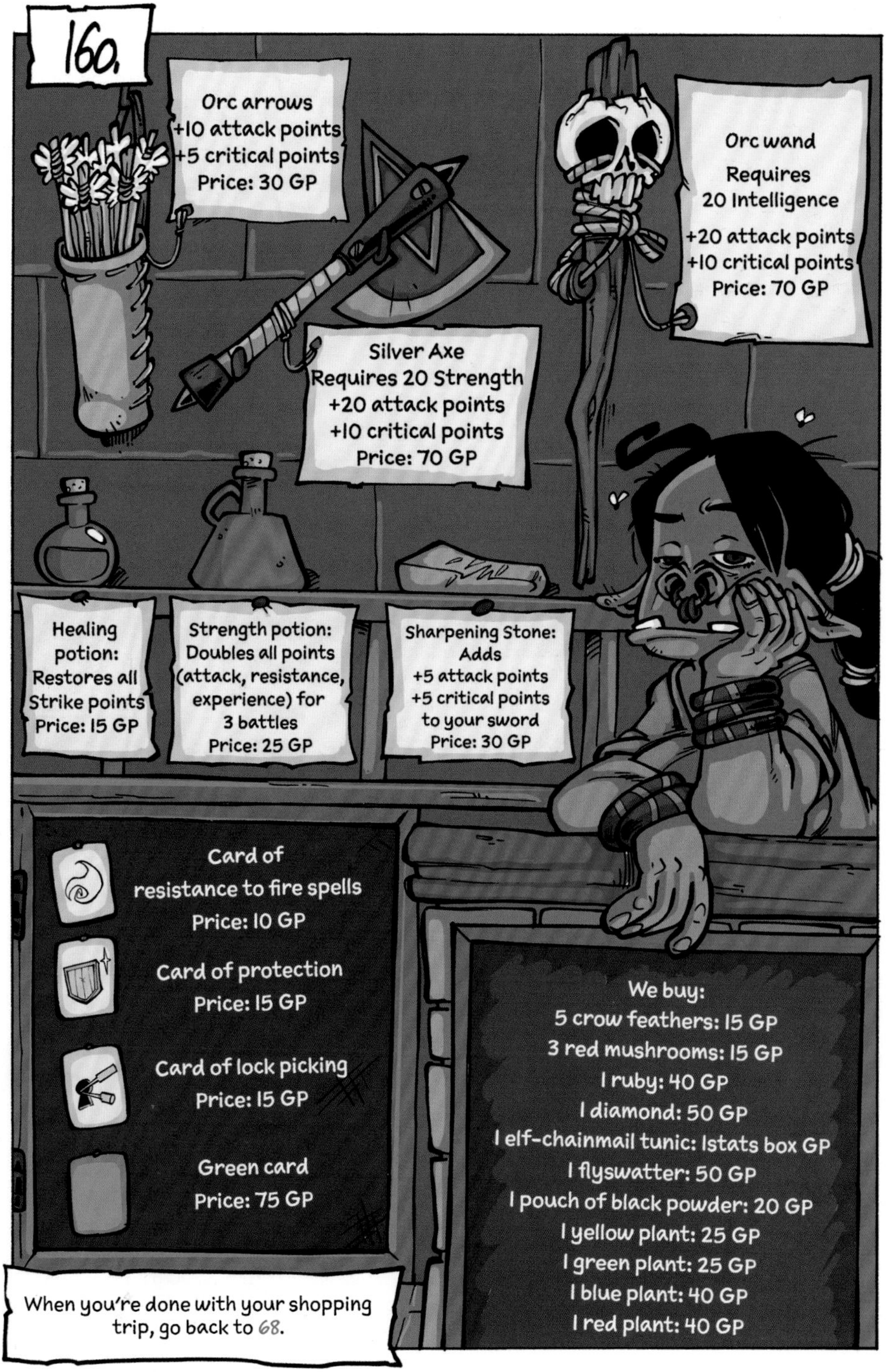
160.
Orc arrows
+10 attack points
+5 critical points
Price: 30 GP
Orc wand
Requires
20 Intelligence
+20 attack points
+10 critical points
Price: 70 GP
Silver Axe
Requires 20 Strength
+20 attack points
+10 critical points
Price: 70 GP
Healing potion:
Restores all Strike points
Price: 15 GP
Strength potion:
Doubles all points (attack, resistance, experience) for 3 battles
Price: 25 GP
Sharpening Stone:
Adds
+5 attack points
+5 critical points
to your sword
Price: 30 GP
Card of resistance to fire spells
Price: 10 GP
Card of protection
Price: 15 GP
Card of lock picking
Price: 15 GP
Green card
Price: 75 GP
We buy:
5 crow feathers: 15 GP
3 red mushrooms: 15 GP
1 ruby: 40 GP
1 diamond: 50 GP
1 elf-chainmail tunic: 1stats box GP
1 flyswatter: 50 GP
1 pouch of black powder: 20 GP
1 yellow plant: 25 GP
1 green plant: 25 GP
1 blue plant: 40 GP
1 red plant: 40 GP
When you're done with your shopping trip, go back to 68.

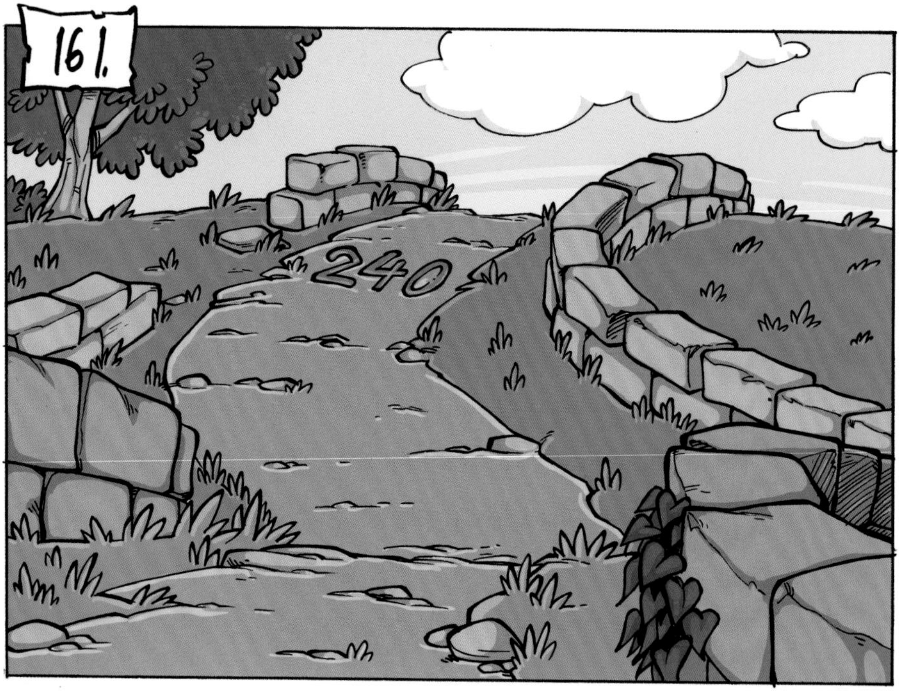
161.
240

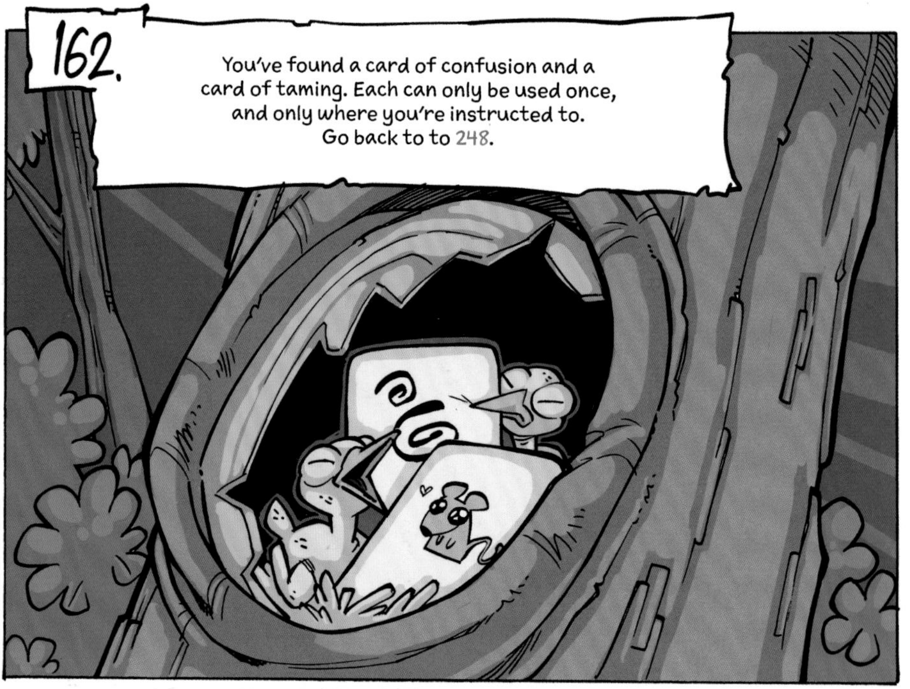
162.
You've found a card of confusion and a card of taming. Each can only be used once, and only where you're instructed to. Go back to to 248.

163.

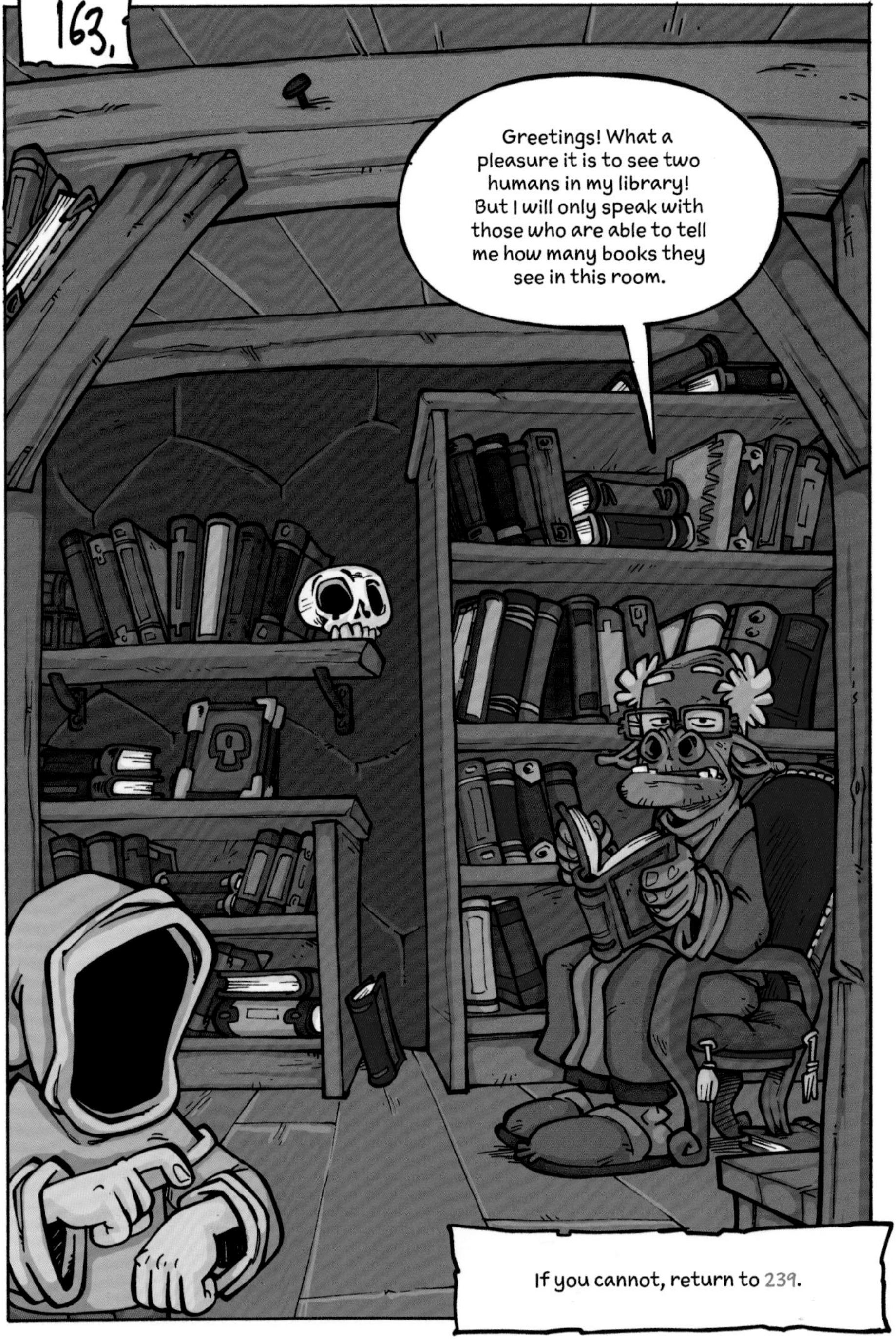
Greetings! What a pleasure it is to see two humans in my library! But I will only speak with those who are able to tell me how many books they see in this room.
If you cannot, return to 239.

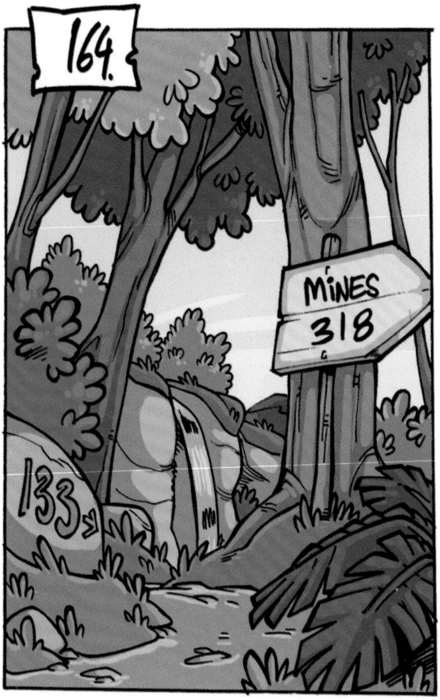
164.
MINES
318
133

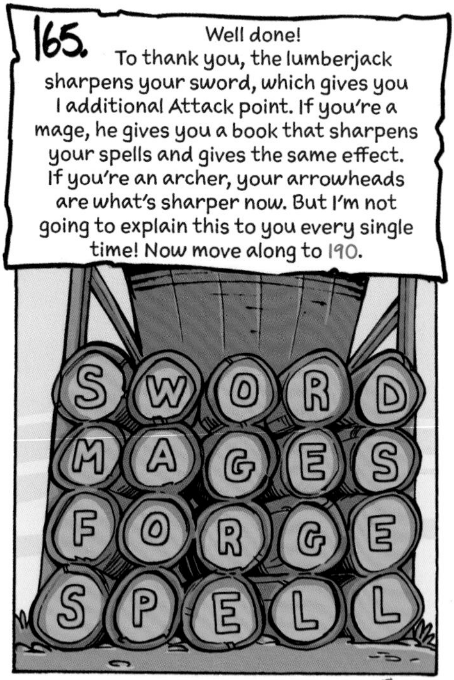
165.
Well done!
To thank you, the lumberjack sharpens your sword, which gives you 1 additional Attack point. If you're a mage, he gives you a book that sharpens your spells and gives the same effect. If you're an archer, your arrowheads are what's sharper now. But I'm not going to explain this to you every single time! Now move along to 190.
SWORD
MAGES
FORGE
SPELL

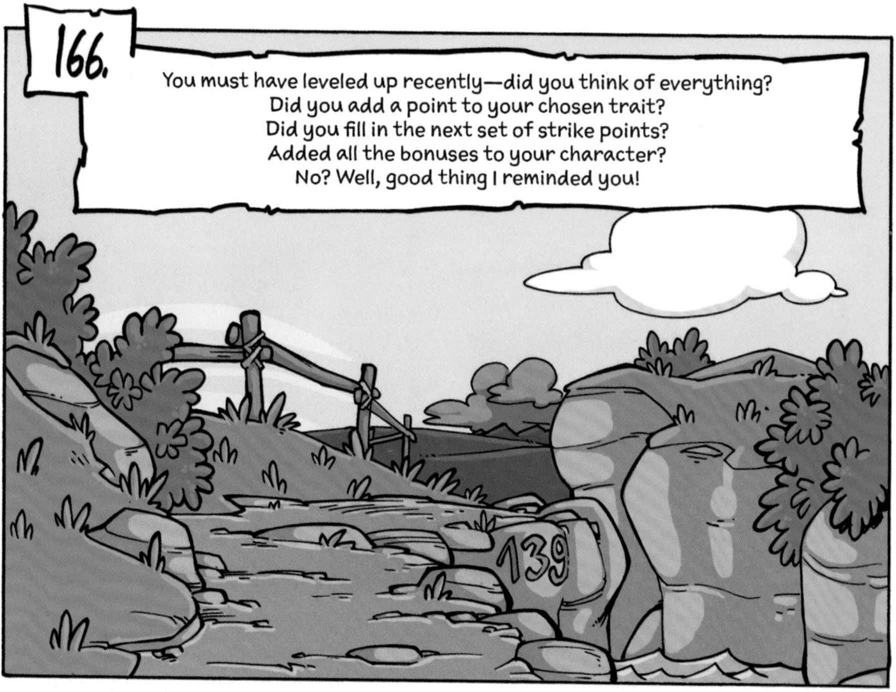
166.
You must have leveled up recently—did you think of everything?
Did you add a point to your chosen trait?
Did you fill in the next set of strike points?
Added all the bonuses to your character?
No? Well, good thing I reminded you!
139

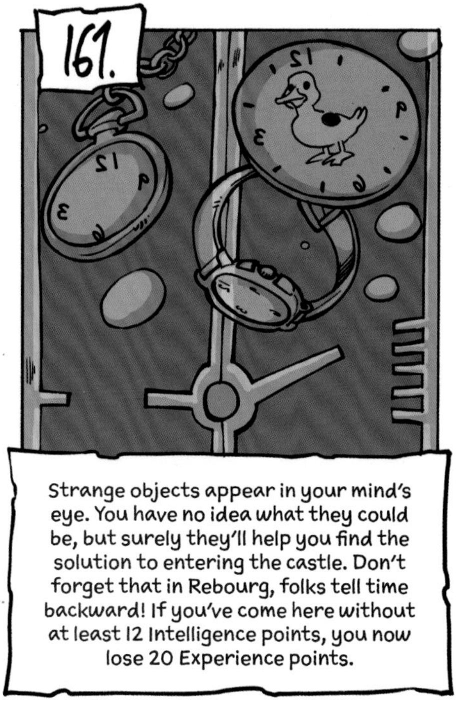
167.
Strange objects appear in your mind's eye. You have no idea what they could be, but surely they'll help you find the solution to entering the castle. Don't forget that in Rebourg, folks tell time backward! If you've come here without at least 12 Intelligence points, you now lose 20 Experience points.

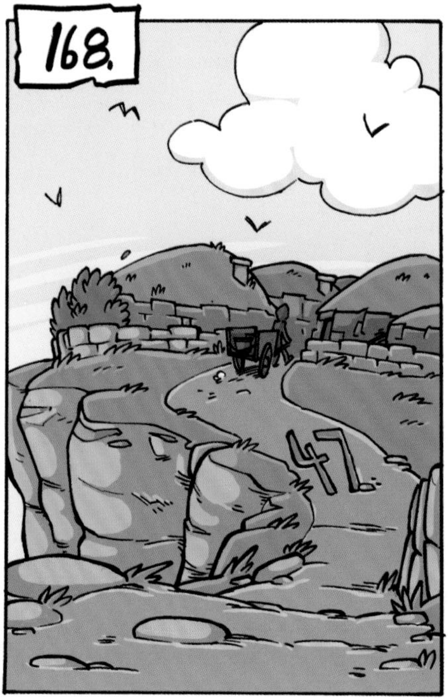
168.
47

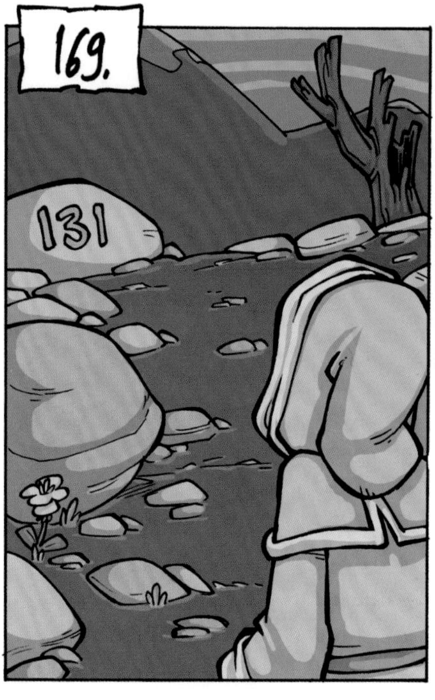
169.
131

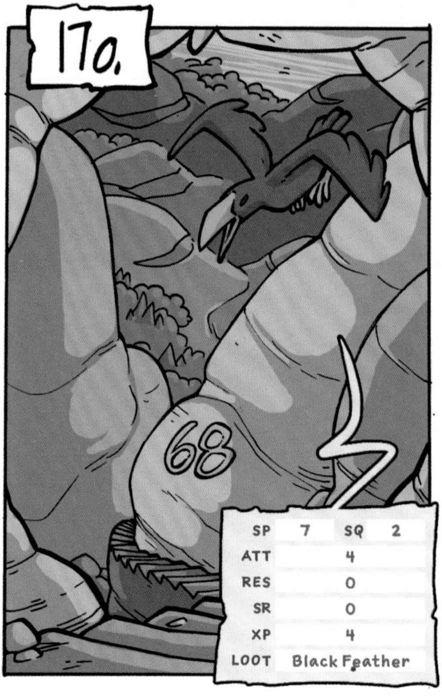
170.
68

SP	7	SQ	2
ATT	4		
RES	0		
SR	0		
XP	4		
LOOT	Black Feather		

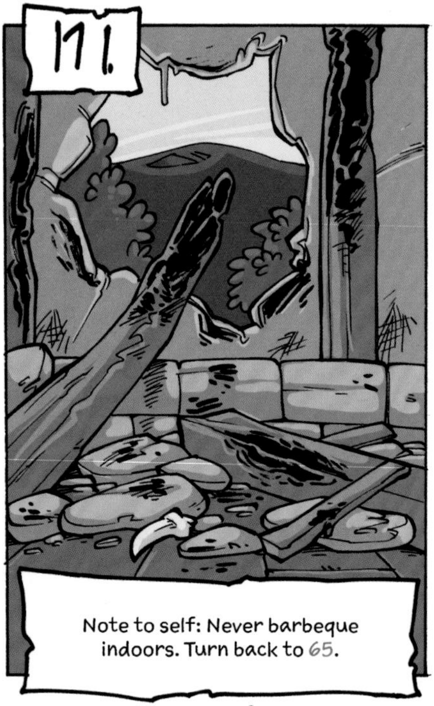
171.
Note to self: Never barbeque indoors. Turn back to 65.

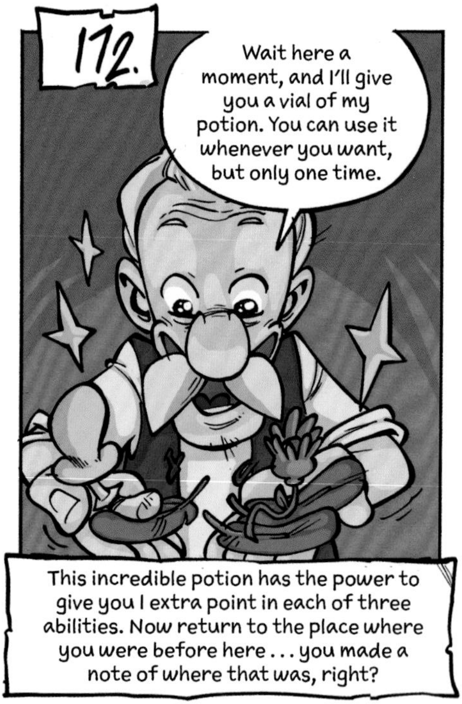
172.
Wait here a moment, and I'll give you a vial of my potion. You can use it whenever you want, but only one time.
This incredible potion has the power to give you 1 extra point in each of three abilities. Now return to the place where you were before here . . . you made a note of where that was, right?

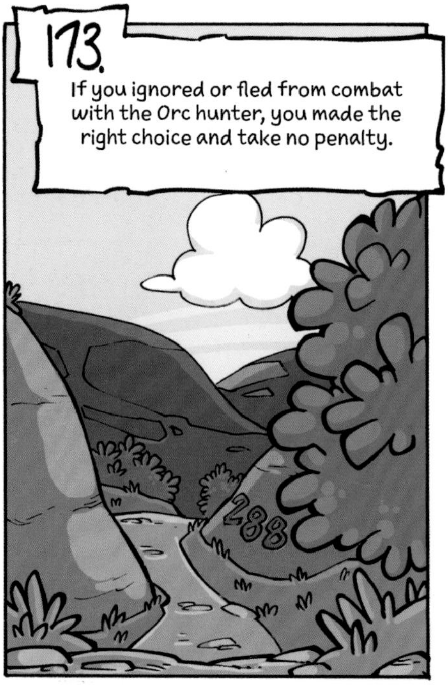
173.
If you ignored or fled from combat with the Orc hunter, you made the right choice and take no penalty.
288

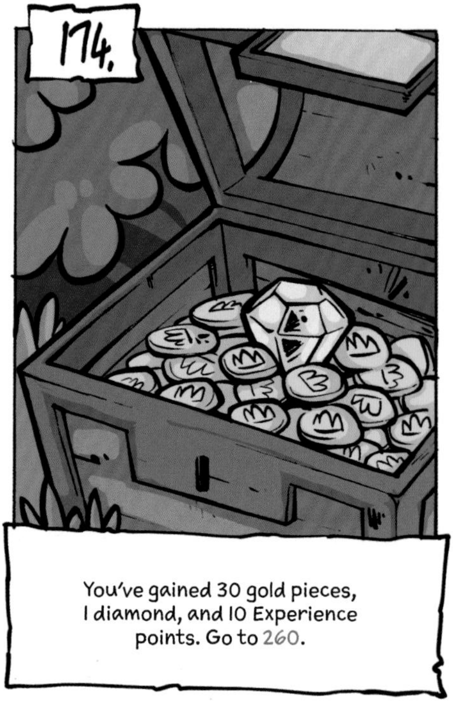
174.
You've gained 30 gold pieces, 1 diamond, and 10 Experience points. Go to 260.

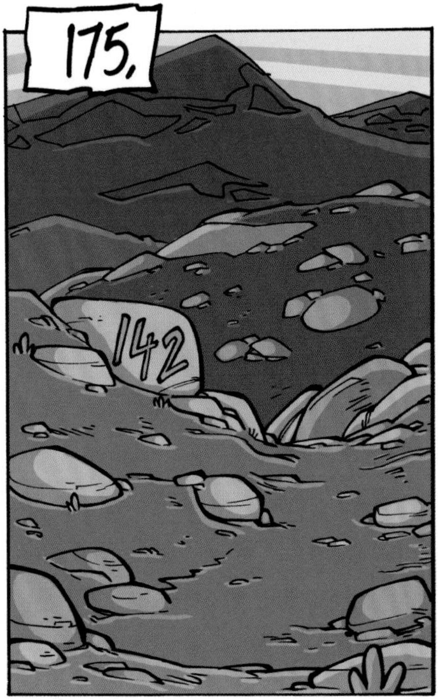
175.
142

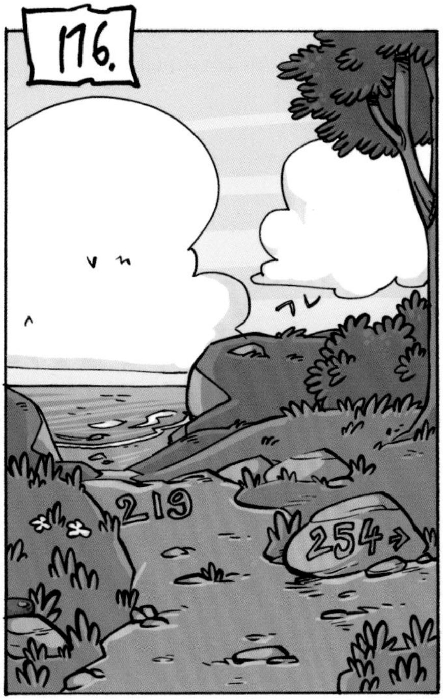
176.
219
254

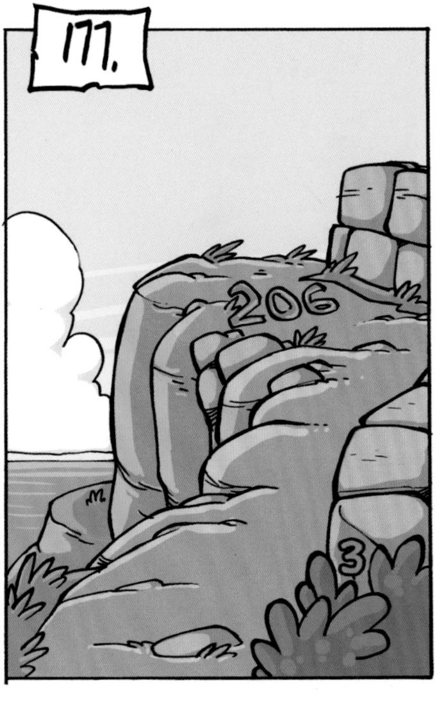
177.
206
3

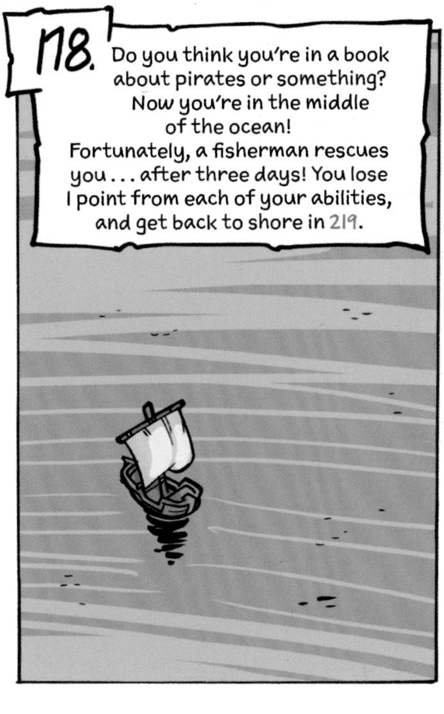
178.
Do you think you're in a book about pirates or something? Now you're in the middle of the ocean!
Fortunately, a fisherman rescues you . . . after three days! You lose 1 point from each of your abilities, and get back to shore in 219.

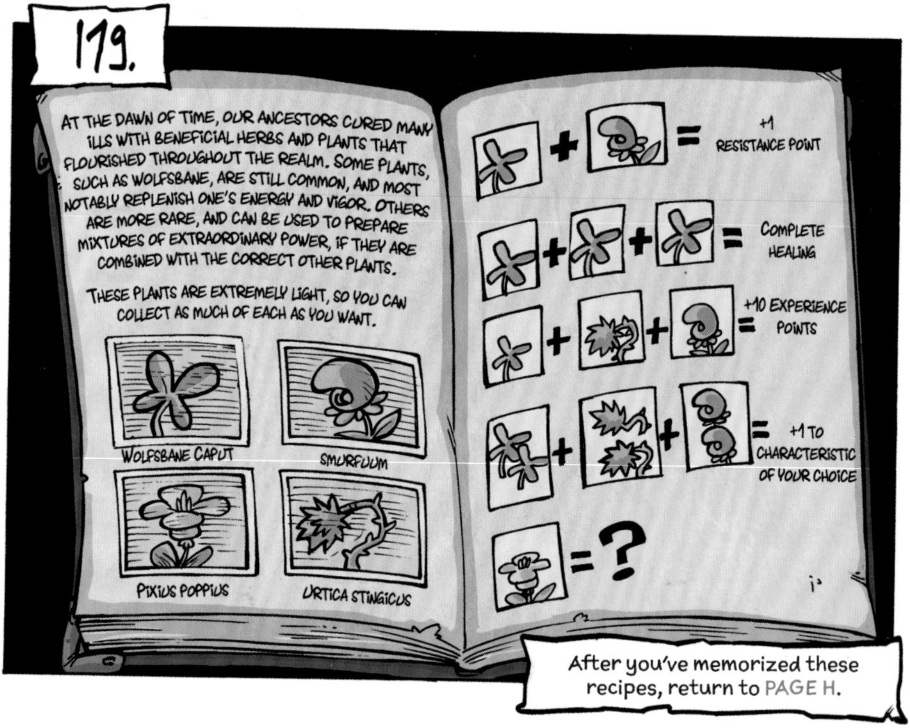
179.
AT THE DAWN OF TIME, OUR ANCESTORS CURED MANY ILLS WITH BENEFICIAL HERBS AND PLANTS THAT FLOURISHED THROUGHOUT THE REALM. SOME PLANTS, SUCH AS WOLFSBANE, ARE STILL COMMON, AND MOST NOTABLY REPLENISH ONE'S ENERGY AND VIGOR. OTHERS ARE MORE RARE, AND CAN BE USED TO PREPARE MIXTURES OF EXTRAORDINARY POWER, IF THEY ARE COMBINED WITH THE CORRECT OTHER PLANTS.
THESE PLANTS ARE EXTREMELY LIGHT, SO YOU CAN COLLECT AS MUCH OF EACH AS YOU WANT.
WOLFSBANE CAPUT
SMURFUUM
PIXIUS POPPIUS
URTICA STINGICUS
+1 RESISTANCE POINT
COMPLETE HEALING
+10 EXPERIENCE POINTS
+1 TO CHARACTERISTIC OF YOUR CHOICE
?
After you've memorized these recipes, return to PAGE H.

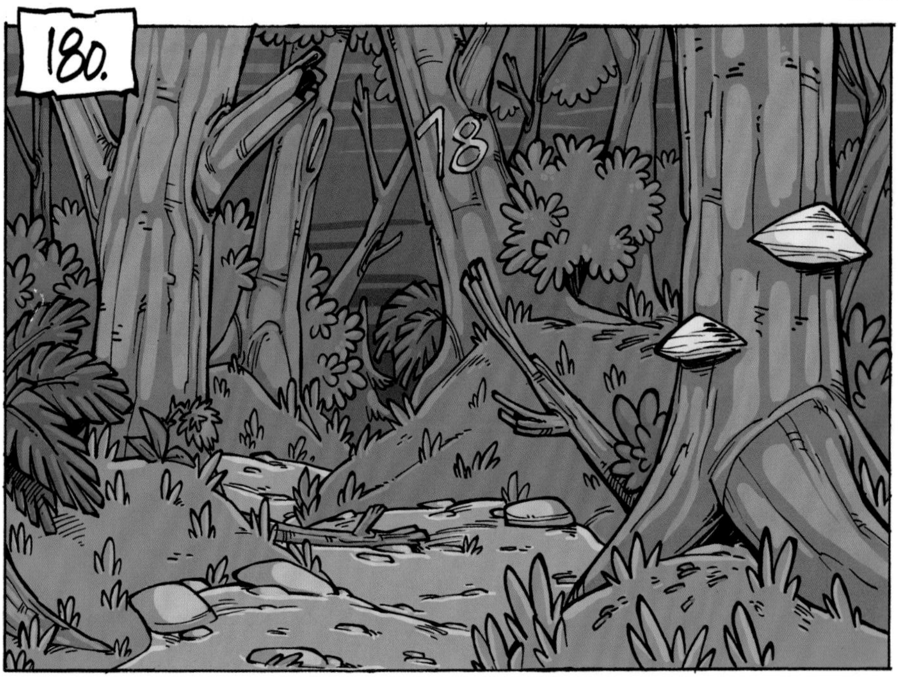
180.
18

181.

Tsk, tsk! Then you have no business being here. Please, go back to 59.

182.

Ouch! Didn't see that coming. Get to fighting, because running away is impossible! It's you or him. Unless you know how to tame creatures? If so, send him to sleep with a simple wave of your hand.

SP	10	SQ	3
ATT	6		
RES	1		
SR	Strength +1		
XP	10		
LOOT	5 Gold Pieces		

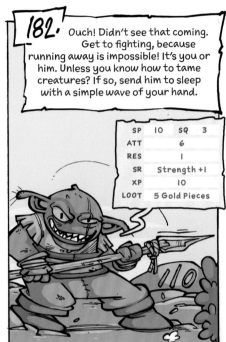

183.

If you fled from battle, you lose 5 Strike points, 5 Experience points, and 5 gold pieces. Yes, I know that's a lot, and no, I don't know what a wolf is going to do with 5 pieces of gold.

184.

Here's some fish pickle sauce to thank you—my wife's special recipe. Drink it before a battle, and it'll double your Attack points. Are you going to stay for some soup?

Stay if you want, but I'll go wait for you in 211.

185.

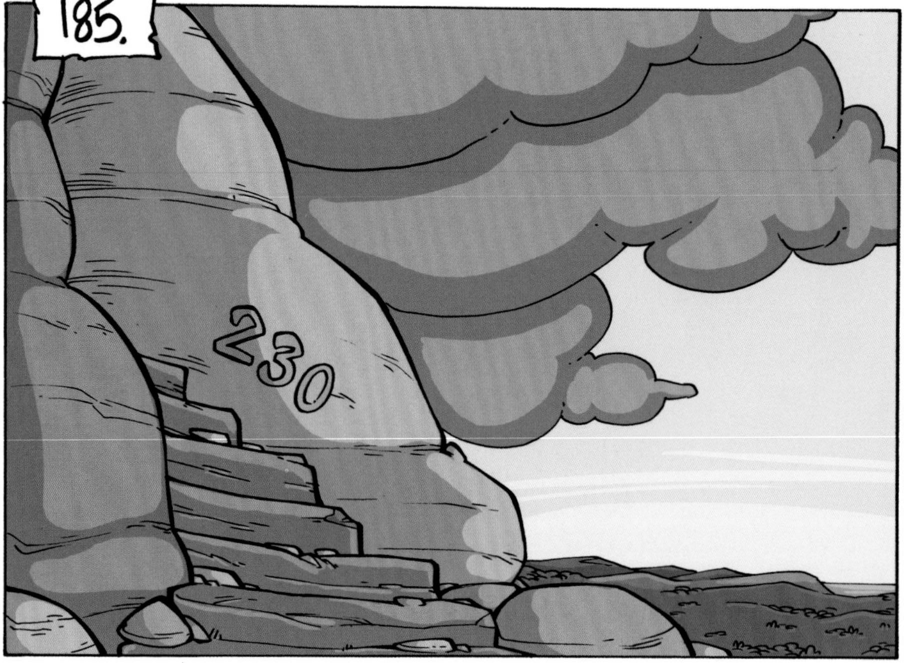
230

186.

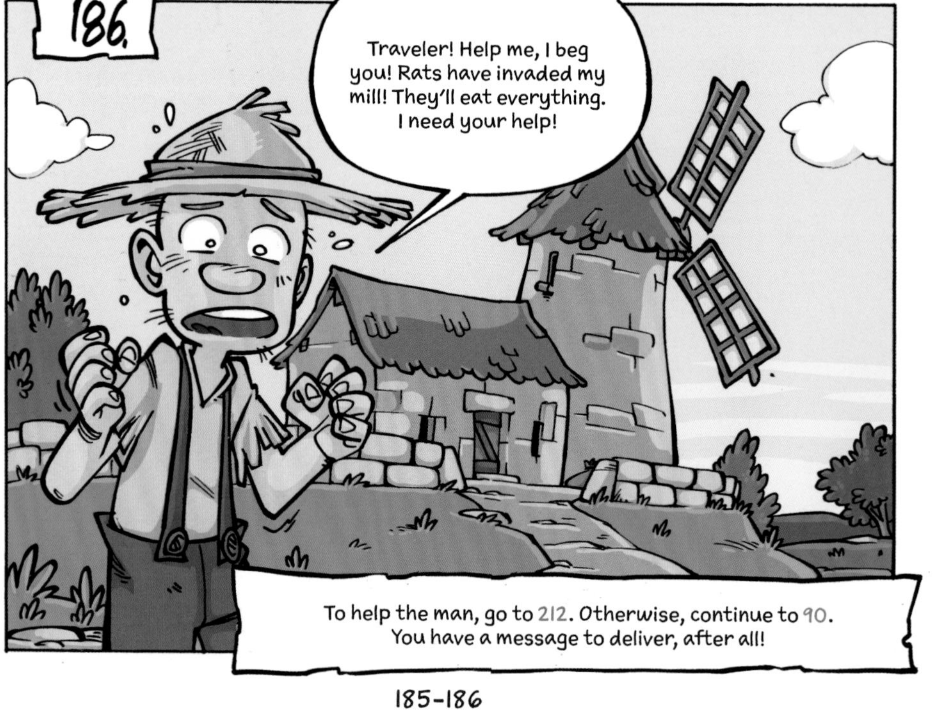
Traveler! Help me, I beg you! Rats have invaded my mill! They'll eat everything. I need your help!
To help the man, go to 212. Otherwise, continue to 90. You have a message to deliver, after all!

187.

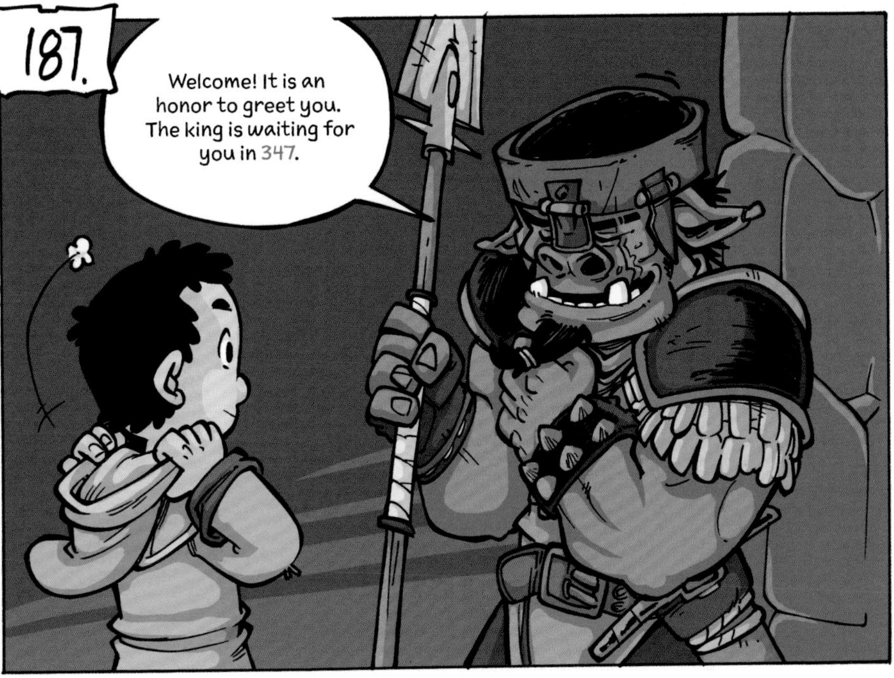
Welcome! It is an honor to greet you. The king is waiting for you in 347.

188.

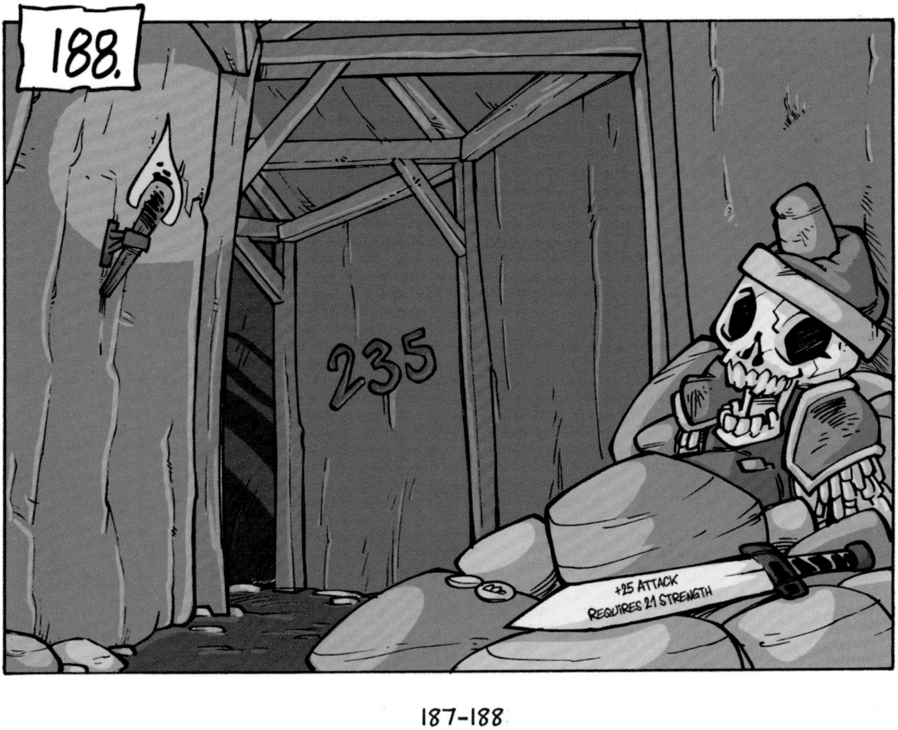
235
+25 ATTACK
REQUIRES 21 STRENGTH

189. Maybe you shouldn't have ignored this fellow. It seems to have upset him. Now he's casting a spell to become more powerful. Do you want to fight? If you win, go to 10. If you have to flee, go to 92.

SP	15	SQ	4
ATT	10		
RES	3		
SR	Fire Spell +2		
XP	8		
LOOT	0		

190. No choice but to fight this creature! Good luck! Don't forget: If you lose all your Strike points or if you're not strong enough to slay him, this is certain death. If you know how to tame creatures, you can change the goblin's mind, and his Attack points will be added to yours during your next battle.

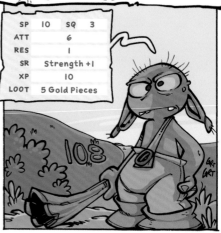

SP	10	SQ	3
ATT	6		
RES	1		
SR	Strength +1		
XP	10		
LOOT	5 Gold Pieces		

191.

192. To climb down the tree, multiply the first branch at the bottom by the second, then divide that by the third, add the fourth, and subtract the last. Or if you have at least 13 Agility (and you're not great at math), you can jump down to 300.

193.

SP	12	SQ	4
ATT	10		
RES	0		
SR	0		
XP	12		
LOOT	10 Gold Pieces		

Hand over yer money or else!

You can flee but you'll lose 3 seashells.
Up to you!

194.

If you have 30 gold pieces, I'll teach you how to increase your attacks and protection by 5 points. You up for it?

Up to you.
Return to 88 after.

195. Well done! Getting this far wasn't easy. You gain 5 Experience points.

196.

Whoa! Careful!

197. Two out of three— not bad! You can return to 259 at any time.

198. What a nasty beast this is! And she seems to be in a bad mood, too! Decide whether you want to battle and then head into the village, or if you'd rather run away on the little path to your left.

SP	7	SQ	3
ATT	6		
RES	0		
SR	0		
XP	8		
LOOT	0		

199.

You should have tried helping him . . . I don't know about you, but I'm pretty scared! If you defeat him, go on to 98.

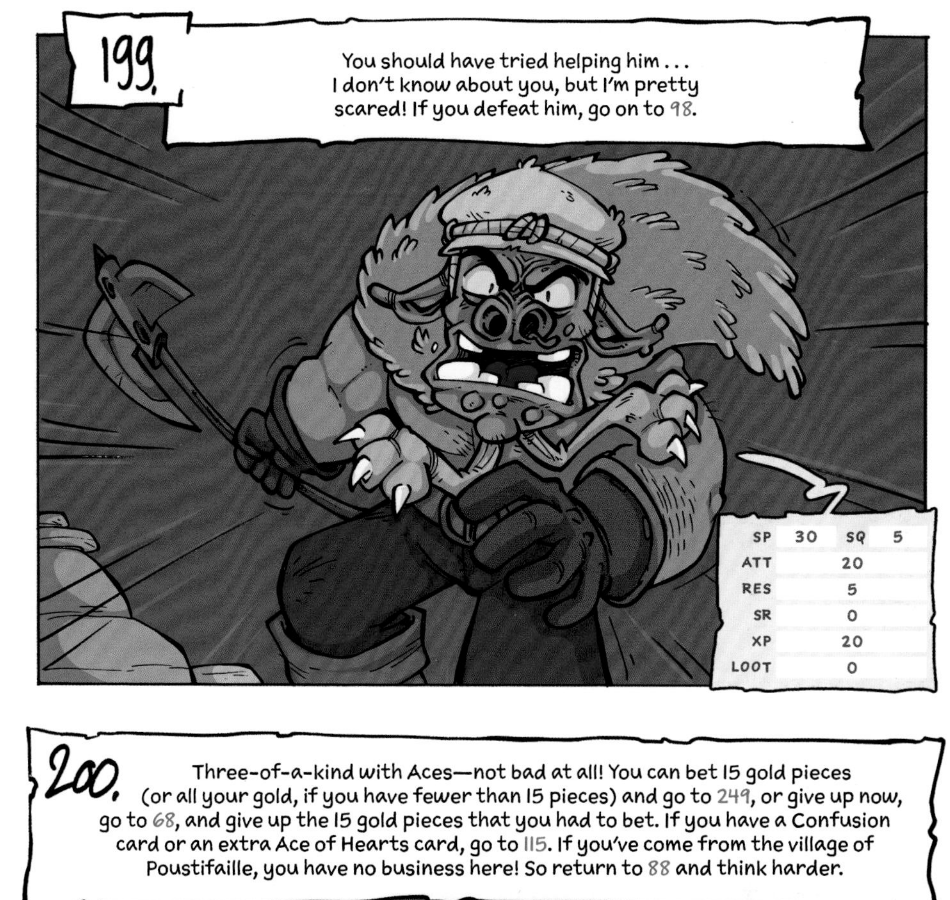

SP	30	SQ	5
ATT	20		
RES	5		
SR	0		
XP	20		
LOOT	0		

200.

Three-of-a-kind with Aces—not bad at all! You can bet 15 gold pieces (or all your gold, if you have fewer than 15 pieces) and go to 249, or give up now, go to 68, and give up the 15 gold pieces that you had to bet. If you have a Confusion card or an extra Ace of Hearts card, go to 115. If you've come from the village of Poustifaille, you have no business here! So return to 88 and think harder.

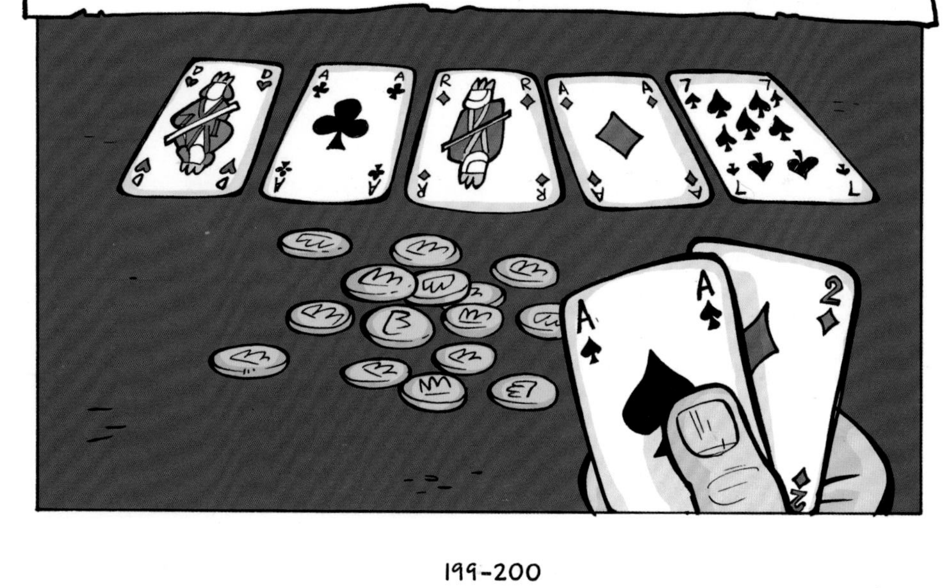

201.

202.

If you have lock-picking skills, you can open the padlock and enter at 257. The door is in bad shape, so you can also force it open if you have at least 10 Strength. If neither of these work, go back on your way in 80.

203.

204.

SP	15	SQ	4
ATT		10	
RES		5	
SR		Fire Spell +2	
XP		8	
LOOT		0	

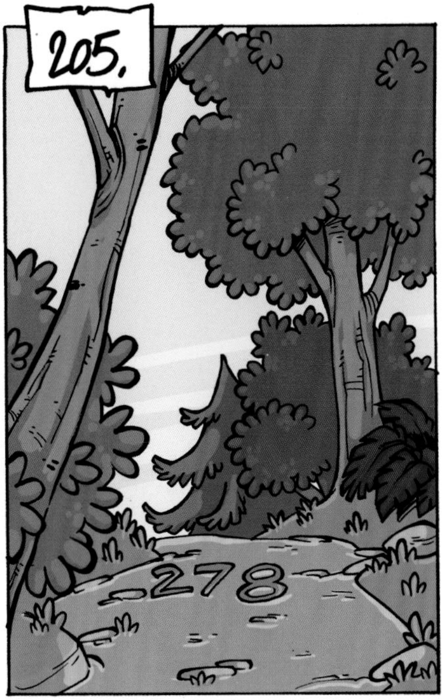
205.
278

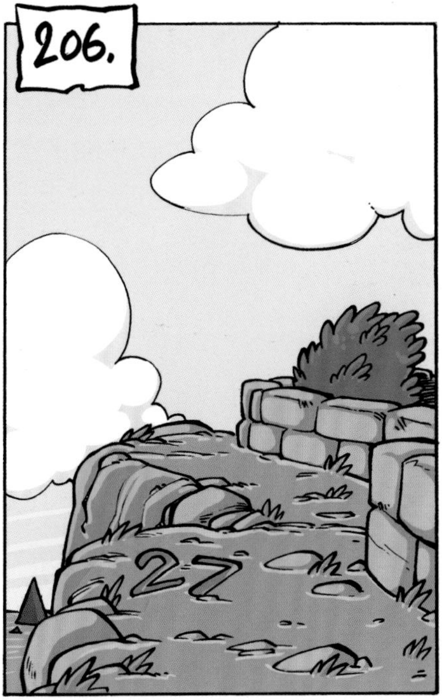
206.
27

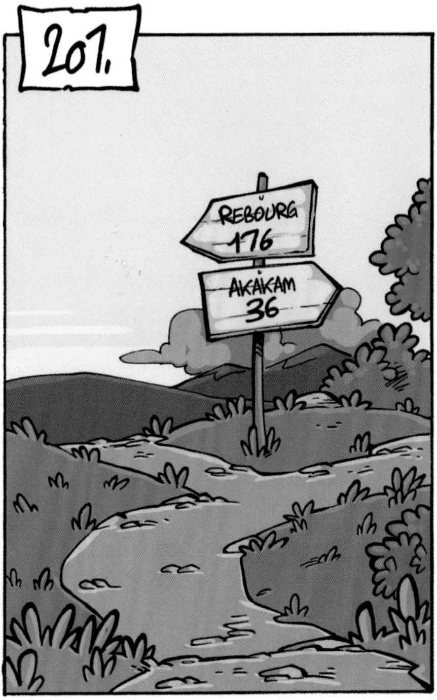
207.
REBOURG
176
AKAKAM
36

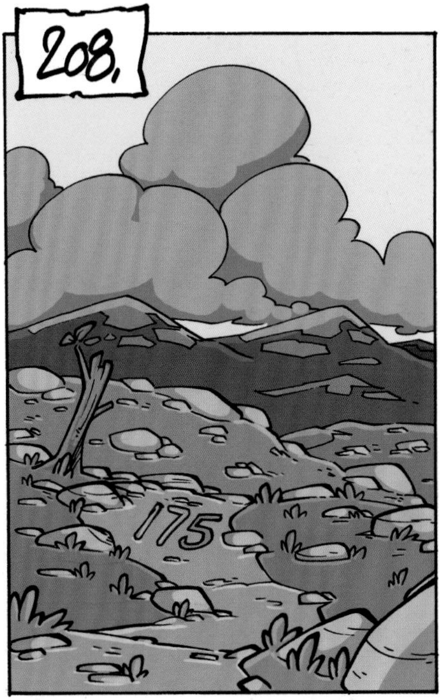
208.
175

205-206-207-208

209.

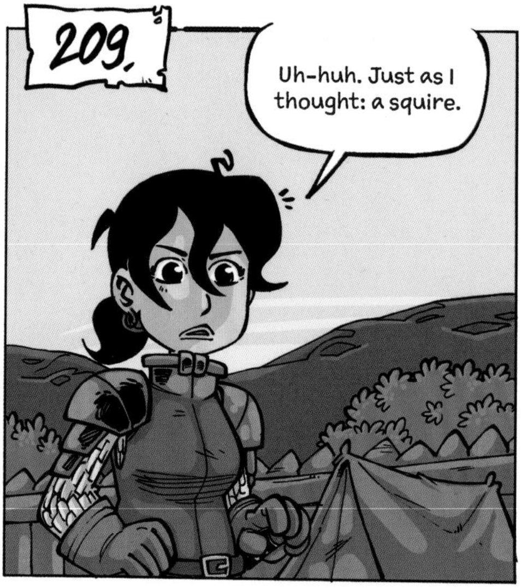
Uh-huh. Just as I thought: a squire.

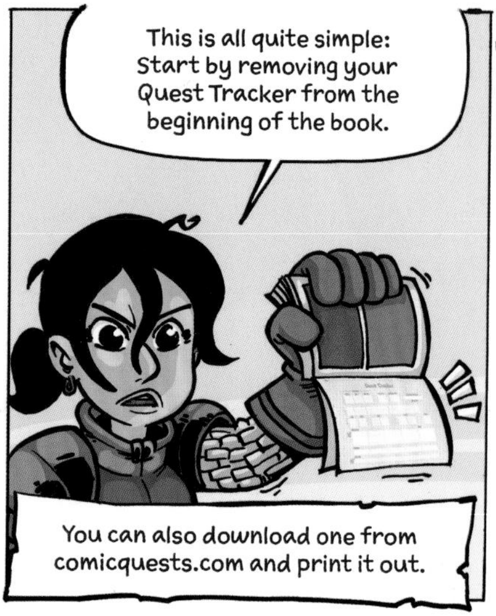
This is all quite simple: Start by removing your Quest Tracker from the beginning of the book.
You can also download one from comicquests.com and print it out.

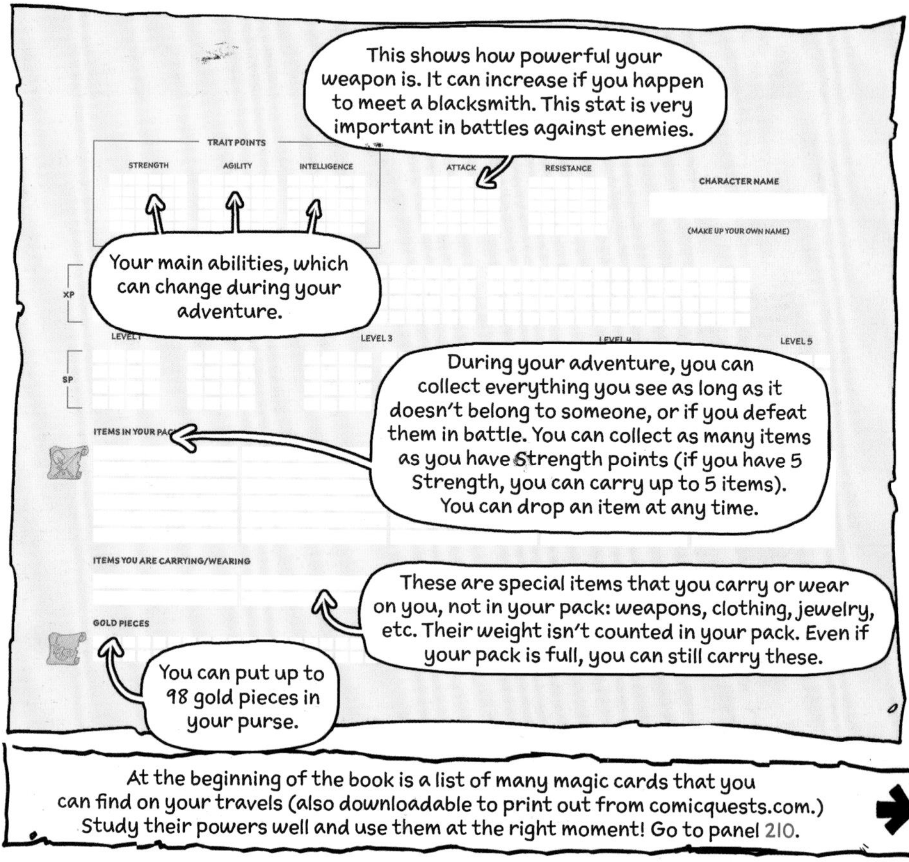
This shows how powerful your weapon is. It can increase if you happen to meet a blacksmith. This stat is very important in battles against enemies.
TRAIT POINTS
STRENGTH
AGILITY
INTELLIGENCE
ATTACK
RESISTANCE
CHARACTER NAME
(MAKE UP YOUR OWN NAME)
Your main abilities, which can change during your adventure.
XP
LEVEL 3
LEVEL 5
SP
During your adventure, you can collect everything you see as long as it doesn't belong to someone, or if you defeat them in battle. You can collect as many items as you have Strength points (if you have 5 Strength, you can carry up to 5 items). You can drop an item at any time.
ITEMS YOU ARE CARRYING/WEARING
These are special items that you carry or wear on you, not in your pack: weapons, clothing, jewelry, etc. Their weight isn't counted in your pack. Even if your pack is full, you can still carry these.
GOLD PIECES
You can put up to 98 gold pieces in your purse.

At the beginning of the book is a list of many magic cards that you can find on your travels (also downloadable to print out from comicquests.com.) Study their powers well and use them at the right moment! Go to panel 210.

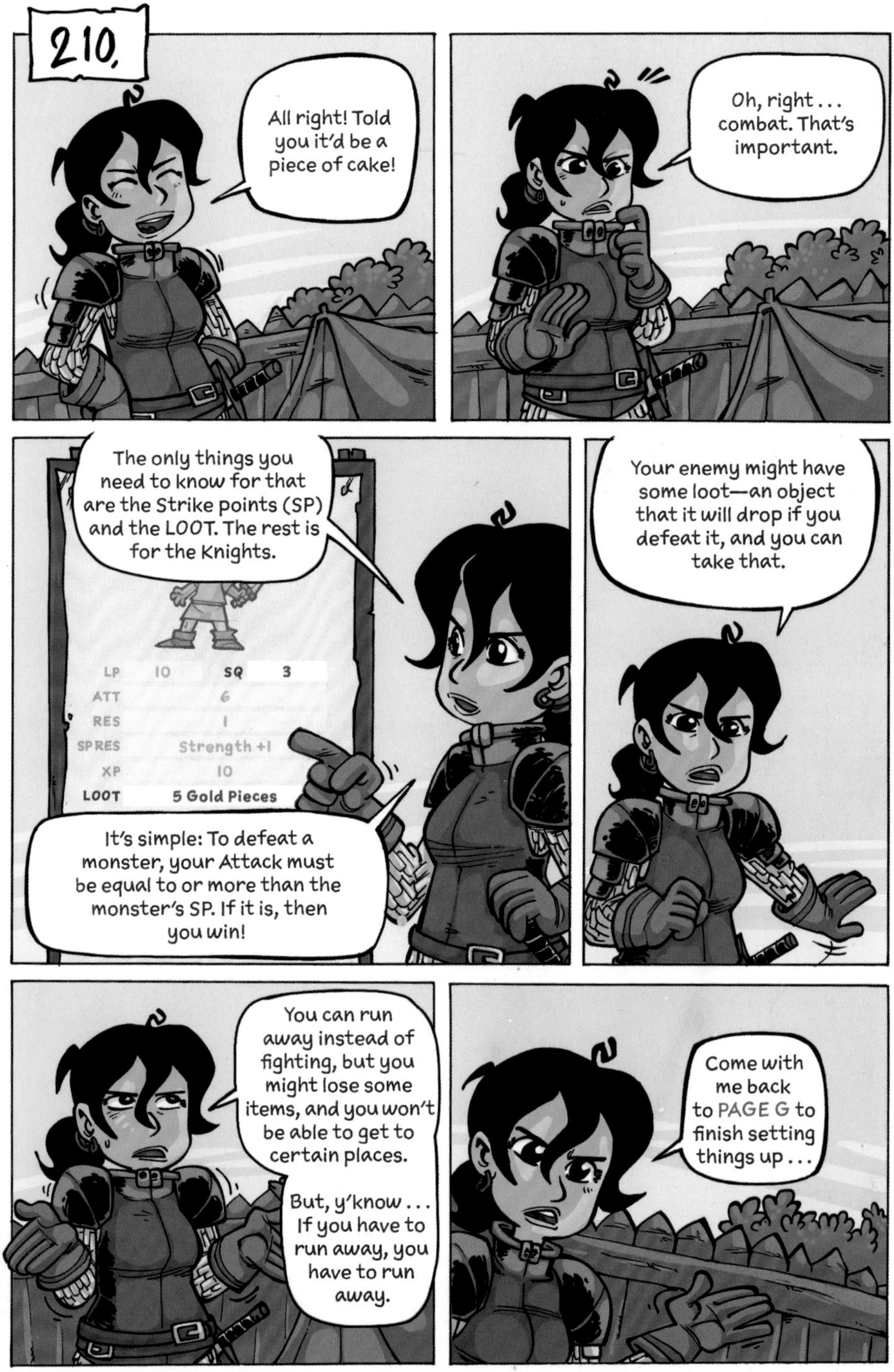
210.
All right! Told you it'd be a piece of cake!
Oh, right... combat. That's important.
The only things you need to know for that are the Strike points (SP) and the LOOT. The rest is for the Knights.
LP 10 SQ 3
ATT 6
RES 1
SPRES Strength +1
XP 10
LOOT 5 Gold Pieces
It's simple: To defeat a monster, your Attack must be equal to or more than the monster's SP. If it is, then you win!
Your enemy might have some loot—an object that it will drop if you defeat it, and you can take that.
You can run away instead of fighting, but you might lose some items, and you won't be able to get to certain places.
But, y'know... If you have to run away, you have to run away.
Come with me back to PAGE G to finish setting things up...

211.

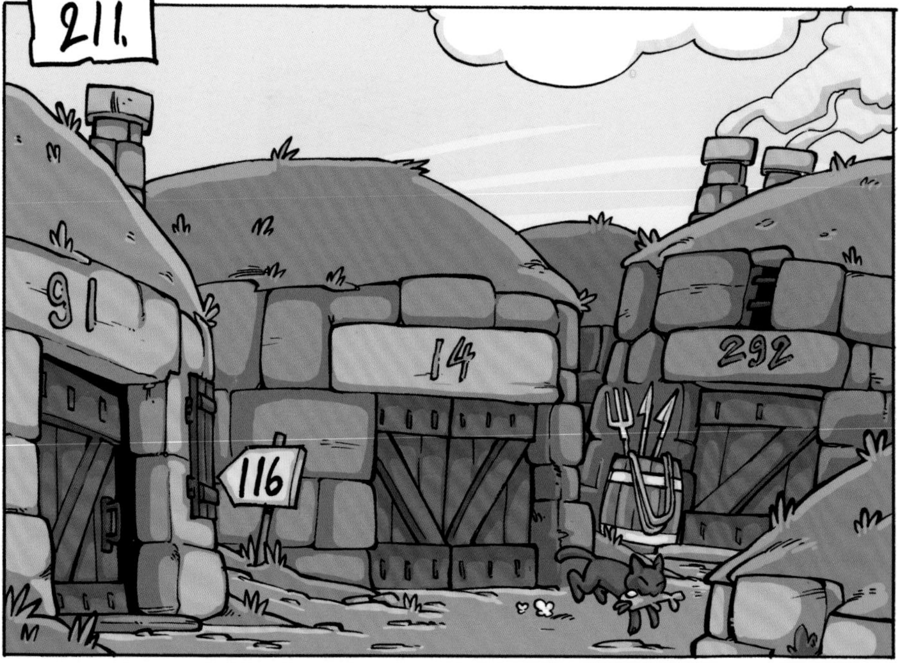

91
14
292
116

212.

Fooey! As always, you can't resist playing the hero—and now you're facing three giant rats! You can't turn around, or you'll ruin your reputation! Fight them one at a time and then head to 18.

Warning: If you lose all your Strike points, you have to start the adventure over, so good luck! If you know how to tame animals, you can charm one of the rats, which will run away. Then you'll only have to fight two of them.

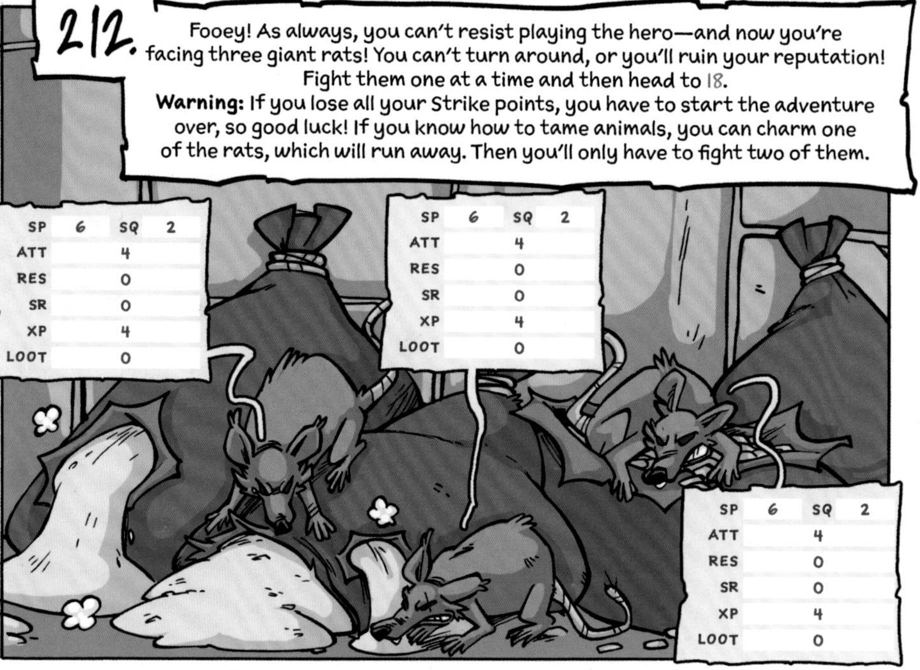

SP	6	SQ	2
ATT	4		
RES	0		
SR	0		
XP	4		
LOOT	0		

SP	6	SQ	2
ATT	4		
RES	0		
SR	0		
XP	4		
LOOT	0		

SP	6	SQ	2
ATT	4		
RES	0		
SR	0		
XP	4		
LOOT	0		

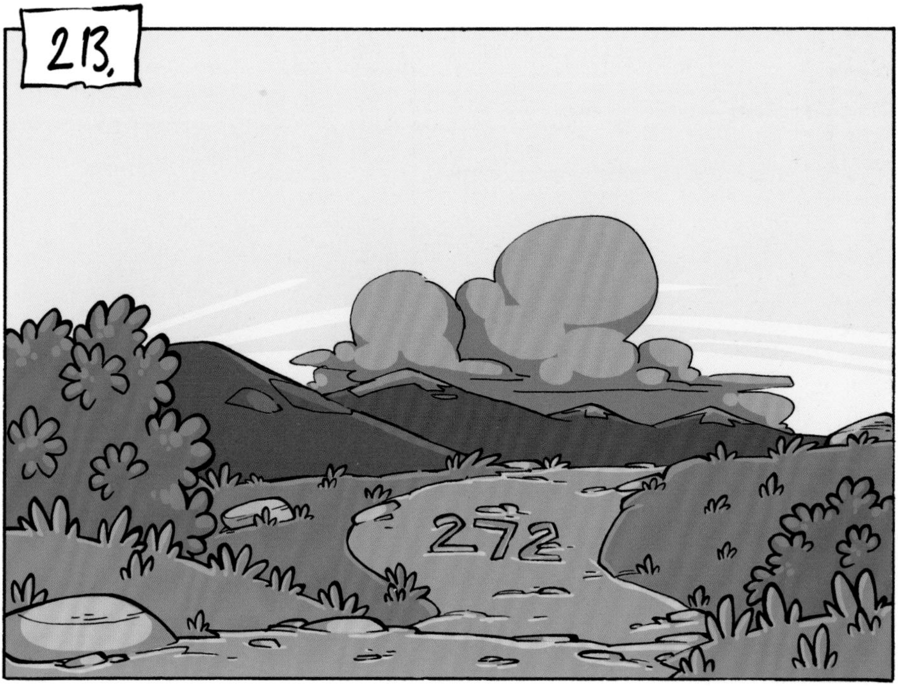
213.
272

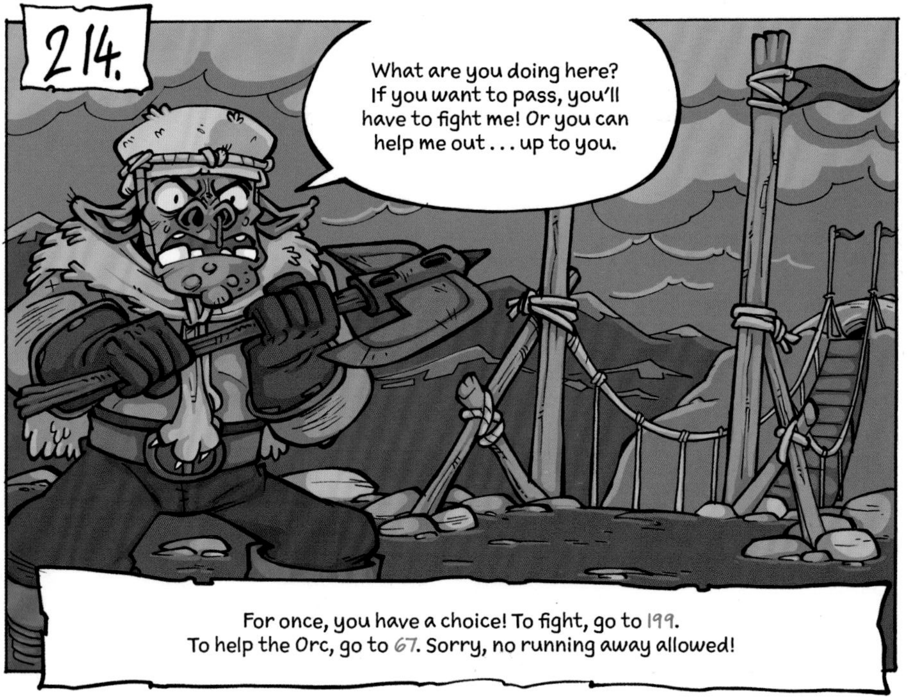
214.
What are you doing here? If you want to pass, you'll have to fight me! Or you can help me out . . . up to you.
For once, you have a choice! To fight, go to 199.
To help the Orc, go to 67. Sorry, no running away allowed!

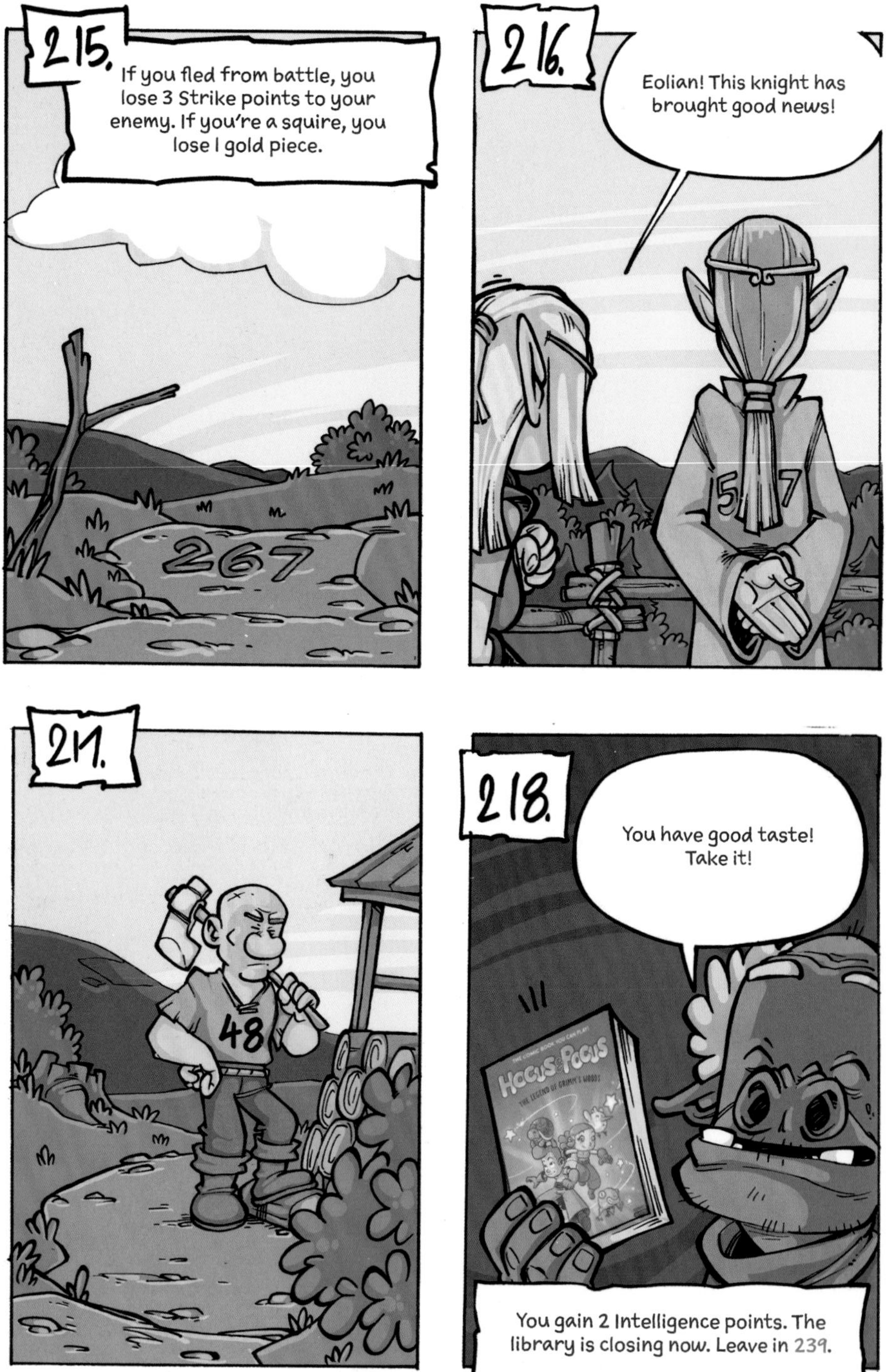
215.
If you fled from battle, you lose 3 Strike points to your enemy. If you're a squire, you lose 1 gold piece.
267
216.
Eolian! This knight has brought good news!
57
217.
48
218.
You have good taste! Take it!
You gain 2 Intelligence points. The library is closing now. Leave in 239.

219.

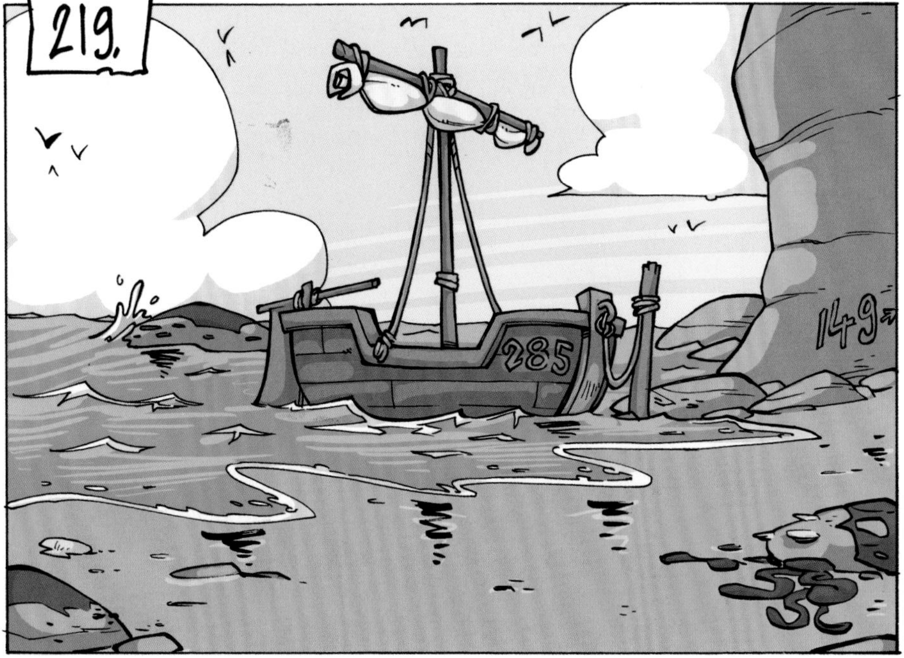
285
149

220.

It was worth it to defeat this brute: you find the elf king's medallion! Do you know what to do with it? If not, you can always take it along with you; it gives you 3 Attack points and restores 3 Strike points after every battle. Now go on to 263.

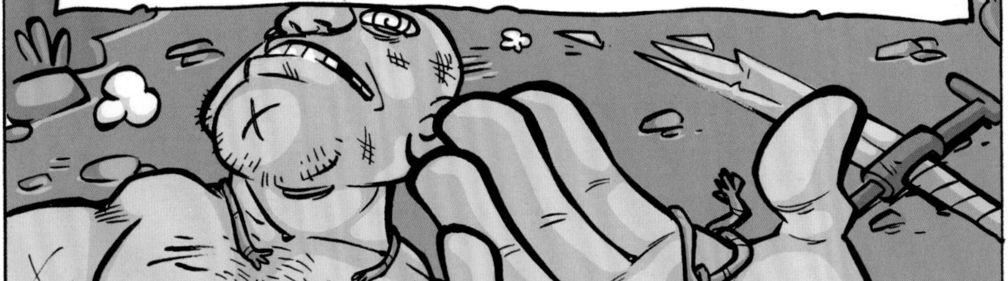

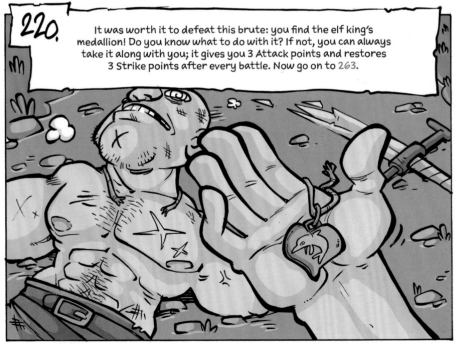

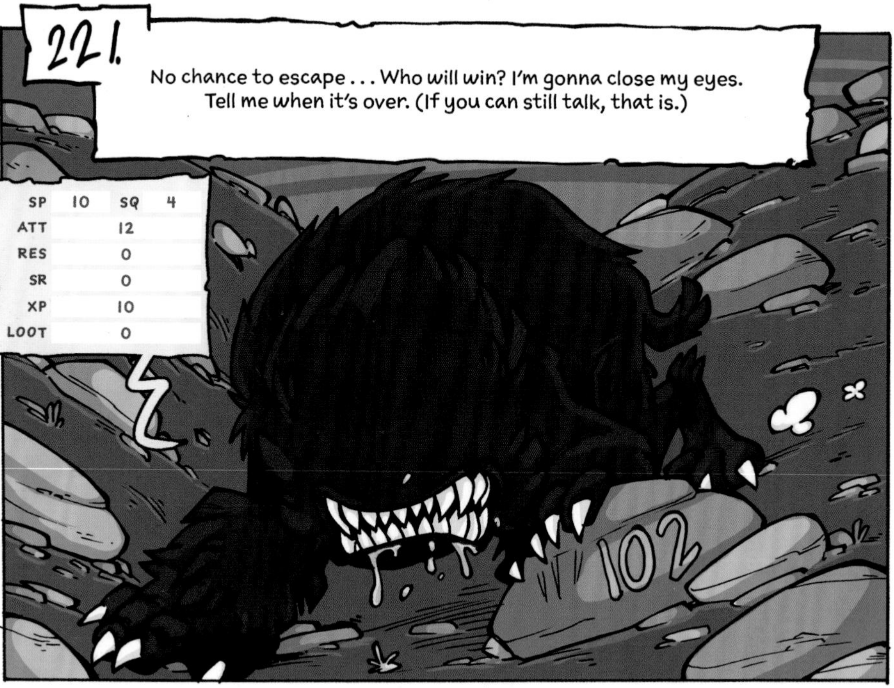
221.
No chance to escape . . . Who will win? I'm gonna close my eyes. Tell me when it's over. (If you can still talk, that is.)
SP 10 SQ 4
ATT 12
RES 0
SR 0
XP 10
LOOT 0
102

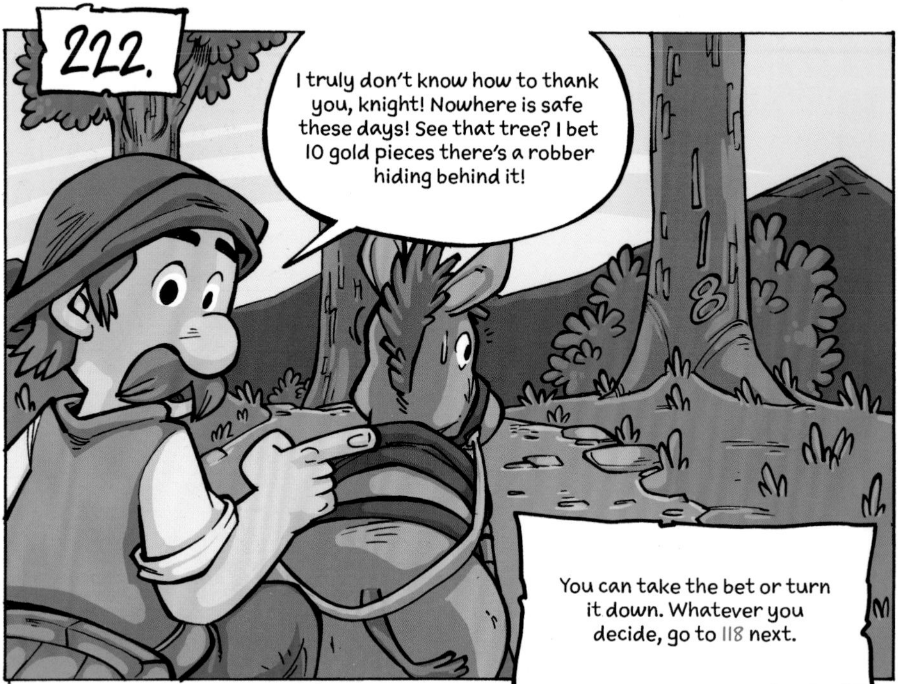
222.
I truly don't know how to thank you, knight! Nowhere is safe these days! See that tree? I bet 10 gold pieces there's a robber hiding behind it!
8
You can take the bet or turn it down. Whatever you decide, go to 118 next.

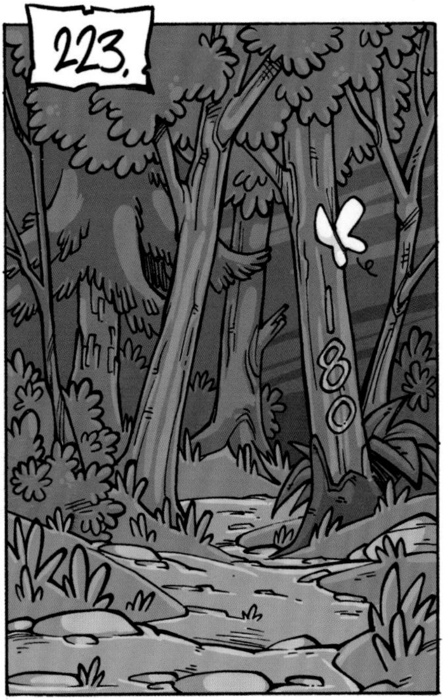
223.
180

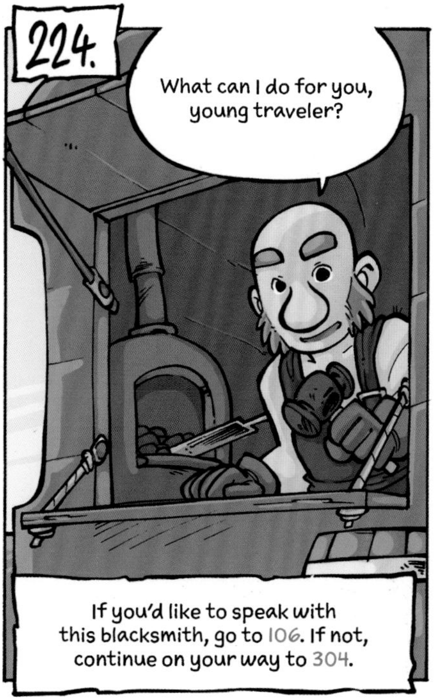
224.
What can I do for you, young traveler?
If you'd like to speak with this blacksmith, go to 106. If not, continue on your way to 304.

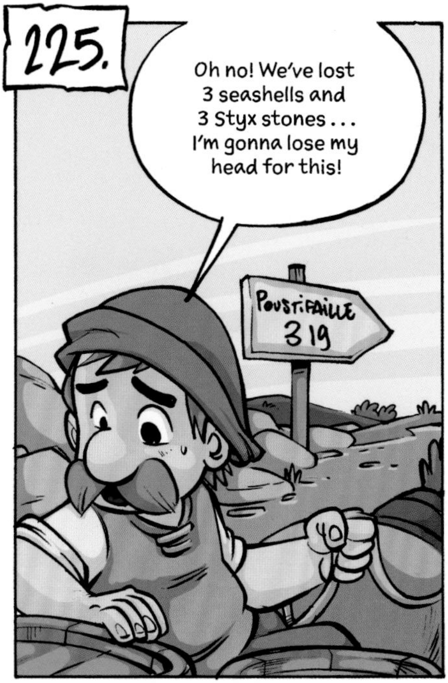
225.
Oh no! We've lost 3 seashells and 3 Styx stones . . . I'm gonna lose my head for this!
POUSTIFAILLE
319

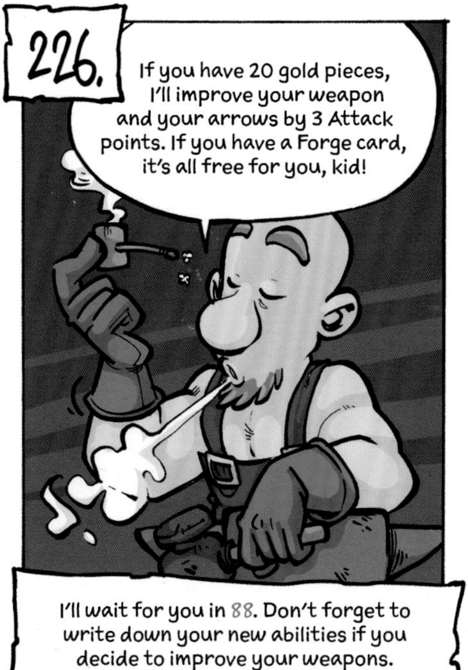
226.
If you have 20 gold pieces, I'll improve your weapon and your arrows by 3 Attack points. If you have a Forge card, it's all free for you, kid!
I'll wait for you in 88. Don't forget to write down your new abilities if you decide to improve your weapons.

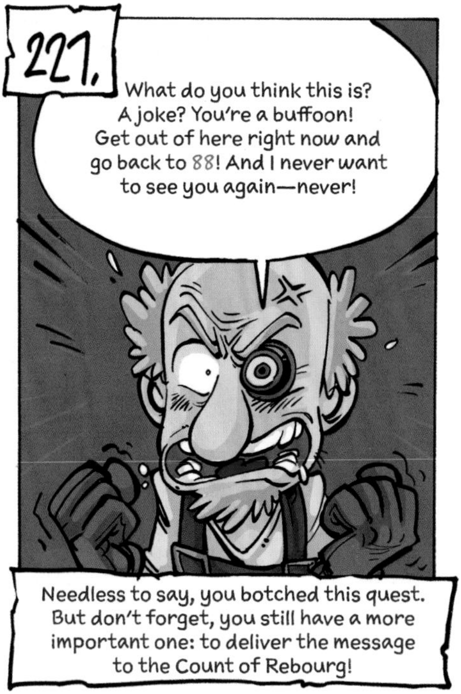
227.
What do you think this is? A joke? You're a buffoon! Get out of here right now and go back to 88! And I never want to see you again—never!
Needless to say, you botched this quest. But don't forget, you still have a more important one: to deliver the message to the Count of Rebourg!

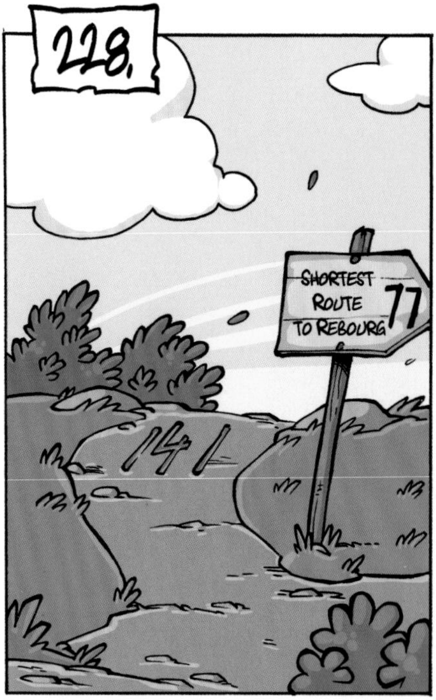
228.
SHORTEST ROUTE TO REBOURG 77
141

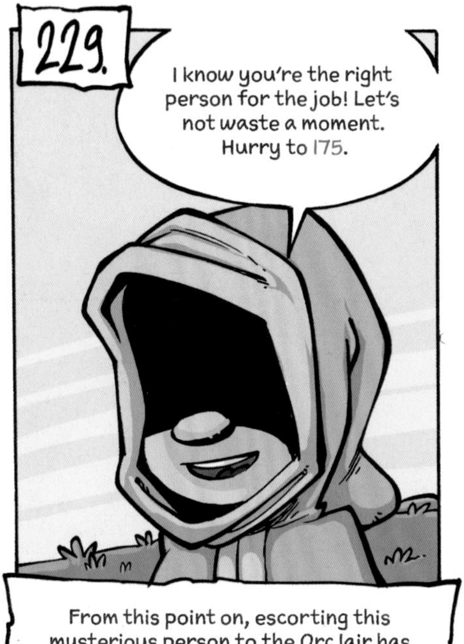
229.
I know you're the right person for the job! Let's not waste a moment. Hurry to 175.
From this point on, escorting this mysterious person to the Orc lair has become your main quest.

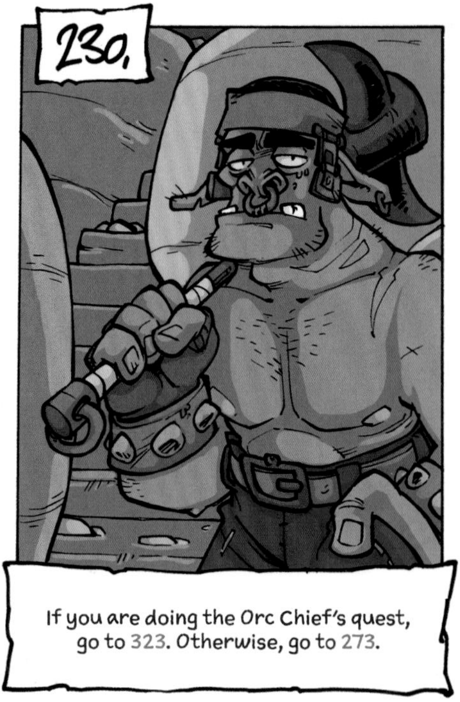
230.
If you are doing the Orc Chief's quest, go to 323. Otherwise, go to 273.

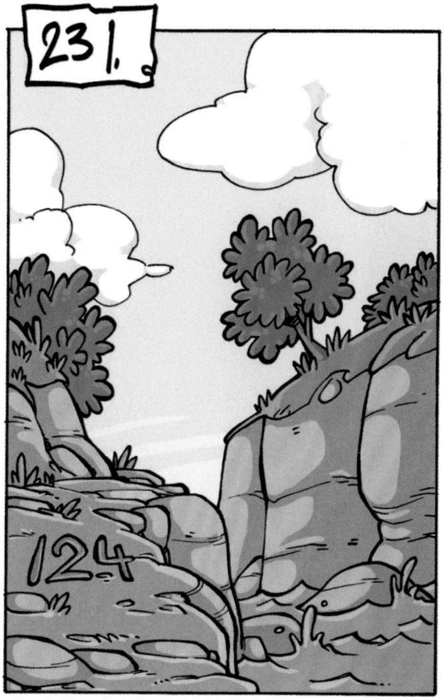
231.
124

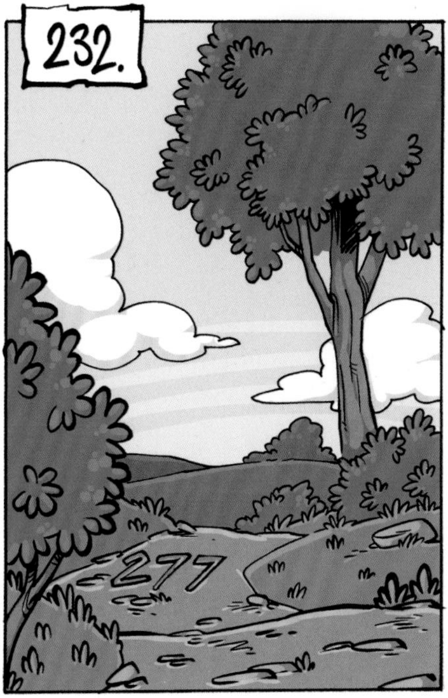
232.
277

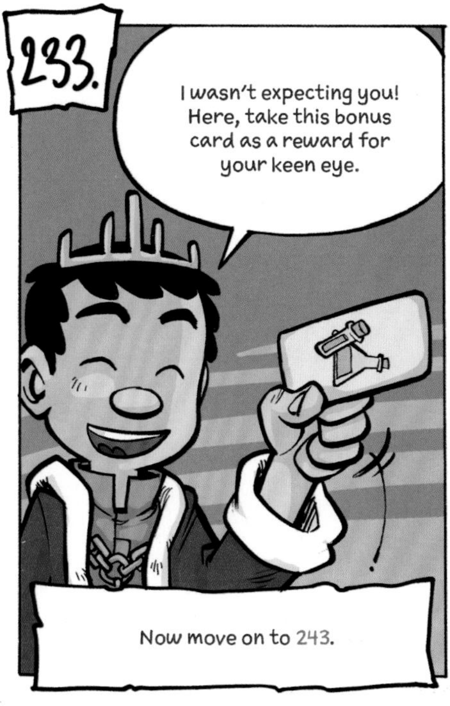
233.
I wasn't expecting you! Here, take this bonus card as a reward for your keen eye.
Now move on to 243.

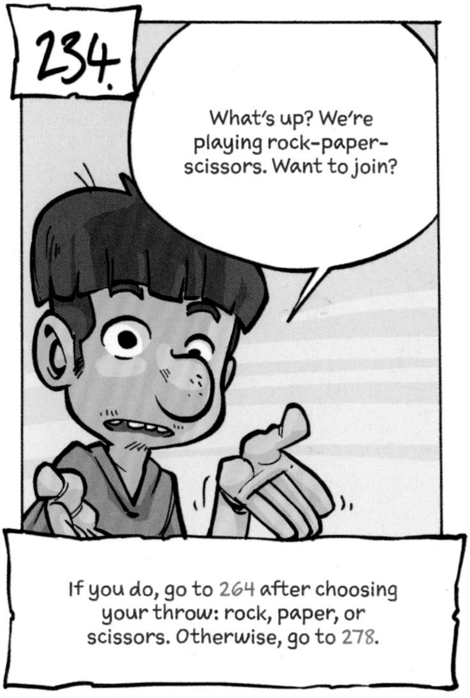
234.
What's up? We're playing rock-paper-scissors. Want to join?
If you do, go to 264 after choosing your throw: rock, paper, or scissors. Otherwise, go to 278.

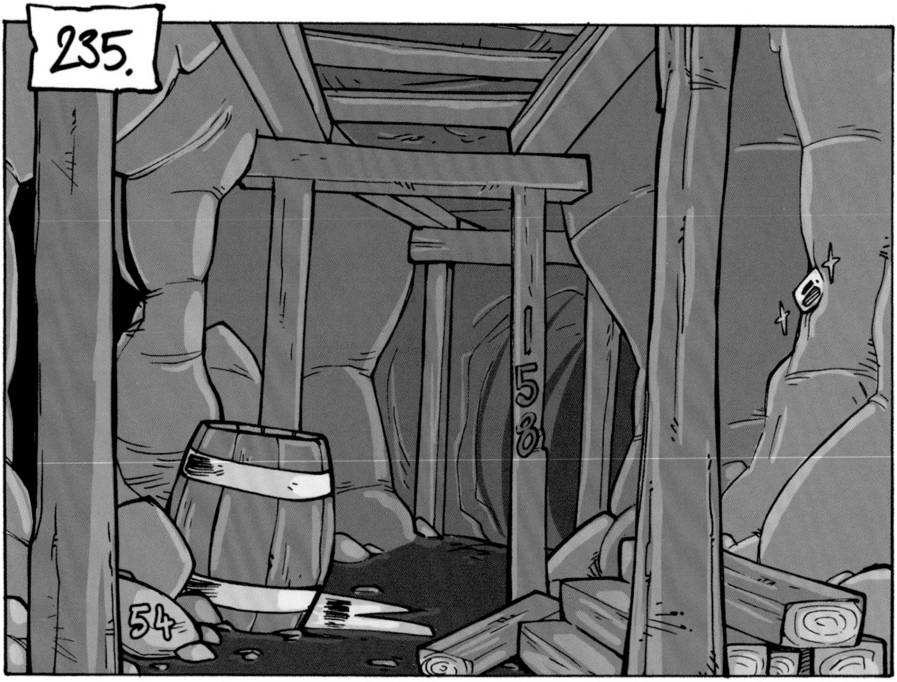
235.
153
8
54

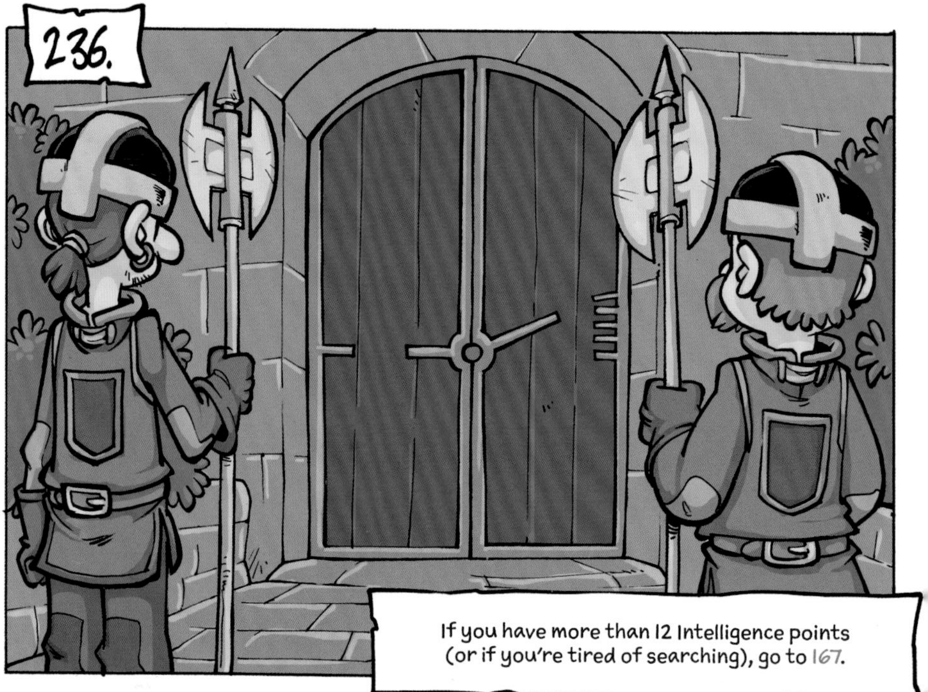
236.

If you have more than 12 Intelligence points (or if you're tired of searching), go to 167.

237.

SP	12	SQ	4
ATT		10	
RES		0	
SR		0	
XP		12	
LOOT		10 Gold Pieces	

Fleeing isn't possible except back to 64. If you really want to pass, you'll have to fight!

238.

Probably a thief. Whatever your Attack points, you get the first strike, since he hasn't spotted you yet. Then, go to 284. Or you can continue down the road without engaging him and go to 302, but that's not as much fun.

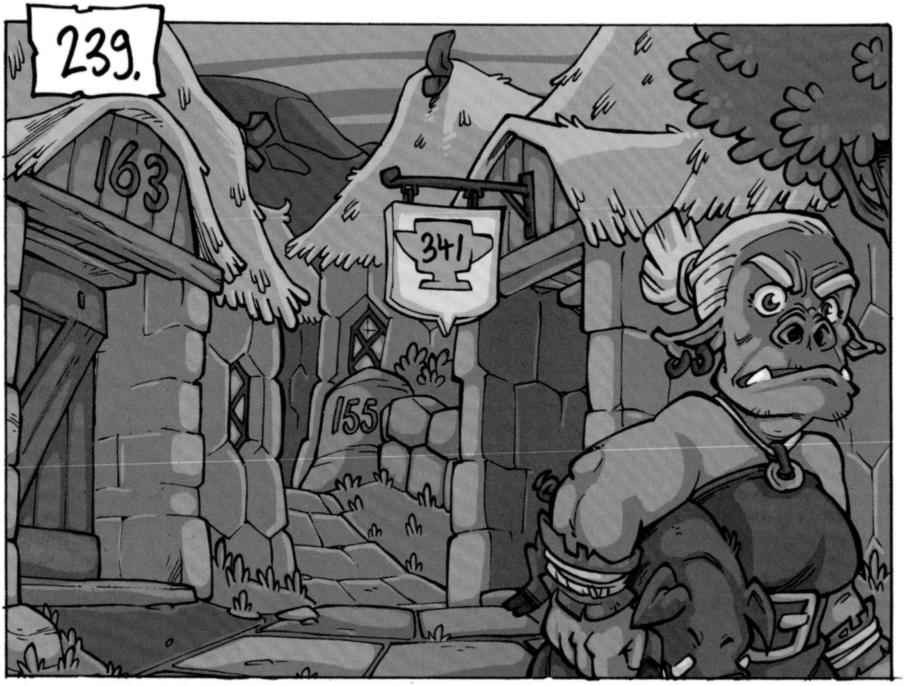
239.
163
341
155

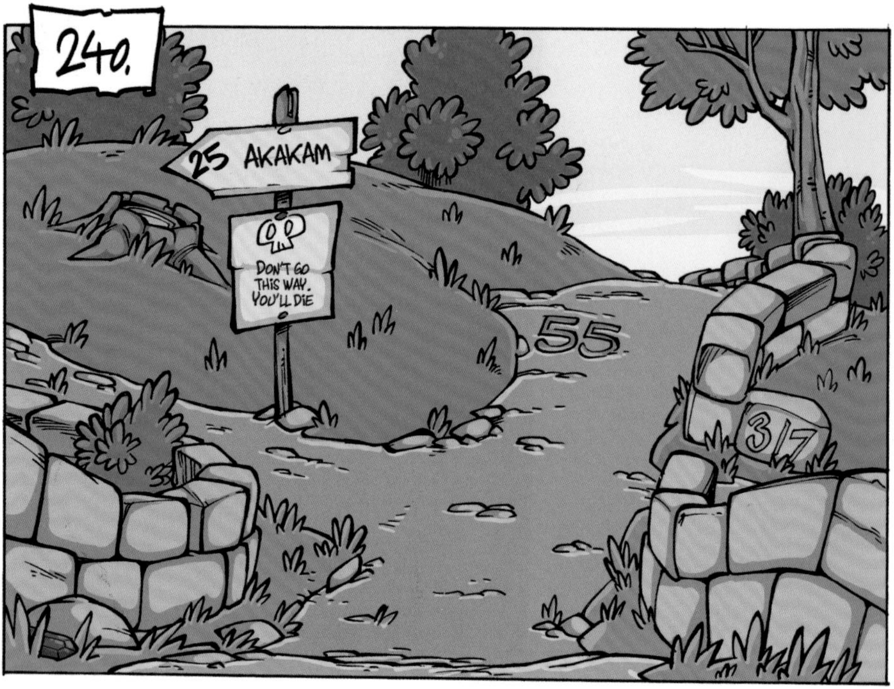
240.
25 AKAKAM
DON'T GO THIS WAY. YOU'LL DIE
55
317

241.

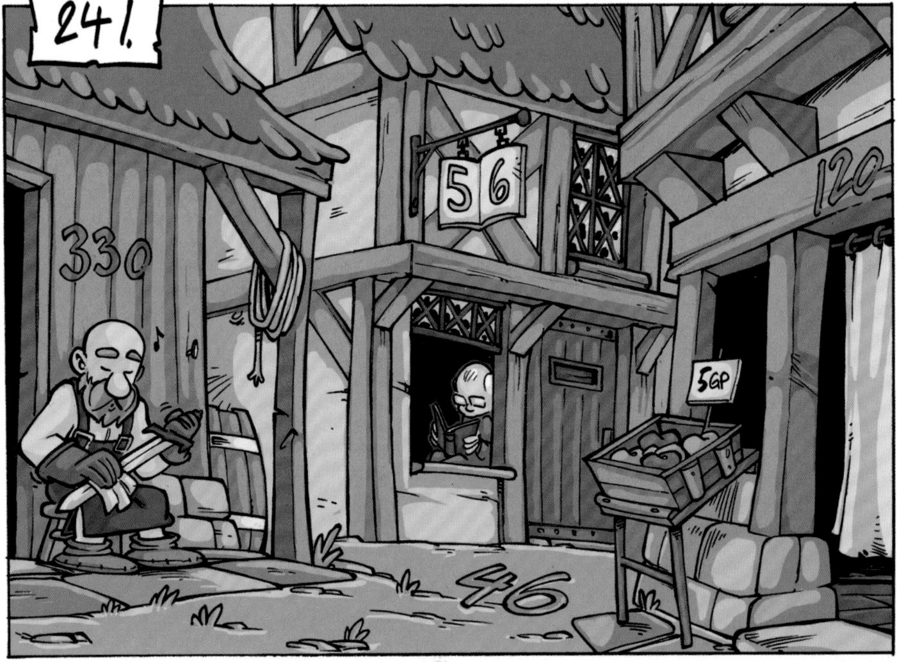
56
120
330
5GP
46

242.

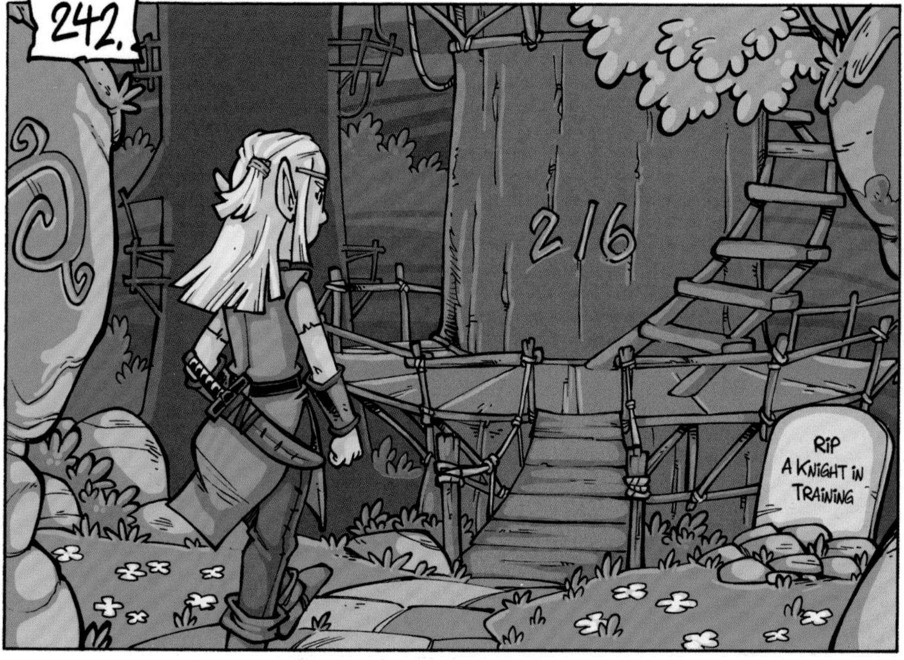
216
RIP
A KNIGHT IN
TRAINING

243.

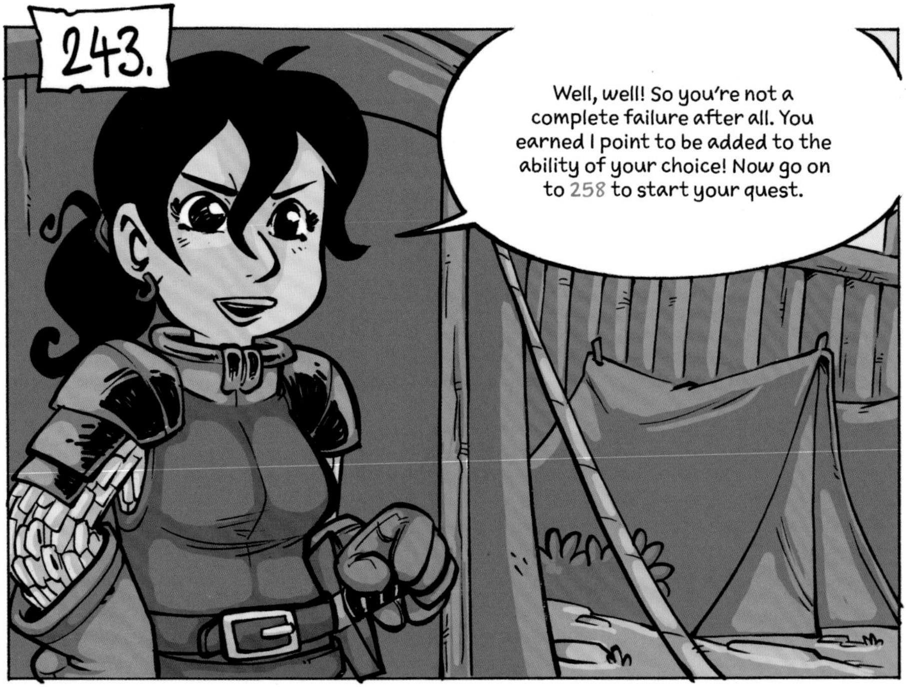
Well, well! So you're not a complete failure after all. You earned 1 point to be added to the ability of your choice! Now go on to 258 to start your quest.

244.

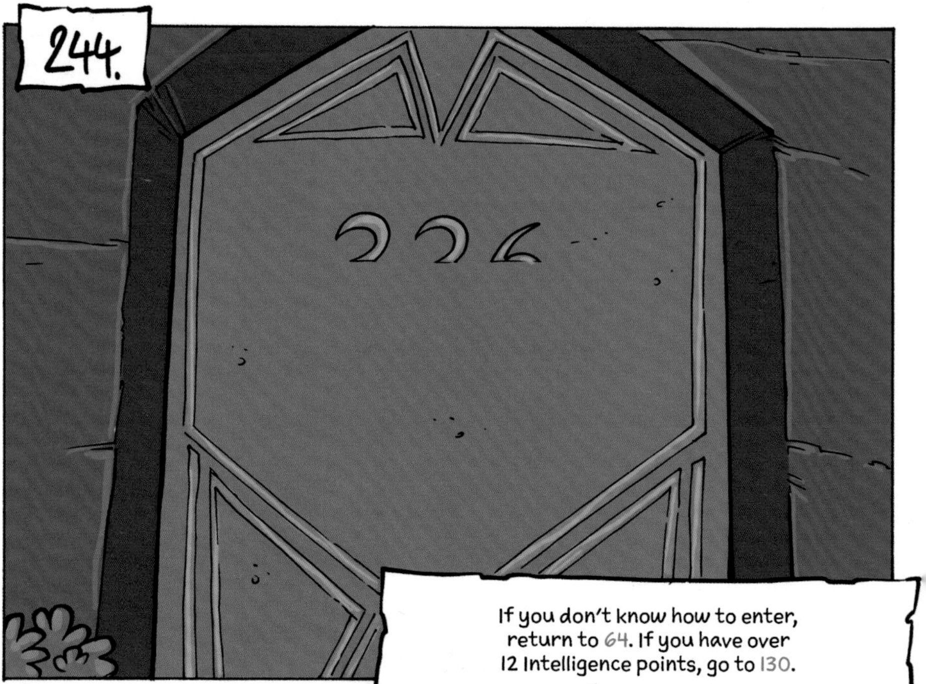
226
If you don't know how to enter, return to 64. If you have over 12 Intelligence points, go to 130.

245.

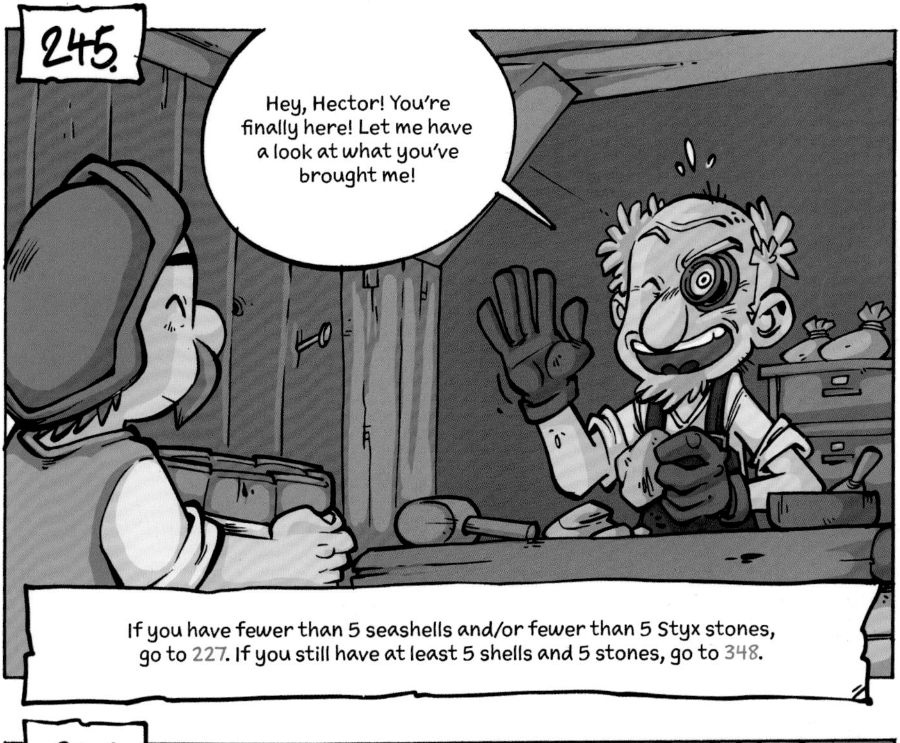
Hey, Hector! You're finally here! Let me have a look at what you've brought me!

If you have fewer than 5 seashells and/or fewer than 5 Styx stones, go to 227. If you still have at least 5 shells and 5 stones, go to 348.

246.

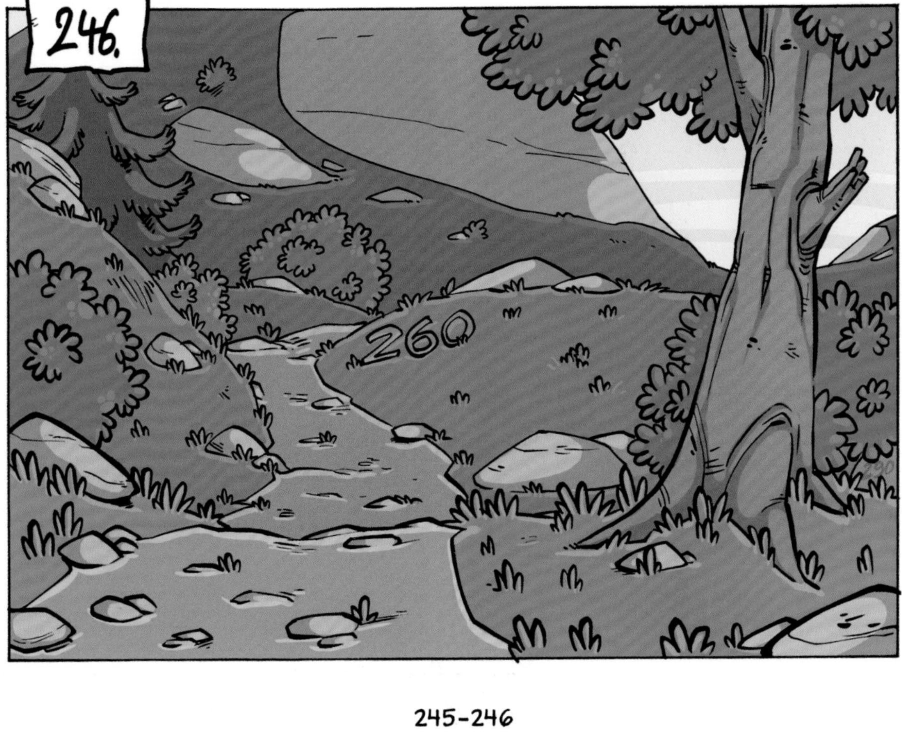
260

247.

You're in luck, friend! I just caught these three lovely sea urchins. My dear, sweet wife loves the taste of them, but she's afraid they'll sting her. Could you show me which one has the fewest spikes, please?

The number of spikes on the correct urchin is the number of the panel where you should go next. If you can't find the right one, head to 211.

248.

249.

Oops! That was a mistake! Go back to 68, but leave 15 gold coins behind.

250.

If you want to fight them before you head to 151, draw your weapon! Don't forget, knight, that each rat gets a turn at attacking you. If you'd rather escape, go to 151.

SP	6	SQ	2
ATT		4	
RES		0	
SR		0	
XP		4	
LOOT		0	

251.

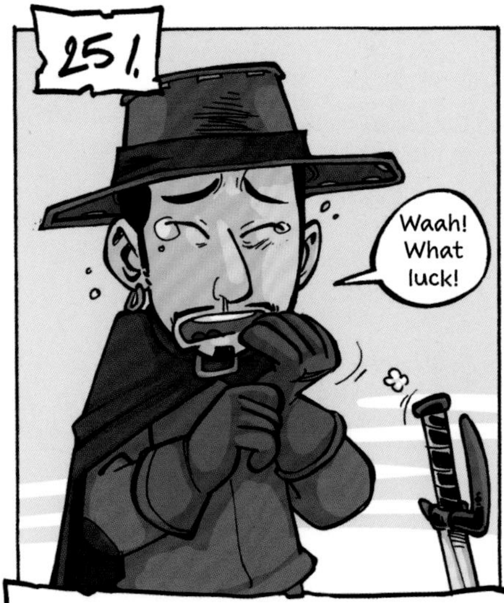
Waah! What luck!

I think you've hurt his feelings. Move on to 166 and take his purse on your way. You get 10 gold pieces and 10 Experience points.

252.

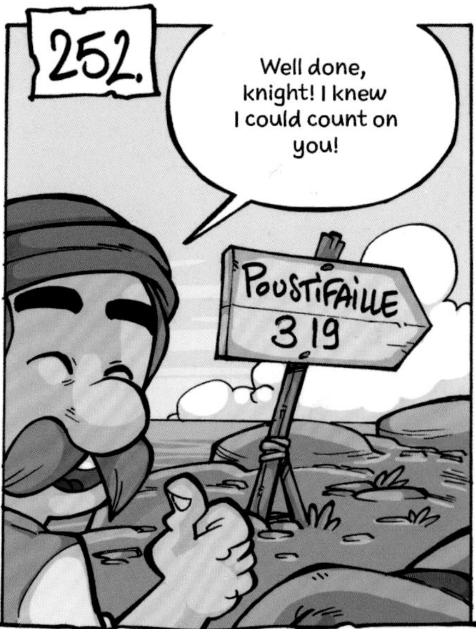
Well done, knight! I knew I could count on you!
POUSTIFAILLE 319

Those stones were heavy! You got a workout, which gives you 2 additional Strength points. You also get 15 Experience points.

253.

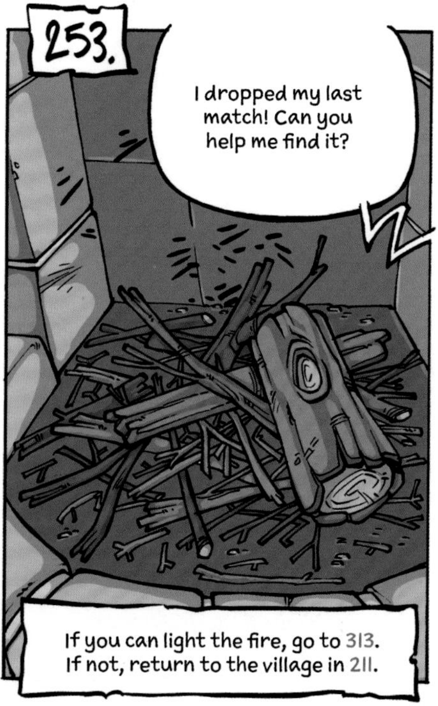
I dropped my last match! Can you help me find it?

If you can light the fire, go to 313. If not, return to the village in 211.

254.

A terrible shadowy beast looms before you. Get ready to fight, for it is impossible to flee! If you have a Taming card, you'll be able to enchant this beast temporarily and attack it three times before it gets a turn.

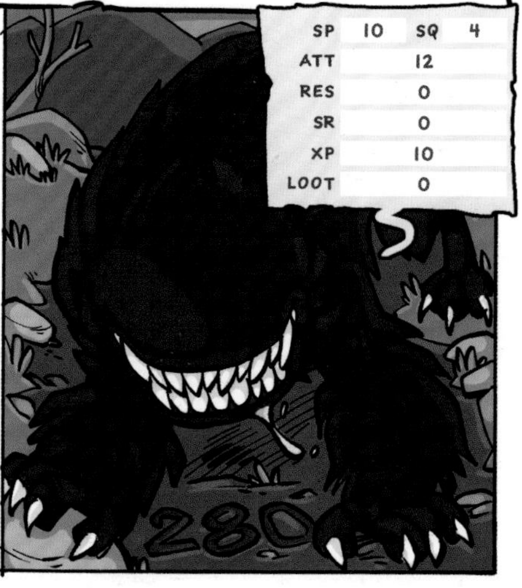
280

SP	10	SQ	4
ATT	12		
RES	0		
SR	0		
XP	10		
LOOT	0		

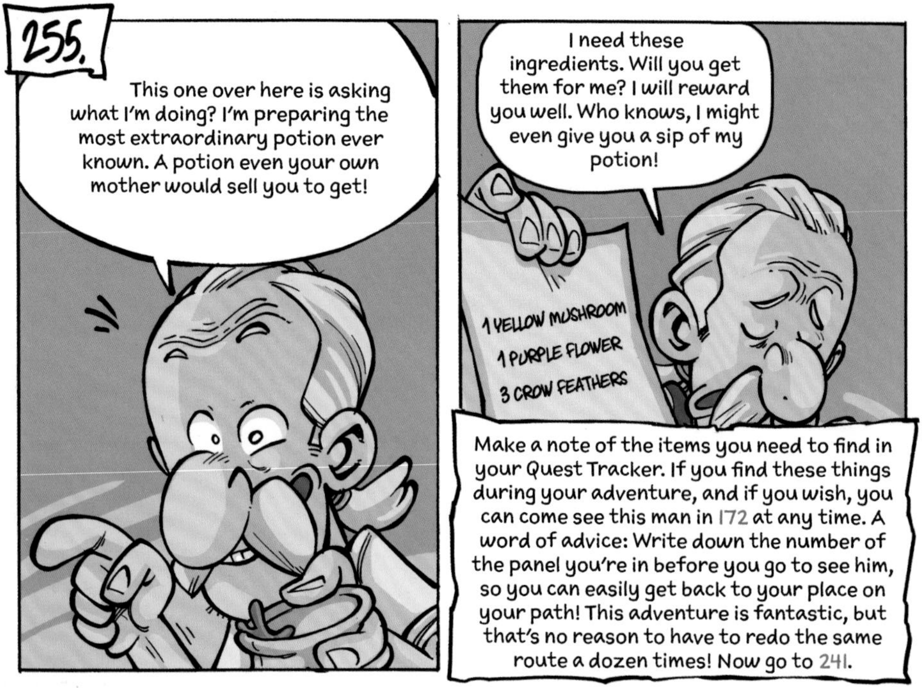
255.
This one over here is asking what I'm doing? I'm preparing the most extraordinary potion ever known. A potion even your own mother would sell you to get!
I need these ingredients. Will you get them for me? I will reward you well. Who knows, I might even give you a sip of my potion!
1 YELLOW MUSHROOM
1 PURPLE FLOWER
3 CROW FEATHERS
Make a note of the items you need to find in your Quest Tracker. If you find these things during your adventure, and if you wish, you can come see this man in 172 at any time. A word of advice: Write down the number of the panel you're in before you go to see him, so you can easily get back to your place on your path! This adventure is fantastic, but that's no reason to have to redo the same route a dozen times! Now go to 241.

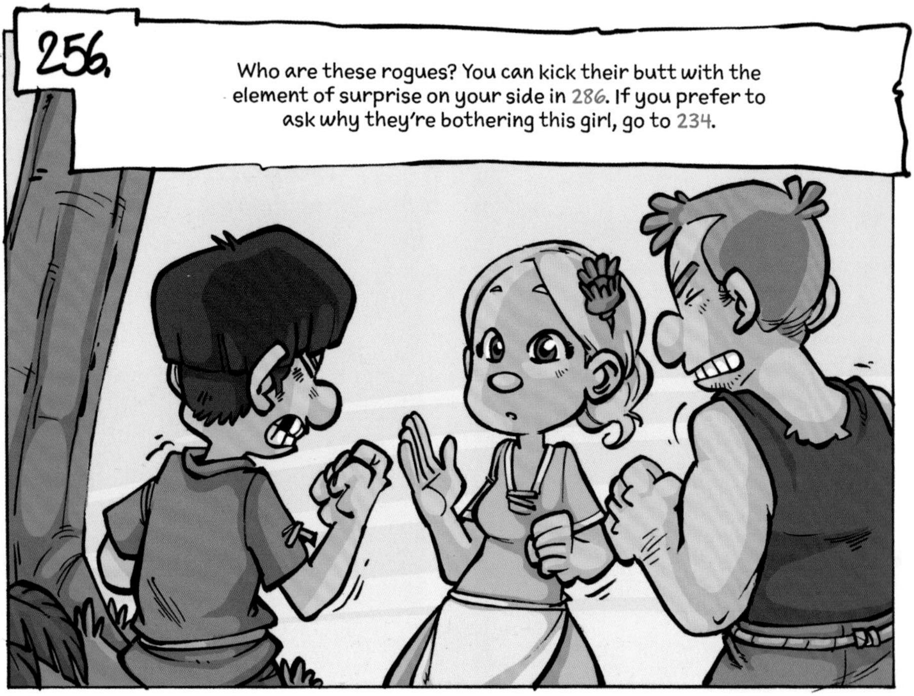
256.
Who are these rogues? You can kick their butt with the element of surprise on your side in 286. If you prefer to ask why they're bothering this girl, go to 234.

257.

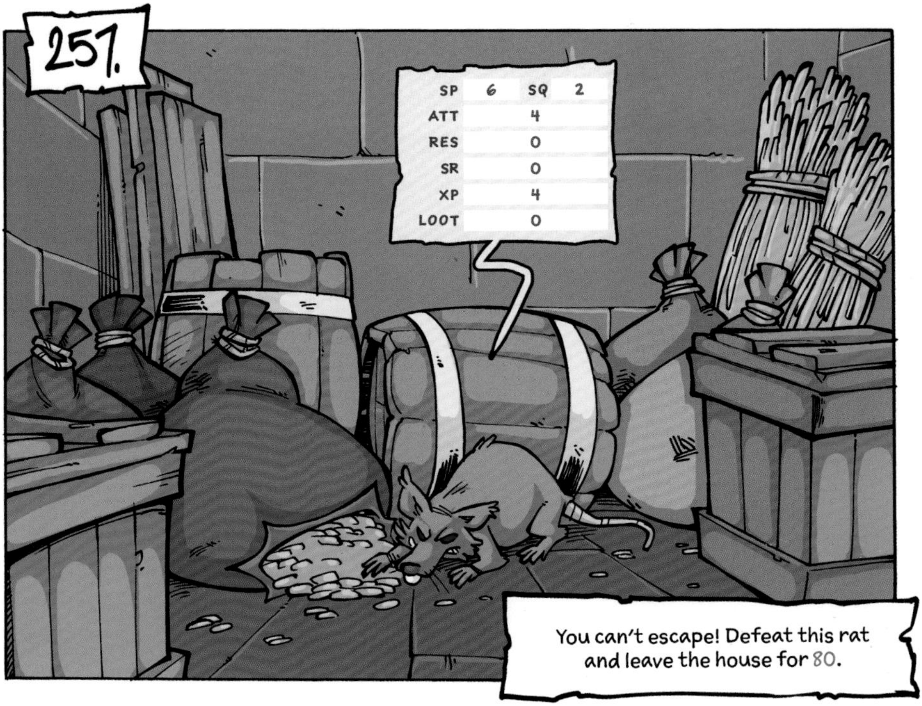
SP 6 SQ 2
ATT 4
RES 0
SR 0
XP 4
LOOT 0
You can't escape! Defeat this rat and leave the house for 80.

258.

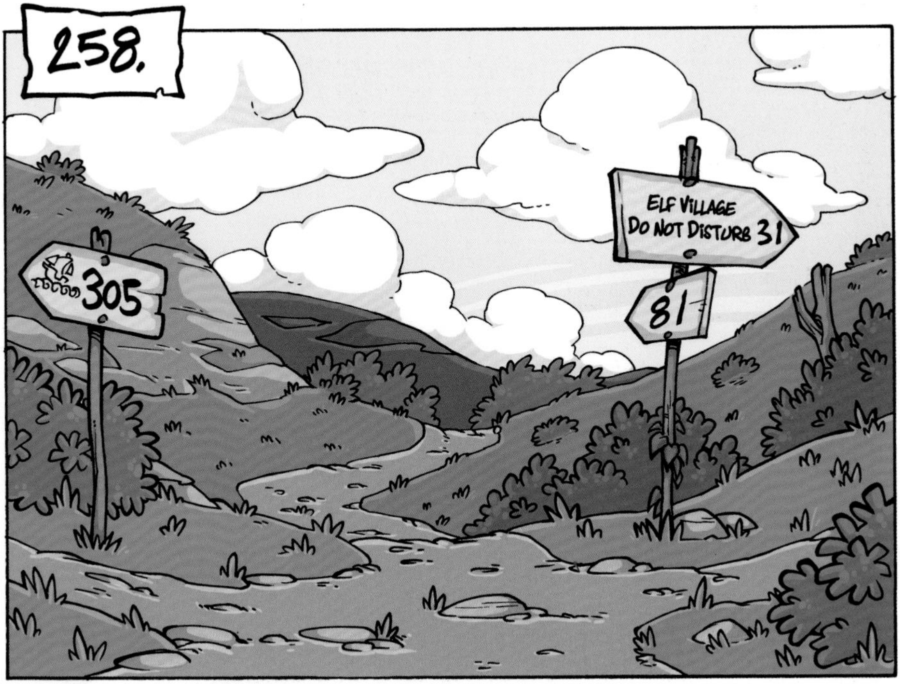
305
ELF VILLAGE DO NOT DISTURB 31
81

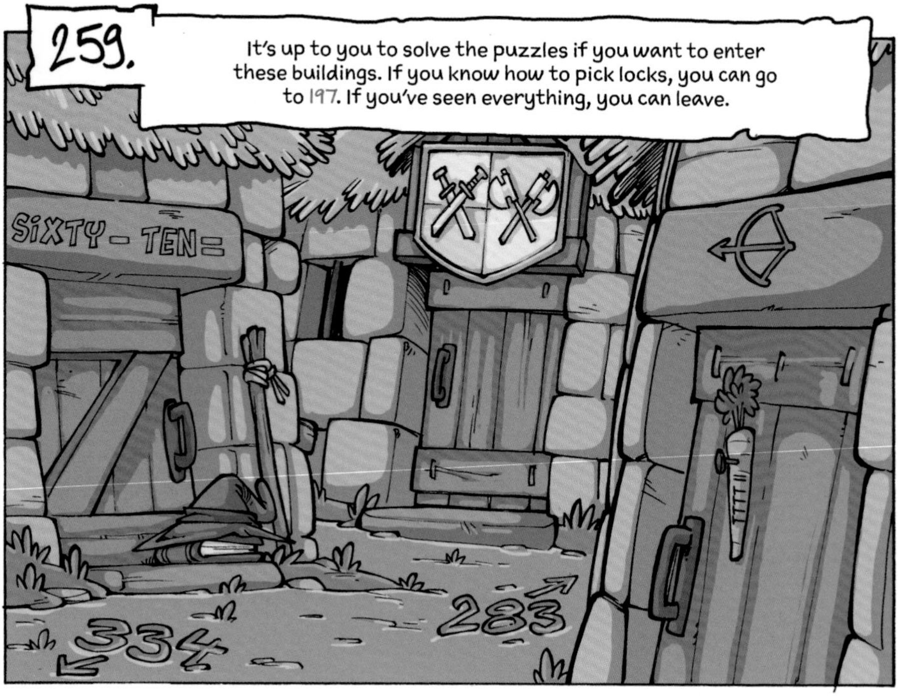
259.
It's up to you to solve the puzzles if you want to enter these buildings. If you know how to pick locks, you can go to 197. If you've seen everything, you can leave.
SIXTY - TEN=
334
283

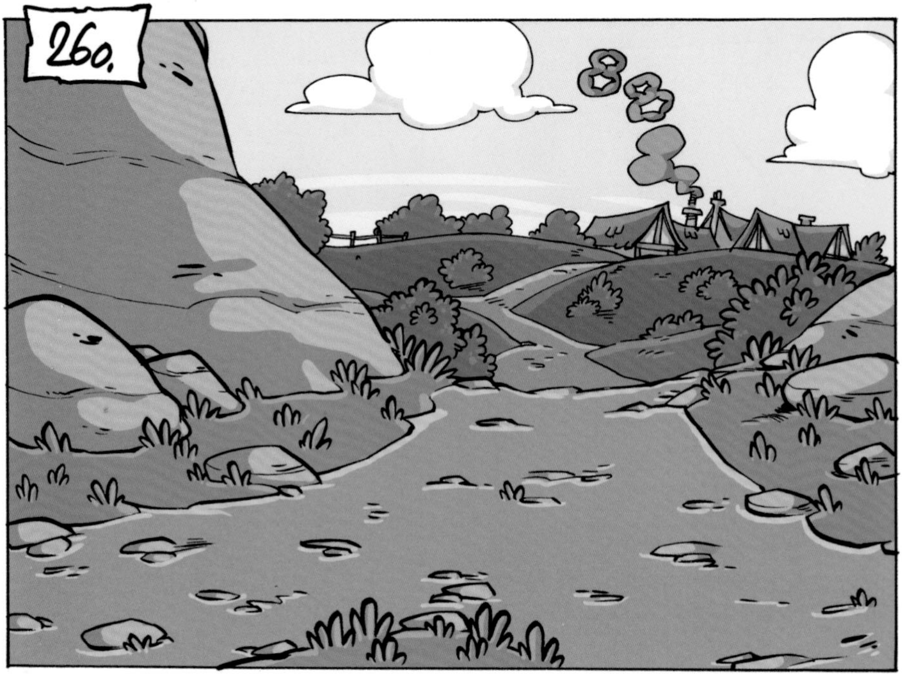
260.
88

261.

If you're a mage, you can take this robe and wand. Together, these two items give you 2 more Attack points and 2 additional Resistance points. Whatever your class, you get an orange card, which doubles your Experience points during the current level. Beware: this robe cannot be combined with other clothing. Go on to 207.

262.

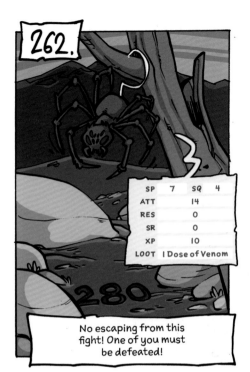

SP	7	SQ	4
ATT		14	
RES		0	
SR		0	
XP		10	
LOOT		1 Dose of Venom	

No escaping from this fight! One of you must be defeated!

263.

REBOURG 134

264.

If you chose "paper," you win. The girl gives you her pretty purple flower as a prize. Win or lose, go to 278.

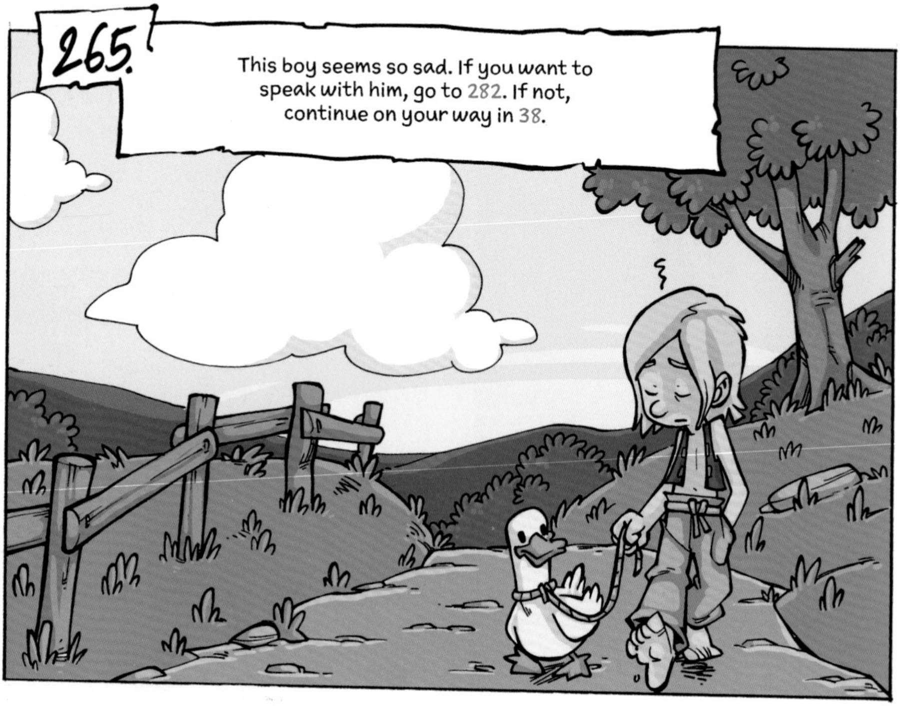
265.
This boy seems so sad. If you want to speak with him, go to 282. If not, continue on your way in 38.

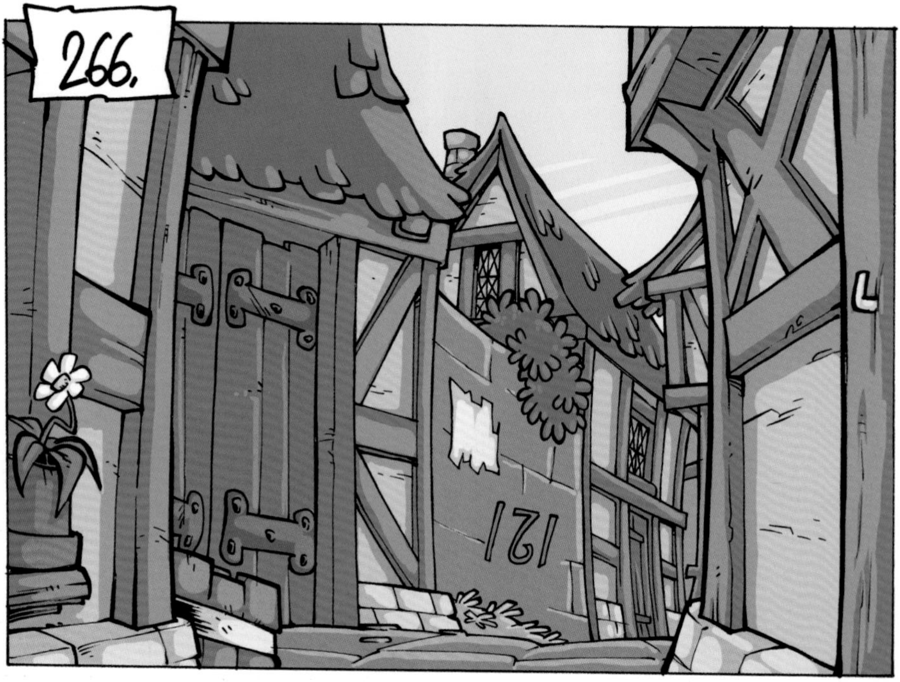
266.
121

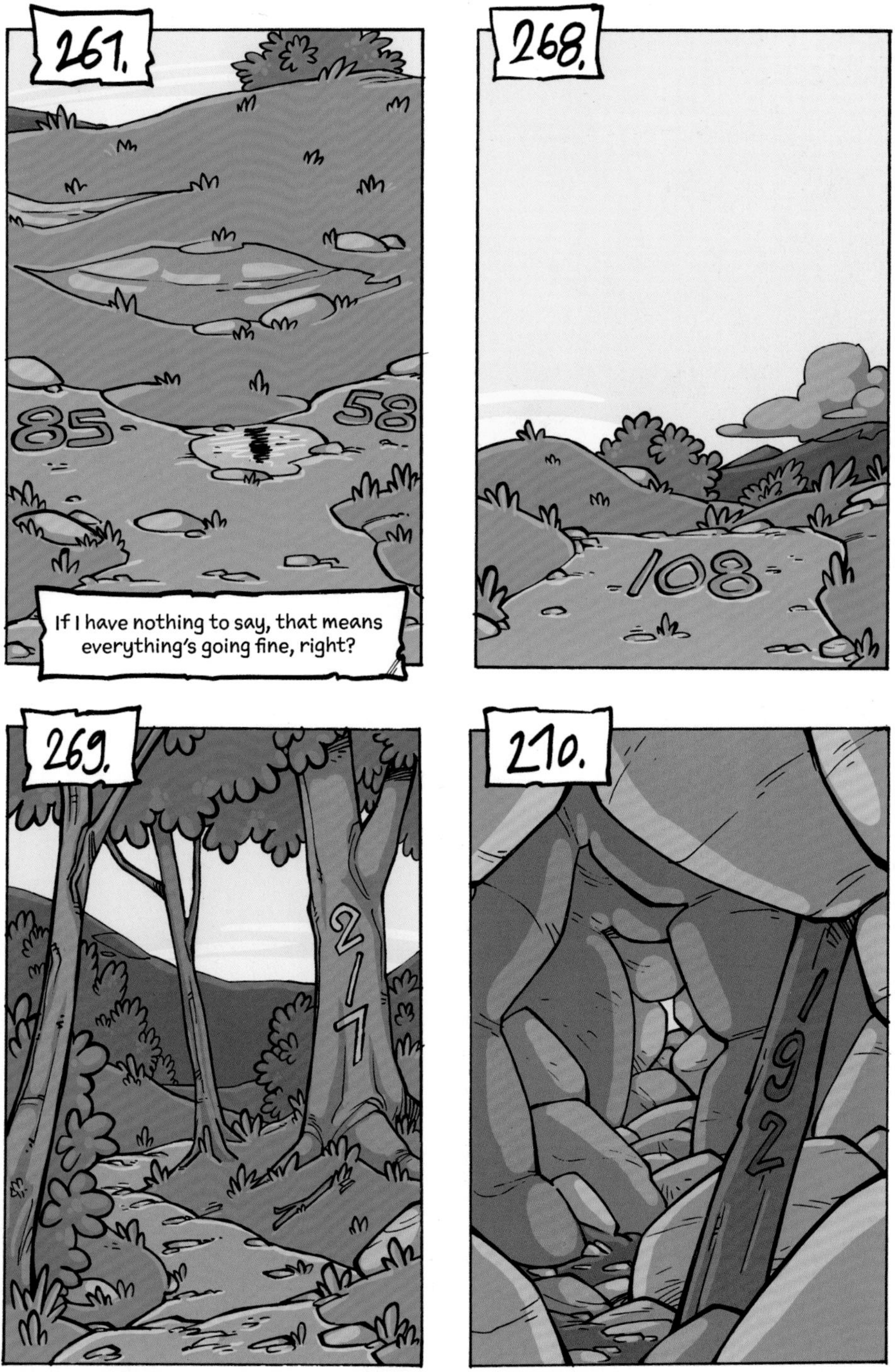
267.
85
58
If I have nothing to say, that means everything's going fine, right?
268.
108
269.
217
270.
192

271.

GAME OVER!
Oh well. We warned you that elves don't kid around. Time to start over!

272.

273.

SP	30	SQ	5
ATT		20	
RES		5	
SR		0	
XP		20	
LOOT		0	

I don't know what he's up to, but it's clear he doesn't want to let you pass. Fight him, or flee to 346.

274.

ATTACK: +10
RESISTANCE: +5

The library is closing. You can exit to 239.

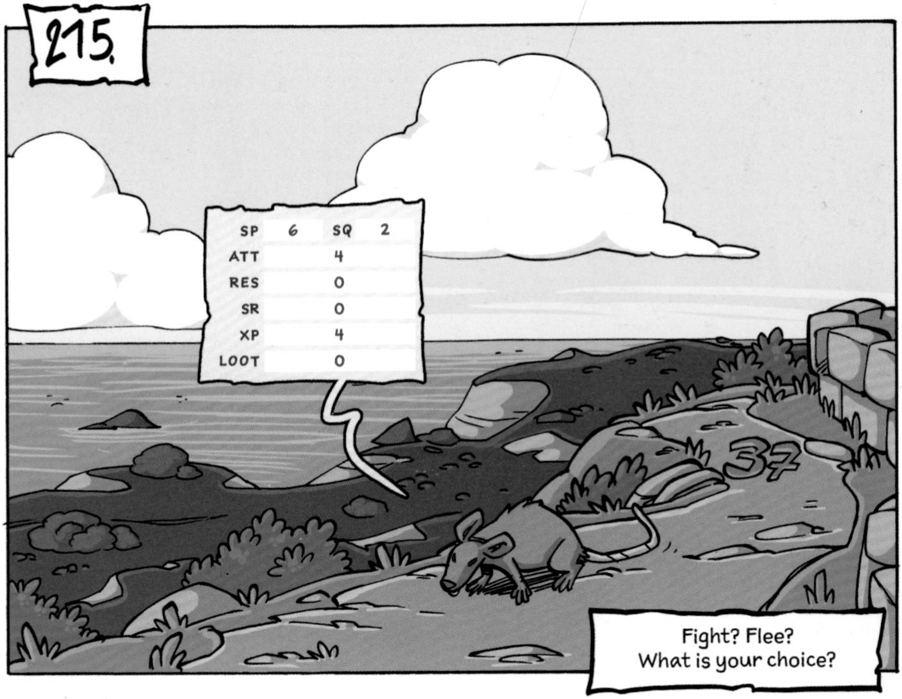
275.
SP 6 SQ 2
ATT 4
RES 0
SR 0
XP 4
LOOT 0
37
Fight? Flee?
What is your choice?

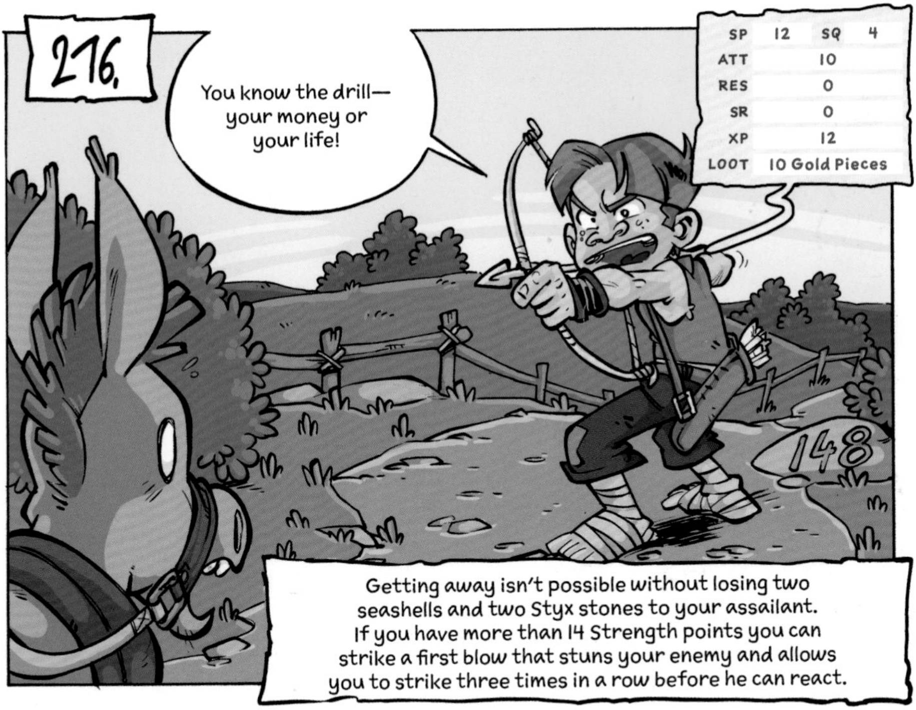
276.
You know the drill—
your money or
your life!
SP 12 SQ 4
ATT 10
RES 0
SR 0
XP 12
LOOT 10 Gold Pieces
148
Getting away isn't possible without losing two
seashells and two Styx stones to your assailant.
If you have more than 14 Strength points you can
strike a first blow that stuns your enemy and allows
you to strike three times in a row before he can react.

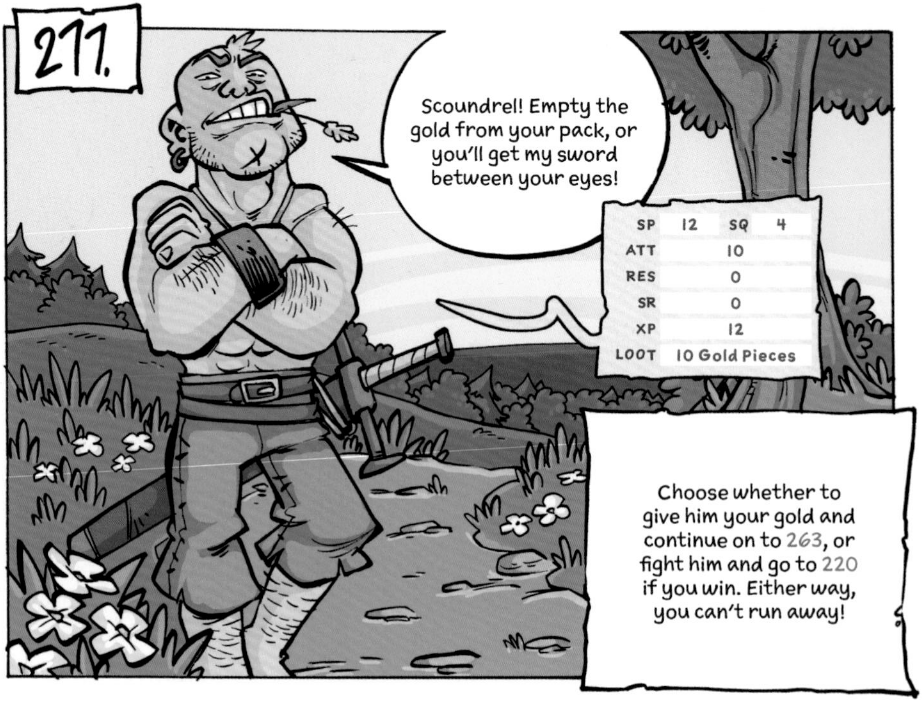
277.
Scoundrel! Empty the gold from your pack, or you'll get my sword between your eyes!
SP 12 SQ 4
ATT 10
RES 0
SR 0
XP 12
LOOT 10 Gold Pieces
Choose whether to give him your gold and continue on to 263, or fight him and go to 220 if you win. Either way, you can't run away!

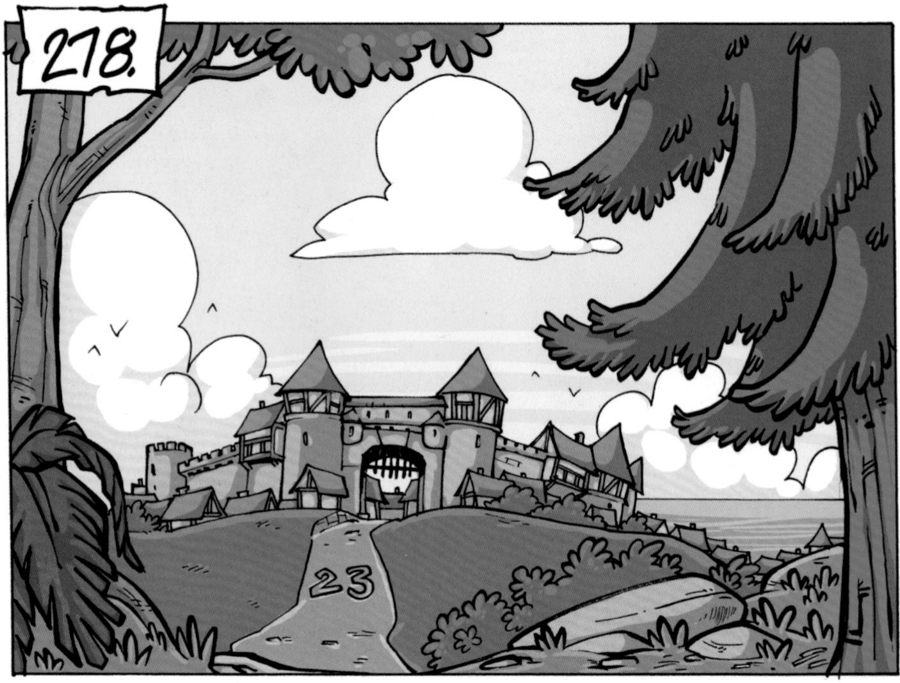
278.
23

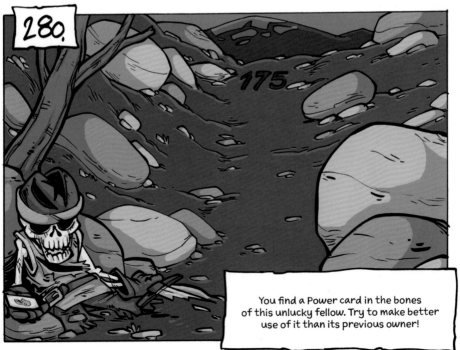

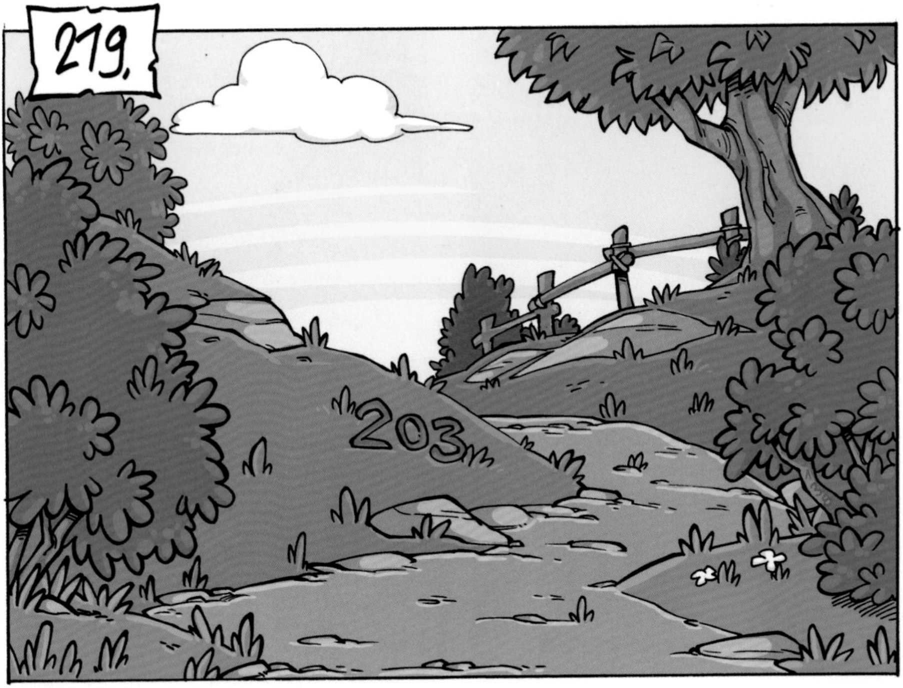
279.
203

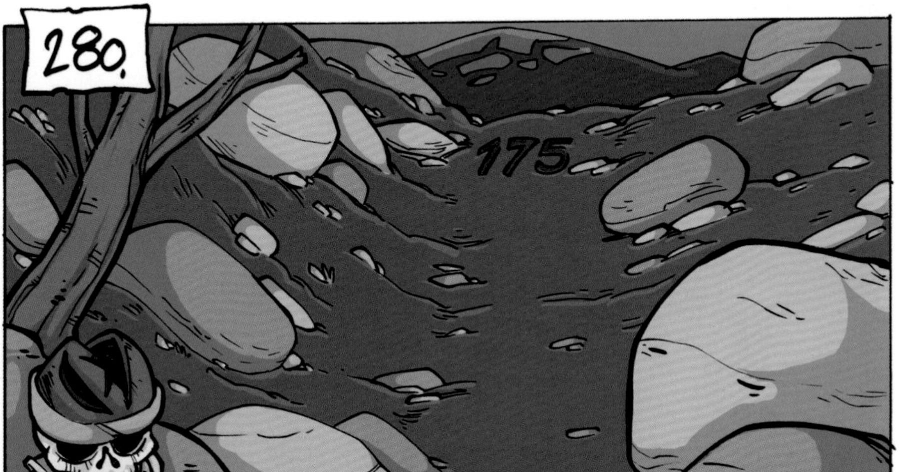
280.
175
You find a Power card in the bones of this unlucky fellow. Try to make better use of it than its previous owner!

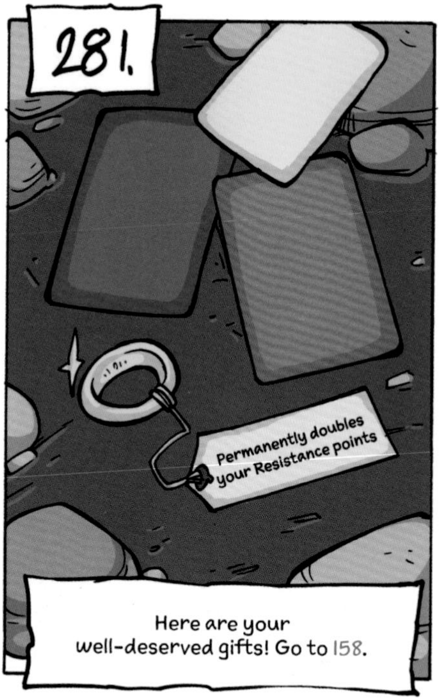
281.
Permanently doubles your Resistance points
Here are your well-deserved gifts! Go to 158.

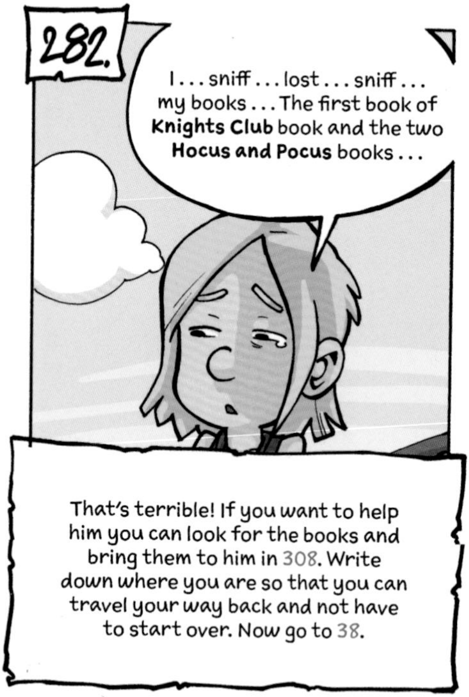
282.
I . . . sniff . . . lost . . . sniff . . . my books . . . The first book of **Knights Club** book and the two **Hocus and Pocus** books . . .
That's terrible! If you want to help him you can look for the books and bring them to him in 308. Write down where you are so that you can travel your way back and not have to start over. Now go to 38.

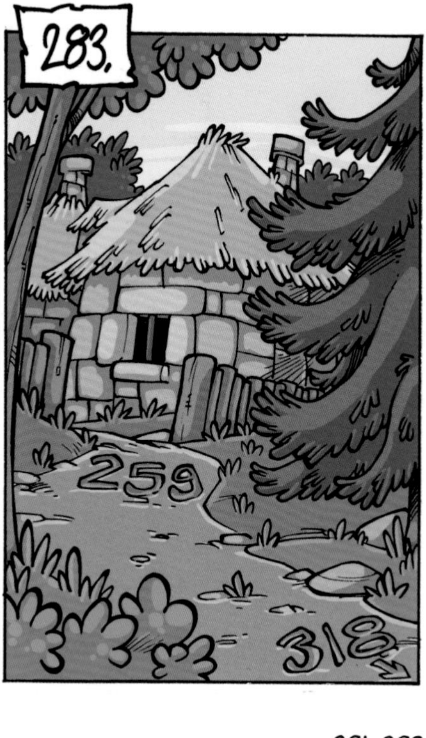
283.
259
318

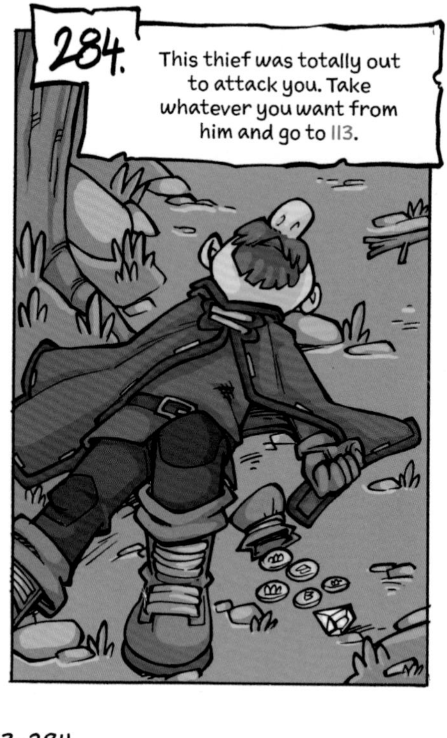
284.
This thief was totally out to attack you. Take whatever you want from him and go to 113.

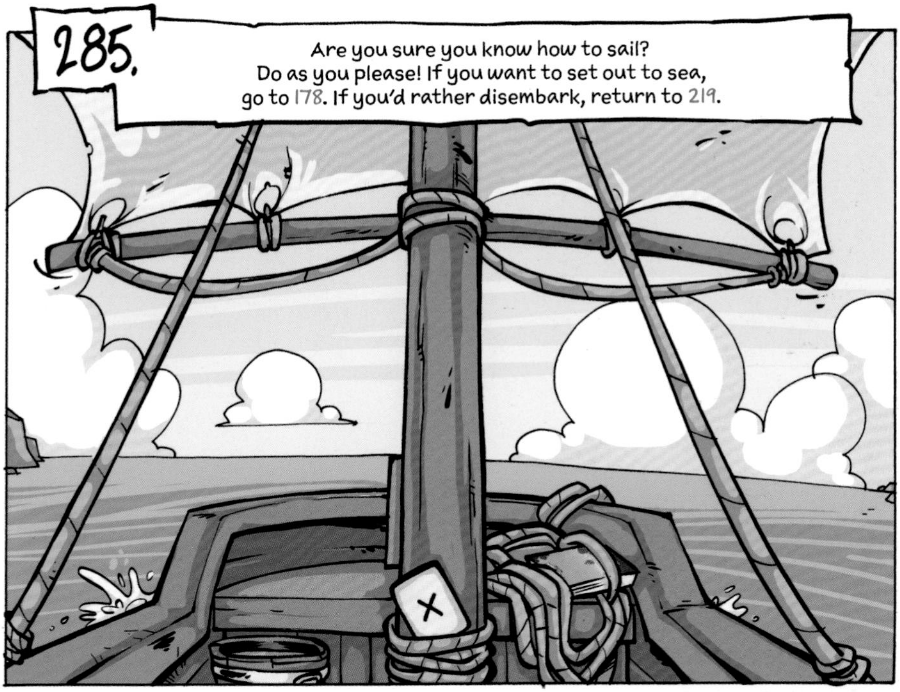
285.
Are you sure you know how to sail?
Do as you please! If you want to set out to sea,
go to 178. If you'd rather disembark, return to 219.

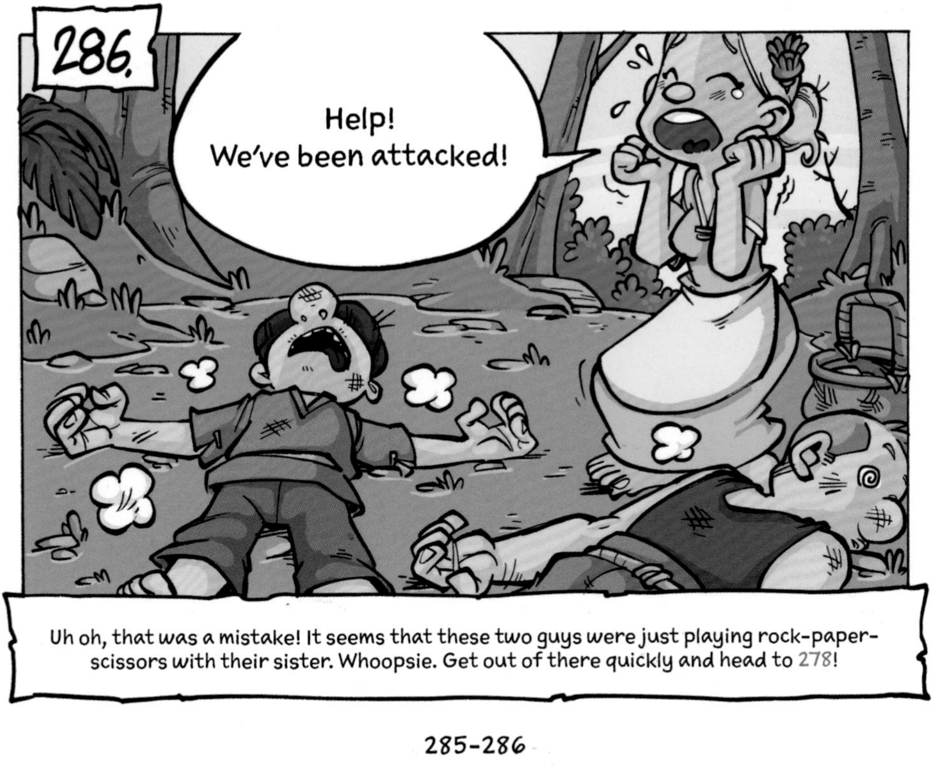
286.
Help!
We've been attacked!
Uh oh, that was a mistake! It seems that these two guys were just playing rock-paper-scissors with their sister. Whoopsie. Get out of there quickly and head to 278!

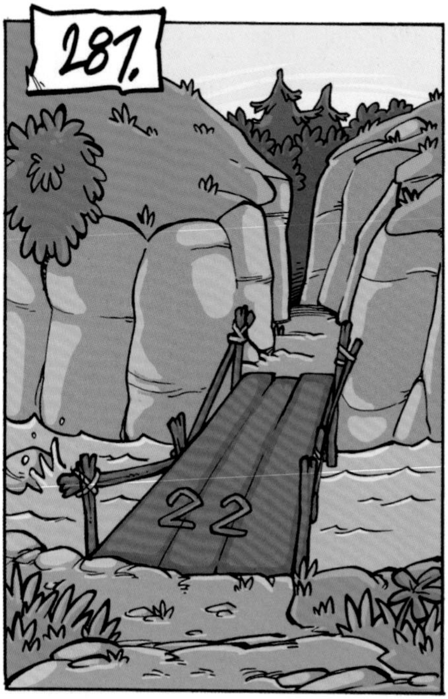
287.
22

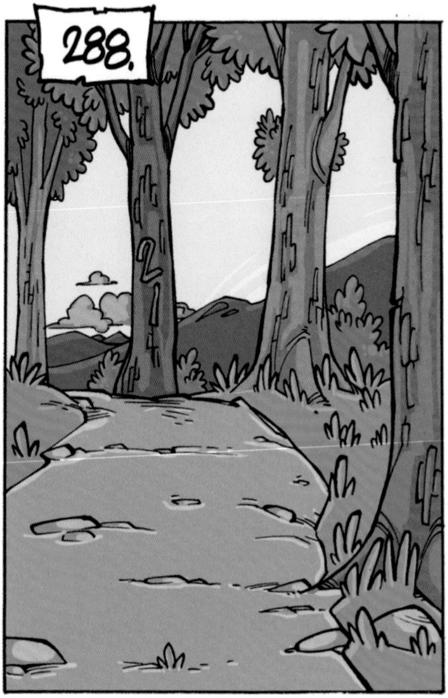
288.
2

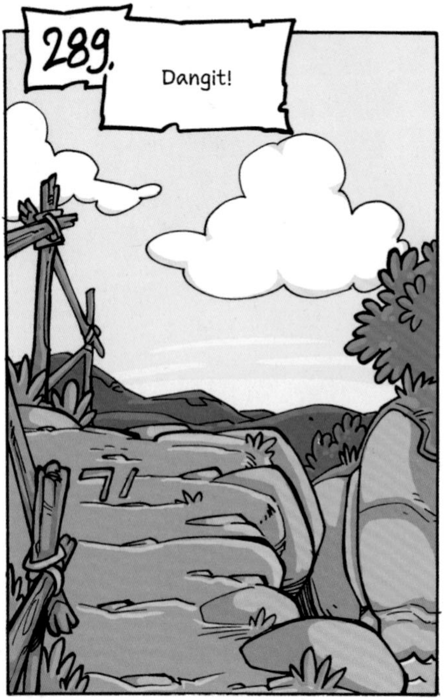
289.
Dangit!
7

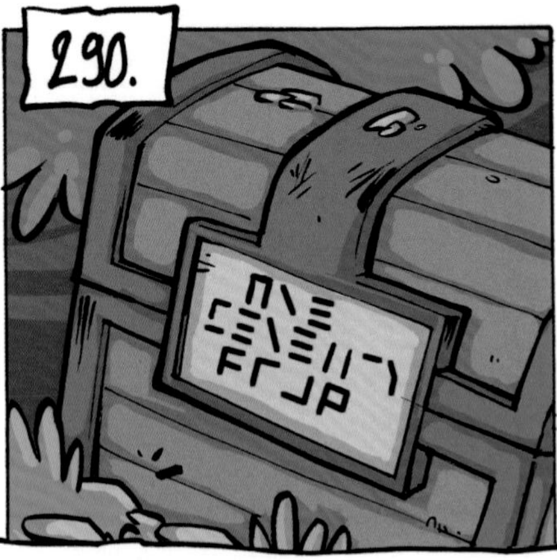
290.

If you have more than 17 Strength points, you can force it open enough to shake out 20 gold pieces. But if you can't bash open the chest or solve the puzzle, you must go to 260. If you have greater than 17 Intelligence points or if you know how to pick locks (thanks to your abilities or a special card) go to 321. If this puzzle just makes your brain hurt, go to 260.

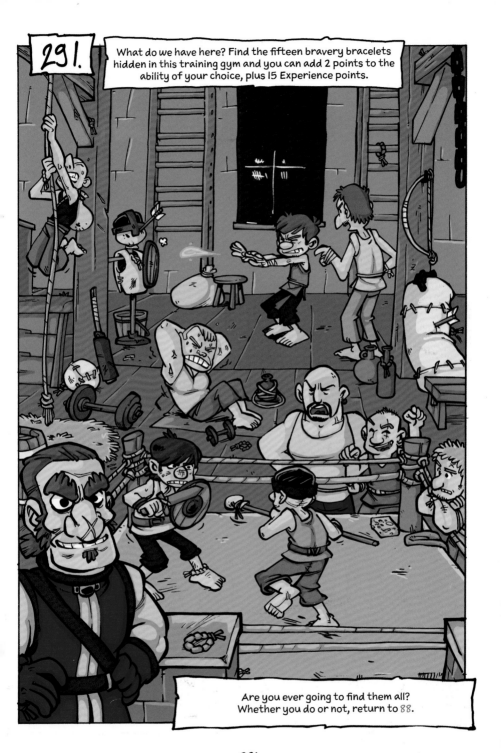

291. What do we have here? Find the fifteen bravery bracelets hidden in this training gym and you can add 2 points to the ability of your choice, plus 15 Experience points.

Are you ever going to find them all? Whether you do or not, return to 88.

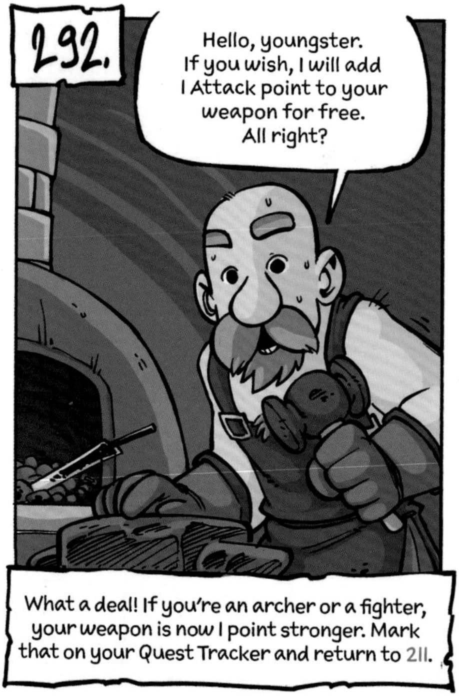
292.
Hello, youngster. If you wish, I will add 1 Attack point to your weapon for free. All right?
What a deal! If you're an archer or a fighter, your weapon is now 1 point stronger. Mark that on your Quest Tracker and return to 211.

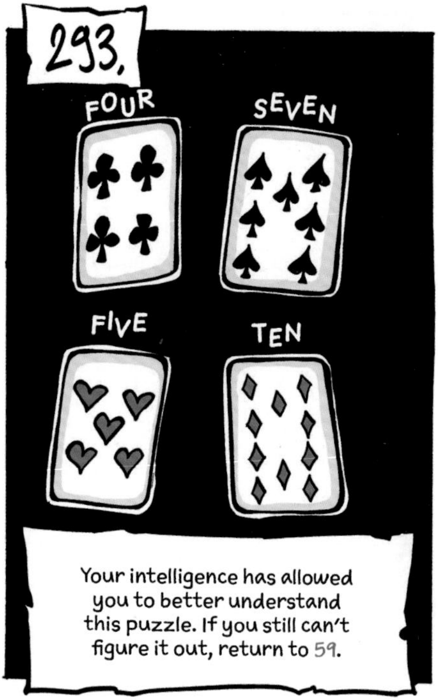
293.
FOUR
SEVEN
FIVE
TEN
Your intelligence has allowed you to better understand this puzzle. If you still can't figure it out, return to 59.

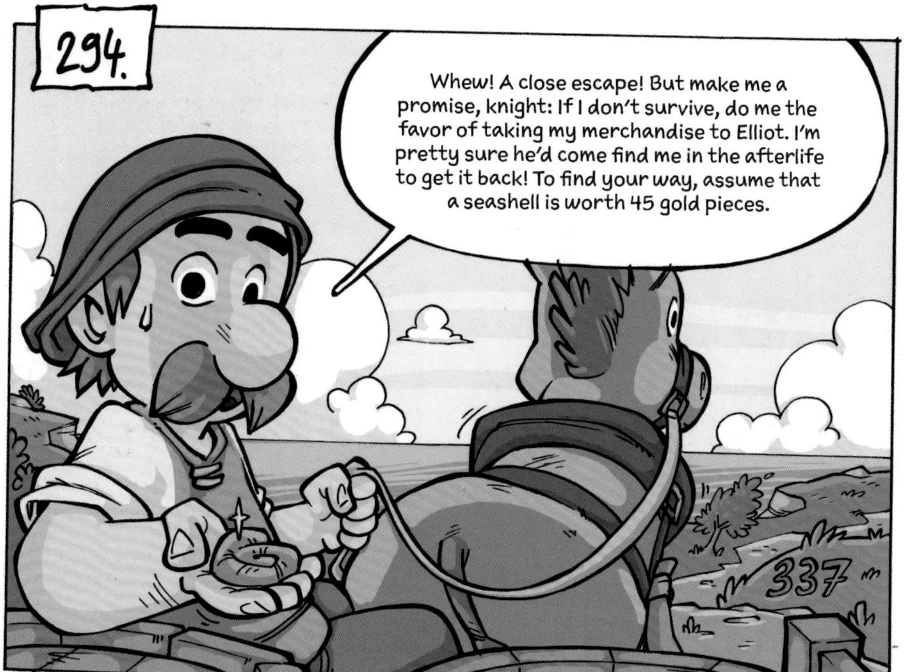
294.
Whew! A close escape! But make me a promise, knight: If I don't survive, do me the favor of taking my merchandise to Elliot. I'm pretty sure he'd come find me in the afterlife to get it back! To find your way, assume that a seashell is worth 45 gold pieces.
337

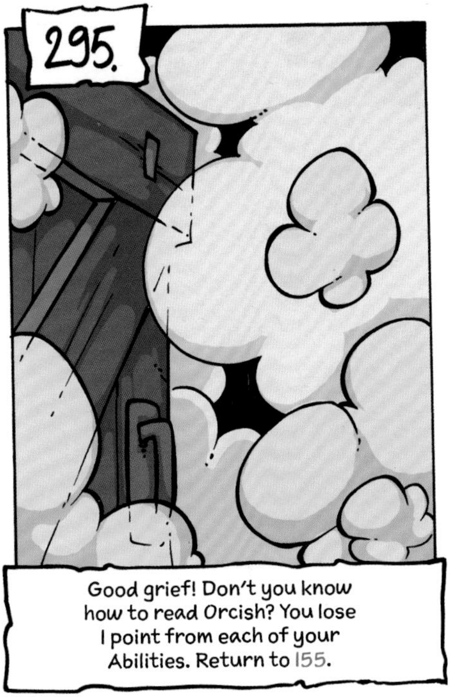
295.
Good grief! Don't you know how to read Orcish? You lose 1 point from each of your Abilities. Return to 155.

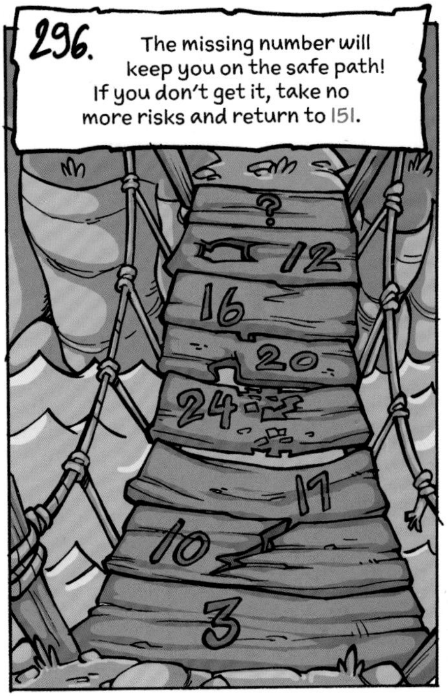
296.
The missing number will keep you on the safe path! If you don't get it, take no more risks and return to 151.
?
12
16
20
24
17
10
3

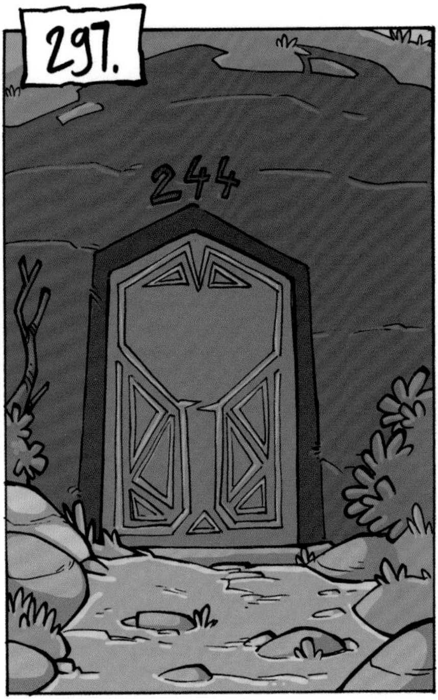
297.
244

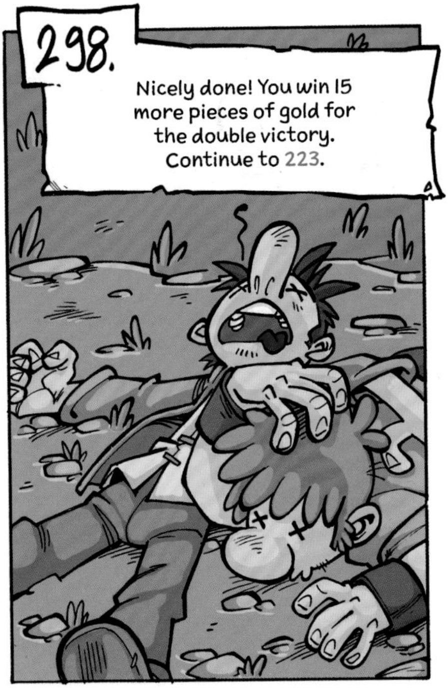
298.
Nicely done! You win 15 more pieces of gold for the double victory. Continue to 223.

299.

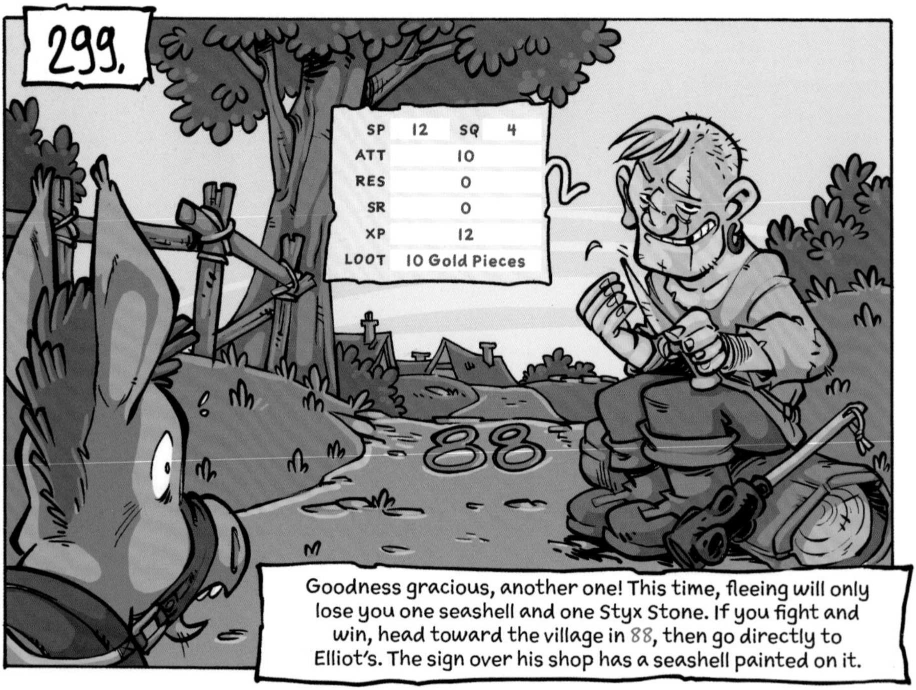
88

SP	12	SQ	4
ATT	10		
RES	0		
SR	0		
XP	12		
LOOT	10 Gold Pieces		

Goodness gracious, another one! This time, fleeing will only lose you one seashell and one Styx Stone. If you fight and win, head toward the village in 88, then go directly to Elliot's. The sign over his shop has a seashell painted on it.

300.

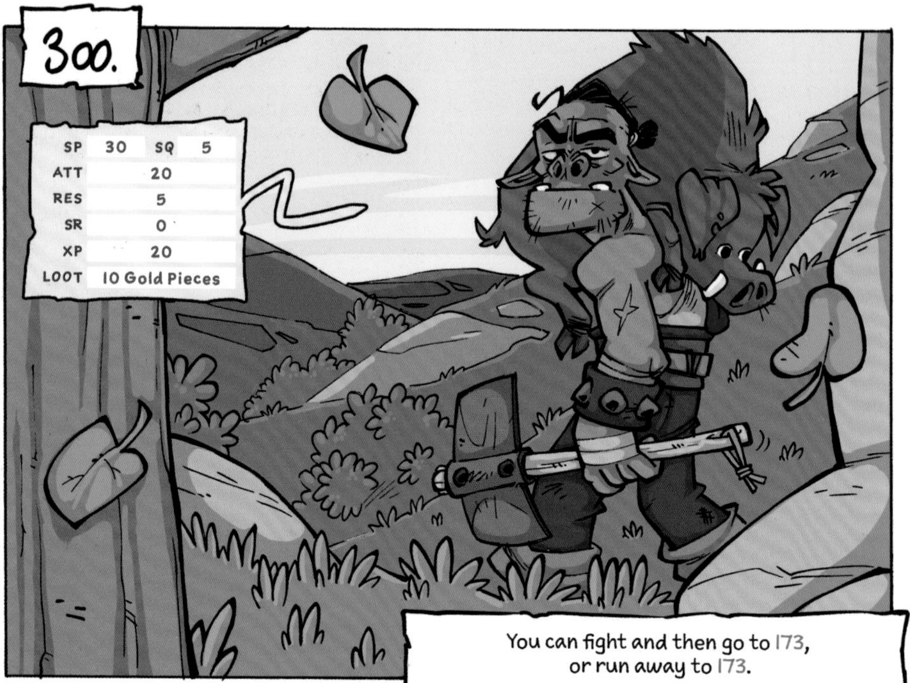

SP	30	SQ	5
ATT	20		
RES	5		
SR	0		
XP	20		
LOOT	10 Gold Pieces		

You can fight and then go to 173, or run away to 173.

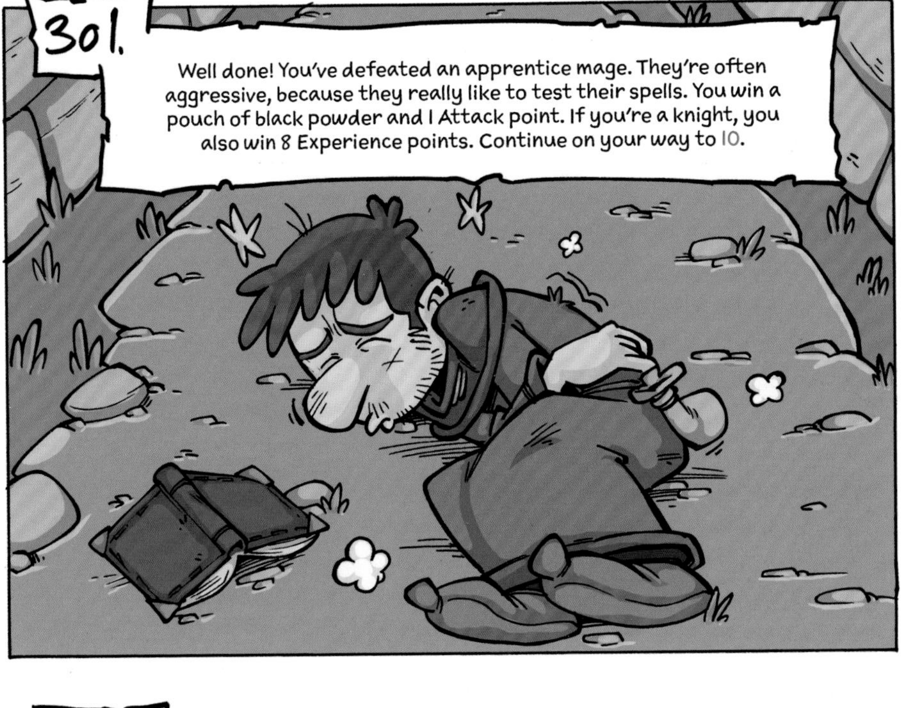
301.
Well done! You've defeated an apprentice mage. They're often aggressive, because they really like to test their spells. You win a pouch of black powder and 1 Attack point. If you're a knight, you also win 8 Experience points. Continue on your way to 10.

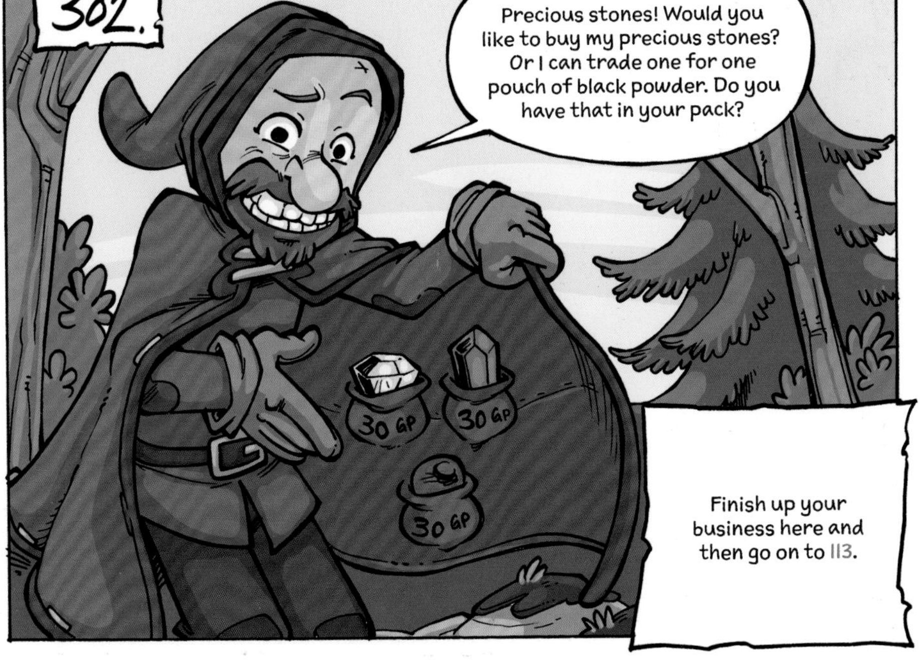
302.
Precious stones! Would you like to buy my precious stones? Or I can trade one for one pouch of black powder. Do you have that in your pack?
30 GP
30 GP
30 GP
Finish up your business here and then go on to 113.

303.

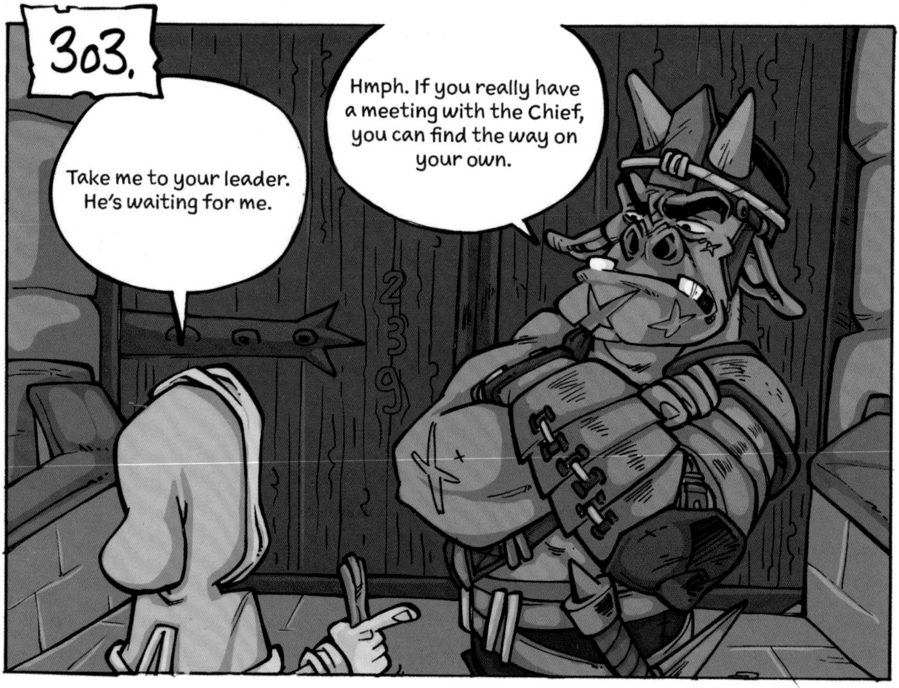
Take me to your leader. He's waiting for me.
Hmph. If you really have a meeting with the Chief, you can find the way on your own.
239

304.

Fight if you like and go to 261 if you win. If you don't want to fight, flee to 96. Warning: You can't flee after you begin the battle—it can only end in someone's death! Decide carefully. If you are an archer and you have greater than 16 Agility, you shoot two arrows that strike the target, but your enemy still gets the first strike.

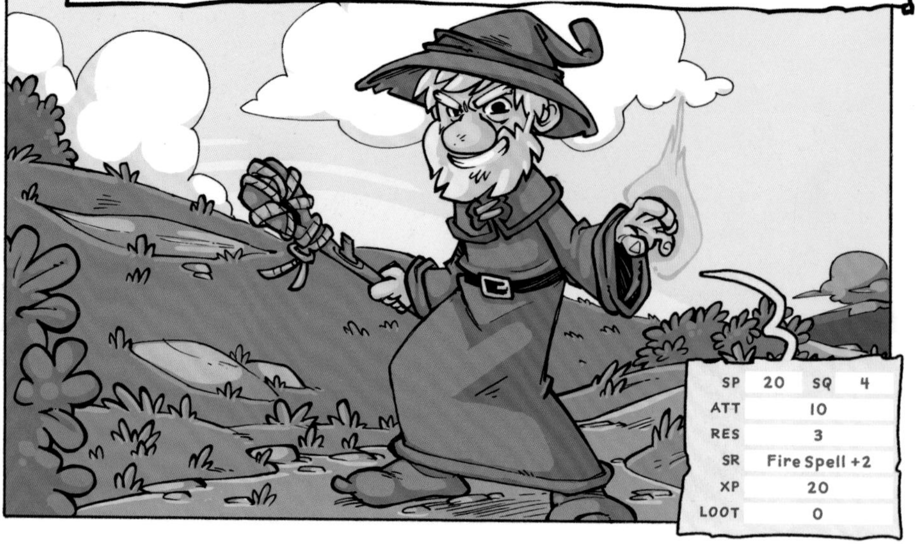

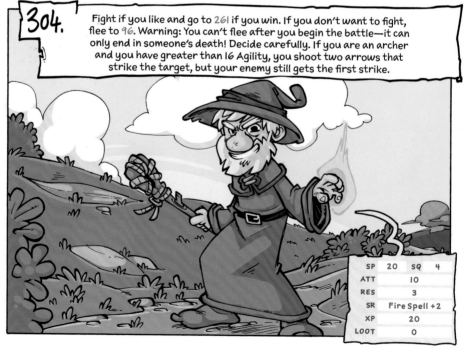

SP	20	SQ	4
ATT	10		
RES	3		
SR	Fire Spell +2		
XP	20		
LOOT	0		

305.

SP	7	SQ	2
ATT		4	
RES		0	
SR		0	
XP		4	
LOOT		Black Feather	

This crow hasn't seen you. Choose whether you want to fight it or sneak by to 145.

306.

Return to 65.

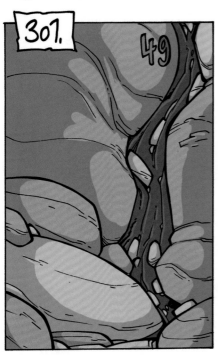

307.

49

308.

You found my books! Thank you so much! Take this card. It multiplies your Experience points by two for the rest of your current level.

That's terrific! Now return to where you came from before helping him. You wrote down that number right?

309.

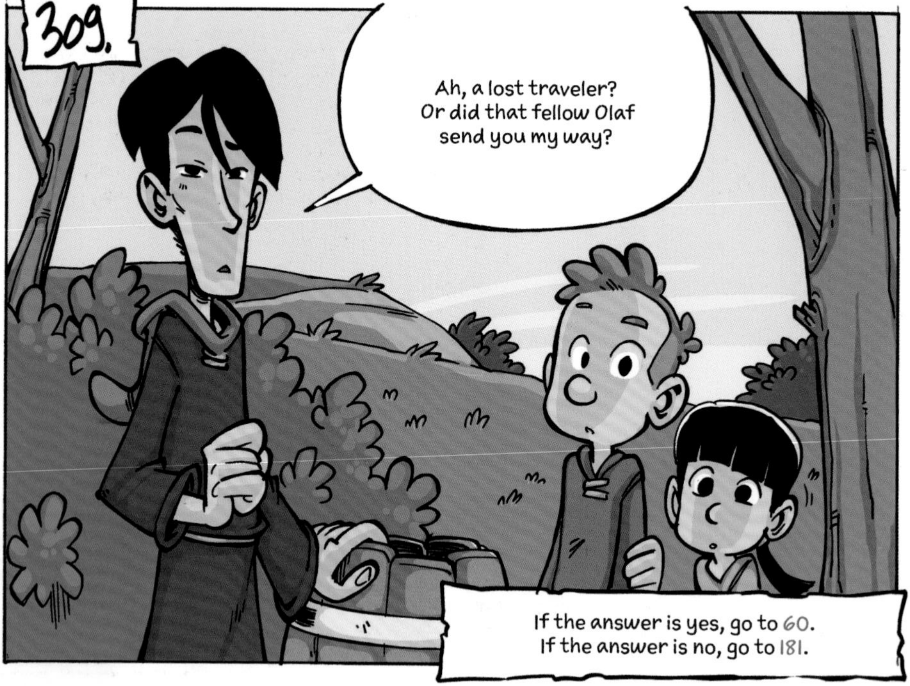
Ah, a lost traveler? Or did that fellow Olaf send you my way?
If the answer is yes, go to 60. If the answer is no, go to 181.

310.

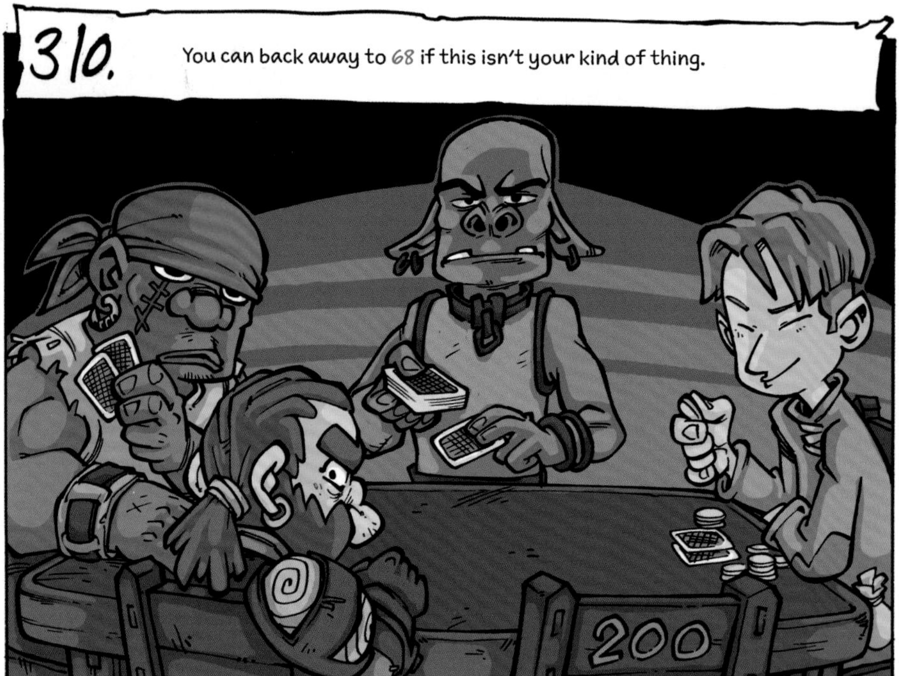
You can back away to 68 if this isn't your kind of thing.
200

311.

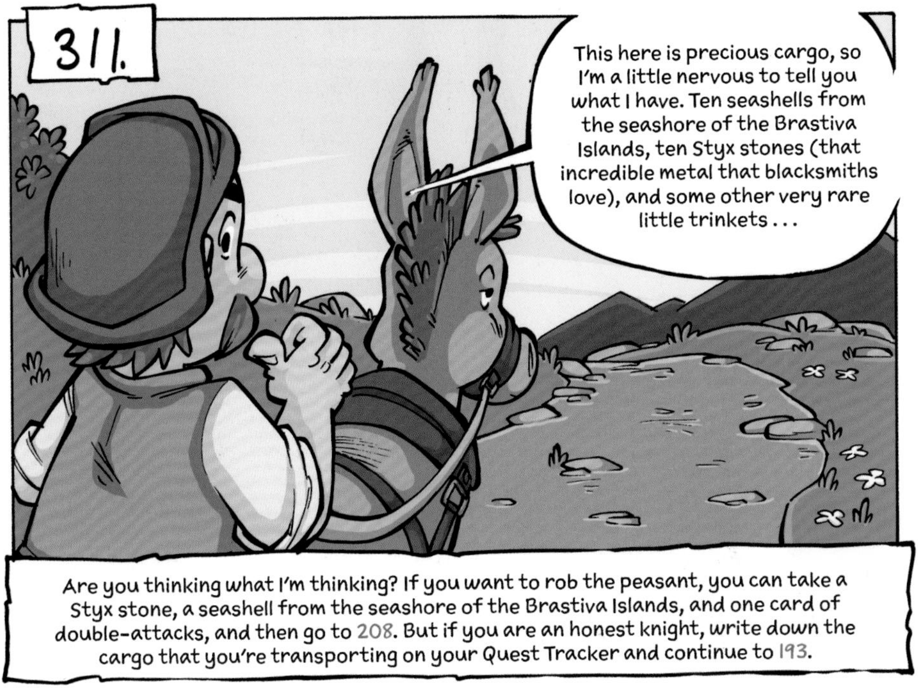
This here is precious cargo, so I'm a little nervous to tell you what I have. Ten seashells from the seashore of the Brastiva Islands, ten Styx stones (that incredible metal that blacksmiths love), and some other very rare little trinkets . . .
Are you thinking what I'm thinking? If you want to rob the peasant, you can take a Styx stone, a seashell from the seashore of the Brastiva Islands, and one card of double-attacks, and then go to 208. But if you are an honest knight, write down the cargo that you're transporting on your Quest Tracker and continue to 193.

312.

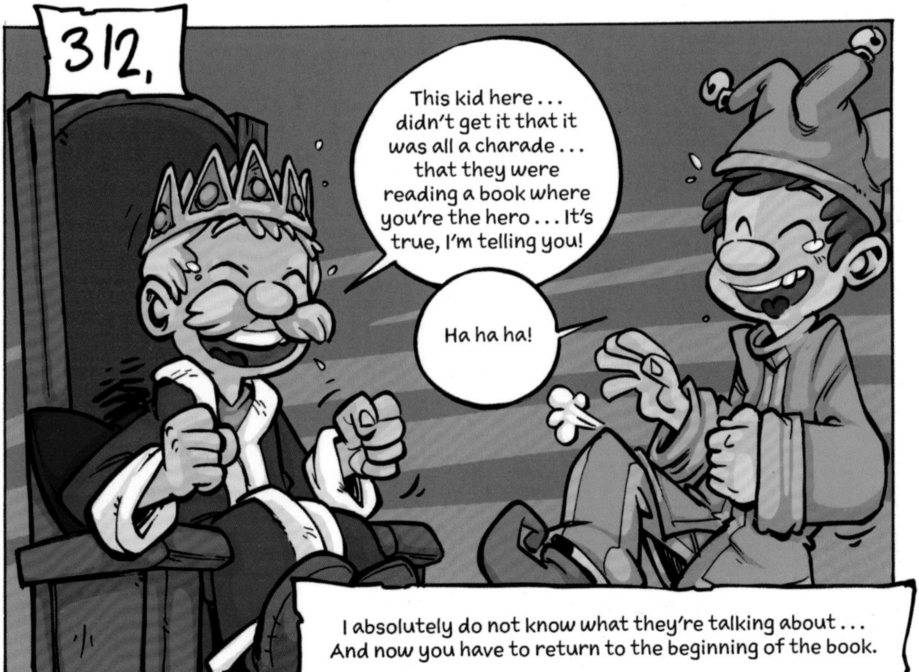
This kid here . . . didn't get it that it was all a charade . . . that they were reading a book where you're the hero . . . It's true, I'm telling you!
Ha ha ha!
I absolutely do not know what they're talking about . . . And now you have to return to the beginning of the book.

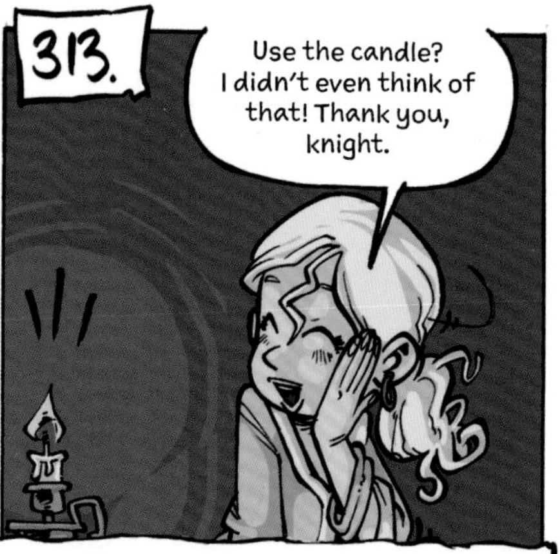
313.
Use the candle? I didn't even think of that! Thank you, knight.

You gain 7 experience points (or 5 gold pieces for squires) if—and only if—you did suggest using the candle or if you lit the logs with a fire spell. It's on you to be honest and return to 211 with or without the reward. It's possible that these points made you go up a level. In that case, add 1 point to the ability of your choice, and add the bonuses that apply to your character.

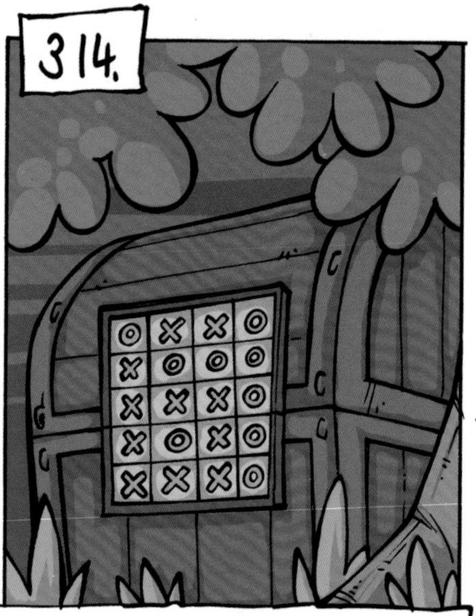
314.

If you have more than 10 Intelligence or can pick locks, go to 82. If you cannot pierce the secret of this chest, turn around and go back to 36.

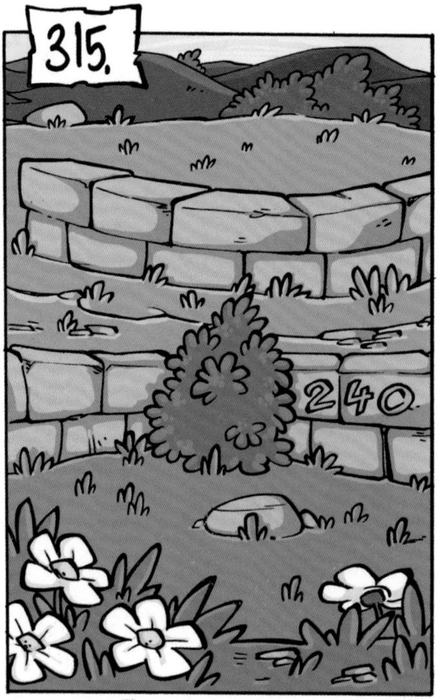
315.
240

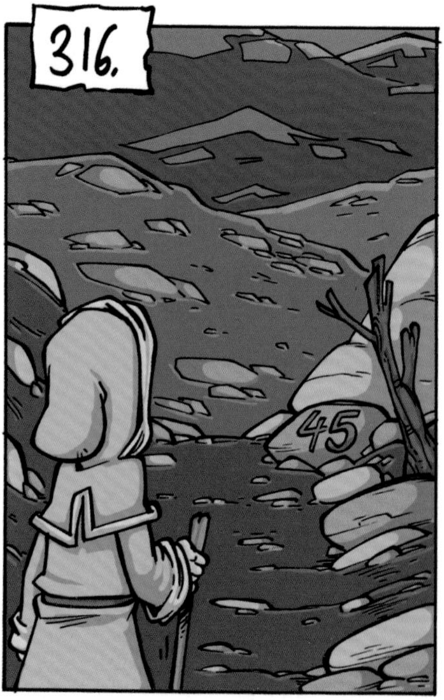
316.
45

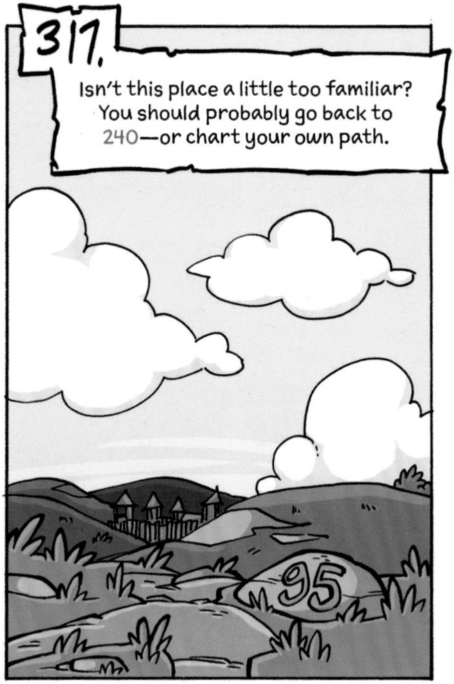
317.
Isn't this place a little too familiar? You should probably go back to 240—or chart your own path.
95

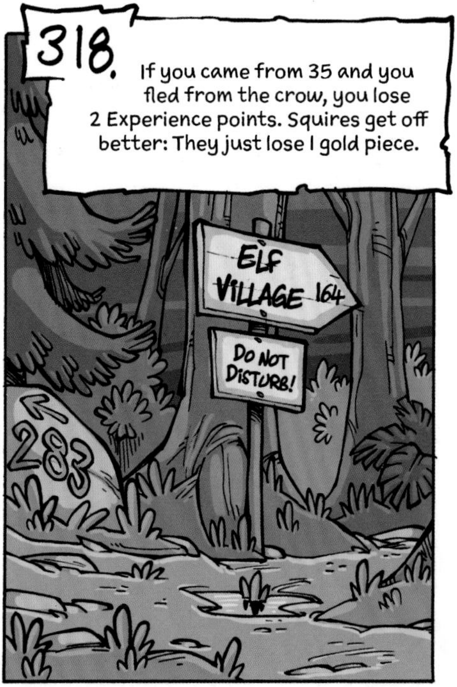
318.
If you came from 35 and you fled from the crow, you lose 2 Experience points. Squires get off better: They just lose 1 gold piece.
ELF VILLAGE 164
DO NOT DISTURB!
283

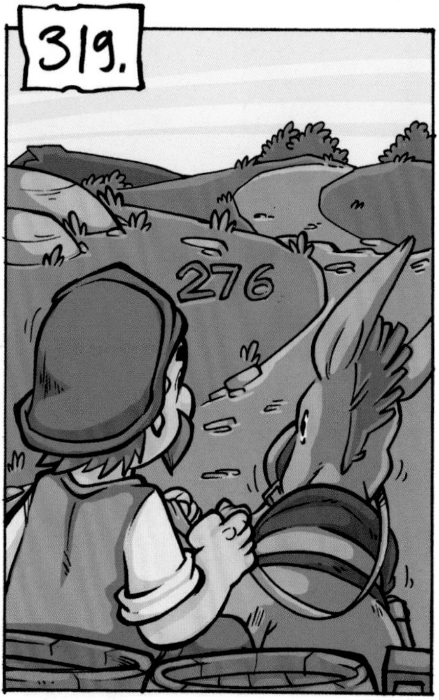
319.
276

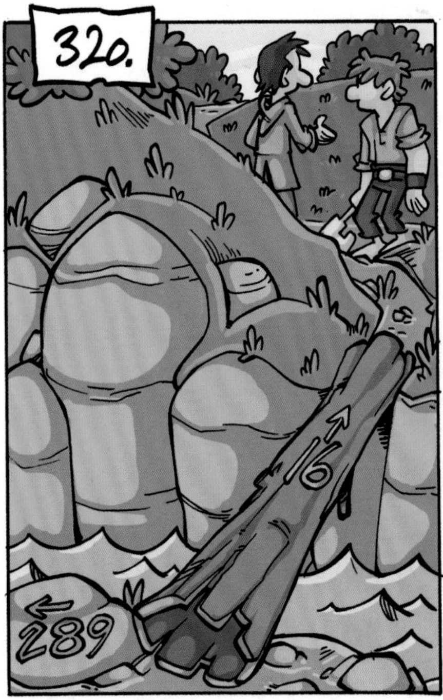
320.
16
289

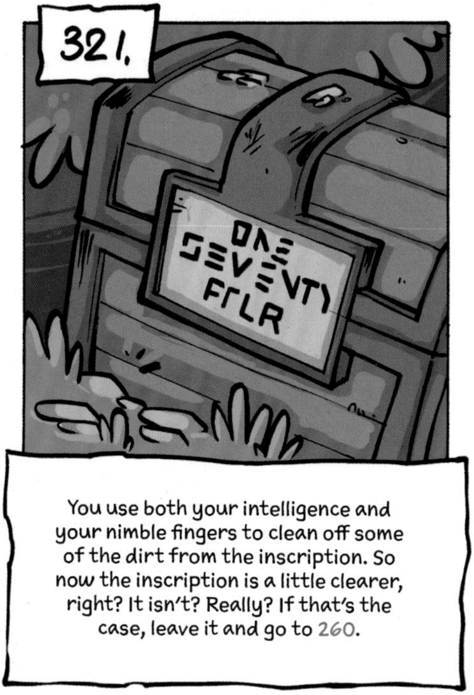
321.
You use both your intelligence and your nimble fingers to clean off some of the dirt from the inscription. So now the inscription is a little clearer, right? It isn't? Really? If that's the case, leave it and go to 260.

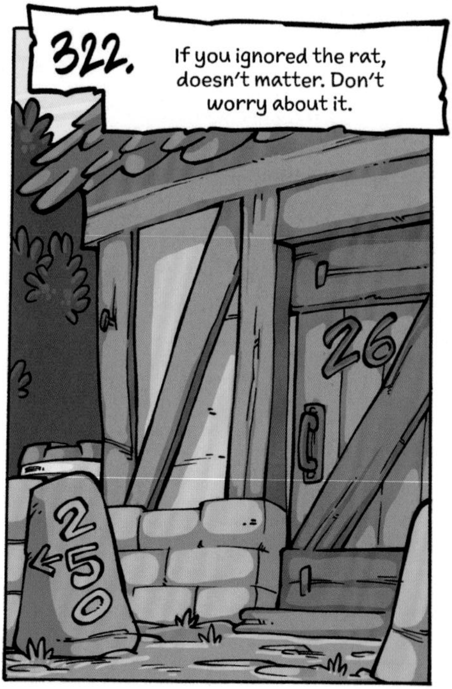
322.
If you ignored the rat, doesn't matter. Don't worry about it.
26
250

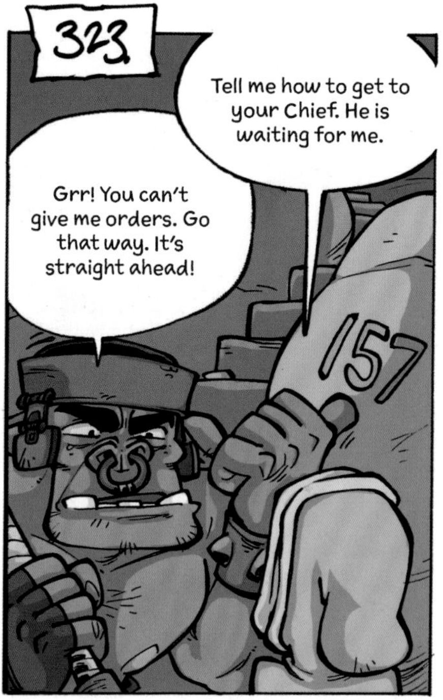
323.
Tell me how to get to your Chief. He is waiting for me.
Grr! You can't give me orders. Go that way. It's straight ahead!
157

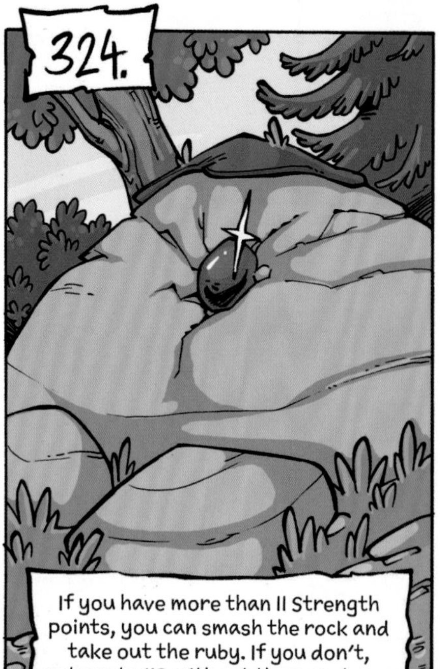
324.
If you have more than 11 Strength points, you can smash the rock and take out the ruby. If you don't, return to 113 without the gemstone.

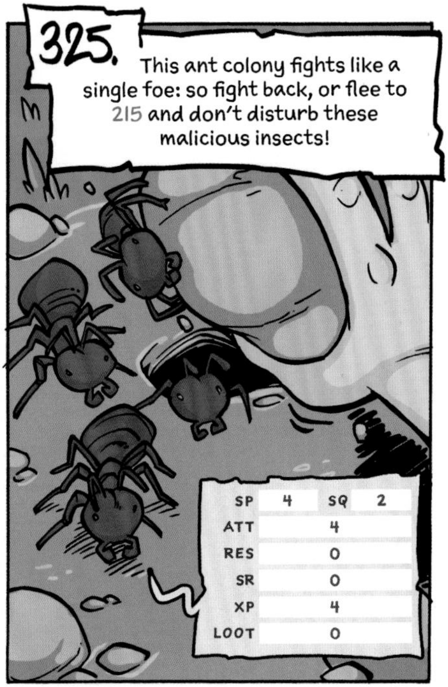
325.
This ant colony fights like a single foe: so fight back, or flee to 215 and don't disturb these malicious insects!

SP	4	SQ	2
ATT	4		
RES	0		
SR	0		
XP	4		
LOOT	0		

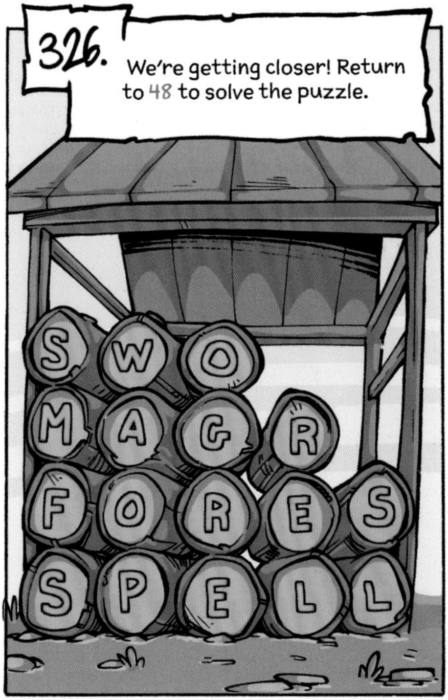
326.
We're getting closer! Return to 48 to solve the puzzle.
S W O
M A G R
F O R E S
S P E L L

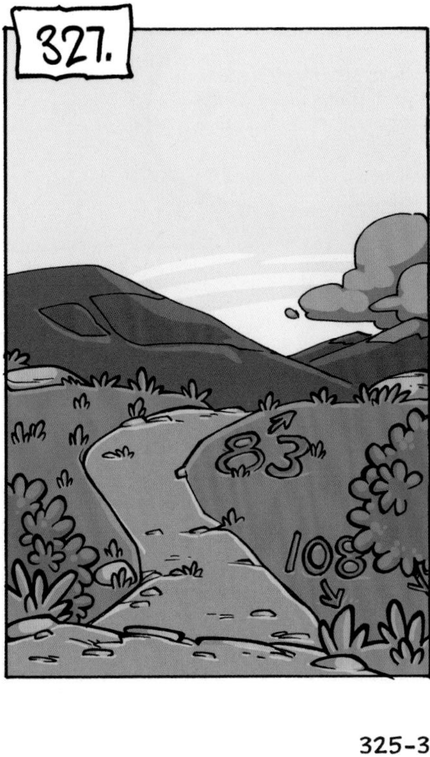
327.
83
108

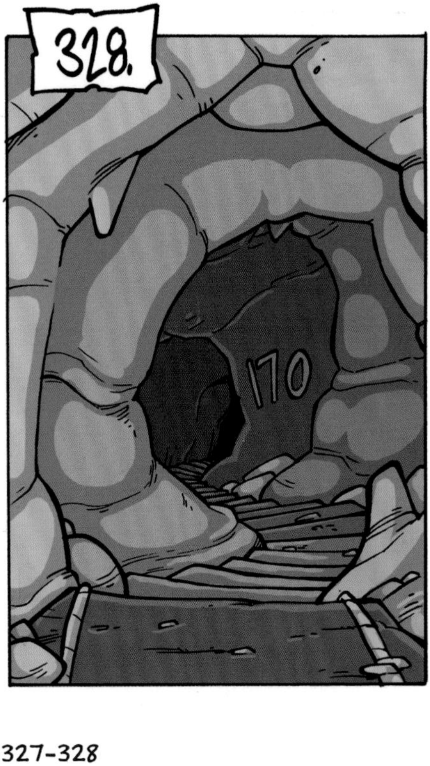
328.
170

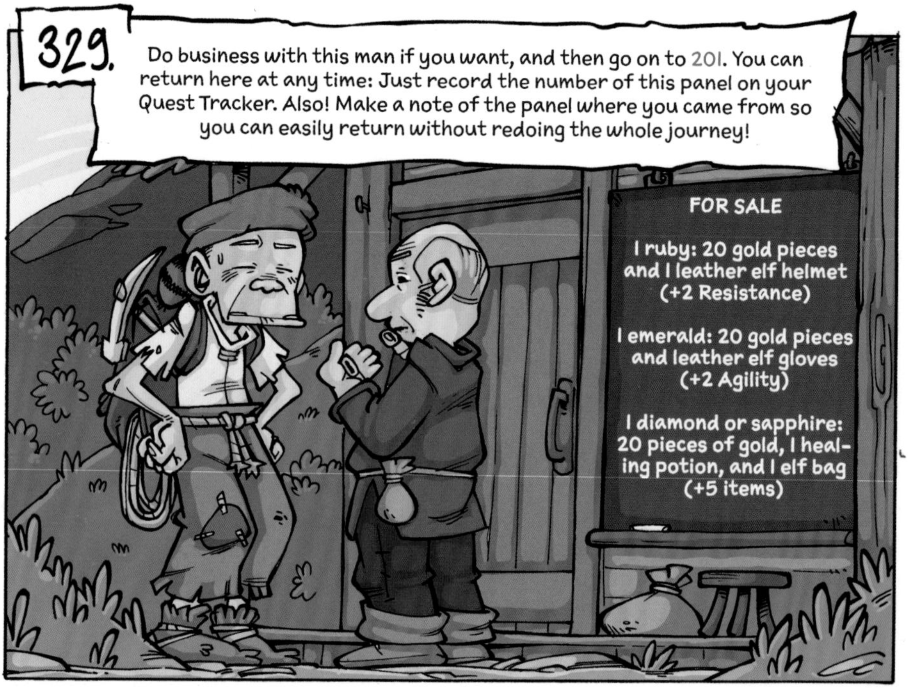
329.
Do business with this man if you want, and then go on to 201. You can return here at any time: Just record the number of this panel on your Quest Tracker. Also! Make a note of the panel where you came from so you can easily return without redoing the whole journey!
FOR SALE
1 ruby: 20 gold pieces and 1 leather elf helmet (+2 Resistance)
1 emerald: 20 gold pieces and leather elf gloves (+2 Agility)
1 diamond or sapphire: 20 pieces of gold, 1 healing potion, and 1 elf bag (+5 items)

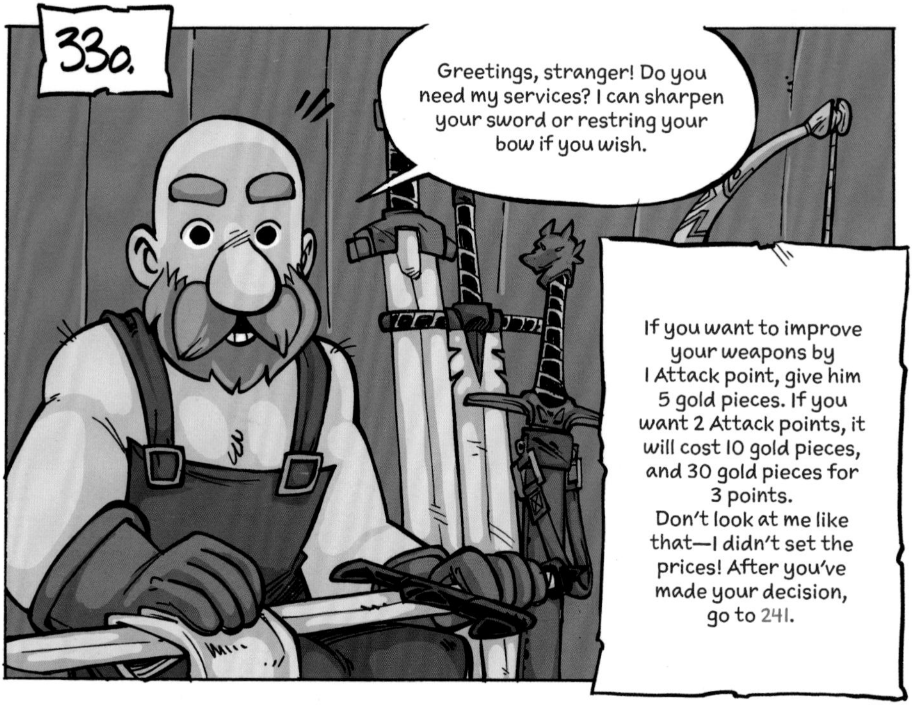
330.
Greetings, stranger! Do you need my services? I can sharpen your sword or restring your bow if you wish.
If you want to improve your weapons by 1 Attack point, give him 5 gold pieces. If you want 2 Attack points, it will cost 10 gold pieces, and 30 gold pieces for 3 points.
Don't look at me like that—I didn't set the prices! After you've made your decision, go to 241.

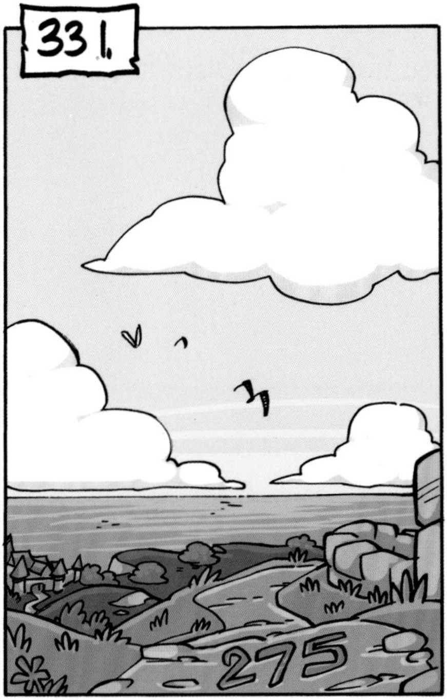
331.
275

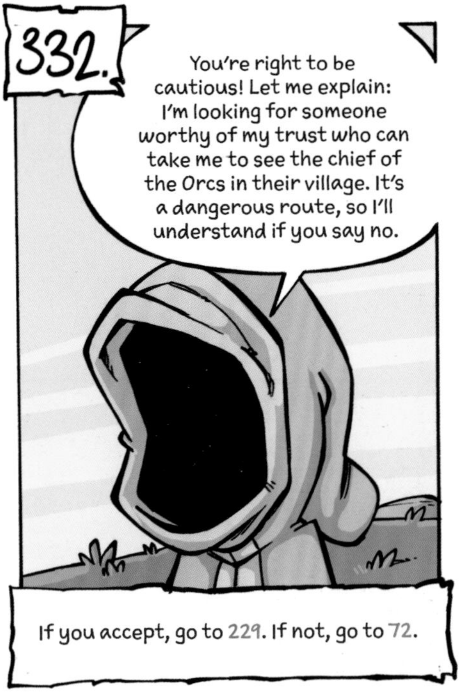
332.
You're right to be cautious! Let me explain: I'm looking for someone worthy of my trust who can take me to see the chief of the Orcs in their village. It's a dangerous route, so I'll understand if you say no.
If you accept, go to 229. If not, go to 72.

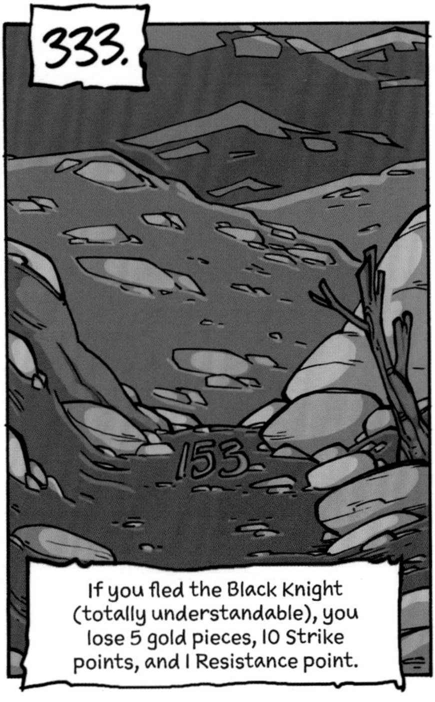
333.
153
If you fled the Black Knight (totally understandable), you lose 5 gold pieces, 10 Strike points, and 1 Resistance point.

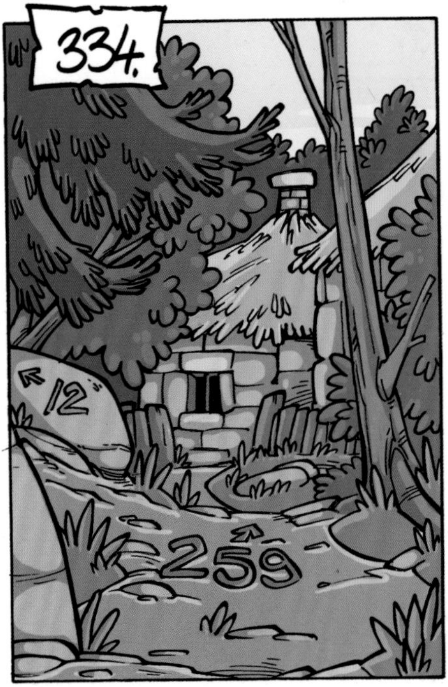
334.
12
259

335.

The blue chest is unlocked, and you find 10 gold pieces. If you have the skill to pick locks, you also open the green chest and find a vial of healing potion, which you can use one time and which restores all your Strike points. If you are a squire, you find 20 pieces of gold in the green chest instead of the vial.

336.

You can take these gemstones if you have over 15 Strength points. This applies throughout your visit to these mines. Each stone you collect weighs 1 point.

337.

Hand over your cargo, knaves, or I'll cut you to bits!

SP	35	SQ	6
ATT	30		
RES	4		
SR	healing + 2		
XP	15		
LOOT	card of concealment		

Looks like someone spread the word about you! You can't flee without losing 3 Styx stones.

338.

Your money or your life! If you give me 5 gold pieces or a bonus card, I'll let you pass. If not, you'll pay with your life!

SP	9	SQ	3
ATT	5		
RES	0		
SR	0		
XP	8		
LOOT	5 Gold Pieces		

You can pay him off to avoid a fight, or you can teach him a lesson. Whichever you choose, head to 69 next.

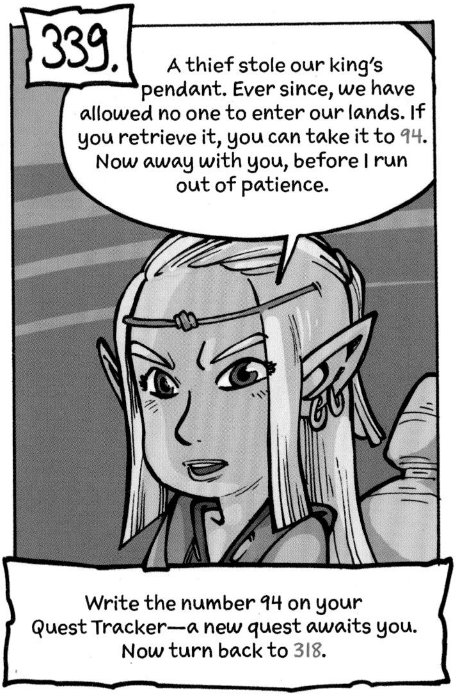
339.
A thief stole our king's pendant. Ever since, we have allowed no one to enter our lands. If you retrieve it, you can take it to 94. Now away with you, before I run out of patience.
Write the number 94 on your Quest Tracker—a new quest awaits you. Now turn back to 318.

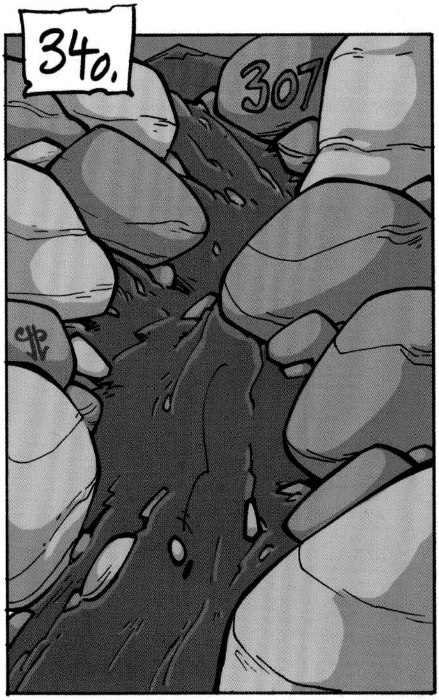
340.
307

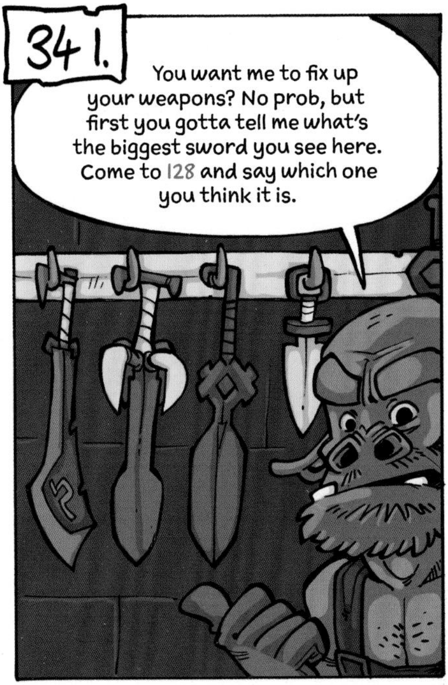
341.
You want me to fix up your weapons? No prob, but first you gotta tell me what's the biggest sword you see here. Come to 128 and say which one you think it is.

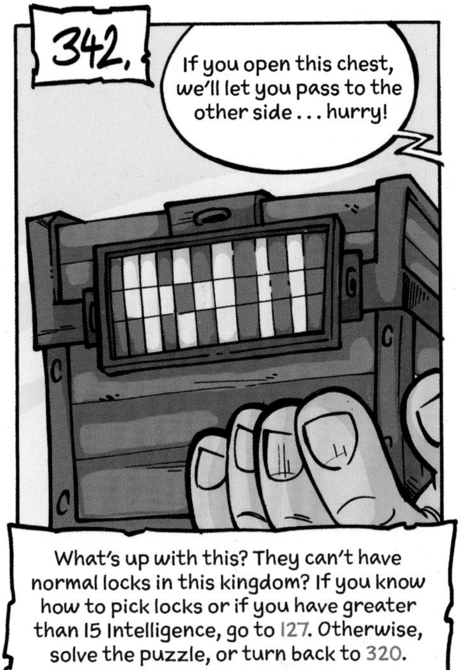
342.
If you open this chest, we'll let you pass to the other side . . . hurry!
What's up with this? They can't have normal locks in this kingdom? If you know how to pick locks or if you have greater than 15 Intelligence, go to 127. Otherwise, solve the puzzle, or turn back to 320.

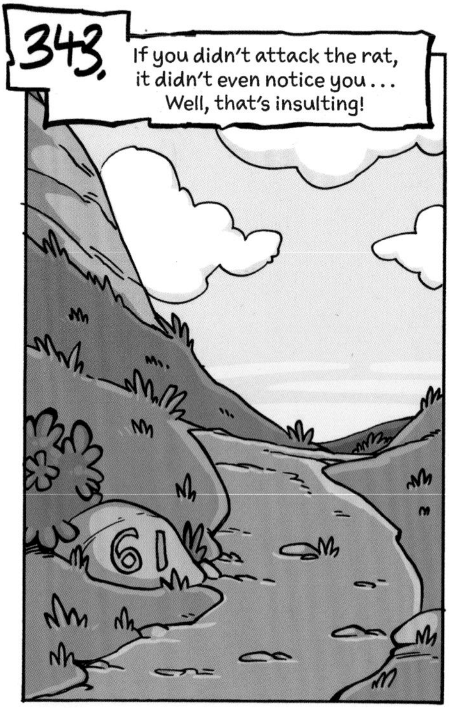
343.
If you didn't attack the rat, it didn't even notice you . . . Well, that's insulting!
61

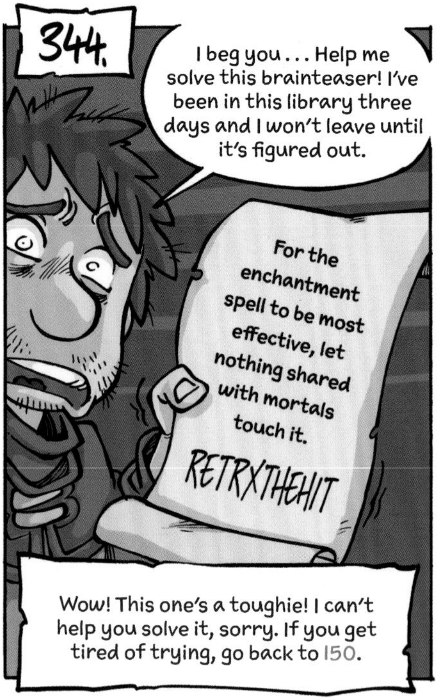
344.
I beg you . . . Help me solve this brainteaser! I've been in this library three days and I won't leave until it's figured out.
For the enchantment spell to be most effective, let nothing shared with mortals touch it.
RETRXTHEHIT
Wow! This one's a toughie! I can't help you solve it, sorry. If you get tired of trying, go back to 150.

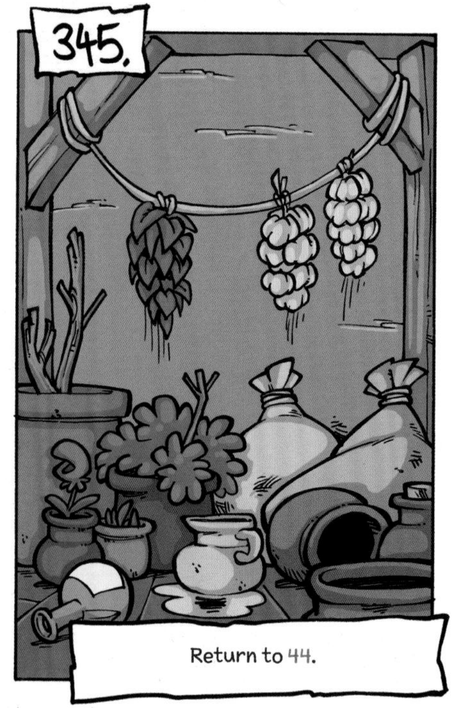
345.
Return to 44.

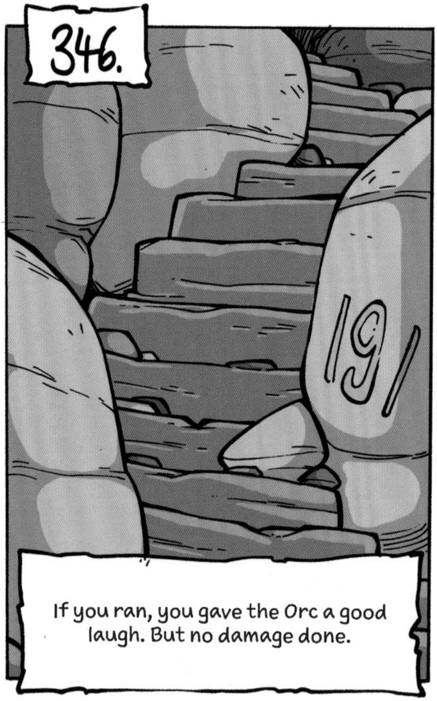
346.
19
If you ran, you gave the Orc a good laugh. But no damage done.

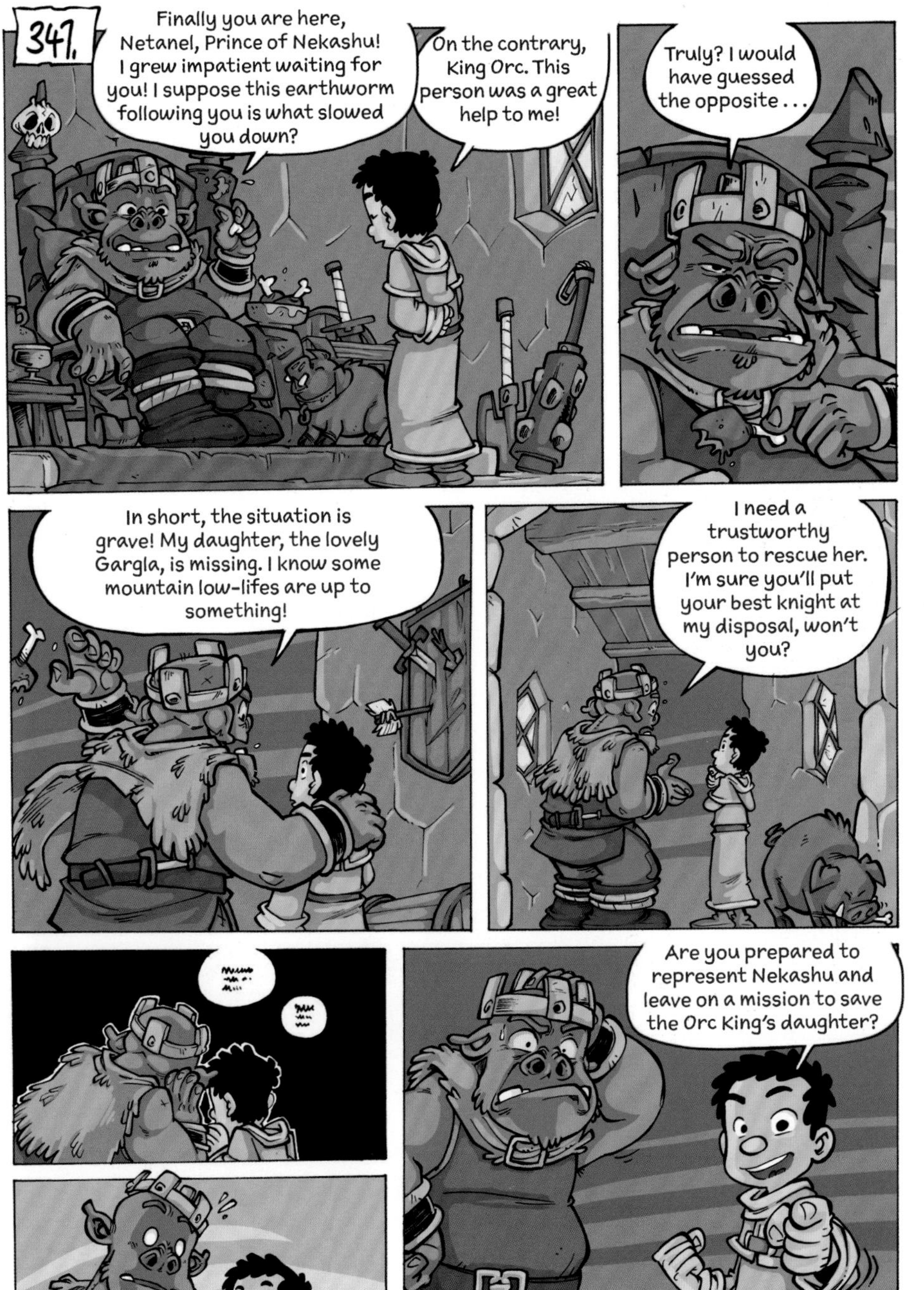
347.
Finally you are here, Netanel, Prince of Nekashu! I grew impatient waiting for you! I suppose this earthworm following you is what slowed you down?
On the contrary, King Orc. This person was a great help to me!
Truly? I would have guessed the opposite . . .
In short, the situation is grave! My daughter, the lovely Gargla, is missing. I know some mountain low-lifes are up to something!
I need a trustworthy person to rescue her. I'm sure you'll put your best knight at my disposal, won't you?
Are you prepared to represent Nekashu and leave on a mission to save the Orc King's daughter?
What have you gotten yourself into? Perhaps you will find out someday. Quickly finish up your current mission by going to 246!

*En 2014, chez Makaka Editions

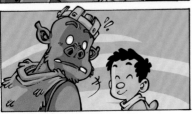

348

Hector, the contents of this barrel positively fill me with joy! I knew I could count on you!

I owe it all to this valiant knight who escorted me. We braved many dangers to get here!

Ahh, so you're a person of honor... a rare quality in these times! If you'll accept it, I have a mission to entrust you with: I'm searching for items of the greatest value, hidden in the most dangerous corners of the kingdom.

Places of which only I know, where the most ferocious of beasts lurk, where the tricks and traps are innumerable, and the puzzles are of the utmost difficulty!

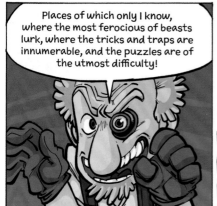

So, will you take up the challenge, knight?

It seems like escorting this unlucky peasant was a pleasant walk in the park compared to what awaits you... Consider carefully, and continue on in the next Knight's Club book, if you are ready for a life of adventure! But don't forget that you still have a message to deliver to Rebourg! Quick, return to 88!

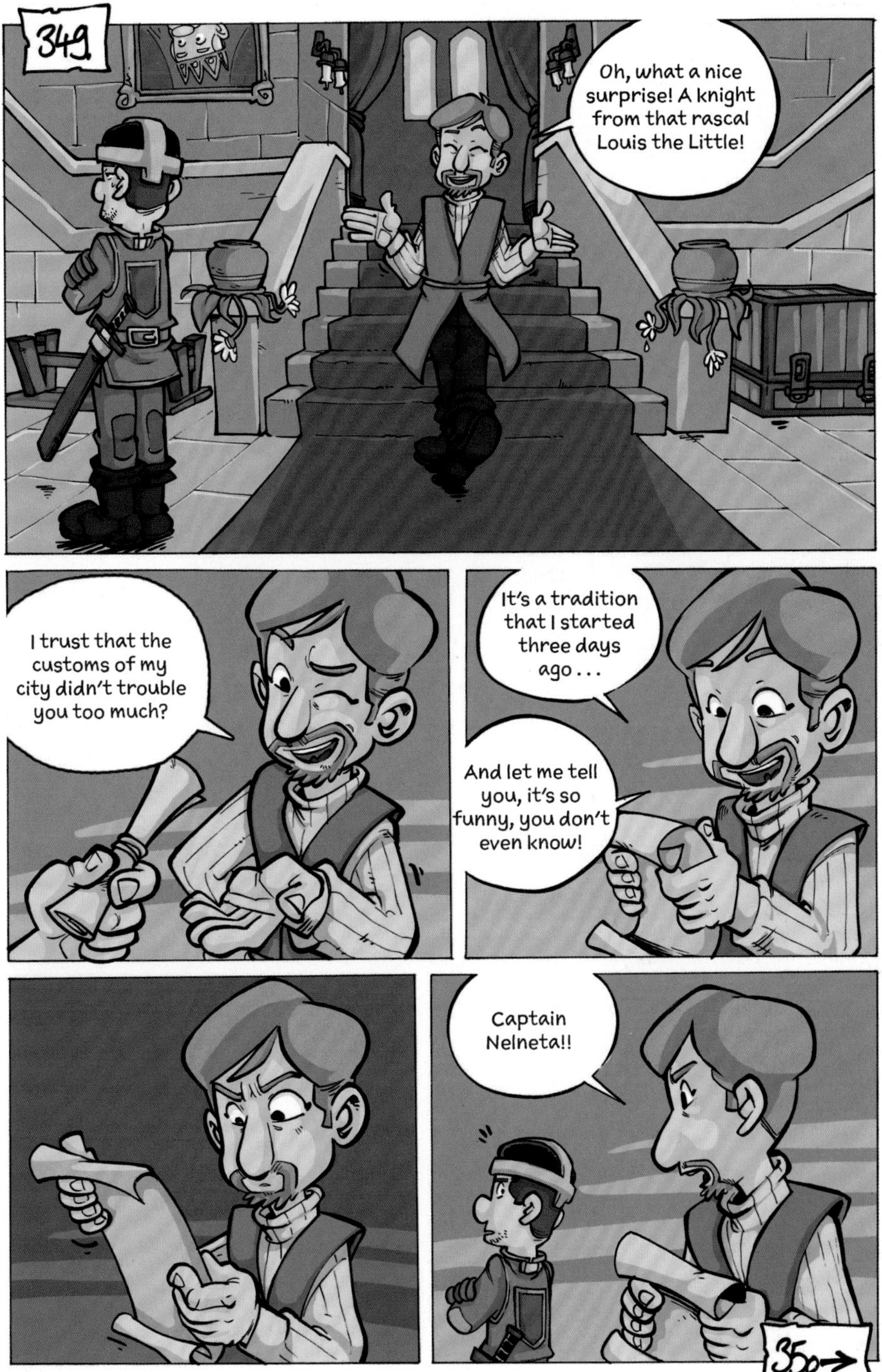
349
Oh, what a nice surprise! A knight from that rascal Louis the Little!
I trust that the customs of my city didn't trouble you too much?
It's a tradition that I started three days ago . . .
And let me tell you, it's so funny, you don't even know!
Captain Nelneta!!
350

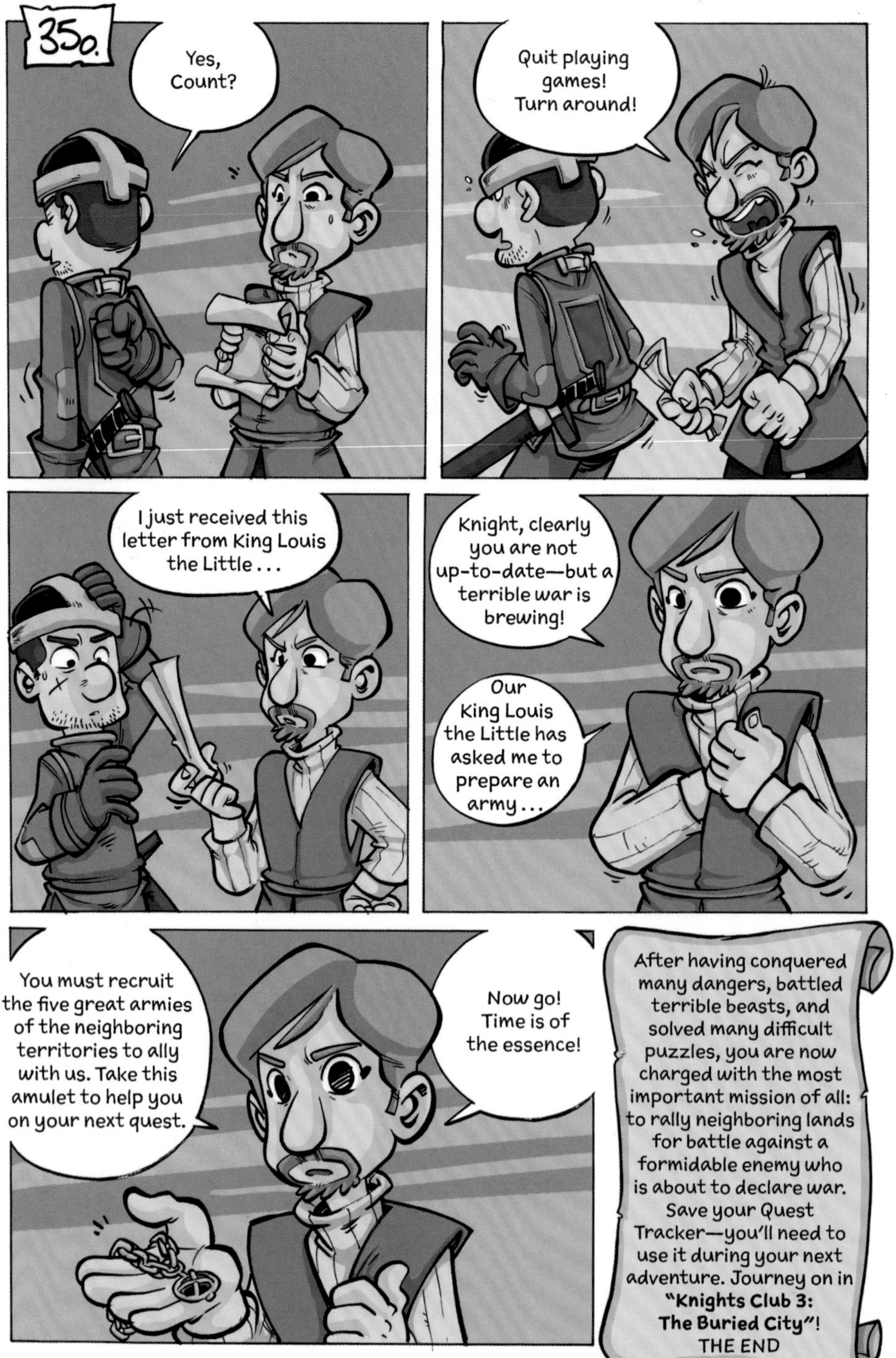
350.
Yes, Count?
Quit playing games! Turn around!
I just received this letter from King Louis the Little . . .
Knight, clearly you are not up-to-date—but a terrible war is brewing!
Our King Louis the Little has asked me to prepare an army . . .
You must recruit the five great armies of the neighboring territories to ally with us. Take this amulet to help you on your next quest.
Now go! Time is of the essence!
After having conquered many dangers, battled terrible beasts, and solved many difficult puzzles, you are now charged with the most important mission of all: to rally neighboring lands for battle against a formidable enemy who is about to declare war. Save your Quest Tracker—you'll need to use it during your next adventure. Journey on in **"Knights Club 3: The Buried City"**! THE END

COMBAT WHEEL

Use this disk to fight the enemies you encounter on your adventure. If you are unable (or don't want) to cut it out, you can download one from comicquests.com. Then spin a pencil on top of the disk. Wherever the pencil tip stops is what you play.

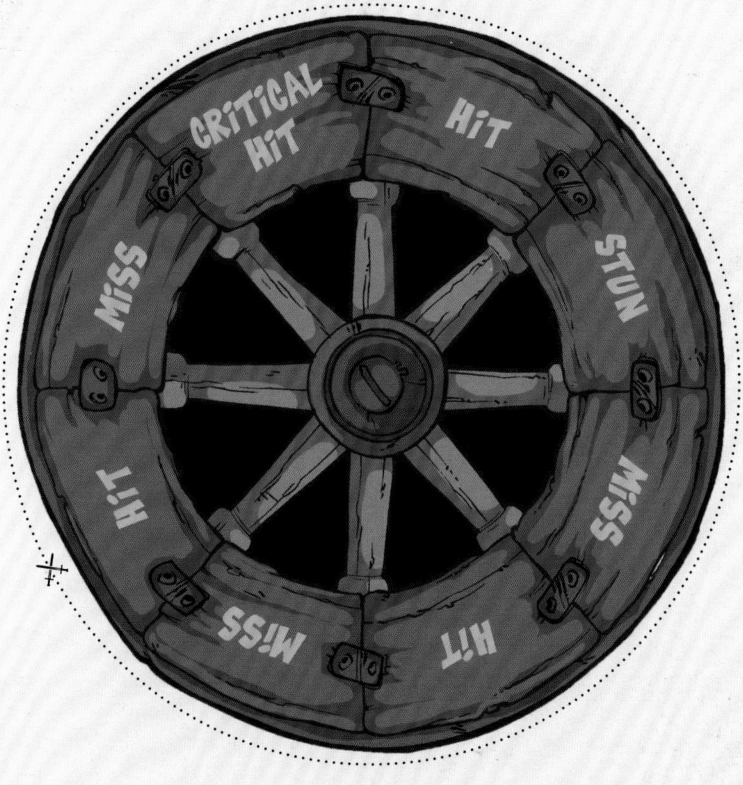

CRITICAL HIT
HIT
STUN
MISS
HIT
MISS
HIT
MISS

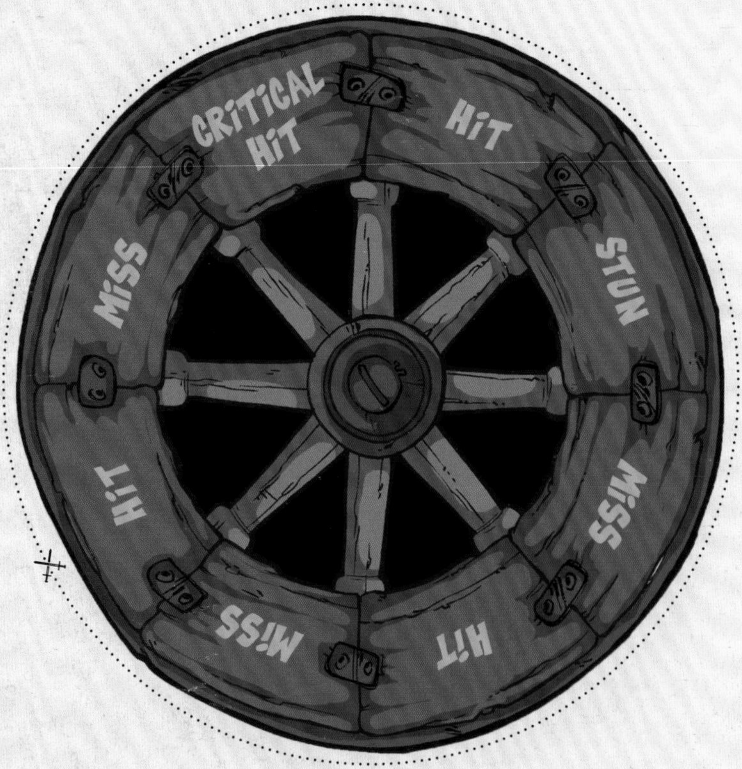
CRITICAL HIT
HIT
STUN
MISS
HIT
MISS
HIT
MISS